Cover design by Alejandro Colucci

Map design by Luan Bittencourt

Author photograph by Felipe Koji

Chapter header designs by Claudio Mello

Internal illustration by Sara Ferrari

ISBN (ebook): 978-1-957237-09-1

ISBN (Paperback): 978-1-957237-07-7

ISBN (Hardback): 978-1-957237-08-4

A SHADE OF MADNESS

THE ASHES OF AVARIN: BOOK TWO

"Sanity is a matter of perspective"

THIAGO ABDALLA

01 Mar/23

T. Abdalla

SIGNED BY THE AUTHOR
in association with The Broken Binding

THIS IS A LIMITED NUMBERED EDITION

THIS IS NUMBER 171/150

A SHADE OF MADNESS

THE ASHES OF AVARIN: BOOK TWO

THIAGO ABDALLA

THE ALTERIAN PRESS

ALSO BY THIAGO ABDALLA

THE ASHES OF AVARIN SERIES

0 - A Prelude to Ashes

1 - A Touch of Light

www.tabdalla.com

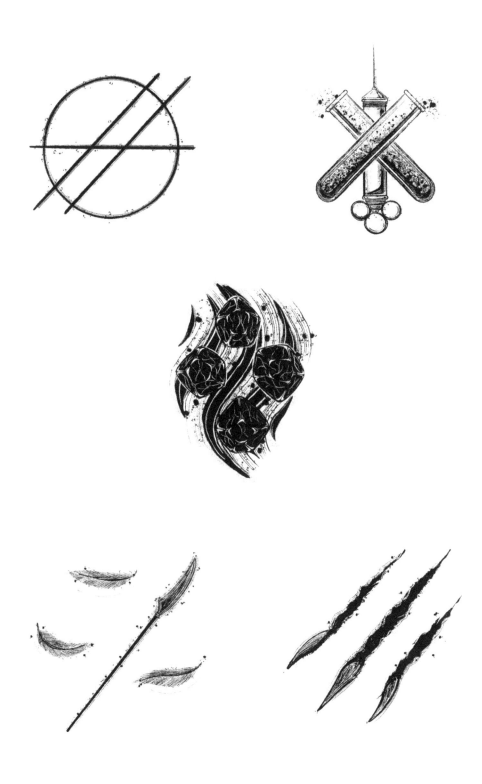

To Matheus and Julia

LIST OF CHARACTERS, ORGANIZATIONS AND PLACES

The Continent of Immeria

The Domain – Notable characters, organizations and places

OTHONEA – One of the largest and most powerful nations in the Domain.

- **Adrian Pell** – Prince of Othonea.
- **Iridan Pell** – King of Othonea, father to Adrian, Jovu and Ellana Pell.
- **Jovu Pell** – Prince of Othonea. Adrian's brother.
- **Ellana Pell** – Sister to Adrian and Jovu. High priestess of Khet in the Church of the Seraph.
- **Queen Dalenna Pell** – Mother to Adrian, Jovu and Ellana. Deceased.
- **Derren** – Former captain of the Othonean army. Promoted by Adrian to General of the Legion. Deceased.

Khet – Formerly a small nation to the north of Othonea. Allied to Dakhra, Othonea's biggest rival nation in the Domain. Taken over by Othonea.

- **Henrik Brandt** – King of Khet, Father to Addo. Deceased.
- **Addo Brandt** – Prince of Khet. A coward.
- **Garrick Brandt** – Henrik's brother. Commander of the Khetish armies.
- **Balt Brandt** – Deceased. Garrick's son.
- **Raklin** – The cleanser at Ultenvell palace in Khet. Deceased.

Dakhra – One of the Domain nations. Othonea's biggest rival.

- **Syvern** – King of Dakhra.
- **Alaya** – Princess of Dakhra and commander of the Dakhran air fleet.
- **Myrra** – Princess of Dakhra, betrothed to Adrian Pell.

Sacantha – One of the Domain nations. Lynn's home nation

- **Niria** – Queen of Sacantha.
- **Lord Keeper Kerr** – Keeper of the prison of Dalhold.
- **Morna** – A priestess that leads Baywater Temple in Sacantha. Ferrin's sister. Found dead by Lynn.

Vizcarra – One of the Domain nations. Protects the southern borders of the Domain against possible clan attacks.

- **Rheda** – Queen of Vizcarra.

The Visslands – One of the Domain nations. Protects the southern borders of the Domain against possible clan attacks.

- **Kadmus** – A potion master seeking to find a cure for the Madness
- **Grunt** – Accompanies Kadmus in search for madmen that serve as test subjects.
- **Bahar** – Emissary representing the Visslands in the southern clans.
- **Lesraile** – Queen of the Visslands.
- **Councilor Carswell** – Part of the council under Queen Lesraile. His son is missing in the clanlands.

The Holy Church of The Seraph – All Domain nations follow the Church of the Seraph. The religion has declared death as the enemy and it is said that the Seraph's blessings extend the lives of the faithful. The Church is based on four tenets of faith: Breath, Body, Blood and Bone

- **The Seraph** – The goddess who left the land because of all the death. It is the duty of the faithful to prove themselves worthy so that She may return in the Promised Dawn.
- **The High Pontiff** – Supreme leader of the Church.
- **The Priests of the Blood -** Priests trained in elite healing. Represent the Blood.
- **The Sentinels** – An elite force of griffin riders answering to the High Pontiff. The only ones allowed to kill in the Domain outside of battle or prison executions. The Sentinels represent the Breath.
- **High Bishop Reznik** – Leader of the Bishops of the Bone, the order of the Church responsible for information and spies. Represents the Bone.
- **High Chancellor Burke** – Represents the Body, which looks out for the faithful of the Seraph. The Body represents the voice and interests of the faithful within the Church.
- **Abbot Orwen** – Lynn's old abbot in the house of Farkhul. Deceased.

- **Abbot Andral** – Standing in for Orwen in the house of Farkhul. Revealed to be taken by the Madness.
- **Priest Talbot** – A priest in the house of Farkhul. Revealed to be taken by the Madness.

The Order of the Sentinels

- **Lynn** – A rogue Sentinel troubled by her past.
- **Vedyr** – Lynn's griffin.
- **Commander Leardin** – Former leader of the Sentinels. Deceased
- **Olem** – The Sentinel's second in command.
- **Rel** – A Sentinel close to Lynn in the past. Supplied her with ruin-stone.
- **Ulenia** – Rel's Griffin
- **Ildred** – A Sentinel from Lynn's past. Does not forgive her for leaving the order.
- **Thain** – A Sentinel who used to be close to Ildred. Went into Dakhra to ask for help.
- **Other Sentinels**: Gwyndel, Deria, Cedd, Wyman, Brehnna, Mirek
- **Elwin** – A high-ranking Sentinel. Mentor to Lynn. Deceased
- **Emida** – Elwin's griffin.

<u>The Church Legion</u> – The army of the Church. Reduced to guard the city of Alteria as years of peace prevailed. Was rebuilt by Adrian.

- **Burnham** – A drunk formerly leading the Legion in Alteria. Now a general. Did not accompany Adrian to Azur.
- **Gotzon** – A Legion captain.
- **Iker** – A Legion captain.
- **Nasir** – A Priest of the Blood found in Khet. Now High Priest of the Legion

- **Hyrkil** – Former captain of the Khetish guard, now a captain of the Legion. Stayed behind when Adrian went to Azur.
- **Bac** – Sent to Azur as a guard for the Othonean delegation. Now serves Adrian.
- **Ferrin** – Close to Lynn. A former prison guard, now a captain of the Legion. Joined the Legion after the Sentinels found it in shambles.

The Hand of The Seraph – A militia formed in Alteria for people to defend themselves where the Legion failed. Led by Commander Ashford. Integrated into the Legion in A Touch of Light. Ashford betrayed Adrian then was executed.

The Southern Clans – Notable characters, organizations and places

The Four Clans: Ronar, Yltigg, Hagun and Lothrak

The Ronar – Live close to a volcano. There is a divide between village dwellers and those relegated to the slopes of the volcano, known as Slopers.

- **Nasha** – A hunter for the Ronar. Came from the slopes and proved herself to become part of the clan. Can feel the emotions of others, considers it a curse.
- **Mansa** – One of the leaders of the Ronar known as Roots. He is the leader of the hunters. His title is Oringo.
- **Tomu** – Chief of the Ronar.
- **Jabillo** – Another Root. Speaker for the Earth. Leads the Speakers: priest-like figures who are spreaders of the tales of the Ronar.
- **Adda** – The Tivezzi, another Root. Responsible for shaping ancestor-stone. Daughter to the Chief. Deceased.

- **Tedros** – An ancient hero and leader of the clans before they were split into four.
- **Razi** – Adda's son. Taken to Azuri with Landi and Uvo.

The Slopers – Live on the slopes of the volcano. Slopers are not considered part of the Ronar until proven.

- **Shai** –a Sloper close to Nasha. Participated in the Proving and now follows Nasha.
- **Ife** – Deceased. One of Nasha's closest friends when she lived in the slopes. Shai's father.
- **Uvo** – Shai's brother.
- **Landi** – Shai's mother.
- **Leku** – Leader of the Zaruni, a militia that dubs itself the protectors of the slopes.

The Yltigg – Rivals to the Ronar. Live on a high peak but their land is more barren. Their peak houses the largest known ancestor-stone mines in the clanlands

- **Ardin** – Chief of the Yltigg
- **Roho** – A high ranking warrior. Leads the Yltigg in battle.
- **Ento** – Recently appointed Speaker of the Yltigg.

The Lothrak – A nomadic clan broken up into tribes that brave the southern icy mountains of the clanlands.

The Hagun – A deeply religious clan. Their village was consumed by a taint and they are nowhere to be found.

- **Zala** – The dead goddess. The clans believe they need to feed blood to the Earth to remain Zala imprisoned within it.

The Continent of Azur

A nation-continent of copper sands. The capital city of Dar Drezji is where the Xakhar rules with the support of the ten consuls, each represented by a noble family.

The Ten Azuri Families – These are the families that make up the ruling council of Azur. The Council answers to the Xakhar but relations are not always smooth.

- **Erhul -** One of the two main merchant families, focused on mining, precious stones and using some of the spice families as allies
- **Rhiall** – The other main merchant family, focused on the wood trade with the east
- **Zarath:** One of the largest families. Dedicated to information and spies. When one needs to know, they seek out the Zarath
- **Attar -** A deeply religious and ancient family that claims to trace its origins back to the original Xakhar. They maintain power through their tradition and wealth, as well as knowledge of the laws.
- **Khorfa -** The main military family. They revolutionized the military with their tactics. They have a strong military tradition with many members of their large family being officers. There are many officers with the Khorfa name who rise rapidly in the ranks.
- **Taraff -** one of the spice families. Less powerful and allied with the Erhul to make a front that can compete with the Rhiall.
- **Fakhin -** Another of the spice families, also branching into the leaf trade. Have had ties with the Rhiall in the past.
- **Mahir** – Another military family. They command the Azuri navy.

- **Bedak -** The main metalworking family. Were the largest but are losing ground to the Yankah after the Khorfa implemented the reforms in the military and started using Yankah blades.
- **Yankah -** Another of the metalwork families. They are smaller so ally themselves with the Khorfa and have grown because of it.

OTHER NOTABLE AZURI

- **Kel Bradaz** – Leader of the blood mages in the House of the Afterdark.
- **Amal ban Khorfa** – A member of the Khorfa family who tried to betray the Xakhar and take over the Khorfa in A Touch of Light.
- **The Xakhar** – Ruler of Azur. Deceased.
- **Kahlia** – Princess of Azur daughter of the Xakhar. Deceased.
- **Niilar** – Prince of Azur son of the Xakhar. Deceased.
- **Jurat order** – The jurors of Azur. Seen in this book: Head Jurat Hasna and Jurat Faruq

THE ASHES OF AVARIN - THE STORY SO FAR

BOOK ONE: A TOUCH OF LIGHT

Adrian, Lynn, and Nasha are all struggling through a changing world.

The world of Avarin is split. The continent of Immeria is divided between the Domain and the clanlands. The Domain worship life, and death is a shame. The dead must be forgotten.

The Domain is made up of six nations: Othonea, Khet, Dakhra, Sacantha, the Visslands, and Vizcarra. They all follow the Church of the Seraph.

The Church considers ruin-stone—a stone that has its origins shrouded in mystery—to be holy. It is used on all the Church monuments, and Church orders like the Sentinels and the Bishops of the Bone use it as an essential component in their magic.

PART 1

Adrian has lost his brother. He counts on Myrra, his wife-to-be, to prove himself to his father, but Adrian soon loses her as well. He decides to prove her worthiness even in death so that the Church may preserve her body to be brought back by the Seraph when the goddess returns.

It is believed that the Seraph will revive the worthy when she returns, an event known as the Promised Dawn.

Adrian heads to Khet to deliver terms for their surrender. The deposed king tries to goad Adrian into killing him, but Adrian sees through it, and the king's brother, Garrick, kills him and accepts Othonea's terms. Addo, the prince of Khet tries to get the guards to attack Adrian, but Garrick calls them off. Garrick becomes governor of Khet, now an Othonean province, and Adrian heads to the cleansing chamber to find Myrra's body before it is burned.

Adrian meets Raklin, the cleanser. He tells Adrian about a strange condition affecting the Khetish. They are calling it a battle fever, but it has nothing to do with battle. Raklin accepts to preserve Myrra's body if Adrian takes him to Alteria to convince the Pontiff to send aid to Khet.

Adrian heads to the holy city of Alteria for the Pontiff's council and brings Raklin with him. On entering the holy city, Adrian is beset by a frenzied man. This is more beast than man, and he injures Raklin, but Adrian manages to defeat him. The man's condition is similar to the disease that Raklin wishes to heal in Khet.

During the council, Adrian is named Light of the Legion, and given the task of rebuilding the Church Legion to clear Alteria of these rising madmen. Raklin fails to get aid for Khet and tells Adrian he was betrayed. Adrian says he will keep his promise, but it will be useless to march to Khet without a large enough army. Raklin returns to Khet leaving Adrian only with the hope that he will not tamper with Myrra's body.

Lynn is a Sentinel, one of the elite griffin-riding warriors of the Church. Sentinels have a connection to their griffins. They can pull strength and speed from their griffins in return for an emotion that they use to connect to the creatures.

Lynn is in hiding. She has been forced to kill her Sentinel

brothers in the past and their memory still haunts her. She fled the Order, thinking death is always pursuing her. Lynn does not want to bring death to the Domain, and thinks she is not worthy of the Sentinel order. Her guilt and fear drive her to hide, posing as a prisoner in the Sacanthan prison of Dalhold.

Lynn searches for redemption to overcome her guilt by saving prisoners who she deems worthy. She is almost getting comfortable with her contribution to life, to the Seraph, when the prison Keeper finds a way to obtain a Church pardon and Lynn is forced to leave the prison.

Lynn walks aimlessly around the Sacanthan capital of Pyrran until fleeing citizens lead her to bloody streets, and a girl standing amid the death. It reminds her of her old enemy—the Madness. An infection that took over her brothers and was the reason she was ordered to kill them.

Lynn finds no signs of the Madness on the girl—no darkness around the eyes or nails grown into claws, and the girl is not taken by a beastly ferocity. Lynn lets her go.

She investigates further murders happening in the city, and discovers that the church guard are doing all they can to hide the bodies of the dead that are appearing around the city. These bodies seem to be ravaged, but Lynn still doesn't want to believe the signs. She seeks out Ferrin, a prison guard who is the brother of one of the Sentinels she killed, and was close to her when she was in hiding. Ferrin sends Lynn to talk to his sister, a priestess at Baywater temple, and the same one who pardoned Lynn.

Lynn arrives at the temple and finds a massacre. The priestess is dead. Ferrin arrives soon after and they decide to leave Pyrran and head to Lynn's old church in Farkhul, where she was trained as a Sentinel, to find help.

Nasha is a Ronar hunter struggling to contain the emotions of those around her. She has what she considers to be a curse that allows her to feel other's emotions, but she has no control over it. The risk of being overwhelmed by external emotion is a big one, and if that happens, Nasha is taken by whatever emotion wins out. Usually a mindless rage.

She is sent on a patrol to find Hagun. The Hagun, a rival clan, have been sighted in the Ronar lands. She doesn't appreciate her companions, who hold the prejudice over the people from the slopes that live above the Ronar village. Nasha grew up in the slopes and eventually grows tired of her company. She walks off, but finds one of the leaders of the Ronar, who are called 'Roots'. This man, Chatta, is the Warden and he is dying. He sits on a rotting patch of Earth. The Ronar believe in strength, and Nasha knows this man's state will weaken the clan. There is no turning back from it. She kills him.

Her companions find Nasha and brand her a traitor. She stabs two of them and buries the last—Iallo—under a pile of rocks. Nasha returns to the Ronar, hoping that her actions to defend the clan's strength will bring her recognition.

Nasha returns to the Ronar village carrying Chatta's head. She tells Mansa, the leader of the hunters, about Chatta. Mansa says he will bring this to the Chief, and Nasha is expectant. She walks out with Bahar, a Domain emissary who has a son among the Ronar. Bahar is here looking for the son of a nobleman from the Domain nation he represents: The Visslands.

When they reach Nasha's home, warriors surround it and Nasha is taken away. Iallo survived and has come back prove Nasha a traitor.

Nasha is brought before the Ronar Roots. Mansa is the Oringo, leader of the hunters. Adda is the Tivezzi, the stone-shaper responsible for the ancestor-stone wards that keep Zala, the dead goddess, at bay. Jabillo is the Speaker for the Earth, responsible for keeping the tales alive and remind the Ronar of their heritage. They all answer to the Chief of the clan: Tomu. Adda is Tomu's daughter.

Nasha is judged and instead of being killed, is named the new Warden to smooth over relationships between the Ronar and the people who live on the mountain above the village, known as the Slopers. Nasha came from the slopes and the Roots believe she will appease their discomforts. After her trial, a new Proving is announced. This is the event that inducts new members into the Ronar. It is the path the Slopers seek for a better life.

PART 2

Adrian builds up the Legion with the help of an old guard who has always served his family, Derren. Adrian makes Derren a general in the Legion and builds the Legion's strength by taking in a militia force that had risen up in Alteria to defend the people against the frenzied attackers. The militia was called the Hand of the Seraph and is led by Ashford, whom Adrian also promotes to general of the Legion. Once Alteria is under control, Adrian marches the army to Khet.

He arrives and finds Addo, the dead Khetish king's son, sitting on the throne. Garrick nowhere to be found. Addo says that he wants to mend relations with Adrian and that Garrick is leading a Khetish force to protect the port towns against the madmen who have beset it. Adrian marches the Legion north but leaves Ashford behind to keep an eye on Addo.

Adrian is betrayed by the Khetish and is knocked out. He awakens in the throne room and learns Ashford has joined the Khetish, who now serve Raklin. Raklin's injury in Alteria infected him with the Madness, but he controls it somehow. He now drops his blood into the mouths of Adrian's soldiers, saying those who are true will be revealed and will resist the infection. He says the Seraph's blood runs through him.

Adrian is thrown into the dungeons. Raklin gives him a choice to be killed so that his men are spared, but Derren convinces Adrian to have faith. Adrian decides the Legion will be judged.

Raklin starts infecting the Legion one by one with his blood, looking for men who will resist. Derren moves to the front of the line in a show of faith, but Adrian soon moves to stop him. Raklin gives Adrian his blood, and Adrian proves himself immune to it. He kills Raklin and takes over Khet.

Adrian frees Raklin's prisoners and meets a priest who had been held in the Khetish dungeons. Nasir is Azuri but is also a Priest of the Blood. It is strange to have a foreigner from the desert nation of Azur as clergy, but Adrian takes him into the Legion when he learns Addo has stolen Myrra's body. The Legion cannot march without a priest, so Adrian makes Nasir High Priest of the Legion.

Adrian goes after Addo but is blinded by rage and falls into a trap. Addo has joined an army of madmen who tear the Legion apart. Adrian has to kill a madwoman wearing the skin of Myrra's face as a mask. He has truly lost Myrra now.

At Nasir's suggestion, Adrian sails to Azur to try to rebuild the Legion.

Lynn reaches the Church of Farkhul and finds that it has been taken by traitors. She is attacked and almost killed but soon finds that her old mentor Elwin has left her a message and is waiting close by.

Lynn finds Elwin in her old training grounds. He is taken by the Madness. The only thing keeping him sane is the Bond he holds with his griffin. He tells Lynn she needs to return to the Sentinels and rally them to fight their old enemy. Lynn is there for Elwin's final moments, but the Madness strings him up as a puppet and she is forced to kill him. She sets off to rejoin the Sentinels, bringing Elwin's body with her.

Lynn goes to Durnn, the city that houses the Sentinel tower. She is met by Thain, a new Sentinel who greets her with a mace to the ribs. Rel, an old companion of hers, soon steps in and Lynn is taken in as a prisoner. Leardin, the Sentinel commander, talks to Lynn and values her experience against the Madness. She is restored to the order, but many of her old companions are not happy about this —especially Ildred.

The Sentinels receive a call for aid and prepare to fly out to help the Legion, which is marching into woods filled with madmen.

The Sentinels are ambushed, and they lose Leardin. Lynn steps forth and brings the remaining Sentinels to what is left of the

Legion. They regroup and decide to send a Sentinel through the pass guarded by the Skygate toward Dakhra to ask for help.

The enemy is guarding the pass, and the Legion have to employ a hit-and-run tactic. They manage to get Thain, the Sentinel who greeted Lynn in Durnn, through the gate to ask Dakhra for help.

Lynn retreats, but her magic is weighing on her. The Bond she has with her griffin that enhances her strength and speed also eats away at her consciousness, and she pushes it to its limit. Lynn falls, exhausted, with the walls of Durnn in sight. She hears wings beating before she passes out and thinks the Seraph coming to take her away.

Five initiates are to be chosen. Nasha participates in the ritual with Tomu and the Roots. It is a ritual performed with ancestor-stone, which Nasha can't touch without become overwhelmed with emotion and losing control. She is forced to touch the stone and is about to lose control, but something pulls back the emotion. She realizes Adda has something to do with this. Five initiates are chosen, Bahar's son Devu, among them. Nasha picks Shai as an initiate. Shai is one of her anchors, a person who helps Nasha retain control when surrounded by other's emotions. Shai is the daughter of her closest friend from the Slopes, who has been killed for trying to steal from the Ronar.

When Nasha is on her way to announce the initiates to the Slopers, Adda stops her and tells Nasha she is to kill Bahar. Nasha tries to resist, but Adda has a similar curse to Nasha's. Adda has control over her curse, though, and Nasha has to accept.

Nasha trains the five initiates to fight in the Proving against the Yltigg clan. There is very little to be hopeful about, and she isn't sure how she'll be able to control all of the emotions that her curse absorbs from others. Nasha uses Shai as an anchor during her training, since emotions in battle are even harder to defend against.

Nasha also trains with Mansa to try to retain control over the emotions. She has lost control in the past; when this happens, she loses sight of who she is and kills everyone around her.

They finally head to the Yltigg for the Proving.

Nasha resists the torrent of emotion. It takes its toll, but she manages to defend the Ronar ancestor-stone prize against the Yltigg initiates. She kills all five Yltigg but finds the Yltigg warden holding a knife to Devu's throat while Shai and another initiate have their hands on the Yltigg ancestor-stone. It is a stalemate. Shai lifts the ancestor-stone off its pedestal, indicating the Ronar victory, but the Yltigg warden slices Devu's throat.

Bahar loses control, invades the arena, and launches a spear through the Yltigg warden's heart. This is an act of war. A Ronar guest has broken the rules of the Proving. The Yltigg attack, and the emotions are too much for Nasha to hold back. She cracks.

Nasha is plunged into a vision of her past. She starts killing everyone around her but also sees what seems to be a Domain city. She is a child in this vision and sees griffin riders as well. They are culling the city.

Nasha doesn't know who she is or who the people around her are. She pushes Shai over a cliff and plummets into the river below after her.

PART 3

Adrian lands on foreign shores and tries to acclimate to a foreign culture. The Azuri prince has been killed, and the Xakhar is in mourning. Adrian is not granted direct audience with the Xakhar, talking to his daughter, Princess Kahlia, instead. He is given quarters in the palace. Derren and Nasir are with him, and there is tension between Adrian's oldest friend and the Azuri priest.

Adrian is called to a courtyard in the middle of the night by Kahlia, the Azuri princess. She poisons Adrian and forces him to agree to help her root out the traitors that are trying to take her father's throne. The ten consul families of Azur keep the nation running but are always a threat to the ruler.

Adrian accepts—he has little choice—but returns to his room and has Derren seek out other allies.

The dead Azuri prince's memory is found worthy, and this is cause for celebration in Azur. When his body is revealed, though, Adrian sees he died from the Madness. There is a blackness around the dead prince's eyes. A feast is held to celebrate the dead prince, and Adrian uses the occasion to question Kahlia about her brother's death. While Adrian is talking to Kahlia, there is an assassination attempt on the princess. Adrian pursues the assassin. Derren follows him.

The assassin leads them to a man who says he represents one of the Azuri consul families and wants to use Adrian's position inside the palace to poison Kahlia. Adrian eventually accepts, thinking this plan will give him more control than depending on Kahlia. He has been a servant to his father all his life. Adrian seeks to take control of his own fate now. He starts planning Kahlia's poisoning with Derren.

Adrian and Derren put their plan in motion, but they are betrayed by Nasir. Derren is killed. Nasir has informed Kahlia of Adrian's new allies, and this is enough to protect the Xakhar for now. Kahlia says she will marry Adrian and he will have his army, but it is clear she is in control and wishes to use Othonea's power for herself eventually. Adrian had ingested poison to try to transfer it to Kahlia. He crawls back to his room and bites off the stopper of the antidote, which had to be kept cooled in his room. The vial shatters and cuts the inside of his mouth, but Adrian survives.

Adrian makes his way to the marriage ceremony, still with a heavy heart. The union takes place, and Kahlia, Adrian, and the Xakhar all drink from the same cup. Because Adrian had just cut his mouth, his blood is mixed in with the wine. Kahlia and the Xakhar are taken by the Madness and die. Adrian realizes that Raklin's infected blood still lives in him, even though it does not drive Adrian mad.

Lynn wakes up in Durnn with Vedyr, her griffin, by her side. The army of madmen is advancing, and they have to prepare for battle.

Lynn is made a general in the Legion and leads troops against the madmen. It seems they will be able to hold the city, but the madmen launch vials with tainted blood at the walls. The defenders of Durnn are infected and start to break from within, taken by the Madness. The walls fall and Lynn pulls back.

They hold as best they can. From the wreckage of the gate, Leardin, the Sentinel commander who was lost earlier, appears. He is infected by the Madness and fights Lynn. Lynn defeats him, and as it looks like Durnn will be lost, a Dakhran airship crests the horizon and drops flaming barrels on the madmen. The Legion celebrate what is certain victory. Lynn has defeated Leardin, but with his last gasp of sanity, he holds out a vial. Lynn discovers the Madness is manmade, and Dakhra is the only nation who could have created it.

The airship keeps advancing and attacks the Legion. Lynn jumps onto Vedyr and, in a desperate attempt that almost takes her life, manages to bring the airship down singlehandedly. They retreat from the burning city of Durnn.

Nasha awakes and realizes she has a newfound control over her curse. Shai is with her, and they must head back to the Ronar. The Yltigg will attack. They are at war.

They return but pass through the Hagun village on the way. It is crumbling, taken by ash, and the Hagun are nowhere to be seen. Nasha brings back this information to the Ronar, but they are preparing to fight the Yltigg.

Iallo drags in the missing Domain prisoner, the son of the nobleman Bahar was after, who seemingly had been taken by the Yltigg. Tomu keeps him safe, thinking he can use the boy to convince the Domain to attack the Yltigg and push the rival clan off the Ronar.

Mansa shows Nasha that the corruption of the land she saw in the Hagun village can only be healed by the blood of Domain soldiers. He reveals he knew about the boy, and Nasha is broken with the knowledge that Mansa could have prevented her from becoming warden. He could have prevented her suffering, but he used her like a tool.

Mansa wants to kidnap the Domain noble and kill him to start a war with the Domain. Nasha goes along with this, but she has plans of her own. She will not let herself be used as a tool anymore.

Nasha manages to kidnap the Domain noble and kill Iallo in the process. They take him to the borderlands, where Nasha has set up an exchange. In return for the Domain noble, mercenaries will take Shai's family to Azur to keep them safe. The noble boy will be returned safely to the Visslands, and there will be no war.

Adda intercepts Nasha and forces her way into the deal with her son Razi. Nasha realizes Razi also has a curse, and he has the power to silence Nasha's curse, sucking out her emotions.

Bahar is leading the mercenaries, though. He escaped the Yltigg somehow and is tortured, his face mottled with scars. He kills Adda, and in the confusion, the Domain boy is killed as well.

Nasha and Shai deal with the mercenaries, but Bahar escapes. They return to the Ronar to warn them of impending war with the Domain.

CHAPTER ONE

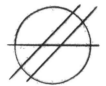

The treachery of the Azuri is well known. One wonders how they've managed to remain united as a single nation for so long. Perhaps there are other, unseen forces at play.

— *Musings on Foreign Politics,* private collection

Adrian had no sword to defend himself. He stood halfway up the low dais, towering over the dead bodies of Kahlia and the Xakhar, eyes moving from the guards closing in, to the Azuri scrambling from their seats.

Lord Attar, the first consul who'd rushed to Kahlia's aid, now stood among the guards. "Murderer!" he cried.

Half-formed thoughts flooded through Adrian's mind: *I didn't do it. I'm still Xakhar. You should be answering to me. Will I lose my army? No, not again.*

The closest guard glared at Adrian, daring him to make a move. Fear had Adrian wanting to run, to attempt some insane jump or roll—anything to get away and live through this.

He held up a hand, palm out. "The union was sealed!" he said. The Azuri language was rough on his tongue, but the guards hesitated.

Adrian took a step back and bumped into something. He turned to find a large, bearded man dressed like one of the Othonean delegates. The delegation had fled in the chaos, but this man stood with a glint of courage in his gaze. More soldier than politician. Nasir and the priest who'd conducted the ceremony stood beside him.

The guards closed in, but Adrian grabbed the Azuri priest and put him in front of the spears. "Tell them," he half-whispered, his fear replaced by an angry will to survive. "Tell them the ceremony is complete."

The man blubbered but failed to obey.

"Nothing to gain from resistance, Prince Adrian." The words came from behind the guards and were commanding enough to hold the men in place.

Adrian's gaze found the speaker. He was gray-haired, clean-shaven, and dressed in silks of green and silver. The silk on his chest bore the image of an upward-pointing sword with ropes coiled around the blade. Lord Khorfa—the leader of Azur's largest military family, and commander of the Azuri army. "Release the priest," he ordered.

Adrian's mind was still working on a plan of escape. He could push the priest down, or try to impale him on the nearest guard's sword . . .

Nasir stepped forward, cutting through Adrian's thoughts. "That will be quite enough," he told the guards. He raised his arms and moved his fingers, as if weaving an invisible thread through the air. The scars on his arms seemed to glow. "He is the Xakhar, Lord Khorfa. It is not for you, Lord Attar, or anyone else to question his actions. The priest's life is his, as are yours and those of all who live in Azur under his grace."

Attar drew closer but remained behind the pointed spears. He fixed his gaze on Adrian. "You come here in rags to beg for our troops, and you think we'll let you take our nation? Seize him!"

A guard advanced, but Adrian shoved the priest into him and

stepped back. The guard swerved clumsily into his companion to avoid putting his sword in the clergyman.

Nasir moved his fingers faster and the scars on his arms bled. Whatever sorcery he was performing pulled the blood from within.

Two more guards jumped toward Nasir, one raising his sword while the other tried to grab him. They tensed midway and dropped their weapons, arms slamming to their sides and staying there, as if bound by rope. Nasir's magic sent a tingle through Adrian. A strange sensation, like a whisper through his veins. The others hesitated at the sight of Nasir's blood magic, but Adrian stood ready.

Another guard stepped forward, but a woman's voice spoke from the back of the chamber and stopped him short. "Tradition dictates he be considered," said the lady in purple and blue. Adrian recognized the colors. Lady Rhiall. He'd seen her husband sitting in the throne room when he'd arrived, but she looked to be the true leader of the merchant house. "Should we squander our ways because of circumstance?" she asked.

"Circumstance, Anisha?" said Attar. "He killed the entire royal line before our eyes."

"There is no proof of that," Adrian said.

"And let us not wade in hypocrisy, my lord Attar," said Nasir. "There was no shortage of plots among the consulate to murder the previous Xakhar."

Khorfa eyed them suspiciously. "He is not Azuri. The consuls must decide who takes the throne."

"The union was made!" Adrian stepped forward. "You cannot—"

"This is an unprecedented event," Lady Rhiall said, "and it cannot be decided here."

"Consuls," Lord Attar insisted. "We cannot let this man get away with this."

Lady Rhiall was already turning toward the door. "Not all consuls are here, Sahim," she said. "Keep them under guard within the palace. We will inform the Jurat and call for a meeting."

Adrian didn't know who the Jurat were. Part of him still wanted to step forward and claim his rightful place as Xakhar, and he might have in the past. But the memory of Derren dying in this foreign land had him holding his tongue.

Nasir kept his gaze on Adrian for a moment, telling him this was the best outcome the situation would allow. Adrian assented, and Nasir lowered his arms.

Khorfa nodded. "We will prepare the bodies for mourning, and the consuls shall judge their worthiness. Remove them."

The customs still sounded strange to Adrian, but saving his own life took precedence over what would be done with the bodies of Azur's previous ruling family.

Some of the guards lowered their weapons and tended to the bodies. Others surrounded Adrian, Nasir, and the remaining delegate and escorted them to rooms in the palace.

Attar locked gazes with Adrian for a moment, then turned and walked away.

Guards were stationed outside Adrian's door. Their chatter bled into the room now and again, but there was nothing of interest in it. The shadows cast by his unused bed and chairs shifted as the day wore on until they melded with the night that crept in through the tall glass window. Adrian paced back and forth before it. His army had been so close. He'd followed the Azuri rituals, suffered their treachery—but it seemed his own blood had betrayed him. Even in death, Raklin seemed tied to Adrian. The priest's plague lived in Adrian's blood, even if it left him unaffected. Adrian had cut his mouth when biting off the plug from the antidote vial. The cuts had reopened during the ceremony, mixed in with the wine, and Raklin's madness had infected Kahlia and the Xakhar. Father's words ran through his mind: *Blood holds ties.* The thought soured Adrian's tongue.

Adrian stopped his pacing. There it was again, that whisper running through his veins. The same one he'd felt in the temple when Nasir used his magic. Kahlia's claw marks burned along the side of his face, but there seemed to be something within the pain that whispered to his mind, directing his gaze toward the gardens outside his window. Adrian opened the glass-paned window quietly and looked over the ledge. Was this an escape? He barely knew, but the call to his blood was inescapable. He had to follow it.

There were no guards at the bottom, but the drop was long enough to break a leg. Adrian looked back at the bed. There were enough sheets there to be tied into a rope. Something he could use to lower himself into the gardens.

He tied the sheets together and pulled them tight to test the knots. He couldn't afford a broken leg. The feeling in his blood rose, and he worked faster. When he was done, he tied the sheets to a bedpost and threw the end over the windowsill. The makeshift rope was long enough for Adrian to slowly lower himself into the gardens, hoping against the warnings of a thumping heart that he would not be seen.

He followed the thrum in his veins, using bushes for cover and taking hedge-lined paths. Soon the thrumming was so strong his muscles all but vibrated with it. He rounded a hedge, alert for Azuri, but he saw no guards. Nasir stood in the shadow of a large tree, hedges all around him. He was so slender, Adrian wouldn't have noticed him if not for the coppery glow that emanated from his long fingers.

Nasir's frayed dark hair seemed almost settled in the moonlight, and his thick beard barely moved as he spoke. "I am glad to see the blood is awakened in you, Lord Light."

Adrian frowned. He hated that it was Nasir doing this. The priest was the one who'd betrayed Derren, and Adrian wished it was the old general—his friend—standing under the tree instead of Nasir. Neither Derren nor Adrian knew the Azuri as well as Nasir did, though, and Derren had paid for it with his life. Adrian had no one else, and he couldn't afford to ignore the priest. "What is this, Nasir?"

"This is where we talk. They have kept us separate for a reason. The consul meeting will be nothing more than a formality if we wait quietly in our rooms. Action must be taken."

Adrian watched as Nasir rounded the tree, remaining in shadows.

"You must prove your strength," Nasir said. "Show that you can be their leader, rather than one who is easily controlled."

"I resisted the Madness that killed Kahlia and her father," Adrian said. "Kahlia knew her brother had been taken by it. Does that not suffice as a display of power? The Madness is stronger than any army."

"That is a start, my Lord Light, but we will need more if we are to survive. And if you are accepted as Xakhar, we will need allies."

"I assume you have a plan?"

Nasir raised a glowing hand. "We show them what the power in your blood can do. I will teach you a simple binding."

"I'm no mage."

"That is a matter of training. One with power such as yours merely needs a nudge onto the path."

Adrian watched the priest's glowing hands. This magic was just one more thing he didn't know. One more thing for Nasir to use against him.

"I know you do not trust me, Lord Light, but this is the way. Blood magic is rooted in sacrifice, in how much you are willing to give in return for all it can bring. I assure you that your sacrifices will taste considerably better with something waiting in return."

"Sacrifice? Are you not a Priest of the Blood?" Suddenly, the title seemed ironic. "You are not supposed to dabble in death."

"On the contrary, Lord Light. The Church is here to prevent death's hold over Avarin. The dead are unworthy, but to deny the use of death as a weapon is to make ourselves weak before it. The Sentinels wield death in favor of life, and the Priests of the Blood heal the worthy through the pain that death seeks to inflict on us. Very few of us are Azuri, of course, and my methods are . . . unique, but the Pontiff has had the wisdom to consider all paths in search of the Promised Dawn. As have I." He pulled out a ceremonial dagger wrought from ruin-stone. "My methods are born of the Azuri mages in the house of the Afterdark, but my faith is in the

Church of the Seraph. That alliance has opened new and unexpected paths."

Adrian narrowed his eyes at the priest. He could be lying, but if Adrian did nothing, he'd fail. He'd die in foreign lands like his brother. No one would come for him. He doubted he'd even be awarded a private cleansing like Jovu's. Father's contemptuous gaze arose in his memory. Father wouldn't care, wouldn't fight the Church to keep Adrian's body preserved alongside Mother's, to be brought back by the Seraph. Adrian gritted his teeth. He would break that gaze. He would make Father care. He stepped forward. "Go ahead."

Nasir stepped from the shadows and held out the dagger. The ruin-stone edge gleamed sharp in the moonlight. "It starts with a cut. Pain is part of sacrifice. It is what will empower you."

Adrian hesitated, watching the pulsing ruin-stone with the image of Derren's dying face in his mind. He could take the knife, stab the priest, and avenge his friend, but that would leave him stranded in a foreign land with no allies. *Time for a new path.*

Nasir's gaze did not waver as Adrian took the knife, placed it on the inside of his forearm, and slid the blade across his skin. It stung, but pain was part of sacrifice.

Nasir nodded. "Follow my movements." He began with a circular motion; easy enough to repeat.

Adrian moved his finger through the air, imitating the move. Nasir nodded once more, then showed him the second sign. Adrian repeated that as well, tracing a horizontal line through the circle, and two diagonal lines across it.

Nasir cleared his throat. "You must let the sting spark the path to where you keep your pain, Lord Light. It will be what gives you power."

Adrian focused on the cut. The gestures seemed to amplify the pain. It dug deep, like a hook in his arm—spreading through his veins and ripping through him until it reached his heart. He held back a scream, but still the pain grew stronger.

"Keep drawing the signs," Nasir told him.

Adrian obeyed, the pain growing stronger all the while—along with the thrumming in his blood. The thrumming took hold of him, so strong he could almost touch it, direct it. The image of Myrra's dead-masked face swam before him, bringing a deep sadness. It was almost like reliving the moment when he'd stabbed the woman who wore Myrra's face as a mask. The grief increased the pain, making the blood that flowed from his cut thicken and coil around his arm. The coils bit into him like sharp blades.

Nasir directed Adrian's arm toward an overhanging branch. The force in Adrian's blood was impatient, aching for release, and he couldn't hold it back for long. Nothing shot from the coiling blood, but Adrian could feel the branch as if it were in his hand. He closed his fingers around it, pulled it left, then right. The wood swayed overhead, as if pulled by invisible strings.

Another pull and Adrian's arm grew heavy, the coils of blood starting to burn. They sapped his strength, like he was bleeding out. He barely noticed Nasir's hands moving before the coil vanished, and the thrumming in his blood suddenly ceased.

Adrian panted as if he'd sprinted around the courtyard. He looked down, expecting his arm to be bloody, but there was nothing other than the shallow cut.

Nasir kept his gaze on Adrian. "You have tasted the power in your blood now, Lord Light. It is not easy to control, but that you managed the binding is proof enough."

"Proof?" Adrian was still panting.

"Blood magic is not about poring over pages, or the study of underlying meaning in texts. It is about the power that comes from within; the power born of pain, and the emotion it stores within us. You have a vast well. You must learn to pull on the right amount of pain, make the correct incision, and use only what is necessary."

Adrian shot a sideways glance at Nasir. He wasn't a mage. Had this always been inside of him? "Can anyone do it?" he asked.

"Most do not hold the same power as you, Lord Light, but to perform the magic, blood must be awakened." Nasir pulled out the cup from the wedding, the one Adrian had shared with the Xakhar and Kahlia.

The notion that the priest had meddled with traces of Adrian's blood from the cup made him want to stab Nasir. "You do not touch my blood again, do you understand?"

Nasir bowed his head. "Of course, Lord Light. But now that it has been awakened, we may move forward. The consuls are testing you. They will not follow one who is weak, who accepts being locked in a room with nothing but wooden doors to prevent escape. . . When they convene tomorrow, we must not arrive as prisoners. Use this power, get rid of the guards at your door, and march into that room as an equal."

As much as Adrian hated following Nasir, it felt good to have the tools needed to once again assume a position of power. "If you have this magic," he said, "why not use it against the consuls earlier?"

"They are warded. To strike at them would require a power few possess. One I certainly do not. You might have that within you, Lord Light, and we will use it to convince the consuls. Khorfa will be hard to sway, but he respects power. Rhiall mentioned the Jurat. Attar has a good relationship with them, but maybe there is something I can do."

"The Jurat?"

"The judges of Azur. It is they who preside over situations like these to ensure that Azur's best interests are served."

"And the others?"

"We do not know where they stand. You will need to keep an eye out in the meeting. Look for cracks, and anyone you can sway."

Adrian breathed deep at last. He barely knew all the consuls' names, but he'd rebuild his legion. He nodded to Nasir and started back, trying to weave the threads of a plan together before morning.

Soon he was back in the garden. Something flashed in the darkness there. A shadow, reddish and fleeting. Adrian halted, hand moving to his hip, groping for a sword that wasn't there. He started forming the image of the signs Nasir had traced, getting ready to paint the air with the circle and lines crossing it, but there was no further movement. He took a tentative step forward, and then another—and noticed a reddish figure standing beside him. He jumped back, and it took him a moment to recognize the face. Not to recognize it, really, but to believe he was seeing it. A second figure stepped from behind a hedge. Both of them were red and translucent, as if made from shifting blood mist. Derren was the first image he saw. Myrra the second.

They were different, though. Derren's face was bloated, his breath rasping. And Myrra's face was not her own, but the mask made from her dead skin.

Adrian understood it then. The pain. Nasir told him that was the root of the magic. But he hadn't expected it to manifest so . . . vividly. Adrian couldn't keep his gaze on either of them. They weren't real, and all they brought was a weight to his chest. He'd lost them. Just like he'd lost Mother. It reminded him of when he'd had no one to lean on, no one to accept or recognize his worth.

Myrra had pulled him out of that hole and fought with him, for him—saving his life more than once. He couldn't help himself. He glanced at her face, and the sight of the dead skin-mask drove a knife through him. It hurt too much, and made him burn for Addo's death.

Myrra stirred and nodded, as if reading his thoughts. The mist that formed her face shimmered, and for a moment, it was whole again. Only for a moment. It sparked a thought, and hope glimmered within Adrian. He couldn't bring Myrra back, but maybe the memory of her would be enough.

The Azuri custom was for the living to judge the deeds of the dead and decide if the memory of them should be kept, but Adrian knew what he had to do. Myrra had given him the answer. The only way to remove the taint of her memory was to kill Addo and make him pay for taking Myrra's body, defiling it, and robbing Adrian of his chance to preserve it. Until then, he'd take the pain, convince the consuls, and rebuild his army.

Adrian closed his eyes and breathed deep, repeating Myrra's ritual to calm himself. He blew out and opened his eyes. The apparitions were gone. Adrian lowered his head and strode back to the bedsheet-rope that hung from his window.

CHAPTER TWO

There are no mentions of Slopers in the Tales because Tedros did not shatter the clans. The leaders did that after he died. We are one, and we will show that to any who threaten our home.

— *Sloper rallying speech*

Shai crouched on a ledge behind a cluster of bushes and pushed her shaggy hair from her face. She looked over the Yltigg force camped before the Ronar village. "What do you think?"

Nasha would have been gritting her teeth in the past, struggling to keep herself from absorbing the girl's emotions, but all she saw now was a misty, leaf-green cloak of apprehension surrounding Shai.

Nasha couldn't blame the girl for the feeling. The Ronar were fighting for their clan's survival. Tomu had sent Slopers out to slow the Yltigg advance, but they'd retreated now and stood atop the walls, their slings and spears trained on the Yltigg camped around the village. The Yltigg surrounded the village on all sides except for the Slopes, but the stones and spears littering the muddy threshold before the main gate of the village made it impossible to mistake where the battle had taken place.

The attackers knew to keep out of projectile range. There was no present assault, but movement in the Yltigg camp suggested it would come soon. Even from the trees surrounding the open space where the Yltigg were camped, Nasha could see warriors sharpening their stone axes, and Yltigg with slings of their own forming up to charge the gate.

Every scrape that sharpened stone in the Yltigg camp sent a shiver through Shai, and her anxiety rippled toward Nasha. The girl wanted to run, to do something. Nasha had managed to get Shai's family on a boat to Azur, but the girl's emotions told her protecting the village was important. Nasha had accepted the girl into the clan, after all. No use fighting for acceptance during a Proving if there would be no clan to come back to. Ironic that this war had started in the Proving itself, and by the hand of a foreigner Nasha had once called a friend.

"What do you think?" Shai's repeated question mercifully pushed the memory of Bahar and his scarred face from Nasha's mind.

It would be a two-hundred-yard dash to the walls, too far for them to go unnoticed, and it was too much to hope the Yltigg wouldn't capture or kill them.

"We're not getting through any of those front gates," Nasha said. "We need to go around."

"Through the Slopes?"

"It's the only way." Nasha nodded toward the Yltigg troops spread in a half-circle around the Ronar village. They were keeping their distance from the area where the Sloper houses began at the base of the Great Mountain. "Even the Yltigg know to stay out of the Slopes," she said. "They'd be lost in it, picked apart. That's our way in."

Even as Nasha spoke, Shai's anxiety crept into her heart. It filled Nasha for a different reason than the enemy at their gates, though. She'd ignored Leku, the leader of the Zaruni, who'd asked for information to exploit the clan. Would that matter now? With the Yltigg at their doorstep? Nasha breathed out. She couldn't let it matter. They had to stop the fighting before the Domain arrived.

Shai nodded, and Nasha started moving along the edge of the forest. "Let's go." *Bahar is coming.* Perhaps it was the thought of him, or perhaps she was just tired, but her dry eyes stung as they crept through the trees, skirting the Yltigg and moving toward the base of the Great Mountain that loomed over the Ronar village.

Nasha had thought they'd be out by now and heading to Azur, away from Mansa's war. Their escape would have fulfilled her promise to Ife: Shai and her family would be safe. Nasha had considered leaving, more than once, before returning to the Ronar village, but she believed what she'd told Shai. The only safe path was through the clans. They would not be forced to live their lives as strangers in another land, and it didn't matter where they'd come from. Nasha and Shai had done more than enough to deserve their place among the Ronar.

Mansa had told her not to be carried away by her title, but she was warden now, and she would be respected for it. She'd learn to control her curse. She wasn't the monster.

Nasha moved through the trees around the back of the Yltigg, making her way toward the Slopes. The scent of the mountain was still thick and pungent, but it was marred by the stench of battle. Even here the smells of the camped enemy and dying clansfolk on the battlefield were strong, tinging the citrusy scent of the trees with the sourness of death. Nasha didn't expect to be seen, but her gaze constantly shifted from the trees to the enemy camp and back again. She used her curse like one of her senses, extending it in search of danger, all the while trying to keep it away from the storm of sensations that engulfed men preparing for battle.

There were too many too close for Nasha to be comfortable. She didn't know if she'd crack like she had in the arena, or if her newfound resistance would be enough to keep her protected from the curse's grip on her mind. There was something different this time. As Nasha crept alongside the Yltigg, she caught glimpses of what seemed to be tall cages within the camp. They were covered with tarps, as if to hide some kind of beast. A few Yltigg stood close, but not too close. Something Nasha was sure only she could see oozed through the tarp. A black mist too thick to be natural. Was that emotion, or something else?

Some of the cages rattled, as if whatever dwelled within was eager to escape. Others were patiently still. Nasha didn't like it, and she didn't want to gamble Ronar or Sloper lives to find out what the cage dwellers were.

Nasha and Shai made their way along the edge of the trees. The sun was sinking in the sky, its light gleaming off the obsidian at the base of the Great Mountain. The uneven wooden houses of the Slopes were visible from their position, but the outpost in their way held smoldering fires, and tents housing hundreds of Yltigg. They were likely there to prevent the Slopers from coming down and attacking their flank.

There were more cages in the outpost. The enemy warriors seemed to be preparing something. The blackness coming from the cages was easier to recognize from here. Grief, but not like the one she'd seen with Bahar when he'd lost Devu. This one was angrier, with streaks of red woven within the black. The nagging feeling at the back of Nasha's mind grew. It was as if something inside them was trying to talk to her, or connect with her curse.

No. You're letting your fears control you. You are not the monster.

Shai turned to Nasha, waiting for the plan.

They wouldn't need stealth. If Nasha could remove the Yltigg in their path and make a run for it, the enemies wouldn't follow. The houses almost formed a wall of their own, and the Slopes were known to hide all manner of traps. Nasha was sure the Slopers would have their most painful surprises awaiting the Yltigg. Perhaps enemy scouts had fallen prey already. That would explain the Yltigg's lack of motivation to advance. Still, there were enough opponents in the way to make Nasha worried about her curse.

You're trusting it too much. She was, but there was no alternate path into the village or onto the Slopes. *Just another risk. You can get past it.*

Nasha pointed around the outpost, to what looked to be the safer routes for them to sneak through. Shai nodded, and they crept from tree to tree, keeping low until they were in position. Fifty paces, maybe more, separated them from where Nasha guessed they'd get enough of a head start to have a chance of reaching the twisting maze of makeshift Sloper houses.

They were close to one of the tarp-covered cages, but she could hear no movement within. It was slightly isolated from the tents, with two men standing beside it, their postures uncomfortable and ethereal dark-green waves coloring the air around them. Much darker than Shai's apprehension. The emotion spoke to Nasha, prompting the smell of burning wood and the taste of iron on her tongue, similar to what she'd experienced in her vision when she'd seen herself as a child. The sensation told Nasha enough. The men beside the cage were afraid, and she wanted to steer clear.

What were the Yltigg doing? Had they found some beast they were too scared to be near? And if so, how would they control it in a battle?

Shai looked at Nasha expectantly, and her shots of anxious anticipation brought Nasha's mind back. This was their opening.

Only two warriors. Ignore the cage.

"You take out the one on the right, then make a run for the Slopes," Nasha said.

"They'll see us." Shai eyed the patch of empty ground between the camp and the Slopes. Impossible to cross without being seen.

"They will, but not in time to stop us. They'd see us anyway, so best to get ahead. We'll be safe once we reach the Slopes." *From the Yltigg, at least.*

Shai looked from Nasha to the Yltigg, then finally took a breath and pulled out a stone-bladed knife. She crept toward the guard on the right.

Nasha made for the guard on the left, her obsidian blades drawn and her curse circling the area in search of incoming Yltigg. She stepped from the trees, picking up speed as she approached her mark. The man heard her approach, but by the time he turned, her blade was buried in his neck. His surprise brushed over her like a breeze, too weak to affect her curse.

A similar emotion came from the spot where Shai had taken out the other Yltigg warrior. The emotion lingered within Nasha for a moment. It had become easier to deal with. There wasn't even the prickling across her skin, the first of her warning signs, but there was something else inside her. A darkness, like a deep pit that filled her with emptiness and spread from her feet, like roots connecting her to the Earth. The emotions were drawn to it and swallowed by this new void.

Nasha felt them running through her, felt the call of the darkness. She moved her feet, and the ground beneath them seemed to have decayed. The sight made her heart push a pulsing dread through her chest, but that emotion was also taken by the void inside her. She didn't like it, but there was no time to stop now.

There was more emotion coming from the cage. Anger. A lot of it. Enough to rekindle the fear planted by the now-dead Yltigg sentries. It prompted Nasha to stride on—each step quicker than the last. They reached the edge of the camp and broke into a run, the sound of Yltigg shouts behind them as they rushed across the open ground.

Nasha looked back to see a dozen Yltigg chasing them as they bolted for the Slopes. A spear flew past Nasha. She lowered her head and glanced at Shai again, hoping the girl could keep up. The Yltigg were hot on their heels with more spears flying. Shai and Nasha dodged the missiles, and Nasha stumbled on a loose rock, sending a chilling wave up her spine. But Shai's determination hit Nasha and kept her upright—legs moving, eyes scanning the Sloper houses for a gap.

Another volley of spears came at them from behind. Nasha was sure they'd be skewered, but there: she found a gap, and the panic forced her into an awkward roll between two Sloper houses. Shai barreled through soon after, spears landing just behind her.

The Yltigg yelled after them but did not pursue. It could have been discipline or fear, but the enemy turned back. A strange sense of satisfaction ran through Nasha, but she cut it off when she felt that darkness within her once more. The curse, eager to be fed.

Nasha stepped forward slowly and let herself be seen so that any

Sloper preparing to attack would hold back. "We are Ronar!" She lowered her voice and turned to Shai. "Stay alert."

Curious gazes might have peeked at them through cracks among the uneven wooden boards of the Sloper buildings, but Nasha pressed on regardless. They moved through twisting streets that soon left the shade of the tightly packed housing behind. The way opened up into a wider earthen thoroughfare flanked by taller houses and crooked alleyways. Nasha kept her head down. Even if the Yltigg didn't follow, the Zaruni could still be prowling the side of the Great Mountain.

As if the thought had summoned them, four men stepped from an alley and blocked their path. Each held a nasty-looking club.

"What do we have here then?" said the first, a bald man with thin pieces of bone piercing each of his ears. He either didn't recognize her or was too confident for his own good.

Another stopped cold a few steps away. "It's . . . the warden."

Shit.

More footfalls behind them split Nasha's focus. How many were surrounding them? Six? Eight? Could she dive into her curse and take them? Would she be able to tap into the speed she'd grabbed on to save Shai?

The dark pit she'd felt held her back. It seemed eager for emotions, as if Zala herself were consuming it.

Nasha's thoughts mingled with the movement of the Zaruni around her, and her skin tingled lightly, not enough to be a warning but enough to tell Nasha that more opponents might be hiding in the shadows.

"You're supposed to be protecting the walls against the Yltigg," Nasha said.

"You come here to supervise?" The bald man said, the sarcasm in his words mirrored by his features.

"Heading to the village," Nasha said. "Your friend has just told you who I am. Best not stand in the way."

"Oh, you ain't getting past here without seeing Leku," a woman's voice said from behind. "He's been asking about you."

"Has he? Well, he can wait until I talk to the Chief. Leku doesn't command the Ronar or hold rank among the . . ."

Emotions rushing toward Nasha stole her words. Anger, exactly like what she'd felt from the Yltigg cage.

All Nasha saw was a blur rushing from an alley as one of the Zaruni was slashed down: a young boy, maybe sixteen. He screamed in pain as a frenzied man with long claws tore through and pummeled him on the ground. The man was Yltigg, but he hardly seemed human. He bit out a chunk of flesh before snapping his head up in search of more prey.

The Zaruni were stupefied, confusion locking them in place. Nasha hesitated as well but was spurred to action as the tainted man charged toward Shai. Tendrils of a desperate anger pulsed off him. Shai tried to roll out of the way, but the Yltigg beast was too fast.

Nasha rushed at him, pulling in the terror from the Zaruni, reaching for her curse to find more speed. The darkness inside her pulled in the emotion, sending chills all over her skin, as if raking it with icy claws. It swallowed the terror like a hungry beast, but as it did, Nasha felt a surge of power that drove her forward. She matched the tainted man's speed and rammed her shoulder into him, making him stumble sideways.

He turned on Nasha. She'd tapped into her curse, and it seemed to open a path for his aura of anger to permeate every piece of her until she was almost taken by it. She screamed it back at her opponent in a rage-filled howl.

The man dashed at her behind a wave of pure rage. All Nasha could do was duck the swipe aimed at her head, then place her foot firmly behind her and thrust her long knife into the man's gut. He was supposed to double over, reeling in pain, but he hardly flinched. He twisted his torso, pulling Nasha's striking blade out of her hands. Nasha was left with only her parry blade, but her display was enough to embolden the Zaruni.

Two of them ran at the man, batting at his back and head with their clubs, but he still showed no pain. He turned on one of the Zaruni—the woman who'd wanted to bring Nasha to Leku—and slammed his forehead into hers, then slashed at her chest with his claws. The woman screamed, but it was the opening Nasha needed. She inverted her grip on the parry blade, lunged at the man from behind, and stuck her blade in the back of his head. His suddenly limp body fell atop the woman, who screamed and convulsed. Two of the Zaruni pulled the body off the woman and knelt beside her, but something hit Nasha; the same rage she'd felt from the attacker. She whirled toward him, but the body lay unmoving. Instead, the woman's wails of pain were turning into growls of rage.

"Get away from her!" Nasha yelled.

The man tending the woman noticed the transformation and jumped back as she lifted herself to one knee. The nails on her hands grew, fast and long, tearing at the skin. Her muscles bulged, body jerking awkwardly. She looked up with a deathly frenzy in her gaze, baring long teeth as a deep blackness spread across the skin around her eyes. The aura of rage and desperation around her grew stronger as well.

Nasha's eyes widened. *It's infectious!*

There was a kind of resistance to it, as if even with her body transformed, the woman fought whatever had taken hold of her. Her struggle shot a familiar sensation through Nasha, similar to the one she felt each time her curse reared its head. The recognition filled her with dread. Was this like her curse? Was this what Nasha would become if she lost control? A mindless, rage-filled monster?

Renewed anger shot from the woman, pulling Nasha into action. The decision wasn't hard to make. She grabbed her striking knife from the dead man's gut, then took two quick steps towards the struggling woman. Nasha hacked twice at her exposed neck, then a third time to cut off her head before she had the chance to attack. The head rolled toward the bald man with the pierced ears. Nasha scanned the strangers, looking for anyone else who might have been wounded. Shai stood beside her, alert but probably not knowing what to look for.

Nasha's skin tingled and her vision was blurred, but as she exhaled and the emotions cooled, her curse, and the warning signs, slowly receded. Finally, she looked to Shai. "Are you hurt? Did he scratch you?"

Shai shook her head. "No, I'm fine."

The Zaruni stood staring but seemed to have lost interest in barring Nasha's path. She made to move past them, but a shadow moved against the setting sun on the makeshift balcony of a building ahead. Leku's curly hair and flat nose were easily recognizable as he looked over Nasha. He eyed the dead bodies with what might have been a shred of recognition, then gestured toward the door below the balcony. "We need to talk, Warden."

CHAPTER THREE

Throughout the centuries that the Sentinel order has watched over the Domain, the Pontiff has never allowed it to grow to more than three-score. Such restraint shows wisdom yet begs the question of what a larger force would mean.

— Excerpt from The Holy Church of the Seraph and Its Orders

Lynn flew on Vedyr overhead as the survivors of Durnn twisted their way on the path below, heading as far from the burning city as possible. They kept to the main roads, which were wide enough for ten abreast, faster and likely safer than the woods that flanked the hard-packed earthen thoroughfare. Fleeing civilians mingled with what was left of the Legion. A few Sentinels formed a perimeter on the ground, while others flew on their griffins above with Lynn—Rel among them, flying close by.

The smoke from the burning city marred the sky behind them. The smell was strong, but they were far enough from Durnn for Lynn to wonder if the scent was in her mind. Like the voices that tried to burn her sanity away.

You brought death into Durnn, Alren said. *You couldn't protect it, just like you couldn't protect us.* He was right, and the guilt turned in Lynn's gut. She tightened her grip on Vedyr's reins and lifted her gaze to the ever-growing Seraph's mark in the sky. It was dimmer now, but large enough to look like a second sun. Whatever that mark was, it hadn't saved them. And if it was the Seraph's eye, as people were calling it, then the Seraph seemed content to watch. Could Lynn still count on Her? And if the Seraph had abandoned them, could they still defeat this enemy?

The refugees below stopped to rest, and the Sentinels steered their griffins to the ground. Lynn aimed for a spot that was far enough away to keep the Durnnish comfortable. No matter the result of the battle, or how close people had lived to the Sentinel tower, the griffins' presence would always instill fear, even from a distance.

Most of the Durnnish had escaped with only the clothes on their backs, and much of those were ripped or in tatters. A few had managed carts, and the elderly struggled to find room among them. There were noblemen at the front of the column, but the Sentinels gave them no special treatment. They seemed even more down-trodden than the poor folk, perhaps feeling they'd lost more. Lynn wasn't sure how long the refugees would last, but she grasped for comfort in the thought that they were all still alive.

This is what the Seraph wants. Death did not get its hands on these people.

The voices laughed at her thoughts. Or maybe it was death's own voice. More Sentinels descended, and their beating wings pushed the laughter away.

Vedyr touched down on a clear patch of grass fifty feet from the road. Lynn jumped off and moved to join the gathering Sentinels. She thought she saw a newfound respect in some of the other Sentinels' gazes. Enough of the Legion had seen her stand against Commander Leardin, and the stories had already spread. Even for a Sentinel, taking down an airship singlehandedly was no easy feat, and Lynn wasn't sure if she could do something like that again.

Olem was still sub-commander and had assumed the leadership of the Sentinels, but there were some—like Brehnna and Deria—

who seemed to walk a step closer to Lynn. As did Rel. Lynn wasn't sure how to feel about that. Brehnna had threatened her with a knife mere days before. But perhaps defeat had left even the Sentinels starved for hope and clinging to what they could, even though Lynn's display had not prevented Durnn's fall.

Taking down the ship wasn't enough, was it? Dentos said, the mockery clear in his tone. Lynn shook her head and kept walking.

Olem had gathered the Sentinels at the edge of a wood. Some of the griffins rested nearby, keeping prying ears at bay. Others patrolled the sky above.

Lynn hadn't been back with the Sentinels for long, but the old roles were still played. They separated into groups of Channelers and Syphoners. Channelers still fought, but the raw power of their Bonds was not as strong as that of the Syphoners. They had other ways of balancing the scales, though. Rel was a Channeler. He provided Lynn and the other Syphoners with ruin-stone during the battle and healed any—admittedly uncommon—wounds they suffered. That Rel and the other Channelers had to be focused on healing instead of fighting now said much about how the perceived supremacy of the Church's elite had been affected, even among themselves.

Lynn could hear Ildred's voice as she drew near.

". . . need to attack." Ildred drove a fist into his open palm. "Their troops are still on the way from Dakhra. We might not take back the city, but if we can strike at their airships, we'll weaken their advance."

Lynn understood why he'd think that. The Sentinels were not accustomed to being beaten, but turning back to Durnn would risk ending them all. Even so, there was no lack of incentive. Elwin's body had been preserved by Leardin and sealed in the catacombs, but the entrance was known only to the commander and sub-commander. Lynn had to keep faith that the Dakhrans would not find it, that her mentor might still be brought back by the Seraph.

"And how will you deal with the Madness?" Lynn said as she approached. Her muscles still ached from the fight with Leardin, and her shoulder flared each time she turned.

"Ah, you're still here!" Ildred said. "Good, I can kill you myself, traitor." He drew a blade and stepped toward her.

Lynn spread her arms. "Are we still doing this? Is the true enemy not clear enough? They're spreading the Madness. This disease, this enemy we thought was sent to us by Death, was created inside the Domain. Fighting among ourselves is what's put us here."

Ildred kept coming, but Rel and Deria stepped in front of him. Olem too, and for once his voice seemed commanding. "She's right, Ildred. If you wish to bring us more death, then you can head to Durnn and start with your own."

Ildred glared at Lynn, but the prospect of taking on several Sentinels held him back. He spat on the ground and strode from the circle that had formed around him. He kept to the edge of the group, with Wyman and Steck, two of the Sentinels who'd followed him from the start.

Lynn turned to Olem. "We can't attack them while they have those potions. If we get infected, we'll add to the threat."

"They can't have planned this without a cure," Brehnna said. "Syvern can't invade the Domain on chaos alone. Some of them seemed more in control than others."

"What are you suggesting?" Olem asked.

"That we take it from them." Brehnna shrugged. "We fly to Dakhra. We're Sentinels. Nothing has ever held us back. We can't let Syvern take our confidence along with our pride."

"That's exactly the kind of thinking that got the commander killed," Rel said.

There were a few murmurs of agreement, and Lynn noticed some jaded eyes.

You're lucky some of them are being smart about this, unlike you, Cara said.

"Rel's right," Lynn said. "We don't know what waits for us in Dakhra, and I doubt Syvern would leave his alchemists unguarded. Besides, even if they haven't advanced from Durnn, we can't abandon Alteria."

Rel looked at Lynn, then a few of the others. "Does the Pontiff still have the Dakhran queen's body?"

Olem shook his head. "He preserved it, but Syvern's only demand was that she be kept in Dakhra. Maybe he was planning his betrayal all along."

Ildred moved back in, his pride seemingly swallowed. "We need to do something. Don't you see what Syvern's doing? He's trying to scare us! We're Sentinels, we can take them down!"

"And what should we do with all these people?" Lynn asked.

Ildred worked his jaw before answering. "These people? What about Thain? He went through that pass to get Dakhra's help on your suggestion. We could have a brother being held by Dakhra. We cannot sit by and watch!"

"I think the Pontiff is the one who should tell us that." Olem was trying to replicate Leardin's tone, but his voice didn't hold the same weight. "The Domain is under siege. We are its protectors. We cannot risk losing ourselves because Durnn has fallen. Rel, gather the Legion generals and push toward Alteria; we will find guidance with the Pontiff."

"Coward." Ildred turned his back, already heading back to his griffin—a massive, black-feathered beast whose silver eyes never left his master. Some followed Ildred, trying to offer support or wisdom, but he was soon mounted and flying off.

He'd never talk like that to the commander. Shame he's dead, Cara said.

Lynn watched Ildred, her earlier guilt rippling through her. Leardin would have known how to deal with this. She lingered close to Rel as the Sentinels dispersed and Olem made for his own griffin, who waited beside a clump of trees.

Rel turned to Lynn, but before he could speak, screams sounded from the refugee area. Lynn dashed toward them, Rel at her side, their griffins taking off overhead. Lynn fed Vedyr all her pent-up anger from the recent defeat and received a burning in her eyes and a power that coursed through her limbs. She leapt as she reached the edge of the road, clearing the crowd, and landing with a cloud of dust on the other side, close to the source of the screams. Rel's bulk thundered onto the ground behind her a moment later, followed by Vedyr and Rel's griffin, Ulenia.

Lynn dashed from the edge of the road and through the trees, pulling out her war-scythe and mace. There was movement up ahead. Growling. Lynn let the growls run through her and burn into anger. She used that to pull on her Bond with Vedyr. She reached a group of soldiers. Ferrin stood before them, holding a tall shield while facing down a madman.

The enemy had all the effects of the Madness: his nails had grown into claws, and the skin around his eyes was tainted black. Two soldiers were already cut open on the ground behind the beast, and he dashed forward, moving faster than the soldiers standing in his way.

Ferrin raised his shield as the opponent pounced with swiping claws. The shield absorbed two blows as Lynn rushed past the soldiers and met the madman with a swing of her mace to the head, launching him into the trunk of a tree. Lynn raced forward and stuck her war-scythe through the enemy's forehead to finish him.

"Behind me," Lynn shouted. Ferrin obeyed, and the soldiers gathered behind him. Ferrin kept his spear raised as shadows flitted among the trees.

The growling rose and more madmen dashed out, only to be crushed when Vedyr's huge form landed on them. He dug his claws into the back of two madmen as he landed, then swung his tail at three more, sending them flying through the trees. Ulenia landed beside Vedyr, snapping off a woman's leg with her beak and swiping at two more who lunged from the shadows, while Rel put his spear through a madman's neck.

The woods were still, the enemy dealt with, but the silence was broken by coughing from a Legion man on the ground. There was a hole in his armor, and blood leaked out. Soldiers gathered around their injured comrade, but Ferrin stared into the woods. "Think they've advanced from Durnn?" he asked.

Lynn looked at the man she'd slammed into the tree: common clothes, and no armor or weapons. She shook her head. "Infected, but not Dakhran."

Ferrin looked to the fallen man. He was hesitant, as if his dead sister still weighed on him.

"I'll deal with him," Lynn said.

Ferrin nodded, features somber. He called to the other soldiers and moved off.

Lynn and Rel walked up to the injured man. Vedyr and Ulenia stalked through the trees like predators seeking another kill. Lynn didn't give the man time to beg. She sank her war-scythe into his heart without looking. Rel looked at her. "What?" she asked.

"When we reach Alteria," he said, "you should throw in for the commander's seat."

"This again?"

"They believe in you."

"Don't know that they'll be believing for long. I'm not sure how much time I have here."

Rel frowned. "The commander took you back, Lynn. You're one of us."

Lynn shook her head. "This isn't about me leaving. The Pontiff will want answers. I was the one who pushed to open the Skygate. Ildred is an ass, but he's right about Thain. We may have lost him, and it was all my plan."

"Olem went along with it."

"Olem hasn't been hiding from the Church. They'll consider everything. The Breath has been weakened, and all the other leaders will be there. Chancellor Burke has always made sure he represents the Body in Choosings, and I doubt High Bishop Reznik will leave the Bone out of it. They'll call for a Questioning before I can even think of the commander's position."

Rel's frown deepened. "Chancellor Burke is a sensible man, and Reznik has never meddled with the Pontiff's affairs. His Questionings have always been focused outside the Church."

The Bishops of the Bone had always been the counterpoint to the Sentinels. Reznik's bishops were focused on obtaining information, working in shady chambers behind closed doors while the Sentinels protected the Church on the battlefield. Lynn wasn't terribly confident when it came to Reznik's impartiality. "Times have changed, Rel."

Other Sentinels approached the source of the commotion, but Ferrin seemed to have relayed the happenings, and they were now herding the crowd away from the trees. Vedyr and Ulenia followed Lynn and Rel from the woods. Rel's griffin was smaller than Vedyr, her feathers gray, while Vedyr's were closer to white. They were as tall as three men, with sharp beaks and claws. Even if Ulenia was smaller, she was just as imposing as any other griffin and had a dangerous glint in her eye.

Rel was silent for a moment. He'd been quieter since the battle in Durnn. It seemed like times *were* changing, and his easy laugh had been absent for some time now. "Becoming commander will end the discussions about you," he said. "You'll be safe."

"And how safe will the Sentinels be with the decisions I make? Look at what just happened to Durnn."

"You think Leardin never made mistakes?"

"None like these."

"He failed to see Dakhra prepare an invasion for a century, Lynn. We all did."

Vedyr nuzzled Lynn, as if feeling her nervous energy.

"I'm not a good leader," Lynn said. "And even if I were, there would never be enough support."

"I can change that."

"No." Lynn's tone was final. Leardin had been a great leader, but she'd seen him struggle under the weight of his office. She would fight the Madness, rally her brothers and sisters on the battle-field if need be, but she would not entrench herself in the politics of the Church.

"There's something else," Rel said. "If this Madness is over a century old, don't you think someone in the Church would know about it? The Pontiff even? You need to be close to them to find out, and you're the only one who can be trusted."

Lynn shook her head. "I know nothing of politics. Our focus needs to be on fighting the Madness and finding a cure. Let Olem deal with the Pontiff and the other leaders."

Rel gave her a look that told Lynn he wasn't done with the subject, but he didn't push it. "Did you see anything that could help during the battle?"

Lynn looked over the Durnnish refugees, who were back to

trudging up the road. Ferrin had moved on, pulled away by duty. Her mind went back to the abbot and the priests in Farkhul: Andral and Talbot. "I met a few madmen before going back to the order," she said. "They were . . . lucid. Didn't seem to be with Dakhra."

"How?" Rel asked.

Lynn was shaking her head. "I'm not sure. Elwin said he'd channeled the Madness away as well, but the priests didn't have griffins or a Bond." She paused. "Did any of the griffins turn in the battle?"

Rel cocked his head. "I saw wounds, some even tearing skin. We watched them for a while, but neither rider nor griffin was affected." Rel's eyes narrowed. His hand went to the pouch at his belt, and he pulled out a shard of white-veined ruin-stone. "You think the stones hold the answer?"

"The griffins' hearts are made of it," Lynn said. "And we use the stones for the Bond. If Elwin was using his Bond to stay sane . . ." Lynn's thoughts trailed off. Could ruin-stone be at the heart of it? The Church had always kept a strong hold over ruin-stone supply. To most people, ruin-stone was merely the material of relics, and the stone's value stemmed from the Church's use of it. As a Sentinel, though, Lynn could feel the power, the anger that could be stored within the stones. Perhaps Rel had a deeper knowledge of how they might alter it to fit their needs.

Lynn thought back to it. Andral had worn a massive ruin-stone pendant around his neck all the while. The memory made her skin prickle with what might be the first glimpse of hope she'd had in a long time. "Can you make it work?" she asked. "Can we use ruin-stone to heal the Madness?"

Rel shook his head. "Not with what I know. I tried during the battle, but got nowhere."

"How did the madman stay sane, then?"

"I don't know." Rel said. "We'll have to experiment in Alteria."

CHAPTER FOUR

Add the previous mixture to two parts Solanum, one part Arcinum. Heat to a boil, stir. Let sit.

—Unnamed cure attempt number 47

Kadmus stood on the roof of the abandoned building, with Grunt at his side. The distant roar of the falls was over-ridden only by the sound of the drunken men from the tavern below.

They were nowhere near the upper city, where the tiered homes of the nobility rose beside the triple waterfall of Pelaket, the Viss-lands' capital. There were too many patrols close to the falls, and Kadmus couldn't afford to be seen.

"The Dripping Bucket." He could hardly imagine how someone would drink in a place with such a name, yet here they were.

The big man beside him grunted, his gaze fixed on the dimly lit street below. Grunt was the first name Kadmus thought of when apprenticing in the Church. The name had stuck, the same way

Grunt had taken to calling Kadmus "Leech" after he'd used the things one too many times in front of him. They'd both failed in their Church training. Kadmus as priest, Grunt as griffin rider, but the names remained.

The building below was the only source of light on the street. Its illumination bled around the silhouettes of men laughing, perhaps even fighting—all of them holding tankards of some kind. Kadmus held back a sneer at the boorish display below. He'd rather avoid places like this, but leaving Grunt to come alone would imply trust, and, well, Kadmus had learned that trust was a trap even before his parents sold him to the Church.

Grunt remained silent, shifting slightly under the padded leather and the mask Kadmus had provided. Kadmus wore a mask himself. Always safer to conceal one's identity when hunting for madmen in a city intent on eliminating the beasts.

Hiding the scars on his face might have been a priority for a vainer man, but Kadmus was focused on function. He was no tailor, and no smith either, but he understood function. The padding would protect Grunt from the madmen's claws, at least initially. The leather mask was a failsafe, to take away the threat of Grunt's teeth in case he became infected and started to turn, but Kadmus didn't have to tell him that.

Even though they'd known each other as children, Kadmus wasn't necessarily fond of Grunt's company—he'd always preferred to be alone—but he couldn't deny Grunt's usefulness.

Kadmus ran a hand over the syringe in his robe pocket. If the padding didn't work, the concoction would end Grunt's life before he could fully turn. His hand brushed over the knife beside the syringe. Cruder methods would have to be employed if the opportunity for a clean stab of the syringe did not present itself.

"Another lost one?" Grunt asked in a muffled voice.

Kadmus shook his head. "No, too early."

They'd tried different spots each night, moving farther and farther away from the upper city that flanked the falls. Now, uncomfortable visits to shady streets had become intimidating. These were the less protected areas of Pelaket. Some might say they weren't even part of the capital city, but Kadmus had to brave them. There was no other choice if he wanted more test subjects.

Grunt hadn't complained, and his quiet was almost galling. Kadmus knew the man's loyalty likely ran deep, but loyalty had a way of pulling up roots when one's life was threatened.

Trust is a trap, he reminded himself. *Even when others are the ones offering it.*

Moving shadows caught Kadmus's eye. At first he thought it was just one of the delinquents stumbling into an alley to relive himself, but as his gaze followed, the shadow's movements became sharper. The laughter on the street turned to silence, then to questions and finally panic as the shadow pounced on the nearest drunk.

Grunt shifted, but Kadmus put out his hand slightly. "Wait."

The madman was moving faster than normal. Not as fast as some Kadmus had seen, but enough that he knew to wait for the Madness to work its way through the man and consume him; then his speed would come closer to normal, and the danger would be reduced.

After a moment, Kadmus descended the dusty stone steps of the abandoned building. Desperate sounds rose outside, but he tried to keep his mind still, calculating possible outcomes as they walked through the gloom. He only needed one madman, but they couldn't take too long. One infected could transmit it to more people, but Kadmus didn't know how they'd react. The Madness could burn through and kill the others. Better to follow the certain path, which meant he had to wait for most of the drunkards to flee or die—but not too long, or the madness would kill the attacker.

Kadmus increased his pace until he and Grunt stood in what was once a doorway. There was nothing to bar their path now, and Kadmus peered out at streets taken by fleeing men and stumbling confusion. The madman had eviscerated three victims with tooth and claw—their bodies were bleeding out on the street before the tavern. None seemed in any state that might indicate survival. A shame. It would have been easier to capture them as they transformed.

Kadmus sighed and looked at Grunt. The man was still beside

him, but the occasional shift of his feet gave away his discomfort. Even after helping Kadmus capture these men for days, seeing them up close still injected him with nervousness, no matter his size. Perhaps it was knowledge that brought him fear. Children are fearless because they don't know the dangers that await them in life, but the danger here was clear. It was depicted in bleeding guts and choking men on red-stained streets.

Most of the people seemed to have fled now. The madman was rounding on the last of his prey: a man too drunk for his reflexes to carry him away, whimpering for help as he backed up against a house wall. Kadmus watched. Perhaps some noble warrior might have the inclination to save the drunkard, but this was the perfect bait.

He nodded to Grunt, who stepped forward gingerly at first, then faster, rushing toward the madman just as he pounced on his victim. It was good that Grunt followed orders without hesitation—he knew it was the difference between life and death, as well as his pay. And Kadmus made sure to pay. No amount of loyalty ever outweighed the clink of gold.

Grunt arrived just as the madman's claws fell, drawing screams along with the drunkard's blood. Grunt grabbed the madman's hair from behind and pulled out a syringe of his own. It was filled with the serum Kadmus had prepared to dull the beast's senses until he fell unconscious. Grunt stuck it in the man's neck, but the madman was more aware than the thug had predicted. He threw back an arm and sent Grunt flying. He fell skidding with his back on the cobbles and the madman turned, furious.

All Kadmus could do was frown. Had the serum been injected? Had he miscalculated? Habit had him looking down as if to search for notes, but he was not in his workshop. The madman rushed at Grunt and swiped down, but the large man rolled away before the claws found him. His opponent didn't stop, and leapt, forcing Grunt to move away, trying to slide back on his elbows. But the sound of tearing told Kadmus the strike had landed.

There were no screams, no grunts either. Grunt got to his feet, and the madman advanced, but stumbled. A thrill ran through

Kadmus. Had the serum taken effect, or was the Madness consuming the beast? Another step and the frenzied man folded forward and fell to one knee.

Grunt was still backing up, and Kadmus found his own syringe. He wasn't sure if Grunt had been wounded. Best be sure.

The madman fell with his face to the ground, panting at first, then slowly closing his eyes. Grunt advanced on his foe now, pulling out a coiled chain at his hip and tying the madman's clawed hands. The beast did not react, already falling into slumber or death. For a moment, the only sounds were the distant screams of men calling for the city guard, and the ever-present rumble of the waterfalls. Kadmus breathed in, perhaps in relief, and only then smelled the stench that permeated the street. Death and liquor mingled, enough to drive any sane man away. Maybe what he was doing was not sane, but there was a certain insanity to protecting loved ones.

He moved toward Grunt, the syringe in his hand. "Is he dead?"

Grunt shook his head and emitted the sound Kadmus had named him for. Kadmus took the moment to check for blood on the big man. There was some on his back from when he'd crawled away, but Kadmus couldn't tell if there was more. As if recognizing Kadmus's intent, Grunt showed him the ripped leather where the madman's strike had landed. There was no blood around it, only peeled-back layers and the glint of chain mail beneath. "Didn't get me," he said through the muffling mask.

Kadmus nodded. "Put the bag over him. We have to get out of here before the watch arrives."

Grunt was already moving before Kadmus finished his words. A moment later, he was hauling the madman over his shoulders. Kadmus's mind worked over the calculations while he waited. Perhaps the spot Grunt had injected the madman had been wrong, or perhaps the serum had been too weak. He gave Grunt a wide berth, just in case the second option proved true and the madman woke.

They kept their heads down and traveled mostly through shadow until they were far enough from the scene that regular city patrols were their only worry.

The sound of the waterfalls grew all the while, and the lights of the palace atop them twinkled in the night. The streets sloped upward as they walked toward the inner part of Pelaket. There wasn't long to go now, and Kadmus's shop was far enough from the fancier areas to be comfortably unremarkable.

They turned the last corner and waited at the mouth of the street that led to the potion shop. There was no movement, but even at this time of night, Kadmus was watchful. He waited, hand held out to Grunt as his gaze flitted between the street and the bag on Grunt's back, searching for movement. He saw nothing and hurried toward the shop's back door. He unlocked and pushed it open for Grunt to hurry through and down the stairs to the workshop.

The big man descended, already familiar with this part of the process after having chained four other captives. Three were still alive—two women and a man. They weren't weak, but too many times, Kadmus had failed to come up with a cure. Perhaps the answer did not live in their blood. Hence the new madman.

Kadmus followed Grunt downstairs and found him opening the bag and shoving the unconscious man into the ruin-stone cage. Grunt slammed it shut, as if the beast might wake at any moment. Behind Kadmus, a woman stirred in another cage, too weak to fight the serum he'd administered.

Grunt removed his mask and looked to Kadmus, who produced a cinched bag that clinked with the familiar sound of coins.

"You saved my wife's life," Grunt said. "You don't need to pay me for every job, certainly not that much."

"I pay you for more than the job." Gold always brought more loyalty than words. Kadmus removed his own mask and tossed the bag to Grunt. "Go home."

Grunt nodded and left, leaving only his silence behind.

Kadmus approached the madman's cage. A small hope tried to flutter within him, but he crushed it. Hope was just the mind's irrational attempt at trust when there was no control to be had. He would be in control now. It had taken him long enough to find another madman, but this would be the one to bring him what he needed: a cure for this mad plague.

His insides burned with anger at the thought that the plague had been created by Dakhra. Part of him considered trying to get past the border to find a cure, but there was too much uncertainty in that plan, and Nima would not manage the trip.

Kadmus checked the lock on the cage, then took a different stairway up to his shop, where shelves of potions, salves, and serums sat in darkness, awaiting his return. He stepped from behind the counter and climbed another set of stairs, making his way to Nima's closed door. Logic implied he should lock it before leaving, but she'd always been his weak spot. He opened the door, heart pounding. He never knew, when he opened that door, whether his daughter would still be alive.

Nima lay on her bed, and Kadmus watched her chest for a long moment. She was breathing softly, as she had been when he left. Her long black hair framed the soft skin of her face and the stubby nose that was just like her mother's had been. The blackness around her eyes was there as well.

Kadmus grasped the shard of ruin-stone around his neck. It was not wrought in any Sign of the Seraph. It was the same stone he'd held in the church when his parents had sold him all those years ago. The same one he'd grabbed onto ever since, not out of faith—the Seraph was just a story—but of habit. He removed the pendant and placed it on Nima, then pulled out another shard of ruin-stone and placed it over her chest. Finally, he pulled out a vial. The one with the serum he used to keep her stable. Alive, but still plagued.

He opened her mouth gently and poured it in, holding her in his arms. There was a slight surge in her breathing, enough for her to keep fighting the Madness. Enough for Kadmus to take another breath of his own.

"Keep fighting. I'll find you a cure."

Kadmus returned to the basement workshop, ready to pursue a thousand paths in search of the one that would prove true. He didn't lock Nima's door behind him.

CHAPTER FIVE

The Seraph's reach extends as far as the faithful will take it, but this world is not without enemies. Keep strong in your faith, but do not let it become a blinding darkness.

—*The Book of the Blood*

The blackness that enveloped Adrian lightened as the morning sun banished the shadows from his room. The velvet on the chairs regained its red and the colors in the room slowly returned. Myrra. Derren. Myrra. Derren. Their images were not as he remembered, but their memories had paced the room with him all night. Myrra's curls framing her bright green eyes, Derren's slight grin showing through his thick beard. The memories, too, were chased away by the sun. All that remained when Adrian closed his eyes was Addo's thin-lipped sneer. How long would the bastard dominate Adrian's thoughts? Even outside the Domain, Addo still commanded Adrian's pain. Death would be too good for him. He would suffer. He'd feel every bit of what Adrian felt now.

Light had taken the room, as had the chatter of the guard outside his door. Words were interspersed with the tapping spear butts; an effort, perhaps, to remain awake until relieved by their morning companions. Time to go.

Adrian opened the door and eyed the guards on either side. They were armed with spears and scowls, but he stepped out all the same. "Return to your room," one of them said.

Adrian's gaze did not waver. "I must talk to my delegate. This doesn't need to be a problem for you. Follow me if you must." He made to walk down the corridor, but the man blocked his path. The second guard moved behind Adrian. "Return to your room," he said, slamming the butt of his spear on the floor as if Adrian were some dog who'd be spooked by it. It set a fire in Adrian's veins, and his words came with little thought.

"Do you know what killed the Xakhar and the princess?" Adrian drew close to the guard before him. "It was a curse. A curse that lives in my blood." Adrian bit at the side of his mouth that still stung from the cuts. The taste of blood filled his tongue, and he smiled at the guard through what he knew were red-stained teeth. "You can stab me, but how can you be sure my blood won't kill you too?"

It was a gamble, but Adrian knew rumors had a way of working themselves up enough that he was confident in the risk. The guard before him stepped back, losing faith in his weapon. The guard behind Adrian seemed frozen in place.

"As I said, this doesn't need to be hard. Just point me to my delegate."

The first guard took another step back and nodded down the hall. The three of them started walking. Adrian kept his eyes trained straight ahead, going over the plan in his mind and breathing steady.

They came to a door with a guard standing outside. Adrian fought to keep his expression masked. The plan would be easier with fewer guards. The sentry at the door hesitated for a moment, but whatever hierarchy ruled the palace protectors seemed to give

Adrian's guards the final word. The door was opened, and they all filed inside.

The sentries whispered among themselves, the one who'd been watching the door probably trying to understand what was going on, but Adrian's attention was fixed on the man standing before him. He'd changed into lighter clothes and didn't seem perturbed by the guards. He seemed solid enough to serve Adrian's purpose; he'd need help to knock out the guards. The delegate looked more like a thug than a diplomat. Adrian was hoping Father had sent him here to help, rather than as a slight. It was a slim hope, but it had grown at the sight of the man, and at how calm he'd been during the wedding.

The room wasn't too different from Adrian's own. Tall glass-paned window at the far end, uncomfortable velvet-backed chairs, low center-table. Adrian rounded the table to approach the delegate, who shifted on his feet as if Adrian himself were a jailer. "You know who I am, yes?" Adrian asked in Othonean.

"They told me you were a prince or somethin'."

The man's Othonean wasn't perfect, but it was good enough. Adrian frowned. Definitely not a noble. "Where did my father find you?"

"I was hired. One of them lords took me from the gallows in Sacantha. Guess I should thank his fear of the desert lands." He chuckled. "Gave me dress and pay to tail him during the ceremony."

"Did King Iridan know about this?"

The man shrugged. "Not my place to tell. Job's a job. Better when it pulls me away from the noose."

Sounded about right. Father must have scrounged the unworthiest of the noble families to send overseas. Not influential or popular enough to warrant Othonean or even their own guards. Only the ones who wouldn't make a difference if lost, and who might have enough fear to bring a bodyguard. "What is your name?" Adrian asked.

"Bac."

"My title is Lord Light," Adrian said.

"Doesn't change my name." Bac eyed a side table supporting a bottle of shraz. Adrian hated the drink, but it seemed the Azuri made a point of having a bottle in every room of the palace.

Some instinct arose in Adrian, one that wanted to put this man in his place, but he held it back. Insubordination was a sign of recklessness or an assertion of courage, and Adrian could use either right now. "Why were you in prison?"

The man shifted again. "I was put in Dalhold for alleged murder."

"Alleged?"

"No one ever proved it. Don't know that no one ever tried either."

"Are you a murderer?"

"Does it matter? I'm disgraced, blessing's gone."

"It matters."

The man looked at Adrian for a long moment. Long enough for the guards to draw a step closer. Good. That would reduce the distance, make it easier to bring them down.

"Man crept up on me in the night, thought he could take me out, then take my sister. Smashed a bottle against my head and thought I'd go down. Grabbed my sister, started groping." Bac's voice darkened. "I didn't cut him with the bottle. He didn't deserve it to be quick. I pulled him off her, beat him down until he was too weak to complain about it. Kept hitting."

"Doesn't seem like that would be hard to prove."

"Way they framed it, I crept up on him. Boy was drunk, close to nobility. Guess I'm lucky, really. If he were any closer to a lord, I don't think I'd even get to prison." He eyed the guards. "How d'you get them to let you in here?"

"Fear and promises. Their usefulness is spent, though." Adrian turned to the guards, hand digging into his cloak where he held the knife Nasir had given him. "You work for me now. You can start by disposing of them." The men didn't shift. They didn't understand the language.

"All three?"

Adrian almost chuckled. Part of him had expected more resistance, but maybe the man was a murderer in his bones after all. "Don't kill them if you don't have to. I'll help."

Adrian pulled out the knife Nasir had given him and slit a small cut into his arm. Smaller than when he'd done it with Nasir. The sight of the pulsing ruin-stone blade was enough for the guards to charge. Two of them came ahead, but Bac was already barreling forward. He met the first one with his lowered shoulder and lifted, throwing out his arm and flinging the man to the floor. The guard hit his head against the low center-table and stayed there.

The other's short spear was stabbing at Bac, but Adrian had already drawn the signs and dug into the pain, performing the same binding he did in the garden. The blood coiled around his arm, the pain of Myrra and Derren's dead, beaten faces empowering him. Adrian threw out his hand, trying to connect the threads of his blood with the stabbing guard. His arm strained as the man tightened, dropping his spear and freezing as if bound. It wasn't a branch this time, and the man struggled against it. Adrian gritted his teeth, the cut in his forearm pulsing. It flared as if he were still dragging the knife across the skin.

Holding the guard gave Bac enough time to take the man's dropped spear and challenge the remaining opponent. The last guard seemed confused, spear raised but confidence lost. Bac hit him across the head with his spear-butt. The man went reeling toward the wall, but pushed away from it and came right back, stabbing at Adrian's new ally. Bac dodged the spear and caught the guard in a bear hug.

Adrian's own opponent was breaking free as the pain rose and Adrian's energy was sapped. Adrian dug deep, focusing on Myrra's face from the garden, and in a flash she was there. *You are stronger than you think.* The words she'd told him before Jovu's Cleansing. They sent a fire through Adrian, and his eyes burned with the pain of the magic coursing through him. He closed his hand and heard a crack. The guard's right arm and leg twisted at awkward angles, broken. He screamed in pain, and Adrian couldn't keep back his own scream as the pain was mirrored in him through the blood-tie.

There was something else in Adrian, though, beyond the pain.

Like a chasm, waiting for him to dive in, seize his strength, and kill the man. Myrra's image became more real, the misty red giving way to an almost solid depiction of the ruin that was her mask. She had black veins painting the area around her eyes, and her gaze held an expression that told Adrian he could do no wrong. She would always be there. But she wasn't there, and he couldn't kill the guard. He needed the consuls to get his army, his revenge.

Adrian let go. Something lingered within him, tugging at his mind as if to say he'd missed an opportunity. The cut on his arm was still burning, and the guard was on the ground, grunting in pain. The magic had taken Adrian's strength again, but it wasn't as bad as the first time.

Bac had knocked the other guard out with a head-butt, if his bleeding nose was any indication. He looked down at the broken-limbed guard. "I thought you said to hold back."

"I said don't kill. Come. Someone will find them. We need to get to the conference chamber."

CHAPTER SIX

Tedros worked with whoever was needed within the clan. That cannot be forgotten now that it is split. Strength must not be held back by borders.

—*Tales of the Ronar*

The Zaruni walked loosely behind Nasha as she made her way to the building Leku had appeared from. Her weapons were not taken, and her hands were not bound. The Zaruni's emotions didn't speak to them treating Nasha like a prisoner, either. Instead, what surrounded her as she and Shai entered the house was closer to awe. Her curse was picking it up, even if she tried to avoid it after what she'd seen in the tainted attacker the Yltigg had let loose on them.

Half a dozen Zaruni stood on either side of the room, their backs to the walls. Their awe was working through Nasha, trying to tell her she should be impressed by the room. It was one of the larger houses, but the wooden walls were thin and made from rough-cut planks that let slim beams of light in through the gaps.

Nothing to be awed by, and Nasha let her own irritation take over. She was no hero, and she especially didn't want to be one for the Zaruni.

She wasn't focusing on her curse, but colors had been bleeding out of people more and more recently. The gloomy room was tinted in a light blue shroud, and her mind seemed to make the connection on its own. Red for anger, green for fear. Yet the green transitioning to blue seemed to represent awe.

Leku waited at the top of uneven stairs. He looked down at them, shadows covering most of his face, then beckoned for Nasha and Shai to follow him.

Nasha hesitated. They couldn't waste time with this. Fighting the frenzied man had shown her enough. Zala was rising from the Earth. The dead goddess had taken the Hagun village, and now her taint seemed to reach the Yltigg. The memory of the dull Hagun warding pillar at the center of their dead village had Nasha gritting her teeth. The Ronar had various smaller pillars instead of one large one like the other clans, but Tomu had told Nasha that the stones were coming back dull from the mines.

Adda had tended to the Ronar warding pillars, and no taint had been seen within the village. But Adda was dead. Would Zala seize Her moment, now that the Ronar stone-shaper was no longer there to strengthen the wards? That the Yltigg were using their tainted as a weapon only made Nasha tighten her jaw.

As if Bahar and the Domain were not enough.

A mad thought crossed her mind. Bahar had killed Adda. Nasha had been sure it was out of vengeance for losing his son in the Proving, but had he known what was happening to the Hagun? Had he seen something during his captivity with the Yltigg? Was he using Zala Herself to strike at the clans?

She needed to bring these questions to Tomu, but the Zaruni always seemed to be in the way. Nasha shook her head and stepped up the straining wooden steps, climbing to a second story built on thin boards that seemed ready to give way at any moment. Leku was unaffected by the threat of creaking wood and led them to a room with nothing but chairs and low stalls. He leaned against the wall beside a crooked window.

The door closed behind them and Leku gestured to a chair. "Sit, Warden."

"I don't have time, Leku. Whatever politics you have with the Ronar can wait."

"This isn't about politics." Leku looked out the window, pointing a finger at where she'd taken down the tainted Yltigg. "That isn't the first one."

"Even more reason for you to get out of my way."

Leku shrugged. "The Slopes aren't safe. If Zala is rising, we need more warding." Nasha frowned at him. He'd come to the same conclusion. The Zaruni feared Zala.

"Where is the tivezzi?" Leku asked.

Shai's irritation spiked in Nasha, a tingling shot that had her shuffling her feet, but she gave the girl no time to speak. "We don't know. She wasn't with us." She tried to keep her tone firm to mask the lie. "The Domain are coming. We can't fight them, the Yltigg, and Zala all at once. If you truly want the safety of the Slopes, you'll help me convince Tomu to make peace with the Yltigg." No use trying to convince Leku to step aside. His own interests would be the only thing to move him.

"Why am I to believe you? This fight with the Yltigg has given the Slopers opportunity. The ones who prove themselves strong will be accepted into the clan."

"And you believe Tomu?" Shai asked.

"He's no fool. He knows not to break a promise to the Zaruni."

Leku's gaze said enough. Nasha had broken her promise to him, but that was not a promise she'd intended to keep. "Promises won't save us," Nasha said. "If the clans don't fight together, the Domain will take us all."

"Then Tomu must provide the Slopes with warding against Zala's touch."

Nasha glared at Leku and took a step forward. Her mind was warning her against the curse, not only because of the risk of the taint, but because she could not show Leku what lived inside her. Leku grinned, as if expecting her reaction.

"You think attacking me will solve anything, Warden? The Slopes are mine." He let out a harsh whistle, and the door banged open behind them. Two dozen Zaruni rushed in and surrounded Nasha and Shai, weapons at the ready.

"You're right," Leku said. "We have little time, but haste cannot be the deterrent to a better future for the people of the Slopes."

Nasha clenched her fists. The man preached as if he truly believed the Zaruni were the only way forward for the Slopers.

"You will go to Tomu, but the Zaruni will go with you. I will have a seat at the table in his hall and discuss the future of the clan."

Nasha considered the man for a moment. She was the warden, but all he wanted was to use her position. Just like Mansa. She was just another tool. It riled her as much as the awe when she'd entered, but there was little time to consider alternatives. Better to be a tool to save the clans than the monster who let them be taken by the dead goddess. "If I accept, you will convince him to make peace with the Yltigg."

"What makes you think the Yltigg would talk peace when they have these beasts keeping us within our walls?"

"They don't control these creatures," Nasha said. "They're held in cages and even the Yltigg keep their distance. They aren't a weapon; they smell more of desperation. Maybe Zala's corrupting them, and they think they can use this corruption on us to even the battle."

Leku considered her. "And what makes you think we can stop this corruption?"

"Our stone-shapers have kept our wards alive. We've kept the taint out of the Ronar." She wasn't sure the stone-shapers were the answer, especially without Adda, but Leku didn't need to know that.

Leku watched for another moment, then nodded, and the men around Nasha and Shai stepped back. The pressure of their emotions receded as the tension diffused. Nasha took a few deep breaths, then turned for the door. "Come on. We have no time."

They left the house with Leku and a handful of Zaruni in tow.

Nasha and Shai walked ahead, while Leku and the Zaruni almost made a parade out of it, as if they were the saviors come to push the Yltigg back. Leku greeted and nodded to all whose gazes lingered on them as they marched down the winding paths of the Slopes toward the Mountain Gate.

"I'm not sure about this," Shai said, but she didn't have to say it. Nasha felt the unease through her curse.

"Neither am I," she said, "but do we have an alternative? There are too many enemies already."

"Can we trust Leku?"

Nasha shook her head slightly. "No, but we'll have to work with him and hope Tomu accepts."

Mansa would also be there, of course, and the thought filled Nasha with dread. He'd probably been the one to tell Tomu to retreat and wait behind the walls. It made sense if he thought their plan of steering the Domain against the Yltigg had worked, but the Domain wasn't coming for the Yltigg alone. Bahar would be leading them, and the Ronar were the closest to the border.

The Mountain Gate was barred and lightly guarded. Tomu had always used the Slopes as a buffer, and it seemed he trusted the Yltigg would not dare venture through them. Nasha marched across the wide bridge that stretched above the moat between village and slopes, pausing before a warrior whom she didn't know. He needed only a quick glance to recognize her and the Zaruni behind. He hesitated, but only for a moment. The confidence of their stride—and, no doubt. the fact that they were led by Nasha—had the man ready to open the gate.

The warriors had no words for Nasha, trusting her rank as she led the Zaruni into the village. A warmth spread through her as she stepped through the gates—part of her appreciating the respect, even if it came from the title. Mansa had told her to not hold on to it too much, but what else did she have? She couldn't reveal what she really was to the Ronar, and the title was better than imagining herself a corrupted beast like the one the Yltigg had set upon the Slopes.

Nasha cut through the village, plunging through the wave of emotions that permeated it. Her mind had learned to protect itself against smaller concentrations of wayward emotions, but the numbers she waded through now gave her no assurances. Instinct had her looking for her anchors: Tanner Hilka and Old Kolg were the first that came to mind, but none seemed to be where Nasha usually found them. They were either fighting, or their emotions were too unstable to grab onto. It didn't matter; Shai was beside her, and Nasha was familiar enough with her pattern of emotions to use them as a shield.

Shai's emotions came in shots, standing out from the curiosity, surprise and apprehension of the people Nasha didn't know. Shai was her anchor, a haven that protected her as she navigated the streets between stone-and-wood housing and an ever-growing crowd.

The houses became more stone than wood as she approached the chief's hall, which towered over them in three stories of pure stone. Not ancestor-stone—the clans would not squander that to build a hall—but solid and tall enough to draw attention from several streets away.

Gazes followed Nasha along the dry-earth streets that led to the chief's front steps, but she focused on the building and blasted through the doors. Only Leku followed her. Shai stayed outside with the Zaruni, the contempt wafting off her.

Nasha hardly looked at the ancestor-stone engraving of the First Tree as she stepped into the room, turning her back on it to face Tomu, Mansa, and Jabillo, who stood around a table beside the fire.

Their gazes passed over Nasha and lingered on Leku, but Nasha eyed them as if nothing was amiss. Tomu grunted, then looked back to Nasha. "Where have you been?" His tone was still deep, but not as controlled as usual.

"Trying to fix things." Nasha shot a quick glance at Mansa. "I failed."

"This is not the time to be cryptic, Warden," Jabillo said. Ironic coming from him, but he had a point, even if Nasha couldn't tell them the exact truth.

Mansa watched Nasha, disquiet bleeding through his gaze. Nasha didn't allow her curse any ground, but even without it, it was clear that he waited to learn whether his plan to start a war with the Domain had proved successful.

"Someone betrayed us," Nasha said. "There was a Domain hunting party, or maybe they were just assassins in disguise. They took the Domain noble boy, killed Iallo. I didn't know what they'd do to him, so I tracked them with the help of two other hunters. Anaya and Bedri. They're dead, and so is the boy."

"How?" Tomu's tone deepened.

"The hunting party met with people from the borderlands, looks like they were trying to sell the boy back." Nasha paused. "Bahar was on the receiving end. Something went wrong. He attacked the hunters, but they killed the boy in the chaos." Silence fell, but Nasha didn't let it linger. "We intervened when things got out of hand, but we couldn't save the noble . . . and Bahar . . . he's angry. Wants revenge for Devu. I'm not even sure what he wanted with the councilor's son." Parts of it were true. It was better that way. Mansa had taught her that the best lies were always rooted in truth. Having so many of Mansa's lessons in her mind, after the way he'd used her, had Nasha's own anger threatening to burn up her throat. There was too much of him in her.

"And Adda?" Tomu asked, his voice taking on a forlorn note.

Nasha shook her head. "I thought she'd be here." Again, the effortless lie had come from Mansa's lessons, and it riled her insides.

Tomu looked away, and Nasha used the opening. "We need to stop this fighting, Chief."

"What?" Mansa said with a scoff.

"We can't count on the Domain pushing back the Yltigg now that we know Bahar is alive. He'll steer them toward us and we can't fight both."

"It was the Yltigg warden who killed the boy," Jabillo said. "Does Bahar even blame the Ronar for what happened?"

"Besides," Mansa said, "he is only one man. Don't you

remember what he said? The council in the Visslands is wary of the cost. Do you think they'd invade us without wanting to take something away? It doesn't matter if we're in the way, the Yltigg have the largest ancestor-stone mines. That's where the Domain will go first."

Nasha shook her head. "You know Bahar has influence with the council. To discard an invasion would be foolish. He'll blame us. He'll blame all the clans if I know him, but Devu was taken to the Proving by the Ronar. We'll be his first target." She paused, looking at Leku, then back at the chief. "That's not all. The Yltigg have some kind of earth-spawn. A tainted warrior they let loose on the Slopes. The taint is . . . contagious. I've brought Leku to represent the Zaruni and the Slopes. We need to fight together."

"As equals," Leku added. "Not as fodder while you pull the clan back into the village."

Tomu eyed the man with enough irritation to stab at Nasha through her curse. It was soon controlled, however. Perhaps he realized the Slopes would be a necessary ally. "And how do you propose we do that?" he asked.

Mansa stepped forward before Leku could answer. "Even if we wanted to stop the fighting, the Yltigg aren't listening."

"We'll have to make them." Nasha turned to Leku.

He stepped forward to meet Mansa's gaze with more confidence than she'd expected. He eyed Mansa for a long moment, then turned to Tomu. "Death has proven to be closer to the Slopes than your promises, Chief, or even mine. There are too many people in their homes, either too afraid to fight, or indifferent to which clan ends up controlling the village below us. That started to change once the Yltigg released the taint within our streets. With the warden's help, we can rally the people and bolster our troops—a show of force so the Yltigg know the cost that lies ahead."

"I assume you want something in return?" Tomu asked.

Leku grinned. "Access to the village and a seat among the Roots. The wards are what will keep Zala's hunger, and her earth-spawn, at bay."

Tomu chuckled. "Impossible."

"Then expand the wards, have them protect the Slopes."

The talk of wards seemed to give Tomu pause, and something spiked within him: a lingering concern that he tried to fight off. It was clear to Nasha, though. He wanted to know where Adda was, or maybe it was Razi he was worried about. Eventually, he let out a sigh. "I'll see what the stone-shapers can do in Adda's absence. Get your people ready, and you'd better be able to convince them, Warden."

Leku grinned and Nasha nodded, but Tomu had already refocused on the crude map of the clanlands on the table before them. "We can't fight on two fronts. Mansa, have scouts report every movement on the road directly to me. I want to know when the Domain are on the move." He looked back at Leku. "You should prepare as well. If the Yltigg agree to talk, you're the one riding out with the warden to meet them."

CHAPTER SEVEN

There have been losses within the order that are not to be spoken of outside of it. In the rare occurrence, the Pontiff is to be informed and the griffin and body brought before him, if possible.

— *The Book of the Blade* (restricted)

The road to Alteria was crowded. Lynn walked beside Vedyr. She tried to keep the refugees moving while focusing on the road—and any shadow that might harbor frenzied attackers.

News from Durnn's fall had reached the cities of Ratha and Dryss, and it seemed the threat of madmen on the road was not enough to strengthen the faith of the cityfolk behind their walls. They'd joined the Durnnish refugees heading for Alteria, hoping the Church and its Legion would know how to keep Dakhra back and the faithful safe. Not all were moving, though. Wagons had been led off the road by the dozen; small groups gathered around them, directing prayers at the Seraph's mark in the sky. One man had even mixed water into the earth of the road and used the mud to paint the Signs of the Blood, Body, Breath, and Bone onto his cart. He'd also painted the drop-like Sign of the Blood on his face. He dropped to his knees as soon as he finished the Signs on the cart, one hand raised up to the Seraph's mark in the sky, the other clutching a small ruin-stone pendant at his neck.

Lynn sighed and moved on. She couldn't stop for every person performing a roadside prayer, even if their faith put their lives at risk.

Vedyr paced close by, and Lynn found herself resting a hand on his side as they walked. His fur was coarse and thick, but he welcomed Lynn's touch with a low rumble that also projected through their Bond. The faint echo of his heart pulsed under her palm, beating in unison with the ruin-stone shard in her own. Even after all they'd been through, it was good to have him back at her side.

Two days after the battle, Alteria's walls came into view. The city had grown since Lynn's last visit. The wall wasn't ruin-stone like the one in Durnn, and some housing had been built outside of it in disorganized fashion, their inhabitants fueled by faith in the Church even if their homes could not be contained within the walls. Lynn wondered what would happen now, with all these people flocking toward the holy city. Surely the Church would not turn them away. That would mean death, and life had to be preserved, now more than ever.

A crowd had formed outside the city's entrance. Not a good sign. Lynn looked to Rel, and they followed Olem toward the Alterian gate. They had to nudge their way through initially, but their griffins soon proved to be a larger motivator than the crowd's desperation. A dozen soldiers stood guard before the closed gate, with more watching from atop the walls. "Watchers," Olem said, nodding to the one closest to them.

The soldier didn't budge. "We have orders to admit only those who've been tested . . . sir." He seemed unsure how Olem should be addressed, but Olem's griffin left little doubt as to what he was.

Rel tilted his head with a smirk, and Lynn stepped up beside Olem. "Whose orders?"

"Captain Brent is looking out for the safety of Alteria," another guard said. He seemed more confident than the first, even when faced with three Sentinels and their griffins.

"And how many have you allowed inside today?" Olem asked.

"Ehm, none, sir. Captain Brent is—"

"Open the gates," Rel said in a tired tone. "Or would you rather we open them for you?"

The guards hesitated, exchanging glances.

Lynn moved closer. "You serve the Legion, yes?"

"Y-yes, my la—"

"I'm not a lady. I'm a Sentinel and a Legion general." Lynn shifted the cloak of her Sentinel mantle to reveal the four Signs of the Seraph on her chest piece. "I command you to open the gate." She looked back. "Unless you want these folk getting infected and pulling it down themselves?"

The guards looked over the refugees for a moment, but Lynn's steady gaze soon had the nervous one calling back for the gate to be opened.

Lynn nodded. "Have the Legion men posted here help set up tents in the barracks." She wasn't sure how many of the refugees would fit, but it was a start.

The guards saluted. "Yes, General."

There was no fanfare as they entered the city. No rush to see the Sentinels, as might have happened in a different time. People on the streets made way, their fear of the griffins obvious. Ferrin walked beside Lynn and Vedyr.

Lynn patted Vedyr on the neck. "Go on," she whispered. He looked at her with thankful silver eyes, telling of his eagerness to spread his wings, and took off, drawing gasps from those around them. Lynn pulled Ferrin close. "What is it?" she asked.

"I . . ." He looked around. "We're losing everything."

Lynn held his gaze, but he looked away. It seemed the faith he'd had in her before the battle was now as shattered as Durnn's gates. "This is what Syvern wants," she said. "Don't let him make you doubt yourself, or the Seraph."

He only doubts you, Alren said. *Tell him. Tell him you killed his brother.*

89

"We were supposed to end this Madness," Ferrin said. "Create a legacy for Morna. Help bring the Promised Dawn." He chuckled mirthlessly. "What if we do bring the Promised Dawn? Is this what the Seraph will return to? Will She bring the worthy back, or will she end us all?"

Lynn put a hand on Ferrin's shoulder and steered him along the road. "The Seraph trusts us to defend Her Domain until She is ready, and we must trust Her in turn. You've come a long way from being a watcher in Kerr's prisons. You're part of the Legion now. You fight for life. That's what matters."

Ferrin walked in silence for a long while before speaking. "I was always trying to impress Morna, you know? Always smiling like everything was all right. I couldn't protect her in the end. I just . . . I wish she could have been kept by the Church. Worthy."

"Now is not the time to doubt your faith. Death will only pull you down to the darkest depths of your mind."

You would know, Roki said. *You've kept us, after all.*

"We don't know the workings of the Seraph," Lynn said. "But the dead are gone. All we can do now is defend those who remain."

Ferrin looked around. The Alterians were still fearful, even with Vedyr flying overhead. "When did we lose their trust?" he asked.

When you brought the enemy through our gates, Dentos said.

"Dakhra is trying to destroy more than our walls," Lynn said. "They are trying to destroy our beliefs and infect us with fear. We can beat them, but we need to believe that we can."

Roki laughed in her mind. *Hollow words.*

He was right, but her words were not meant to protect Ferrin; she'd already failed in that. He needed to trust himself, so that he didn't need to rely on her.

"Faith is not always easy," Lynn said, "but we can't win without it." She tried a smile, but it was taut on her lips. Ferrin nodded and kept walking.

The cathedral's towers cast blade-like shadows over Lynn's group. It almost made her feel safe, but there was no safety to be had while Dakhra and its Madness advanced. Lynn sighed and moved forward until they reached the barracks.

The high tower at the back of the four-level, U-shaped barracks building overlooked the training yard, where the tents would be set up for those who didn't fit inside.

The Legion had taken enough of a hit in the battle. A thousand men remained, maybe less; but the internal quarters were still not enough to handle the roughly thirty thousand refugees, with more on the way.

Lynn walked among the refugees that flooded through the gate, searching for signs of the Madness: the jittery movements, the blackness around the eyes, a raised voice that might lead her to something. She closed her eyes. *Don't let Syvern infect you with fear.* The refugee numbers would have to be discussed with the Pontiff, though.

When she opened her eyes, Olem was heading toward her. "The Pontiff wants us."

Lynn swallowed the dryness in her throat and followed, meeting up with Rel and a scowling Ildred along the way. They strode through crowded streets on their way to the cathedral. The building was flanked by four immense statues of the six-winged Seraph. Each held one of the four gleaming Signs in polished ruin-stone: Breath, Body, Blood and Bone. People were crowded around the base of the statues, but there hardly seemed to be a place in the city without crowds now. Prayers were being uttered, and some groups even had priests leading the people's words.

The cathedral's short entry chamber was a rectangular room with openings on both sides. It led to the darker and much larger reflection chamber. The bigger room had faithful in groups no larger than five or six, focusing on the scriptures written in sunlight on the floor. There were even groups trying to make out the texts on the perforated walls. Everyone desperate for some shred of solace. It was impossible to keep much distance among the hundreds of people crowding the chamber, the discomfort clear with every bumped shoulder and brushed arm.

The Sentinels were less recognizable without their griffins, but a path still opened up as Olem, Lynn, Rel, and Ildred made their way through the chamber. Lynn paid little heed to the sunlit texts in the reflection chamber and walked straight into the next room, which was dominated by the huge Ever-Tree that stood beneath a vast circular opening in the ceiling.

Lynn suppressed a gasp. This was the largest Ever-Tree she'd known. Its leaves had always been a vibrant red, with shades of orange and yellow that lost themselves in the sunlight pouring down from above. The leaves were dull now. Even the bark was tinged with gray, and petals littered the floor around it. No one had removed them. Perhaps the priests thought the tree would heal itself if they didn't meddle.

"This can't be Dakhra's doing," Lynn said. "There's no way they've poisoned the trees."

"If they're striking at our faith," Olem said, "the Ever-Trees would be their first target."

Lynn didn't argue, but it didn't seem right. The Dakhran brew drove people to an uncontrollable madness. She still didn't understand how some of them maintained control, but the Madness itself was furiously quick. What was happening to the trees seemed slow and patient, and even the earth around the tree's base was ashen and black. It was impossible to believe any potion was strong enough to do this. Her eyes sought Rel, but he was already following the others down the hall that led to the Pontiff's audience chamber. She followed.

The walls of the passage rose a hundred strides or more on either side and opened into an enormous antechamber. Parts of the chamber wall had the white veins of polished ruin-stone, while others had been fitted together with a duller gray stone, polished to give a sense of cohesion to the whole. Carvings of the Seraph sat atop the room's exits. The largest carving—a full-body depiction, its bottom pair of wings framing the door—was above the entrance to the Pontiff's audience chamber.

The Alterian cathedral had always bathed in grandeur, but would intricately wrought stone and huge statues be enough to maintain the foundations of faith? Or had Dakhra's blow already struck too deep? Lynn eyed the glowing veins that ran along the walls, then followed the others into the audience chamber.

The gloomy stone room was long and wide, the steps at its center leading up to a raised dais and a throne-like chair crafted from ruin-stone: the Seat of the Seraph. The Pontiff sat upon it, flanked by men in other, less grand chairs. High Bishop Reznik, the leader of the Bishops of the Bone, sat to his right. To his left was Chancellor Burke, a man of common birth who represented the faithful, the Body of the Seraph's faith. Each man wore a ruin-stone pendant that indicated his position. Bone and Body for Reznik and Burke, and the Sign of the Blood for the Pontiff. Lynn's Sentinel coin, shaped in the sequential crescent shapes of the Sign of the Breath, weighed heavy around her neck.

High Bishop Reznik was a slight man, as if he'd decided to demonstrate his faith by showing as much of the bone under his thin skin as he could. He appeared to be the eldest of the three, but his movements were unhindered, and Lynn wouldn't put it past the leader of the Church's questioners to make himself seem frail to catch others off-guard.

Burke was as common as they came, and very little about him stood out. So little, in fact, that she wondered if he strived for that effect. His hair was close-cropped, his clothes plain. He had a young look to him, and soft eyes, like someone ever ready to aid the faithful. But men did not occupy such seats of power solely by granting favors.

The Pontiff did not stir as the Sentinels approached the dais. His deep green eyes and perfectly combed white hair all but glowed in the chamber's gloom. There were texts on the wall to the left, the sunlit projections one of the few sources of light cutting through the shadows. The Sentinels kneeled.

The Pontiff rose a hand. "Welcome, Sentinels. Rise." He had a slight pull to his lips that wasn't quite a smile. Not the expression one would expect from the leader of the Church, after the loss of the Domain's main defensive bastion. Lynn felt her brow crease. The man had always been hard to read.

"You fought bravely and did well in preserving the lives of the faithful. And for that, I thank you." Lynn couldn't tell what the other two thought. Reznik was stiff in his chair while Burke regarded her with a slightly cocked head.

"However," the Pontiff said. "It is our duty to stand watch not only over the faithful, but the integrity of the Domain, and in that we have all failed." He looked over the Sentinels, his gaze seeming to linger on Lynn. "We cannot repeat that mistake in battles to come."

Lynn frowned. She'd always assumed Leardin would be taken into the ranks of the worthy. He'd led the Breath, after all. But it seemed the tarnish of dying a madman had been too much. The failure to speak his name was proof enough that the Pontiff had discarded the old commander. Would he do the same with Elwin? Lynn found herself almost grateful that her mentor's body was sealed away in Durnn, even if it was at risk of being found by the Dakhrans.

Ildred seemed less concerned about the worthiness of the dead and stepped forward. "If there is to be a Choosing, High Pontiff, I—"

"There most certainly will be a Choosing, my boy. But there are other matters before that. I hear whispers that it was the idea of one of your own to open the Skygate?"

He sees you for what you are, traitor, Roki said.

Lynn stepped forward, struggling to keep the quivering nervousness out of her muscles. "I was the one who called for it, High Pontiff." She looked at each of the Church leaders. "The situation was desperate, and a decision had to be made."

Olem nodded beside her. "Her loyalty is not in question, High Pontiff. Lynn has the remains of a Dakhran airship at her feet to prove it."

"The idea came from her, but we all followed it," Rel said.

"Not all of us agreed," Ildred said.

"Yet we all charged." Rel's tone was dangerously sharp.

"We stood united, yes," Ildred said. "Yet not all of us have always been here." He gestured toward Lynn. "It is regretful, yet I must inform that the Sentinels followed the suggestion of one who has abandoned us before. Loyalties must always be confirmed, High

Pontiff. Especially in times like these."

The Church leaders were silent for a moment, their gazes heavy on the Sentinels.

"We have ways of confirming loyalty," High Bishop Reznik said at last.

"Preposterous, Reznik!" Chancellor Burke waved a hand at him. "Your techniques have never been meant for use inside the Church. What will be next? Questioning Priests of the Blood?"

Lynn fixed her gaze between Ildred and the leaders. Doubt had always been as big an enemy as any. Doubt about what the Madness was and how to fight it. Doubt about her loyalty, her worthiness. She'd already failed to protect those close to her. And with doubt surrounding her, she'd fail again. Breaking the shroud of doubt was the only way to help Elwin as well. He'd died a madman, after all.

Do it, they whispered. For once Lynn followed her voices. "If there is uncertainty as to my reacceptance into the order, I will gladly be questioned."

Rel looked at her with wild eyes, as if she was a child who didn't know what she'd asked for. They'd talked about avoiding this, but the matter had to be settled.

"The Questioning can be a . . . dangerous process, Sentinel," Burke said.

The Pontiff nodded. "I would prefer the precedent not be opened within the Church."

"This will set no precedent, High Pontiff," Lynn said. "The Questioning is based on my request. This Madness threatens to take everything from us. I will not fight it with the shadow of the Church's doubt hanging over me. I request to be questioned. Let the Seraph judge my worthiness and take my life if She sees fit."

Olem moved up. "High Pontiff, I—"

The Pontiff's upraised hand silenced him, but the old man's eyes remained on Lynn. "There is a thin line between bravery and foolishness," he said.

"There is nothing brave about it, High Pontiff. If anything, I am a coward. Tired of the scrutiny."

The Pontiff flashed a grin at this, but it was fleeting as a breath. "Reznik?"

"A Questioning can be prepared within a day, High Pontiff."

"Very well. You will get your wish, Sentinel. Now, Sub-commander Olem. Have any besides brother Ildred stepped forward for a Choosing?"

"The ones in this room are the only ones I'd trust to lead the Breath, High Pontiff."

Ildred stepped forward, but the Pontiff was on his feet. "I see. Including her?"

"Yes, High Pontiff."

"Then the Choosing will have to wait until loyalties have been proven. In the meantime, I need you to plan a defense and rebuild the Legion. Sacantha is overrun with madmen. They are fighting, but I fear Queen Niria is losing ground. Pyrran might soon be threatened."

"My informants say King Henrik's son, Addo, is leading the madmen," Reznik said. "We are looking into the boy, trying to find a weakness."

"We will consider a strategy to aid Sacantha," Olem said.

"Their troops will be invaluable if you do," Burke added. "The Visslands have rushed to close their northern border, but the clansmen are stirring in the south, and Vizcarra has taken the worst of the attack. We cannot count on them."

The Pontiff nodded. "That leaves Alteria and Othonea. We must not fall, Olem, and we cannot have threats rising from within. The Durnnish you brought into the city . . ."

Lynn found herself frowning. The Pontiff was a placid man, but very little escaped his gaze.

"They must be tested," the Pontiff continued. "The ones that are fit for battle, armed and trained. Keep a close eye on them. Times are dark, I'm afraid, and we have seen groups take matters into their own hands once before."

Olem nodded. "And how are the troops to be sustained, High Pontiff?"

The Pontiff seemed to consider this for a moment. "Rations will

A SHADE OF MADNESS

be provided twice a day. The barracks should be enough to house the current contingent. If not, have the newly trained set a perimeter around the city. We cannot keep all the faithful within our walls, but we will protect them as we can."

Olem bowed his head. "Yes, High Pontiff."

"Good. Sister Lynn, please remain within the city. High Bishop Reznik will question you tomorrow."

CHAPTER EIGHT

It is the duty of every Visslander to watch over the southern border of the Domain, but our duty goes farther than that. Our dams are the heart of life in the Domain. They are never to be risked or forgotten.

— Excerpt from The History of the Visslands

K admus frowned as he wiped the counter. His knuckles whitened over the cloth; too much pressure. Not because of some stain he was trying to wipe away—his mind was occupied with the pieces of the equations he'd failed to resolve. He'd used the new madman's blood, but the cure—if there was one—still eluded him.

He stopped wiping and gazed out the large window. His mind screamed at him to race downstairs and continue his work, but he couldn't. Appearances must be maintained, and so he'd opened the shop as he did on every other day. He'd already risked too much by healing Grunt's wife. People were talking, wondering how to gain favor with a healer who wasn't hidden behind the requirements of the Church.

The priests wouldn't have it, of course, but word hadn't yet spread far enough to inspire a search. At least, not to his knowledge. He accepted few requests, always wore a mask, and did his work in patients' own homes. No one suspected he was using their diseases to look for similarities to the Madness, but why should that matter? He healed them all the same.

He glanced down. He was gripping the cloth again, knuckles white, and he hadn't even noticed. He let go and massaged his forehead. He was letting his emotions get the best of him, and that slight voice of doubt he constantly suppressed was mocking him at the back of his mind.

The Seraph is punishing you. This isn't a disease; this is Her intervention.

Kadmus shook his head.

The Seraph is a lie.

He rarely had to remind himself of that, but Nima's affliction had changed things. He resumed wiping the counter, even if there was nothing left to clean. The movement helped him think. The street was empty, had been for a while. People were generally too afraid to go out at night, but empty streets in daylight were rare. A hooded man walked past the front window and stopped at the door, coming inside a moment after.

"Afternoon," Kadmus said, trying to sound nonchalant. His mind had already shifted to new calculations. He started listing the poisons he carried, watching the man to determine which would be most effective. Hooded men were never a good thing.

The man walked with a heavy limp, using a cane to bear his weight. He didn't lower his hood or the cloth that covered most of his face. The covered visage made Kadmus strangely aware of his own scars, the lines over his cheeks where the Weeping had bled pus. The scars had always bothered others more than they did him, but there was something about the man in his store that set Kadmus on edge. He'd never been a fighter; surprise and men like Grunt had always been his weapons, and Kadmus's unease was only compounded by the visitor's silence.

The visitor scanned the shelves for a moment, then turned and nodded at the open door. Two more hooded men walked in, holding a third man between them. The captive had bound hands and was hooded as well, but Kadmus didn't need to see his face to know who he was. His concern teetered on dread as they revealed Grunt's apologetic face.

Damned brute. I knew I should have paid him more.

The pair who'd escorted Grunt left the store and closed the door, likely standing guard outside. Kadmus felt sure they'd cleared the street earlier. Were they from the Church? They wore no Signs of the Seraph. Had they already made their decision, and come to take his life? He knew from his failed training as a Priest of the Blood that they couldn't do that. Not officially, anyway—these men weren't Sentinels. Still, he wouldn't put secret assassinations past the Church.

Grunt looked like he wanted to say something, but fear seemed to hold his tongue. He wasn't bruised, but Kadmus was sure a threat of some deeper wound, likely to his family, was what had brought him to stand here.

"I'm told you're a healer," the hooded man said.

"I sell all kinds of cures and toxins," Kadmus tried a smile. "What do you need?"

"I'm not here to play games, potioner, though I understand my entrance might have intimidated you."

Kadmus's left hand continued wiping the counter as his right dipped beneath it in search of the poison. He knew which one: palatium, second one from the left. If he threw it hard enough at the ceiling, it would burst into a cloud of smoke and have the man choking in seconds. Grunt wouldn't escape, but some sacrifices were unavoidable. "What do you need?" he asked again, fingers tightening around the vial.

"Your ear. Your help, perhaps."

Kadmus's fingers slacked a touch. The Church had always been too proud to ask for help, but this could be a Bishop of the Bone, deceiving him to make his job easier. Still, there was no ruin-stone about him. There could be some under the cloak, but the Church was never shy about flaunting its signs and trinkets.

"A masked man walks into my store with . . . I don't even know what this one is supposed to be." He jerked his head at Grunt. "Your muscle?"

The man raised his hand and slowly pulled down his hood. "As I said, there is no need for games. Your activities here do not concern me. My only interest is in your abilities. There are rumors, and if there's one thing I am very good at, it's tracking down those that are both real and useful." He lowered the cloth covering his face, and a strange sense of recognition came over Kadmus. He silently chastised himself, certain the surprise revealed itself in his features.

The man nodded. "You know who I am then."

Kadmus did. He was not with the Church. This was the man who could have been a consul but chose instead to become an emissary to the clans: Bahar. It seemed he still held enough power to close off a street for a private conversation, even if it was a street in the Mannis quarter and too far from the falls to matter.

Bahar's features were not as he remembered. His face was marred by deep, half-healed wounds, stark red against his pale skin. One side of his mouth had been cut, as if to open it wider.

Kadmus almost brought his hands to his own scars, but part of him settled down after identifying Bahar. It was unlikely the Church would send such a man for him. "What do you want?" he asked, his tone taking on the comfortable coldness it always held.

"I told you. I need a healer. One who can attend to my needs in a more private manner."

"The Priests of the Blood can be private, especially for one in your position. My focus is on potions." He didn't deny he was a healer—trying to keep up appearances would only rile the man—but Kadmus wanted nothing to do with him. Every cut on his face told a story of a different kind of trouble, each deeper than the last.

Bahar grinned. "If your friend here is to be believed, you have enough experience with the Church to know their privacy extends only so far."

Kadmus looked at Grunt, who avoided his gaze. Kadmus shook his head. "This man knows nothing about me. He's a hired hand when I need an assistant. Wanted to learn how to brew, but his fingers are too stubby. All he does is move the furniture."

Bahar reached into his cloak and, before Kadmus could react, drew a knife and cut Grunt's throat. The movement had been efficient and would kill Grunt in moments. The big man took a moment to realize what had happened, then fell to his knees, his bound hands clutching at his throat.

Kadmus tightened his grip on the vial, surprised at the sudden violence but ready to respond with a surprise of his own.

Bahar pointed the dagger at Kadmus. "He doesn't have much time. You can show me the prowess people whisper about on the streets, or you can attack me with whatever it is you have under that counter."

Kadmus's gaze moved furiously from the bleeding Grunt to the grinning Bahar. He'd never seen officials act this way, but the scars on Bahar's face indicated a radical change in behavior. Part of his mind scolded him for not expecting this, another part for losing focus earlier. Kadmus sighed, directing his thoughts to where they always went when swift decisions were required: what was there to gain, and what was the cost?

He could let Grunt bleed out, but would that make Bahar leave? Would Grunt's wife come looking for him? If Grunt had told Bahar about Kadmus, what had Grunt told his wife?

If he saved the man, Bahar would know what he could do, and that was too close to finding out that Kadmus had a living daughter and not the dead one he claimed. Nima was in danger either way, but things would be less messy with a live Grunt than a dead one.

Kadmus grabbed a shard of ruin-stone and rounded the counter. He took a serum from a shelf and knelt beside Grunt, pressing the stone to the wound as he emptied the vial into the big man's mouth. He held Grunt's mouth shut so he wouldn't choke out the serum.

Slowly, the wound began to heal under the ruin-stone's pulse. The skin knitted itself together until the blood stopped gushing, but the outer layers would take more time. Healing wasn't a fast process and was never without pain. He could see it now, taking over the initial relief on Grunt's face. Kadmus stood, noticing the blood on his robes. He glared at Bahar, who grinned back at him.

"There are many generals," Bahar said, "who would kill to have you among their ranks."

"My potions are not made for the crudeness of battle. They are slow, deliberate. One small wound I can handle, especially when it's fresh, and I saw it inflicted. Thousands, I cannot repair."

"My wounds are not fresh," Bahar said, "but you will find a way to heal them all the same."

Kadmus didn't hide his fury, half of it over his ruined robes. He didn't mind blood, but if it would ruin his clothes, he preferred to be the one spilling it. "I suppose there'll be more cutting if I say no?"

Bahar dug into a pocket. Kadmus stiffened, telling himself he was ready, though for what he knew not. Bahar held out a small disk bearing the Visslands' triple waterfall: the seal of entry to the capital city's more noble parts.

"Most nobles," Bahar said, "find their vices in the outer quarters, and are followed as they do. You will treat me in the upper city. A new location will be relayed to you whenever you are summoned."

Kadmus eyed the man, his mind unintentionally evaluating the damage to his face—which obviously bothered the man the most. Kadmus could try, but they would leave a mark, especially days after the original infliction. The limp seemed to be something deeper and harder to fix, but Bahar had made it clear that Kadmus had little choice in the matter. He could not fail.

Bahar moved to the counter, no longer trying to conceal his limp. He set the disk down and turned to leave. "When I call, you come," he said over his shoulder. "Or it'll be the Church that visits you next time."

Kadmus was left shaking his head for a long time, with only his anger and the passed-out Grunt at his feet. He'd always had everything planned, calculated. Where had he misstepped? His answer was probably right in front of him, passed out on the floor, but there was no point in beating himself up about it now. Maybe later. Right now, he had to attend to Bahar. The man was dangerous, and as ruthless as they came. His actions seemed almost too ruthless to be seeking only a healing, but perhaps men's vanity grew with their station.

He breathed out a long sigh, locked the door, and drew the curtains. Grunt would know to clean up when he woke up. Kadmus went down to his brewing chamber. Appearances be damned. He had to find a cure for Nima.

CHAPTER NINE

The dead's deeds in life shall be judged to determine the worthiness of their memory. To be deemed worthy of remembrance is a joy that will dull the pain of the living; to fail is a test to the faith of the perished's kin. One that is necessary for the continued growth of our people.

— *The Azuri Book of Memory*

Adrian was ready to convince the consuls to rebuild his army. He walked away from Bac's room with the man beside him.

"I don't know how the consuls will react," Adrian said. "But you stick close to me."

Bac nodded. "Wouldn't want to end up like those three."

Adrian was glad the display had bought him a measure of respect, even from a man that was a perceived murderer. Bac had held his own against the Azuri guards, and even if one man might not make a big difference to the consuls, arriving with followers would strengthen Adrian's image. Maybe it would buy a measure of their respect as well.

Bac wore a mix of armor taken from the felled guards. Adrian had found enough red and white for Bac. Not the traditional Othonean red and black. Adrian was carving his own path, building his image with new colors.

They finally reached the long corridor to the chamber where the council waited. Two guards stood by the chamber's entrance, wearing the green and silver of the Khorfa. They drew curved blades as Adrian and Bac approached. "Where are your guards?" asked one.

"I brought my own." Adrian jerked his head toward Bac, who walked ahead and faced the guards, defiant.

Nasir came round a corner. No guards with him either. "We are here as equals," he said. The guards were now outnumbered, and their insecurity was clear.

"No need for heroes," Adrian said. "We'll be sure to tell Lord Khorfa you had no choice." He walked past them and opened the doors, Nasir and Bac close behind. The guards kept their weapons handy but let them pass.

The chamber was the same one where the decision on Prince Niilar's worthiness had been delivered to the Xakhar. That was weeks ago, but to Adrian, it seemed like a distant lifetime. Perhaps they meant to send him a message by picking the smoky room. Wanted him to remember Niilar's dead body. Wanted Adrian to know he could be next.

There was less smoke in the room this time, but a thin mist twisted in the light that streamed into the rectangular chamber. Tall windows flanked the high platform where the Xakhar had once stood with Kahlia to receive the news regarding his son. That platform was empty now. The ten consuls stood along the rectangular walkway beneath it, some with guards behind them.

The consuls had their attention on the pit-like space where the dead Azuri prince had once lain. Adrian was sure he was supposed to enter on that lower level, and the consuls must have been eager to look down on him. So much so that most of them failed to notice his entrance. It gave him time to search for the wards Nasir had mentioned. Or try to; a ward could be anything—a pendant, a ring—and the gloomy room did him no favors.

Khorfa stood to Adrian's right and was the first to spot him. Khorfa's hand went for the sword at his hip. Mahir, a consul with deeply sunburnt skin, stepped behind Khorfa, also ready. Bac made to step up to meet them, but Adrian gestured for him to stand down. Soon all turned to Adrian, but none approached. His lack of Azuri escort sent a clear enough message.

Adrian caught a mixture of disapproving and curious gazes from the consuls. It reminded him of his audiences with Father. He'd never been welcome there either.

Attar pointed at Adrian from the far side of the walkway that surrounded the pit-like depression. "T-traitor!" he said.

Nasir spread his arms, as if the situation were inevitable. "None of the guards are dead, Lord Attar. We have simply come to the meeting on our own terms."

"This is not a meeting," snapped an old woman with pursed lips and a pinched face. "It is a judgement."

"The consuls may discuss, Lady Yankah," said Nasir. "But in the absence of a Xakhar, Azuri law is clear." He snapped his fingers, and another man entered the room. He wore light silks of black, white, and gray. If they represented a house, it was one Adrian didn't know. The Jurat?

Nasir smiled around the room. "I am sure not having a Jurat among you is an oversight. One I am happy to remedy."

Adrian watched for a reaction, but none came.

Lord Attar smiled back as if he'd won some kind of game. "An admirable attempt," he said, "but your lack of knowledge about our families is clear." Attar was known to have a strong influence among the Azuri Jurat order; Nasir had said as much.

"Jurat Faruq," Attar continued, "please remove the murderer from our presence. I am sure the order will issue swift justice unto him." Attar waved a hand and turned away.

Jurat Faruq did not move. "The Jurat are sworn to serve justice for the greater interest of Azur, Consul Attar. That is not done with the simple wave of a hand."

The outrage was plastered on Attar's face. "You do not decide over the Consulate! We are the future of this nation. If you have allowed yourself to be bought, justice will be swift to you as well."

Faruq eyed Attar coldly. "I will ignore that slight as a result of the current circumstance, Consul Attar. I will not ignore another."

Nasir suppressed a smile now. "Perhaps circumstance has clouded your memory of our customs, Lord Attar," he said. "Understandable, as you have lived in the comfort of the Xakhar's shadow for long enough. I'm sure you know that in the absence of a Xakhar, the Consulate may discuss, but the Jurat decide." Adrian could not fathom how Nasir had gotten hold of this Jurat, but the man seemed to be on their side.

Attar watched Jurat Faruq but did not argue. Nasir had told Adrian that the Attar family was always the one to be consulted on legal matters, the ones who kept the Jurats amenable to the consuls, under their control. It was clear that Attar knew the law, and just as clear that he had not expected Nasir to know it as well.

Attar turned toward the door, trying to seem unscathed, but his expression was fraying. "We shall see how long you can keep up this little game, priest." He stomped out, leaving the other consuls to gaze at the Jurat.

Faruq remained silent.

"The Jurat is not here today to lead the proceedings," Nasir said. "He has come simply to see that the agreement is favorable to the nation of Azur. Now, if there are no more departures . . ."

None of the consuls moved, but Khorfa stepped forward. "And how does your presence among us warrant a favorable agreement, Lord Light?"

"Lord Khorfa," Adrian said, "as I told Princess Kahlia when I arrived, I've not come in search of enemies. There is a plague spreading through Immeria. I had hoped it would take some time to arrive in Azur, but it's already here."

"And how do you know that?" a bald man in orange and red asked.

"It was on the prince's dead face, Lord Erhul," a woman in the shadows said. This had to be Lady Zarath, the consul responsible for dealing in secrets and information. "We did not give merit to the foreigner, but after what happened to Kahlia, it would be folly not to look into this further."

"How can we be certain?" asked Lady Yankah, the old woman in brown and gray. "Stained skin on a dead man proves nothing. How do we know the foreigner didn't poison the Xakhar and Kahlia?"

A man standing beside Zarath stepped forward. "We can be certain."

Yankah scoffed. "Another Bedak nugget of wisdom?"

The man was the leader of the Bedak house then—rival metal-workers to the Yankah. He looked at one of the men standing guard in the shadows. The soldier bounded off. A moment later, the doors to the lower tier opened up. Guards dragged a struggling man into the space, hooded and chained.

Adrian caught movement on the other side, where he recognized Lady Rhiall, the leader of the largest Azuri merchant family, shifting for the first time. Rhiall had been the one who convinced the consuls to gather instead of striking at Adrian after the wedding ceremony. She had kept a stony visage. Something slipped in her expression now, a slight frown and parting of the lips that lasted only for a moment. *She knows what this is.*

Yankah seemed unimpressed, but the consuls beside Rhiall were almost leaning over the parapet in anticipation. Bedak nodded, and the hood was removed.

Adrian recognized the madman instantly, but his unveiling pulled gasps from the room. Some of the consuls stepped back, while others gazed down in disbelief. "This is my nephew," Bedak said. "He has been afflicted with the same curse as Prince Niilar."

The madman growled and struggled against his chains, but the guards held them tight. "It is contagious and easily spread, but the Lord Light has shown resistance to it." Bedak gestured toward Adrian's face, where Kahlia had scratched him in her madness. "The Xakhar had accepted him into his family, and so had Kahlia. Should we not follow what the Xakhar himself envisioned?"

Lord Mahir, the naval commander of the Azuri, frowned,

moving his considerable girth farther from the steps that led down to where the madman struggled against the guards holding his chains. "This goes beyond a threat. If it was brought to us by the foreigner—"

"Niilar was afflicted before I arrived," Adrian said. He gestured toward the madman. "And I have never seen this man."

"The Lord Light comes to us as an equal," Bedak said. "So let us consider him as one. The deaths of the Xakhar and the princess were a tragedy, but dwelling on them will not move us forward."

"You would have him lead us?" said the man in orange and red, almost gasping the question.

Mahir cleared his throat. "Resistance to this plague does not ensure the ability to lead us against it."

"The Admiral is right," Lady Rhiall said. "A leader cannot be decided in this"—she glanced down at the madman— "circumstance."

Bedak nodded, then turned to Jurat Faruq. "Very well, then; a vote must be called. Every name among the council considered."

There were mumbles among the consuls, but it seemed they were inclined to accept the proposal. The Jurat gave them a moment, then nodded. "I will inform High Jurat Hasna."

Adrian breathed out in the smoky gloom and thought he saw a reddish tinge shift in a shadowed corner. It could have been a glimpse of Myrra's smile, and Adrian did all he could to keep back his own. He'd arrived as an escapee; now they were discussing whether he should rule them.

"My guards will not hold you to your rooms, Lord Light," said Khorfa. He gave a brief nod to old lady Yankah and left without ceremony, most of the consuls following behind him.

Lady Zarath's gaze lingered on Adrian before she approached him. "You have shown yourself an able maneuverer, Lord Light. And your priest, he is a disciple of the Afterdark, yes?"

Adrian nodded.

"We should talk. You will not do this without allies." She left without waiting for a reply, moving silent as the shadows.

Bedak nodded down to the guards, who drove their spears

through the madman's heart. Bedak looked to Adrian, and his gaze said enough. The man had exposed a member of his family to convince the council of the threat—and persuade them to consider Adrian as ruler instead of fodder for the executioner. A prisoner could have been infected for the demonstration, but that wouldn't have spoken to the personal urgency of the spreading plague.

Adrian wouldn't put it past a consul infecting a member of his family to further his own interests, but he'd been in Azur long enough to know that, even if he hadn't requested a favor, he now owed Bedak one.

The consuls were allowed inside the palace and had taken up rooms. Nasir had told Adrian it was all part of picking a new Xakhar, but to Adrian, it seemed more like an effort to project an image of strength to their peers. Not all would place their names up for consideration, and it was unclear who Adrian's competition was. And who—aside from Bedak—his allies might be.

The families had been allowed their own guards, but Jurat Faruq had taken command of the palace guards who'd served the Xakhar. It would be little more than a week until the consuls convened again, and Faruq seemed intent on keeping the peace. There would be no shortage of politics, though, and Adrian could think of only one path forward.

He made his way down the corridor with Bac close behind. Their boots echoed off the copper and blue-tinted marble floor as they moved toward the steps that led to the dungeons. The Khorfa boy who'd plotted against the Xakhar would still be down there. Kahlia had said she'd been interrogating him, and Adrian doubted the Jurat would let him be removed by Lord Khorfa. Adrian couldn't rely on the consuls for information. Amal ban Khorfa had been involved in trying to kill the Xakhar. If Adrian offered him his freedom, perhaps he could get enough information to understand which families might be allies.

Two guards stood by the stairwell. Adrian ignored them, but

they barred his path as he tried to pass. He considered using Nasir's blood magic, but killing guards would likely jeopardize his recently earned freedom. Adrian eyed the men. "Do I need to get the Jurat, or would you like to keep your lives?"

"There is no entry to the dungeons, Lord Light. Not even by the consuls."

"The Jurat it is, then."

Someone chuckled behind Adrian. "What would you desire down there, Prince Adrian?"

Adrian turned to find Jurat Faruq behind him.

"These men are my own," Faruq said. "Access to the dungeons is restricted until a Xakhar has been chosen."

"A sensible course of action." Nasir had turned a corner and held a posture of deference to Faruq. He looked to Adrian. "I have urgent news, Lord Light."

Adrian sighed. If he couldn't get to Amal, maybe he'd need to take Lady Zarath up on her offer. He moved away, following Nasir down a corridor with Bac looming behind them.

"What is it?" Adrian asked.

"There is news from the Domain. Not good, I'm afraid."

Nasir opened a door halfway down the corridor and led them into what seemed a disused room. Bac stood guard outside.

"Dakhra has turned on the Domain," Nasir whispered. "They are behind this. This plague, this madness, comes from one of their potions."

What? How could it have come from Dakhra? Myrra had been infected! How? Memories flashed in Adrian's mind. The Othonean battle with Dakhra, still with him over a century later. Myrra coming to his aid; their talks about controlling their fathers; Adrian's burning desire to see the Domain united, as was his mother's vision. Himself standing in Erez, defending the Dakhran capital against the Azuri invasion. Myrra had stood with him, convincing her father to join the Domain. It had never been a smooth relationship between Father and Syvern, but there had been no outright war. Now it seemed that Syvern had been biding his time all along.

Had Syvern sacrificed Myrra? Adrian closed his eyes, hands

balled into fists. He took a deep breath, and then another. Syvern had sacrificed Myrra. Adrian picked up one of the chairs and smashed it into the wood-paneled wall. *Bastard!* He smashed the wall again. Nasir merely watched, waiting for him to regain control.

"I'll kill the bastard," Adrian said, more to himself than to Nasir.

"We must keep on our path, Lord Light."

The cuts along Adrian's arm from the recent bindings pulsed as if calling out to him, and that same tingle was in his blood again. He paced around the room, questions jumbled with the frustrated rage growing in his heart. Addo wasn't the only one. He'd make Syvern answer all his questions. Painfully.

Adrian took a few more heavy breaths, trying to recompose himself. He'd smash as many chairs as he could against Syvern, but he could not get to Dakhra without an army. *Just get through this.* "I can't get to the Khorfa boy. Can we count on Zarath?" He was past using the word "trust". He wouldn't get any of that here.

"It seems we'll have to," Nasir said. "She is the only one who has offered alliance."

Adrian nodded. "I would speak with her today." His voice came out loud, still loaded with anger. "We need to get this over with and return to the Domain."

"Yes, Lord Light."

Nasir left Adrian alone in the room, but Adrian wasn't alone. He took out the ruin-stone knife, rolled up his sleeve, and cut at the scab that throbbed from his last binding. He didn't draw signs this time. He wasn't even sure why he'd cut himself. Something just made him do it, as if to bleed away the pain. His gaze searched the gloom. His eyes found Myrra in a corner, more distinct than ever, though her face was still a patchwork of skin torn and sewn together. It made the pain and anger cut deeper.

"I'll kill them," he whispered. "I'll kill everyone who hurt you."

Myrra gave him a broken smile. "I know you will."

Adrian rolled down his sleeve, letting the blood seep through. Then he stepped out and returned to his room.

Adrian paced for what felt like an hour in his room and was still pacing when the knock came at his door. He'd left Bac there, and the man peeked through the crack as Adrian opened the door.

"One of them consuls." Bac jerked his head over his shoulder.

Adrian looked past him, but the man who stood in the hall was a guard. "That isn't a consul, Bac."

Bac shrugged. "Says he has orders to take you somewhere."

He looked at the man behind Bac. Lady Zarath calling on him, most likely. Adrian stepped out. "Stay close behind," he told Bac.

The guard led them to a room on a middle floor. There wasn't much traffic in the halls, even with the consuls occupying the palace. The guard pointed at a door and kept walking, as if on patrol.

Adrian looked to Bac and pushed the door open. Bac went through first, with Adrian close behind.

The room wasn't much different from the one Adrian had initially occupied in the palace. The antechamber opened onto a balcony, and there were tables inside and out. Bedak sat in a high-backed chair with a glass in hand, Lady Zarath behind him.

"Caution is always a good course of action," Bedak said. "But it is unnecessary in here." He lifted the glass of shraz and took a swig. "You can leave your dog outside."

Adrian nodded to Bac, who left, seemingly without offense.

Lady Zarath moved around the chair. "I'm glad you accepted my invitation, Lord Light."

Adrian was in no mood for politics, but he'd lost everything to brashness once before. He held his tongue, waiting for the consuls to continue.

"Your Priest of the Blood is quite efficient," Bedak said. "An amusing title for one trained as a blood mage in the house of the Afterdark. Yet I find a short leash is always best." It seemed like every word the man spoke held some underlying jab.

"Like your leash on your nephew, Lord Bedak?"

The man chuckled. "Precisely. A sacrifice that had to be made, yet one that gained your freedom, and a chance at the army you came for."

Adrian watched them for a moment. "What do you want?"

"To help you," Zarath said.

"You do not wish to be Xakhar?" Adrian asked.

Lady Zarath chuckled. "Oh no, my dear boy. We are most comfortable in the shadows. Isn't that so. Lenir?"

Bedak nodded. "There is no true freedom in the light. Too many eyes on you."

"And how will you help?"

Lady Zarath smiled broadly now. "With information, my boy."

Adrian was gritting his teeth again. He'd probably lived twice as long as this woman, yet she treated him like a child. "I'm no boy."

"Of course, Lord Light." The words came with the expected deference, but they seemed to veil an amused curiosity.

"What will you want in return?"

"A favored eye," said Zarath. "Contacts, access to resources. And to the palace, naturally. Even when you are Xakhar, timely information is the difference between life and death."

"That didn't seem to help the previous one."

Zarath grinned. "He had no deal with me."

Adrian looked to Bedak. "And you?"

"Khorfa favors the use of Yankah's blades, but her family does not forge like we do. It's been too long since we fought a proper war. To fight one, your army will need proper weapons. You will make Khorfa use my steel. Exclusively."

Adrian eyed them for a long while. "How will you make me Xakhar?"

Zarath strode to a side table and filled two glasses with shraz, then walked up to Adrian and handed him one. She sipped at it, but Adrian didn't.

"To sway them, you will need Rhiall," she said.

Adrian thought back to her reaction when she'd seen the madman. "She knew about the Madness."

"I'd expect so," Zarath said. "It broke out within her house and almost took her son."

"Almost doesn't give me much to work with."

"The boy was irresponsible. He was doing his own deals in the dark. Found more than he bargained for, then ran away."

"And?"

Zarath smiled. "I know where he is. The blood mages are keeping him."

"Why?"

"We think he found something," Bedak said. "Something that interests the mages. It seems he is not free to leave until they have what they want. The house of the Afterdark, like the Jurat, has a certain . . . independence in the absence of a Xakhar. Retrieving the boy will require some convincing."

"Your priest will help," Zarath said.

"He's not part of their order anymore," Adrian said. "He turned to a different religion on a foreign continent."

Bedak grinned and shook his head. "You'll find the blood mages are more tied to what flows within the veins than the bonds we create without."

Blood holds ties. Does Father have something to do with this?

"Kel Bradaz is the leader of the mages," Zarath said. "If you have him on your side, and retrieve Rhiall's son, I believe Lady Rhiall will be more than favorable to your cause."

Adrian still wasn't sure, but if this was the path, best to get on with it. He raised his glass, and all three downed the shraz. It burned down his gullet, but not as hot as the fire within him, aching to avenge Myrra.

"We will stay in contact," Bedak said.

Adrian nodded and left the room. Bac waited in the hall, by an open window that looked down on a courtyard. Nasir was with him. "I trust your work with the consuls has been fruitful, Lord Light?" Nasir said.

"They want us to meet your old friends," Adrian replied. "Looks like they have Rhiall's son hostage."

Nasir's eyes widened a touch, but he soon regained his composure. "Kel Bradaz will sense your strength. He'll take a special interest in you."

"Then I'll need protection. I won't be at his mercy, Nasir. Or yours."

"You can be warded, but Bradaz's skill will not be thwarted, merely delayed. Perhaps enough for an escape if it comes to that."

"I'll have you do it all the same."

Nasir bowed his head. "Of course, my Lord Light. Let us find a more private place for the ritual."

CHAPTER TEN

It is the duty of the Bone to provide the Church with information on the happenings in the Seraph's Domain. The bishops are given the power of Questioning not only to be used against the Seraph's enemies, but to stand as a reminder that the power of other orders within the Church is not absolute.

— Excerpt from The Holy Church of the Seraph and Its Orders

Lynn had taken up rooms in one of the cathedral towers that had been closed off for the Sentinels. Whether for their comfort or because it made it easier for the clergy to keep an eye on her was impossible to tell.

Her room was one of the smaller ones, but it was still far larger and better furnished than she needed. The bed had silken sheets, and the chairs were inlaid with ivory and silver, and covered with velvet. Lynn stood before the large window, gazing out at the night sky and tracing Vedyr's circling path. He kept close, as if he shared her trepidation. The urge to jump on his back and fly off was almost overwhelming, but Lynn had promised. No more running.

You can't run from what you are, coward, Alren said. *You'll get what you deserve.*

Rel's footsteps pulled Lynn from the voices. It had to be Rel—no one else would take the trouble to climb those steps to see her. He knocked, but Lynn kept her eyes on Vedyr for a moment before calling him in.

"I'm not sure you know what you got yourself into," he said.

"Sometimes the only way past is through, Rel."

"Elwin's words?"

"Leardin's."

Rel chuckled. "As long as you know you'll reach the other side."

"I'll get somewhere. It's better than running circles with Ildred."

"Just won't let go, that one." Rel moved to stand beside her.

Lynn still watched Vedyr. Ulenia seemed close by as well. "He isn't wrong," she said. "Why should he trust me? Alren, Roki . . . they were all following me, just like now. I couldn't protect them. I couldn't even see the true enemy."

"None of us did. Punishing yourself isn't the way."

"This isn't punishment. I just need to . . ." Lynn sighed. "I've promised myself. No more running. We need to stop the Madness. The Questioning is the first step."

"You're taking this too lightly. There's a reason they don't allow the Questioning within the Church." Rel's tone rose as it never had before.

Part of becoming a Sentinel was shedding a previous life, but whatever Rel had endured was clearly present. He looked away, then back at Lynn. "You think they'd let an Azuri into the order without a Questioning?" he asked. His tone was resigned now, tired. "The High Bishop will dig deep, and it's more than just physical pain. It can change you."

Lynn put a hand on his shoulder. "Things are already changing. Maybe it's time I did as well. If I get through this, we can focus on the Madness. Have you found anything that might help stop it?"

"Not yet, but we should look into your theory about the ruin-stone. I'll need to check the archives."

Lynn lifted her eyes to the Seraph's mark in the sky. It was larger than ever, more than a second moon now. "Do you think She's coming? Finally lost Her faith in us? Do you think the Ever-Tree is dying because She's taking her gifts back?"

She's only lost faith in you.

"If She is coming, we'd better clean up before She gets here," Rel said. "I'll pray to Her that you get through this. You're the one who should be leading us."

"We need unity, Rel. Even if I wanted to be commander, I wouldn't unite the Sentinels. Olem needs to keep the chair, or you. Make sure the Pontiff knows that."

Rel chuckled. "We'll see tomorrow." He turned for the door but paused before leaving. "Lynn? At the Questioning tomorrow . . . Don't forget who you are. You're one of us. You've proven you're strong enough to stand against Death."

She watched him leave. He might think she was strong enough to face Death, but did she know who she really was? She thought she'd known, all those years back, but now that she asked herself, she struggled to find an answer. She'd run away as a child, tried to face Death with Elwin, but that only led to more running. She'd even run from the Sentinels. Death was the only thing that always followed her.

Don't fight it, said Dentos. *Death isn't following you. You are Death itself.*

Lynn shook her head, and Vedyr's shadow flew close by. She was sure he could feel it, even if he didn't know her thoughts. She stepped out onto the window ledge and looked over the city. A light flickered outside what might have been a tavern or an inn, but all was quiet. She closed her eyes, trying to let the city's silence seep into her mind, then jumped off. Air rushed past her, cold and cutting, until she landed on Vedyr's soft feathers.

"You know who I am, right?" she whispered.

Vedyr's answer came as a low rumbling that vibrated through Lynn. She wouldn't run again, but sleep was hard to come by, and there was more comfort on Vedyr's back than she'd ever find in her room.

The next morning, she was ready when the knock came at her door. She'd dressed in her Mantle, still adorned with the Signs of the Seraph, which labeled her as a general of the Legion. She'd considered it temporary, but maybe her service to the Legion would help convince the Church leaders of her worthiness. Everything would be considered.

Two of the Church guard walked before Lynn. She closed her eyes for a moment and reached out to Vedyr. He was still close. Still connected.

We'll get through this, Vedyr. She received a flood of recognition through her Bond, enough to make her chin rise as she stopped before the audience chamber doors. The Alterian guards opened them, and Lynn stepped inside.

The chamber was darker than before. The three chairs had not been moved, but only two were occupied: the Pontiff in one, Burke the other. The one reserved for High Bishop Reznik held only shadows, while the man himself stepped from the soft glow of the sacred sunlight texts that filtered in through the wall on the left.

Another chair had been brought in and positioned at the base of the steps, clearly meant for Lynn. Reznik indicated the chair. "Please take a seat, Sentinel."

She sat.

The Pontiff rose. "This proceeding is not standard Church fare," he said, "yet times are trying, and we must seek all paths that may bring us to the light. Let it be clear that this is carried out only by request of the questioned herself, and shall not be taken lightly, or likely repeated. Sentinel Lynn, do you consent to this Questioning?"

"Yes, High Pontiff."

"Then let us begin."

Reznik stepped close. Lynn had expected some kind of tool or aggressive questioning, but the man seemed as collected as he'd been the day before. He dug a bony hand into his robes and pulled out a fist-sized rock of ruin-stone. Its veins glowed more than any light in the room. "Please remain still." He pressed the stone onto Lynn's forehead.

There was nothing but the cold touch of the stone at first. Then the burning began. It started in her ribs, as if she'd taken a blow from a mace, strong enough to crack bone. The feeling spread as if streaks of fire were running all over her skin. She could even smell the burning. There were chills, followed by searing lashes all over. She didn't want to scream, but the scream was pulled out of her all the same. It didn't sound like her voice. In her ears it was Alren, then Roki, Dentos, and Cara. They were all with her in this, and they weren't laughing now.

The chamber faded, and Lynn found herself in a smaller room. There was shouting, and a girl crouched in a corner beside a bed. She was covering her head with her hands, crying and averting her eyes. Her dirty blond hair was framed in a dark green light, almost like an aura. A man stood before her, older. Surrounded by a bluish-purple aura. The girl was Lynn, the man her father. He had a long blade in one hand. A young boy lay bleeding on the room's floor, while another rounded on her father. Lynn's brothers: Jeck and Pyth. It was Pyth on the floor. Lynn averted her eyes, just like her younger self.

The vision flashed and for a moment the walls of the room became rough stone, like a dungeon's, then reverted once more to her parent's estate: Pyth bleeding and Jeck feral.

"Look," a voice said. She didn't know why, but she did.

Jeck lunged, filled with nothing but rage and surrounded by a blackish aura. Lynn screamed, reliving the scene. She hadn't seen her father stab Jeck as a child; she'd been huddled in the corner. The little-girl Lynn ran, pulling the image away behind her.

Lynn's world swirled and reformed until she stood on a hill as a city burned just below. Gheria. Lynn's skin felt aflame. She squeezed her eyes shut.

"Look," a voice said, sharp and cold. So cold that Lynn hung on to it, like a final shred of sanity amid the burning madness. Some people were close enough to see, and they all had auras, like the ones surrounding her father and brothers—swirls of green and blue all around them.

Lynn raised her head. People were running, escaping the winged shadows from above. Griffins. Vedyr! She reached out, almost regretting it, but she knew Vedyr could feel the burning as well. She pulled back, but the griffin held onto their Bond. He took some of the heat into himself, enough for Lynn to pull in a breath and return her consciousness to the chamber.

"Look!" Reznik had something in his hand. Lynn tried to focus on it but couldn't tell what it was. "Take it," he said.

She stretched out a hand, but something held her back. There was a glint to the object, but it was not aglow like the ruin-stone. Reznik pushed the item into Lynn's hand, and her fingers closed around a hilt. A sword? She brought it close. A long knife. She wanted to drop it, but Reznik grasped her hand and kept her fingers tight around it. "Do not let go."

He pushed the ruin-stone harder onto her forehead, and her vision blurred again. The chamber fell into darkness and was replaced by Gheria. She was close to a square now. The heat from Reznik's ruin-stone still sent tongues of flame all over her skin, but it was like Lynn was watching herself from above. A slightly younger version with confident steps, sure of who she was and what she was doing for the Sentinels.

Someone put a spear in her hand. Lynn surveilled the square, brushed away her dirty-blond hair, then launched the spear straight through a woman's chest. It seemed like a clanswoman, one of the slaves the Domain folk took in certain cities. She couldn't remember why she was doing it, but it was clear to her younger self that it should be done. There was no hesitation. Even Vedyr was unwavering as he flew above. The burning had only grown, though, and Lynn's Bond with Vedyr seemed to be fraying. It was starting to break her consciousness, threatening to hollow her out.

It made no sense. She wasn't consuming Vedyr's strength, just holding onto her sanity, but whatever Reznik was doing seemed to be enough of a drain. She looked sideways and there they were: Alren, Roki, Cara, and Dentos, her voices taken form. They'd been running from her after they were infected, hiding in Gheria, but now all they did was laugh. Their necks were sliced, but the wounds had been crudely stitched shut, and blood was leaking from them.

A flare from the ruin-stone sent a searing pain through Lynn's forehead and down her neck. She screamed again. Her dead companions' laughs became screams of their own, and she unconsciously channeled her pain across the Bond to Vedyr. Lynn tried to let go, but it wasn't only Vedyr holding on this time; the ruin-stone seemed to keep her bonded to Vedyr.

Her body weakened, and she was back in the chamber, breathing heavy. The blade was in her hand, but her ears were ringing and her vision was still blurred.

"Look!" Reznik snapped his fingers, drawing her useless blurry gaze to something else. It had a gleam to it, but was small and transparent. A vial. Lynn recoiled, remembering what Leardin had shown her. And then there he was, as if summoned, the dead commander standing behind Reznik with his hands on the bishop's shoulders.

Take it, Lynn. Join me.

"No!"

"Take it." Reznik said. "I will not force this upon you."

Lynn blinked, trying to sharpen her vision. Leardin was still there. He nodded at her. She gritted her teeth, ears ringing. She'd asked for this. There was no point in denying it now. She took the vial and swallowed its contents. The liquid flared her insides and spread, lighting her veins on fire, but it faded a moment later, and the burning on her skin subsided.

She was in the battle at Durnn now. Slashing at madmen, urging the Legion first to fight, then to fall back. The chill ran through her again. The same one she'd felt when she realized the silhouette coming toward Durnn's gates had been Leardin, and when she realized the Madness she'd fought her entire life had been engineered by Dakhra. The revived feeling crushed her heart, pressing her with a mixture of guilt, disappointment, fear, and helplessness. The emotions were too many and too entwined for Lynn to know what she truly felt, beyond the pain clawing at her chest.

Leardin's dead body lay beside her, and the sight of it almost took what strength was left in Lynn's muscles. Her skin went cold, so cold it burned again. It was a different kind of burn, but insistent. And it was rising.

She pulled on Vedyr's strength to aid her, but it did nothing to lessen the pain. She knelt beside Leardin in her memory. "I'm sorry," she whispered, her voice thick with grief, her shoulders heavy with the burden of all she'd been through. She pressed a hand to Leardin's chest and let the tears fall for a moment, as if shedding the weight that had been pent-up within her for too long.

Lynn rose and ran back to the Sentinel tower and to Vedyr. The wind blew past her, tearing away pieces of her mind. She crashed through the doors of the Sentinel tower, but what greeted her was not the common hall; it was the Pontiff's audience chamber.

She was on her feet, the vision gone, skin going hot and cold and the blade she'd been given held tight in hand. A clergyman stood before her, pressing the ruin-stone to her forehead. What was his name? She couldn't even remember her own. The stone pulsed anger through her, and it felt almost good. Anger she knew. Anger she could control. Something was pulling it from her, though. A source high above. There was something else, too. Calling to her from the back of her mind.

Kill him. End your pain. Take your place as my herald. She knew the voice. She would never forget death's icy tone.

Alren was beside her now. That name she remembered. Not only him, but all of them. They surrounded her, guiding the blade in her hand while Leardin stood behind the bishop, still nodding.

She breathed deep. Her limbs seemed to move with a mind of their own. She gave her anger to the source high above, but the more she gave, the more of herself she lost. Her legs shook, and a whiteness crept into her vision. The clergyman stared at her unwaveringly, like he was trying to read something.

L . . . what was her name? She held the man's gaze, pressing her teeth, then pushed against the stone on her forehead. Instinct gathered her anger and directed it at the stone, pushing back its flaming tongues with a scream. The Bond was released, along with the blade. Lynn. That was her name. She would not kill the bishop. She still believed in the Church, in the Faith. She was a Sentinel.

Lynn fell to her hands and knees. She stayed there, gasping as her mind slowly recomposed itself. Her skin still tingled with memory of the burning from Reznik's ruin-stone, and her veins pulsed as if trying to push the fire out of her. It gathered in her stomach and came rushing up her throat. Lynn vomited a hot bile on the stone floor.

The pulsing in her veins became a pounding in her head, and her mind slowly pulled back the pieces of itself from the hollow pit where the Bond drew its power. The place where it had threatened to trap her sanity. No one spoke, the only sounds Lynn's heavy breath and Reznik's soft steps as returned to his chair.

"There is a lot in this one's past," Reznik said, his voice distant, "but her intention in the battle was clear. As clear as in the present moment. She did not betray the Church and does not wish to strike against it. In this, she can be trusted."

Two guards helped Lynn stand on trembling legs. She clutched her ribs with one arm, the burning still rippling through her innards. A hunched stance was all she could manage as they helped her out of the audience chamber and led her back to her room.

CHAPTER ELEVEN

The path to the First Tree is known by few and quickly forgotten. Only by ritual can it be remembered, and many believe the ritual depends on the whims of the Earth. Those with less faith claim it is the whims of the dead goddess herself.

— *Tales of the Yltigg*

"What happened?" Mansa had pulled her aside after the meeting with Tomu, and they'd locked themselves in Nasha's room in the Great Hall.

Nasha walked around the bed and stood with her back to the window. "I was serious in the hall. We need to stop the fighting. The Domain is coming."

"Yes, like we wanted them to."

"No. Bahar . . . He's not going to let go. He's coming for us."

"He's not coming for us. I know Bahar, and I know the Domain. The Yltigg ancestor-stone will speak louder."

Nasha shook her head, but Mansa was set in his ways. "You did good," he said, "involving Leku. The Slopers will help to keep the Yltigg at bay."

"And if you're wrong? If Bahar comes for us?"

Mansa frowned, but Nasha didn't pick up much emotion from it. "What happened out there that makes you so sure he'll come for us?"

"Adda followed us. She was trying to get out. She . . . was like me."

"Was?"

"I just told you she had my curse, and you're more interested in whether she's dead?"

"If she is, her having your gift doesn't matter, does it?"

Nasha had always counted on Mansa for her training, to keep her curse under control. Now she'd found others like her, and all he cared about was his own plans. She was still just a tool to him, and the thought tied a knot of frustration in her chest. "She's dead. We were taking the boy to be killed on the Yltigg border, but Adda followed me. She wanted the boy. She thought she could use him to bargain her way out of the clanlands. She said she would never be safe, and I wouldn't be either."

"None of us are safe. But your gifts make you safer than most."

Nasha was tired of arguing. He didn't know her curse, didn't know the strain of keeping it under control.

"And?" he asked.

Nasha was slow to answer, but she had to finish the lie. She still needed Mansa, just as he needed her. Perhaps he'd be her own tool to help her keep her standing in the clan—and avoid Tomu's suspicions. "Maybe she knew Bahar escaped," Nasha said. "Thought she could broker a trade for the boy and told him where we were somehow, I don't know.

"All I know is that Bahar found us... The Yltigg cut him up, scars all along his face. He's angry, Mansa, too angry. Perhaps Adda thought she could take his anger away with her curse, but he didn't give her the chance. He had people with him. They killed her and the hunters." Nasha had practiced the story carefully, and she was ready for questions about the parts that weren't true.

"How did you get away?"

She couldn't lie about that. Mansa was too smart. "I found something. In my curse. I used it."

Mansa grinned. "I always knew you'd learn to control it."

"I haven't. Not yet. Don't know if I ever will. It was quick and barely enough to get away. Bedri killed the Domain boy before Bahar could take him, though. You're getting your war, but I can't keep relying on this curse."

"I taught you better than that. You're letting fear take hold."

Maybe he was right. She'd relived the fear of her past: that little girl in the Domain town under the floorboards, watching people die, with the smell of burning wood in her nostrils and the taste of blood on her tongue. The sensations had followed her, infecting her senses whenever fear's cold fingers dragged against the back of her neck. There was a certain safety to fear, though. She'd seen Zala's taint up close. She would not let herself become that. "This is a different fear."

"It's still holding you back from what you need to do," Mansa said. "Embrace your gift. Use it to give us an upper hand."

No, it was too much of a risk; she couldn't let herself be lost and turn on the clan—on Shai again, like she did in the Proving. "The clans have always been free without the need for cursed warriors on our side."

Mansa chuckled. "No one is free. Half the people wouldn't even know what to do with freedom."

"If you won," Nasha said, "do you really think this new order of yours would accept people like me?"

"I'd make them accept you."

"Then how are you better than the Domain? Besides, none of that matters if the Silent Earth is rotting away. The Hagun are gone, and the corruption's already taking the Yltigg. Zala is creeping out and we need allies, not new enemies."

Mansa nodded. "You're right. We need the Yltigg by our side; their monsters will be useful against the Domain."

"You want to use them?" The incredulity in Nasha's tone was clear even in her own ears. "Mansa, not even the Yltigg get close to the monsters; they're contagious. We need to kill this, not spread it."

"And then what? We keep the Earth whole so the Domain can keep exploiting us? The Earth is giving us a chance, Nasha. Let Jabillo tell his tales of Zala. Don't you find it strange that the Domain worship life while we live with the fear of death?"

"The clans don't fear death; we embrace its necessity."

"Oh, there's no courage in killing," Mansa said. "Wars are just a consequence of the fears of those in power. Fear for their lives, fear for their comfort. You think what's done to the Slopers is wrong? We are all the Slopers, Nasha. The Domain is the true clan. It's time we had our own faith. Maybe the Earth will choose the ones who should live."

Mansa's anger hit her hard, and it almost infected her, breeding an unexpected outrage that was not her own. But there was something behind his words. something he struggled to keep hidden. "Why do you hate them so much?" she asked.

"I don't hate the Domain, Nasha. I just don't want to serve them. Talk to the Yltigg tomorrow and broker a peace, but remember to show them who the true enemy is. Then remember the Earth has given you a gift. One that should be used to fight those who try to take our lands from us."

Nasha sighed. It seemed they couldn't even agree on who the enemy was anymore. She wouldn't convince Mansa now, though. Better to get the Yltigg on their side and talk about it later. "I had to bring in Leku, but I don't trust him. He'll find a way to exploit the situation."

"I'll have warriors riding out with you," Mansa said. "They'll keep an eye on him."

Nasha nodded and made for the door. Perhaps she'd still have to trust Mansa on some things. She'd never love him like she had. Like a father. He'd broken that in her, and the more he talked about what she should do to further his cause, no matter the risk, the less likely things were to be mended. Still, she'd said it herself: it was time to find allies, not enemies.

Nasha, Shai, and Leku stood ready on the outside of the Ronar village's stone walls. A dozen Ronar, along with three Zaruni, accompanied them. Slopers had gathered at the base of the wall as well. Enough for Nasha's intended show of force.

The severed head of the Yltigg madman was displayed beside the Ronar's flag of truce. The flag was dirty-white and painted with an old sign: a circle with four connecting lines, representing the roles of Tedros's officers when the clans had been united as one. The clans had been split, but the roles of warden, oringo, tivezzi, and speaker had survived. Jabillo had suggested the sign, and Tomu hadn't argued. The Yltigg would certainly recognize it, but both clans had lost leaders, and Nasha was unsure whether the symbol would convey peace or just another reminder of what both clans were lacking.

The risk seemed necessary, though. The Yltigg had to believe the Ronar could deal with these frenzied men. A severed head did not speak to peace, but Nasha hoped it would show strength in the face of enemies who would not distinguish between Ronar or Yltigg.

Nasha didn't know what Mansa was counting on. Maybe he had faith that some hidden power would choose the ones to protect the Earth. He might believe that Zala would not corrupt those who remained after the Domain swept through the clans. Or maybe that was the plan—to have Zala's taint bring down the Domain, and hope the taint would not consume the world. Nasha couldn't rely on that kind of faith. She wasn't an Earth-Breaker and would not let herself become one. Zala would not escape from her prison.

They started a slow march toward the Yltigg camp. Nasha was still avoiding her curse—the corrupted Yltigg man was enough to keep her from using it—but some unconscious instinct had her searching for Leku's emotions. He was trying to hold something down.

Leku had always tried to veil his true intentions. Perhaps it was only natural that he hid his emotions as well. Still, Nasha caught an underlying thrum of nervousness from him, which betrayed his previous words about not fearing the Yltigg. He was afraid, and Nasha was glad for it. Men too calm in situations like these were the ones to be feared.

She kept her gaze straight ahead, advancing slowly toward the Yltigg camp. She breathed in the smoky scent of the Great Mountain and the biting smell of citrus trees. That, and the scent of the death from the crow-picked bodies on the battlefield before her.

The space was open enough that there was nowhere for Yltigg troops to hide for an ambush, but the ground had become barren and beaten after days of fighting. There were patches of black on the ground, like the one Nasha had seen Mansa heal in the glade with the Domain officer's blood. The blood of the clans healed nothing here, though.

The Ronar stopped when a Yltigg spear came singing through the air and sank tip-first into the earth before them—a warning shot meant to tell Nasha that the Yltigg commander was willing to listen but didn't want them getting any closer.

Leku dug the makeshift peace-standard into the ground, while Nasha surveyed the Yltigg as they stepped from their tents and firepits.

"A larger enemy looms," Nasha called out to them. "One that will make our quarrel unimportant. We must talk."

No one stepped forward, but no new spears flew, either. After a few moments, the Yltigg opened a path, and a man rode toward them on horseback. He stopped before them.

"Tomu sends us in peace," Nasha said. "The Domain is coming."

The man scoffed. "Good, they'll finish you off, then."

"They won't stop with the Ronar. The prisoner—the one whose face you cut up. Bahar. He wants revenge."

That seemed to give the man pause. "So do we."

"Revenge will weaken us in the face of a common enemy. You've set tainted among us, and still failed to break our lines." Nasha gestured toward the gathered Slopers. "How high a price are you willing to pay for your revenge? Would you weaken yourself enough for the Domain to destroy you?"

The man's gaze moved along the Ronar for a moment, then he urged his horse to one side. "March ahead. I'll not have backstabbers behind me."

Nasha released a trapped breath, and her heart beat a touch slower. If they'd failed here, the clans would likely be done for. She bowed her head, thanking the Earth for the Yltigg man's sense, and led the Ronar toward the enemy encampment.

The Yltigg watched as the Ronar walked through. There were spikes of anger and frustration aimed at Nasha. Not strong enough to threaten her, but she still grabbed onto Shai's emotion, thankful again for having the girl at her side. Shai was afraid, but the dry throat and the shooting sensation of her anxiousness were familiar enough to keep Nasha grounded. Soon, they reached what looked to be the chief's tent. Nasha, Shai, and Leku entered first, followed by the three Zaruni and the dozen Ronar. The Yltigg man dismounted and came in last. There was more than enough room inside.

The Ronar and Zaruni escorts stood to the back, while Nasha, Shai, and Leku approached a low bench before a crackling firepit. Ardin, chief of the Yltigg, sat on a raised chair on the far side of the pit. He was a plump, dark-skinned man with thin lips, hard eyes, and close-shaved hair. The fire cast a shifting light across him.

Another man stood beside the Yltigg chief. He wore a veil-like headdress, his face hidden behind a curtain of uneven beadstones. Most of them had blue-glowing veins—ancestor-stone—but their pulse that was stronger than any Nasha had ever seen from ancestor-stone. She was glad to have some distance between herself and them. The Yltigg rider took a seat near the chief's feet.

The veiled man whispered in the chief's ear as the Ronar took their seats. Nasha hadn't seen the standing man at the Proving, but he had to be the speaker.

"I am Roho," the Yltigg rider said. "You will not address the chief. I have been allowed to accept you into this camp to listen to your terms of surrender."

Nasha eyed them. "We are not here to surrender," she said. "We have come with a warning. Our fighting will have no victor. The Domain is coming, and they will not pick between clans. Bahar will bring the full strength of the Visslands upon us all. If we are weak from battle, he will destroy us both."

Roho grunted. "You come here outnumbered, with nothing but warnings?" His anger hit Nasha's curse stronger than anything he could say. It was a different rage. Deep and personal.

"We come here offering life," Nasha said. "You might outnumber us in this tent, but look at our walls. You use Zala's taint, and neither the Ronar nor the Slopers will stand for that. If you do not take our request for peace, the battle will be a long one." She shot a look at Leku, who nodded.

Roho worked his jaw for a moment, then waved a dismissive hand. "The Domain are fighting battles of their own."

"That may be so," Leku said. "But the focus of the Visslands has always been on the clans."

Nasha shifted uncomfortably on the bench. Bahar had always been a friend, and talking about him this way was foreign. "There have been losses on both sides," she said. "But what is done is done. We must look ahead if we are to preserve the clans."

The speaker leaned close to the chief and said something.

Roho shook his head. "We cannot trust warnings on your word alone. The son of a chief was killed. If the Domain comes, we will let them roll through you, then fight a weakened enemy."

"You don't believe you'll be safe," Nasha said.

Roho raised an eyebrow. "And how do you know what we believe?"

"We wouldn't be sitting here if you did."

"You assume too much."

Nasha narrowed her eyes at Roho. There was something beyond the anger that came from him. Not quite fear exactly, but a kind of disquiet. If he did not fear the Domain, then there was only one other option.

Leku seemed to read the man without needing the curse. "If the Domain does not worry you," he said, "then you seek our help with something else." He grinned at Roho. "The earth-spawn you set upon us are not under your control, are they?"

The Yltigg chief rose. "We may consider a truce and leave you to prepare for the Domain. But we will not bleed for you. And Roho is right: grievances must be settled."

"And what would you have?" Leku asked.

Shai had been silent, seemingly out of her depth, but Nasha didn't need her for her words.

"We will get you Bahar," Nasha said. The words still tasted sour, traitorous, even after what he'd done. "You went far enough as to torture him. We'll get him back to you."

The Yltigg chief laughed. "It is amusing that you think he escaped. We let him go."

Shai finally broke her silence. "Why?" she said, the word angry and laced with bitter accusation.

Roho shrugged. "We took what we needed from him. Living with his scars and his memories will hurt him more than death."

The satisfaction emanating from Roho burned hot through Nasha. Whatever grief had twisted Bahar, some part of her still felt his pain, and the Yltigg had brought that pain onto Shai as well. Bahar's actions had kept her separated from her family.

Leku seemed more focused on the negotiation. "If you do not wish to have the emissary, then we will compensate a warden"—he glanced at Nasha with an infuriating grin—"for a warden. And her prized initiate."

Every hair on Nasha stood on end. The betrayal took a moment to settle in, her mind not wanting to make sense of the words. They made no sense. Leku did not have the power to do this, but then she remembered his emotion. This was what he was afraid of—not the Yltigg, but her—of being caught before he could offer her up.

Nasha rose, instinct driving her muscles, but the Zaruni had already closed in, as had the Ronar escort. Nasha lost all caution the moment the first Zaruni laid a hand on her. She let the curse burn, saw the lines of emotion bursting from everybody in the tent—her anger heightening her perception.

She let the anger rush through her, infusing her muscles with power as the other two Zaruni advanced. She kicked the first away, sidestepped the second and shoved him at the firepit, but more hands were already grasping at Nasha. The rush of battle fueled her. The image of the earth-spawn that attacked the Zaruni in the Slopes was at the back of her mind, but she couldn't hold back now.

She reached for a line that seemed to be fear. The emotion didn't matter; she'd burn it into strength to get out of this. Even as she reached, though, something stirred inside her. That dark pit that feasted on the emotions. It sent burning tendrils through her, pulling at more than the emotion that fed it. It pulled at parts of her mind. A growl rumbled within her, wanting to rise up her throat. The same guttural growl that she'd heard from the tainted.

Nasha recoiled on instinct, cutting off her enhanced strength at the risk of what seemed to be a rising taint. The fear she'd pulled into herself prompted her to run, but she could not run from what dwelled within her. A body hit her from behind, and she was pushed to the floor. She'd dealt with the Zaruni; it had to be the Ronar.

Someone spoke over the grunts coming from the warriors struggling to keep Nasha down. She looked up. The ancestor-stone glowed on the veil that covered the speaker's face. The air shimmered before it, and Nasha saw the threads vanishing into the stones.

Nasha struggled, desperation winning out over fear. She grasped for more emotions but couldn't grab onto them. It was as if they were fleeing her touch, moving toward the speaker's veil. "Gah! Leku, you traitorous bastard!" she yelled.

Leku looked to the Yltigg chief. "Do we have a deal?"

The chief and Roho stood side by side. Both turned to the speaker, who nodded. The Yltigg mirrored the motion. "We have a deal."

CHAPTER TWELVE

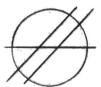

The Azuri hold a mysterious kind of magic. One that has never truly been accepted or taught in the Domain. Perhaps the Domain nobles value their blood too highly to trust it to foreign hands. But what of the lowborn? Could an advantage be had? Soldiers enhanced?

— Excerpt from the Dakhran treatise Military Magic

Adrian followed Nasir into a small room. The chamber had no desk or chairs. It was situated along one of the many cloisters that overlooked the palace gardens with a view of the palace gates. It could have been a servant room or guardroom, but Adrian was sure Nasir used it to keep an eye on the comings and goings of the palace.

The priest knelt before a stone basin filled with copper-red sand. Adrian knelt on the other side, eyeing the ceremonial ruin-stone knife beside the basin. His eyes lingered on the edge, and his scabbing wounds itched in response. Nasir wrapped his slender fingers around the knife. "I know your faith in me is shaken, Lord Light."

It was more than that: asking Nasir to teach him—allowing the priest to perform this ritual—felt like a betrayal. It wasn't the magic itself, but the guilt of Derren's last expression that refused to leave Adrian's mind. He'd never forgive the priest for sacrificing Derren, but he needed this to ensure that justice would be done to Addo. Besides, he needed to know more. The images of Myrra and Derren felt dangerous. They had him wanting to wade into this strange blood-magic more and more, just to be near shades of the people he'd loved, and who'd loved him in return. "Let's get on with it," he said.

The priest nodded. "The warding ritual requires your blood, but the connection is mutual. We will be bonded, but only through a token. That is what will keep you protected."

"A token?"

Nasir pointed to the pendant that hung from Adrian's neck: Myrra's medallion of the Bone. "Your father's words are not wrong. Your blood does hold ties. It is ancient blood, and powerful. Ruin-stone is the only thing that can hold such power."

"The consuls didn't have ruin-stone about them."

"Because their blood is not as strong as yours, Lord Light. They have different tokens."

"And how will this make me trust you?"

"Your blood will be open to me, as mine will be open to yours. Our vulnerabilities will be the same."

Adrian eyed Nasir for a long moment. He wasn't comfortable with this. Whatever he might learn of blood magic was still a life-time behind what Nasir already knew. If he was telling the truth, Nasir's vulnerability was better than nothing, but Adrian would likely have little skill to take advantage of it. Still, knowing where the chink in Nasir's armor lay could be useful.

The other option would be to remain exposed while walking into a building of blood mages who, like most of the Azuri, would certainly look to take advantage of him and his blood. Not to mention blood mages who could be in the consuls' employ.

Better to go with the monster I know. This has to be done. Waiting for someone I can trust will only delay my return to the Domain.

He breathed deep, took the pendant from his neck, and placed it between them. "Go ahead."

Nasir scooped a handful of sand and spread it between them, covering a large portion of the floor. He then traced glyphs in the sand, revealing the floor beneath.

Once he was done, he raised the knife he held in his other hand. "Give me your hand."

Adrian held it out, palm up. Nasir sliced, letting the blood well there for a moment. "Trace the glyphs with your blood."

Adrian closed his hand and moved it over the glyphs so that his bloody palm dripped onto the signs drawn by Nasir. The priest did the same, leaving the floor painted in glyphs of their mixed blood.

Nasir took the knife to his own forearm and slashed close to a scar, then set the knife down. He didn't mix this blood into the glyphs but spoke words in a language Adrian didn't understand. Smoke plumed from the blood that flowed from Nasir's arm. Soon, the blood in the glyphs was bubbling and emanating smoke as well. Nasir moved his other hand, fingers weaving through the air as if pulling at threads.

The blood in the glyphs started to move, lines coiling into the air like hungry snakes, tracing their way toward the ruin-stone pendant of the bone. The blood-lines sizzled where they touched the stone, and were sucked into Myrra's old pendant. Slowly at first, then faster. The blood darkened the ruin-stone, making the gray move into black, and causing the white veins to glow orange-red. Once the ruin-stone absorbed all of the blood, Nasir stopped moving his fingers. "Touch it," he said.

Adrian paused, but he couldn't hesitate now. He touched two fingers to the stone, and the world around him was yanked away.

He was back in Khet, but things were not as he remembered. There were no veiled glances filled with fear, and no madmen either. This was earlier. Yes, Adrian remembered this. Dakhran soldiers marched through the Khetish capital of Ultenvell. It was the day his father had ordered him back to Talnea. It was the last day he'd seen Myrra alive. Adrian could see himself from outside his body. He was sparring with one of the Othonean captains whom Derren had insisted he take to Khet, while Addo watched from afar. The sight of Addo put a fire in Adrian, but it was only a memory, and there was nothing he could do.

Their session ended with Adrian nursing a broken lip. He could taste the blood, even if it was only a vision. Addo was there, handing Adrian strips of linen to clean the sweat and blood. The strips were coated with the ointment Addo always held ready for the inevitable bruises after Adrian's sparring sessions. Adrian dabbed the cold cloth on his lip, and the vision shifted.

He was suddenly standing before his carriage, embracing Myrra. Her face was whole, and she had a smile that said they'd see each other again. It cut straight at Adrian's heart. Like the claws of the woman who'd worn Myrra's face as a mask, tearing through flesh and muscle to the bone. Elwin, the Sentinel Father had left with them, stood behind her. "This will be over soon," Myrra said.

Adrian nodded, and she gave him a fierce kiss, paying his cracked lip no heed. It was only a memory, but Adrian's lips felt the kiss all the same. It spread a warmth through him the like of which he thought he'd never feel again. The aching in his heart settled just a touch, and his lips burned as if Myrra were fire on a cold night.

They finally broke apart and she looked up, the blood from Adrian's lip painting her own. "I'll always be here for you," she said. Then the vision was pulled into darkness.

Adrian was back in Azur, panting, the wisps of Myrra's warmth chased off by cold reality.

"Tell no one what you saw," Nasir said. "Not even me. That is what will root you, what will ward you against wayward blood magics. You must draw power from that experience."

Nasir had told Adrian that blood magic was based on pain. If that were so, the memory had given him more than enough to keep himself warded. Thinking about it put a clamp around his heart. The memory might have been a good one in the past, but now it only showed him all he'd never have again. The amulet was still on the ground between them, black with pulsing, blood-red veins.

"Put it on," Nasir said. "That is your token."

Adrian placed it around his neck. It was warm to the touch. "Can I see it again? What I saw just now?"

Nasir shook his head. "No."

Adrian stood. "Then let's go meet Kel Bradaz."

The streets of Dar Drezji were crowded and as hot as ever. If the knowledge about the Madness had spread, it did not seem to affect the Azuri. Adrian kept a cautious gaze on the people as he and Nasir followed behind Bac as he made way through the crowd.

Adrian heard singing and turned to see a large group dressed in multi-colored silks. It was led by two women holding torches, and those in the middle held something over their heads. It looked like a stretcher.

"Are they carrying a body?" Adrian asked Nasir.

"Yes, my Lord Light. A dead one. Look at the fires." He indicated the torches held by those in front. They burned a clear blue, even in daylight. The color was similar to the torches used by the men who'd declared Prince Niilar worthy. "This man has been considered worthy. His body will be taken to the river so it can float into the lands of memory. He will be remembered in high regard by his family."

"They celebratin' death?" Bac asked. He was still learning how to be a bodyguard and hadn't picked up on the desired silence.

"They celebrate his memory," said Nasir. "Would you not celebrate the Church bringing your loved one into worthiness?"

The question stung at Adrian. His recent memories of Myrra and Derren were nothing to celebrate, just a new kind of pain. He suddenly understood these people, though. He might not have Myrra back, but untainting her memory would bring him no small measure of peace.

The group passed by them, and Adrian's gaze lingered on the dead man. How much would they be celebrating, had he been taken by the Madness? How many would he have killed? Adrian shook his head and kept walking until they reached the end of the street.

"We are far from the Domain, Bac," Adrian said. "Best forget what you know. At least for now."

Bac shrugged. "Didn't know much to start with."

They kept moving through the crowded streets until they could see their destination.

The House of the Afterdark had not been built to stand out. It was made of the same coppery sandstone as the surrounding houses, while lacking the actual copper that glinted around the palace. There was no azure stone, like that found in the dome of the palace throne room. The building was squared with hard edges. Three sides held windows only on the upper floors, but one wall had ground-level, prison-like grills on the outside.

The door was unlocked. From what Adrian had seen of blood magic, locks would be the least of an intruder's problems. Nasir pushed the door open, and Adrian followed him in. Bac waited outside.

The missing exterior grandeur seemed to have been reserved for within. The square entrance hall was wide and open, tall pillars supporting an azure stone-coated ceiling illuminated by rounded windows. It was like looking at the sky. Blood mages ambled over cool tiles and around a fountain that burbled at the room's center. Some disappeared through arched doorways that led to corridors on either side. Adrian couldn't deny the chamber was enticing after the sun-scorched streets of Dar Drezji.

"Do not be fooled," Nasir said. "Everything is a test."

Adrian didn't advance or drink from the fountain, as some mages did. Most of them paid no mind to Adrian or Nasir, but one man strode their way. He was bald with a thin beard framing his jaw, forming a short goatee. As he drew closer, Adrian noticed a calmness in his gaze that seemed rooted in confidence, as if there was nothing in the world that might threaten him.

Nasir bowed his head. "We ask for admittance into your house, master Kel Bradaz."

It might have been a formality, but Kel Bradaz seemed glad for it. "It is good to see you have not forgotten me, or your manners,

Brother Nasir. Even if you have abandoned our ways and committed to a foreign faith."

"I go where the power of blood takes me, great master, and I too am glad it has brought us together once more."

Kel Bradaz looked at Adrian, his gaze lingering for a moment on Myrra's pendant with the Sign of the Bone. "Welcome, Lord Light. We have been watching your exploits since you entered our city, and are honored by your visit."

Adrian bowed his head. "The honor is mine. I was hoping for a word in private."

"We will get to business, though rest assured the privacy of your words is guaranteed within these walls, wherever you may be. Now, walk with me."

They walked through an arched passage and down a narrow, well-decorated corridor. "How do you like our house, Lord Light?"

"It's, ahm, not what one would expect from the outside."

"Are surprises not the best part of life?" Kel Bradaz smiled, but Adrian had trouble returning the gesture. He'd had enough surprises and hadn't come here for more.

"You seek the support of my house in the coming decision of who is to be Xakhar, yes? I am sorry to disappoint, but we do not involve ourselves in the politics of the families."

"Is that why all the consuls are warded?"

Bradaz smiled again. Nasir watched in silence, as if letting Adrian take part in some unspoken test. "I see you are not without warding yourself. It is powerful blood that requires such a powerful vessel."

They entered a wider corridor lined with doors on the left and archways to an open courtyard on the right. The doors were made of heavy wood and had barred windows. Almost like prison doors.

"If I am to be Xakhar," Adrian said, "it would be unwise not to follow the precautions of my competitors."

"Naturally." Bradaz stopped and turned. "And which of your competitors do you seek to sway, Lord Light?"

"Lady Rhiall." No use skirting around it. "I've heard you have dealings with her son."

"Yes, he is with us."

Sounds came from behind the heavy doors. Strange sounds, as if beasts waited inside.

"Release him," Adrian said. "Let him go back to his family."

"That, I'm afraid, is something I cannot do."

Adrian frowned. "I took your people for negotiators."

"We will haggle when there is something to haggle about. This is different."

He pulled out a keychain and put a key to one of the doors beside them. Something rattled on the other side, like a creature throwing itself against metal bars.

Bradaz opened the door and a madman lunged from the shadows, stopped only by vertical bars that cut the chamber in half. Bradaz stepped inside.

The madman reached through the bars with sharp claws, spittle flying from his mouth. The claws didn't reach Bradaz, who appeared unperturbed. "This is Resh Ban Rhiall, Lord Light. He sought us out when he noticed something was amiss. We are not holding him against his will; we are keeping him alive. Treating the frenzy in his blood as best we can."

That was a surprise. Whatever the look on Adrian's face at that moment, it seemed to please Kel Bradaz.

"We have a duty to Azur that goes beyond politics. We must watch for this madness and keep it at bay for as long as we can."

"You can't control it," Adrian said. "You may stay out of politics, but they will still affect you. I'm your best chance at fighting this thing. I'll root it out at the source."

"On that I do not disagree, yet I cannot release the boy. Not in this state. We have prevented the plague from consuming him, but a cure is still out of our reach." Bradaz pulled a copper sphere from his robe. "There have been attempts, however. Enchantments of all kinds. But there is one thing missing." The mage eyed Adrian's pendant again, then gazed into his eyes.

"You want my blood."

"It is the first that we have seen resist this disease, Lord Light.

Perhaps a demonstration is in order?" Bradaz offered him the sphere.

Seemed like they were in a negotiation, after all. Adrian looked to Nasir, and back to Bradaz. There didn't seem to be much of a choice; just one more sacrifice he'd have to make. Adrian closed his fingers around the sphere. Small spikes pierced his palm and funneled his blood into the sphere. Adrian was becoming accustomed to pain and barely flinched. The Rhiall heir was still throwing himself against the bars in a frenzy. Bradaz gave it a moment, then a reddish smoke rose from the sphere. He put it close to Resh, and the man's fury wavered. He stepped back, breath heavy, and Adrian thought he saw a glimpse of sanity in his eyes.

There were other figures there in the dark, though: Myrra and Derren, standing behind the Rhiall boy. Derren had a hand on his shoulder, and Myrra offered a hand to Adrian. His half-healed cuts stung, as did Kahlia's claw marks on his face. The fury taken from the boy seemed to be trying to take hold of Adrian. He ground his teeth, remembering Nasir's words: "Everything is a test."

Adrian's cuts hurt more every second, and the area around the eyes of Myrra's twisted mask grew darker. He closed his hand into a fist, trying to resist the pain. The rage eating at Resh Ban Rhiall was unending and whatever enchantment Bradaz had placed on the copper sphere seemed to use Adrian's strength to fight the boy's Madness. He felt a burning around his own eyes, and with it came a new vision. A red path connected him to Resh. A blood binding. Adrian could feel the rage, the Madness creeping through it, but he didn't falter. He held the Madness at bay, suspended within the path that connected them. It gave Resh a momentary shred of sanity, but Adrian had no notion of how to destroy the Madness. The pain rose again, seeping Adrian's strength. He pushed the pain back to Resh and stepped away, panting. The Madness resumed its hold on the boy as soon as the bond was broken.

Kel Bradaz ushered them out and followed, closing the door behind him. "Maybe there is hope, after all. I will support your claim to the throne and promise Rhiall to return her son on two conditions. First, you must frequent the House of the Afterdark for the next week. We will refine our enchantments and see what can be created for the protection of Azur. Second, you may only return him to her once he is cured."

Adrian hated being treated like some exotic animal to be experimented on, but there was no denying it felt good to be recognized. There was power in his blood, and he would use it. He nodded.

Kel Bradaz produced an empty vial and held it out. Adrian held his hand over it, still bleeding where the spikes had punctured his palm, until the vessel was full.

"That will be enough for now. Blood is most powerful when fresh from the host. We await you here tomorrow for more."

CHAPTER THIRTEEN

It's a common misconception fomented by smaller minds that griffins are some sort of hybrid creature. It's improper to classify them in the kingdom of the birds and insulting to place them in the felidae family. The griffin does not defy classification, but sits within a class of its own, along with the various griffidae orders below it.

— Kadmus's notes, taken from the studies of Ander W. Demerith

I t didn't take long for Kadmus to be summoned. The knock came on a late afternoon, when he was ready to try a new serum on Nima. Kadmus knew what it was the moment the man entered the shop.

The man walked in, wearing a wide-brimmed hat that covered his face, but he bore no colors or signs. He looked around, then placed a neatly folded parchment on the counter. To anyone looking in from the street, it would look like a standard transaction. The man looked long enough at Kadmus to feign conversation behind his hat but uttered only a single word before leaving. "Now."

Kadmus rubbed his temples as the man left. He gave it a long moment, then walked toward the door, locked it, and pulled the drapes on the window. He took his latest attempted cure and held it tight, as if that would somehow help it succeed.

He paused at the top of the steps, just a few strides before Nima's door. It would work this time. He'd upped the dosage of Solanum. It could be fatal in large doses, but was the best agent he knew for fighting infection. It kept Nima asleep, and the larger dose would likely prolong that, but that was a comfort. Better to have her in her bed than on a frenzied rampage. He let himself believe that pain did not trouble her dreams.

Kadmus dug a hand in another pocket and pulled out a handful of ruin-stone shards. Part of him almost wished he'd spent more time in training with the Priests of the Blood. He'd learned the basics of their stone-work, but his mind tried to convince him there was more to it. Maybe even something that could have healed Nima by now.

Don't be a fool. If that were true, the Church would have a cure.

He placed a shaky hand on Nima's door handle. He hated this. Hated losing control of his wits and his body to emotion. But he took solace in knowing that Nima was the only one who could cause that.

Kadmus opened the door and went to kneel beside her bed. He placed the ruin-stone shards against her skin. He'd treated them with the concoctions he'd learned from the priests. The ones meant to open the veins of the stone, so their power could be more easily extracted by Sentinels and Bishops of the Bone.

Kadmus did not have the talent for healing. Not like the Priests of the Blood, at least. There was no mystical use of ruin-stone that would funnel life into Nima. Kadmus had rarely seen the Priests cure true diseases, though. The ones deep inside that wounded the body in different ways than cuts and bruises. His potions had always been better at that, but this Dakhran Madness seemed to be some-thing more. Stronger than any disease he'd ever come across.

The stones flared as they touched Nima's skin. They seemed to keep her stable, at least while she slept. Once the stones were in place, Kadmus eased Nima's jaw open and poured the potion into her mouth. He held his breath and watched.

Nima's breath was steady, perhaps slowing down a touch. She stirred, and Kadmus stood, watching the serum fight the plague that infected his daughter. She twisted in her bed, eyes still closed, whimpering a little. Kadmus breathed again and gave her time to fight it, but the blackness that had tainted Nima's skin since she'd been infected did not recede from the skin around her eyes.

Nima quieted, her breathing returning to the slow rhythm of sleep. Nothing. The Madness persisted.

It took an effort for Kadmus not to hurl the vial across the room. He'd been certain this one would work. His grip tightened around the vial, but he remembered himself. No frustrated cry, no shattering vials. He didn't know who might be listening. Leading others to believe his daughter was dead was the best way to keep her alive. No one dared talk about the dead, especially now that a plague threatened the Seraph's faithful. Kadmus scoffed. Steering the faith of the people was such an easy thing, and even now that the Church's enemies had exposed weakness, the people's belief in some invisible miracle only grew.

He left the room, closed the door gently, and went downstairs. Perhaps he needed more ruin-stone, but that was scarce, even in a nation bordering the clans who mined it raw. He grabbed the seal with the triple waterfall of the Visslands, tucked Bahar's potions into his robes, and set off.

The roar of the falls filled the streets as Kadmus approached the upper city. He'd never enjoyed venturing close to the palace and often wondered why the nobility accepted the ever-present noise of crashing water. In truth, appearances were more important than comfort. Appearance guaranteed the nobility's position, and their blessings from the Church. That and their tithes, of course. Kadmus had never figured out how the Church extended life; that was a secret he'd probably have to sacrifice too much to unveil. He'd stopped trying when Nima was born. He'd lost Brenna in the birth process and was cast out for it. Shunned by the Church for the unworthiness of his family, and for fathering a child while in the practice of becoming a Priest of the Blood.

Kadmus didn't mind the exclusion. Like most things in life, it was merely the repetition of a cycle. His parents had given him over to the Church when they found out about his disease. At first he thought it was their faith in the Seraph that had prompted the separation, but then he realized that he'd been given to the Church in hopes that his parents would be healed. They'd believed that some invisible being—the Seraph—would reach out and remove the Weeping from them.

It had taken him a while to get over seeing himself as the cursed child that had infected his parents with the Weeping. Ironic that their lives were taken while he survived with little more than a marred face; pockmarks and scarred lines where the flesh had wept pus at the height of the infection.

The priests had kept him, even if the Seraph had discarded his parents. A cruel joke by the goddess, perhaps, but one for which Kadmus was thankful. It had opened his eyes and planted the seed that made him question why a benevolent entity would let Her people suffer, then throw them away. The more he'd grown within the Church, the more the seed grew with him. The more he saw of men's actions, the more he saw the hypocrisy in their words—and the more certain he became that the Seraph was not real.

The priests had insisted on his training, claiming he had the talent even if Kadmus displayed no taste for it. He'd never felt bound by their rules and hadn't held back when Brenna caught his eye. She was going to be his wife, and she'd even planted a sliver of her own beliefs in him. Perhaps there was some merit to the existence of the Seraph, in that she might explain the things his logic and calculations could not.

Kadmus scoffed as he climbed the steps that flanked the fifty-foot-high triple waterfall, approaching the gate to the upper city. If any of what Brenna believed was true, the Seraph would not have let her die.

He paused before the guard and flashed Bahar's seal. It was enough to make the guard stand aside and avert his gaze. The soldier's motion sent a chill through Kadmus. Bahar was known to have relinquished power, though none knew why. Kadmus had never given himself to trust anything so vile as rumors—no point in that—but if this was the kind of power the man wielded, Kadmus had to redouble his caution.

The steps evened out after the gates. The upper city had been constructed in tiers along wide stone shelves that rose like massive steps themselves, inaccessible to the common folk below.

The homes were solidly built, with thick layers of stone and small windows, both necessary to dull the water's roar. The people on the streets moved slowly, almost leisurely. There were no open markets here; commerce was kept within stores, where people could be heard above the din of the falls. Kadmus appreciated the lack of rudimentary screaming and haggling, and couldn't deny the pleasant scent in the air nor the crispness of the greenery that grew all around.

There were at least six more levels before the top of the mountain, where the palace of Pelaket was built at the edge of the triple-falls. Fortunately, there were only two levels between Kadmus and Bahar. He'd rarely ventured to the upper city, but even from the outside, he could tell the building was a steam-house.

Once inside, he found the structure empty but for the man who'd let him in. Kadmus was led past steaming pools that clouded the building's yellow-tinted stone columns. He didn't enjoy the humidity but was soon taken to a smaller room with stone benches lining the walls. Bahar sat on one of them.

Kadmus' guide retreated with barely a rustle, leaving him to stare at the ruthless man who'd forced him here.

"The heat helps the pain in my leg."

Kadmus nodded but had little more in the way of an answer. He stepped close to Bahar and watched him for a moment, forming the words carefully in his mind. "There is something I will require if we are to do this."

Bahar chuckled. "Are we not past this? Will you need another demonstration?"

A lesser man might have let fear take him, but Kadmus had run out of fear long ago. "You made your show, but you've undoubtedly learned enough about me to know simple threats will not cloud my judgement."

Bahar looked up at him with a sharpness in his eyes, but Kadmus pushed on. "You need me. You wouldn't have gone to the lengths you have if that weren't true. You can threaten me with the Church, try to convince me you can find another healer, but we both know I'm your favored choice."

Bahar gave him a slight grin. "That's better. I was beginning to worry I had the wrong man. What do you require?"

"Ruin-stone. Enough to cause the Church envy if they found it."

Bahar eyed Kadmus through the steam clinging to the air between them, then nodded. "That can be arranged."

"Weekly," Kadmus said.

A slight frown creased Bahar's brow. "That will be decided once I've seen the result of your work."

Kadmus paused, considering, then pulled out the leather-bound roll that held his vials. "Where would you like to begin?"

Bahar waved a hand before him. "The face."

Kadmus looked at the wounds and surveilled his vials. A place with better light would have helped, but he wouldn't complain. All he needed was to get this done, then get as far away from Bahar as he could. He'd already negotiated for ruin-stone, an important step in healing Nima.

His hand hovered over the vials but shifted to pick out a salve. "I'll need to apply this first."

He didn't tell Bahar it would sting, or what the salve was supposed to do, but it seemed the emissary had suspicions all the same. "There is a level of trust that is necessary here. You have shown yourself to be the kind of man I need, but rest assured, I am not unprepared. If I suspect even the beginning of foul intent, there will be consequences."

Kadmus had to hold himself back to not roll his eyes. Threats were such a crude thing. If the intention was to intimidate, there were better ways to do that than with words. And if intimidation was the goal, one acted or didn't; there was no point in warning your opponent in advance.

He nodded and scooped the salve with a flat wooden rod already beading with droplets of steam. He smeared it onto the largest wound on Bahar's face. He expected a reaction, some kind of complaint, but all he received from Bahar was a grimace. At least the man understood that pain was part of the healing process.

Kadmus had learned that long ago, when the Weeping had taken him. If the pus that formed yellow scars on his face dried, the pain would stop, but that was the danger. It became poisonous, and as the body tried to heal itself, pieces of the dried pus could enter the bloodstream. There was no coming back from it then. The only protection was to keep the pus in its liquid state. Sometimes even by taking hot metal to the wound.

Bahar kept his gaze on Kadmus as the wound reopened. Kadmus needed it fresh; that was the best way for the serum to rebuild the skin. It would still leave a scar, but a lesser one.

Kadmus let the blood well for a moment and gave Bahar a piece of cloth to keep the blood from running down his cheek. The emissary held it to his face while Kadmus handed him the serum. Bahar downed it without a second thought. There was a deeper grimace this time as the skin started to stitch itself together. It was a slow process, and Bahar's breathing became heavier. He gripped the stone bench and let out a grunt of pain.

Kadmus waited patiently until he became used to it. The pain would not recede for a long time, not until the skin was fully healed. That could take hours.

"That is all you'll be able to stomach today," Kadmus said.

Bahar brought his breathing back under control and pulled out a small mirror. He removed the cloth that covered the wound Kadmus had just healed. Even through the clouded gloom, Kadmus could see the man's eyes widen a touch. Bahar nodded. "Keep going."

Kadmus shook his head. "This is not about how much pain you can take. It is about how much strength your body can spare to heal itself. Too much of the serum takes from the body. It becomes a poison."

Bahar looked up with a clenched jaw, but Kadmus couldn't tell if it was out of pain or frustration. He finally nodded and slid the mirror across the bench. He leaned back and closed his eyes. "If your healing proves adept, there is another matter to discuss."

Kadmus held his tongue; he wanted nothing more to do with the man.

"The Visslands will march against the clans," Bahar said. "I don't need to trust you to let you know that. There might be resistance in the council, but it will soon be quelled. Queen Lesraile sees the signs. They've killed a councilor's son and are gathering their forces."

"War is not my area of expertise, Emissary."

"Indeed it is not. But to leave your home, you must make sure that what you leave behind is safe. We cannot march with the Madness running rampant."

As much as Kadmus had tried to steer clear of rumors, he'd heard that Councilor Carswell's son had been lost in the clanlands. So he was dead then. Bahar was right; Carswell was too powerful for the Visslands to let this pass.

"I need you to find a cure," Bahar said. "I will put you before the council and convince them you are the person to find it. We would have to replicate the Madness first, of course, to have something to work from."

Many might have jumped at the opportunity, but Bahar's words were clear enough. This disease, the Madness, had taken Nima—Kadmus would never replicate it. Bahar offered resources, but Kadmus had not failed for lack of resources. He would find a cure, he was sure of it. And Nima would hold strong.

"I'm not the man you're looking for."

Bahar opened his eyes and gazed at Kadmus, who was already

packing up his vials. Kadmus didn't expect Bahar was a man who took "No" lightly, but the emissary simply nodded with renewed pain and leaned back again.

"We will speak again." He waved a hand, and Kadmus left the chamber.

CHAPTER FOURTEEN

The breath is a gift given by the Seraph so that Her word may be spread. A held breath that hides words of truth can be the difference in preserving life. Do not be silenced by fear of the enemy.

— The Book of the Breath

Lynn awoke in bed, in a dim room, her head pounding and faint candlelight flickering on the canopy above her. Instinct had her mind reaching out to Vedyr. She knew the griffin would be close, and walls would not deter him if he sensed danger while she was in her weakened state. He was flying close, but there was nothing to suggest he thought her in danger.

She sat up and rubbed her eyes. Every muscle ached like she'd just been through a battle. It had been a kind of battle, and her mind was slow to piece it together. Lynn squinted. A silhouette was lighting the candles on the mantlepiece at the far side of the room. She coughed, and the figure turned. Lynn almost jumped out of the bed when she saw his face. "High Pontiff. I—"

"Rest, my dear. You've been deemed worthy."

Worthy. She'd longed to hear that word in her past. She thought it would be what she needed to drive the shadow of death from her back, but it did little for her now, even coming from the Pontiff. Lynn knew what she'd done, and what she had yet to do. She doubted a word would loosen death's grip on her. She let out a small part of the tightness in her chest, and before she knew it, the question was already on her lips. "Why couldn't I release the Bond?"

The Pontiff tilted his head, as if expecting some other question. "The secrets of the Bone are theirs alone, I'm afraid. The Seraph gives us power through Her grace, but if one order of the Church grows stronger than the other, it can bring us all down."

Lynn frowned, but even that slight movement worsened the pounding in her head. More came back to her. What Reznik had done.

Sentinels could channel their emotions toward their griffins and draw on the creatures' strength and speed when needed. Only one emotion. The one they found when bonding. They could use emotions stored in the ruin-stone to help keep them from hollowing out for longer, but the concept was the same: give and take. What the bishop had done was different. If he could use ruin-stone to manipulate the Sentinel Bond, manipulate memories, make the voices and the insanity within her tangible—could he use that power to control the Madness as well?

Could the bishop's power be strong enough to dig into the mind of a madman and keep him controlled? Was that what Andral and Talbot had done in Farkhul? The more she thought about it, the more certain she was that ruin-stone was at the heart of controlling the Madness. And that the bishop's power could be the key to it all.

Lynn opened her mouth for another question, but the Pontiff shook his head and walked toward her bed. He sat on the edge and folded one hand over the other. Even in the candlelight, the greenness of his eyes was still clear. "We will beat this Madness, Sister Lynn, but we cannot do it at the expense of what keeps us safe. Unfettered power is how nations fall, and we have enough enemies trying to pull us down already."

Lynn didn't argue, but it was hard to accept the Pontiff's calmness in the face of all that threatened them.

"A new commander was chosen while you slept." Lynn's heart jolted in her chest. "Some wanted you to lead, but unity speaks louder in times like these." He gave her a soft smile. "We all have our limitations. Better to remain with the leader we know, yes? Olem has been chosen."

Lynn let out a sigh of relief, both for avoiding the burden and because the choice proved that her trust in the Church leaders' wisdom was well-placed. Olem was the better choice, the safer choice. She nodded and almost fell back on the bed.

"What you have done, though," said the Pontiff, "is not to be taken lightly."

Here it was. Had she really thought he missed her mistake? She was so afraid of being chosen as commander, she'd forgotten she still had crimes to be judged. Her heart ached for Vedyr. As if in response, his shadow flew across the window beside her bed.

Fool! Roki said. *You thought you would get away?* The words were delivered amid irritating, satisfied laughter.

Lynn was still trying to think of an argument, but the Pontiff pressed on.

"Your decisions were rash, but such is the nature of war, is it not?" He ran a hand over the sheet at the edge of the bed. "Your worth has been proven, your loyalty questioned and answered. There are few people who can claim to be in such a position." He chuckled. "It would be almost foolish to spend that on a commander's seat, and as I said, our enemies are numerous. There is much more you can do for the Church, if you are willing."

Lynn eyed the Pontiff for a long time. For so many, his face had always been a sign of hope. But it had been her death sentence for years. Things were always blurry in her mind when she thought of him, but those eyes had always been with her, rising in the darkness of her mind when fear or doubt threatened to take her heart. Now here he was, offering the chance to help the Church without the constraints of hierarchy or politics. Was the Seraph guiding him?

Lynn wasn't sure why, but she wanted to follow him. Wanted to have faith in what he offered. "What would you have me do?"

The Pontiff's soft smile touched his eyes, only for a moment, and then it seemed like the room's shadows gathered over his expression. "There is more darkness within the Church than I care to admit." He rose and paced slowly. "Dakhra has hidden false prophets in the darkest corners of the Domain. They call themselves the True and seek to destabilize us from within. I fear there are priests who preach blasphemy within our very walls."

"The Sentinels never received word of this. Does Olem know?"

The Pontiff sighed. "They are not fools. It is done under the veil of their own interpretation of the texts. Interpretations that eventually lead people astray and into Dakhra's arms. I'm sure you can see that an inquisition against our own priests in a time like this can be . . . complicated, yes?"

Lynn thought back to their retreat from Durnn. Dakhra had not given chase. Perhaps this was why; they could be trying to end the war without a battle. To defeat the Domain from within. She nodded. "You wish me to find them?"

The Pontiff shook his head. "There are few I can fully trust, but little escapes Reznik's gaze, especially within Alteria. The enemy are cunning enough to notice when they are being watched. Results from those detained by Reznik have been . . . inconclusive."

"Reznik has been questioning priests?"

"Oh no, my dear. I'd never let him go as far as that, but we have been replacing preachers in certain quarters and watching for results. Those removed have been kept safe, but it is a long and tedious process, I'm afraid. You, however, present a rare opportunity. I have never had an agent I could trust so fully. One that has been through a Questioning." He smiled at her again, without showing teeth. "The Seraph cannot have these enemies within Her city. Reznik is alert, but I fear true danger brews silently, and might be closer than we imagined."

"Where do I begin?"

The Pontiff considered the question. "One of the churches in the Lower East Row has doubled its masses in the past weeks," he said. "I would never judge that a bad thing, but there seems to have been an exodus from other churches in the outer quarters, and whispers of blasphemy have begun to spread."

Lynn nodded. "I'll get there tonight."

The Pontiff rose and made his way to the door. "I will pray to the Seraph that your foray is a swift and fruitful one, my dear. Oh, and Sentinel?" He turned, one hand on the door. "Discretion is paramount in this. We cannot have the streets taken by panic, and we do not know who to trust within the Church. If you have to tell someone, keep them close."

Lynn nodded, and the Pontiff left the room with slow steps and a softly rustling robe. Lynn got to her feet. Everything hurt—from her legs as she got out of the bed to her arms and back as she moved to don her Sentinel mantle-but something in the Pontiff's words had filled her with a drive she'd not felt in a long while. It was time to defend the Faith again. Stop false prophets from recruiting the faithful. Time to be a Sentinel. Lynn finished donning her Mantle and put on the oldest cloak she could find to cover the steel. She stepped onto the window ledge and jumped, her mind reaching out for Vedyr to catch her.

It didn't take long to reach the outer quarters of Alteria. The Lower East Row had always been, as the name suggested, on a level below the surrounding streets. That made for a somewhat isolated area with sloping lanes and deep shadows. Ideal for hiding. Lynn approached on Vedyr, leaning close to speak above the howling wind.

"Circle close by. You'll know if I need you." Lynn knew the griffin didn't understand the words, but the intent was shared through the Bond. She had a sliver of his ruin-stone heart beating in hers, after all.

Lynn flew Vedyr closer to one of the taller buildings in a neighboring block and leapt from his back. She made her way down the street, and then the Lower East Row. She headed for the small church that, while not exactly tall, still rose above the low-roofed housing clumped together at odd angles along the up-and-down, narrow paths that formed a patrolman's nightmare. There were too many places to hide, and the looming city above cast more shadows on already dark streets.

Lynn used the shadows, creeping along with an old comfort in knowing she was veiled from the world, and alone. Vedyr flew overhead, but there were enough griffins flying over Alteria these past few days that his proximity would not be viewed with alarm.

The streets were mostly empty, save for the movement of an Alterian hurrying toward the church. Firelight streamed off the sidewall where sconces held burning torches that illuminated the carved-out scriptures for those outside, while painting them in light for those within. A priest stood by the door, welcoming the faithful as they flocked inside. Even from a distance, eager eyes and hopeful steps were easy to spot.

Lynn watched from the shadows, avoiding as much of the firelight as she could. She was cloaked and dirty, but having the priest see her face would be a risk. It could bring questions. She waited until the front doors closed, then headed to the back streets behind the church. She let the image of the people's eagerness sit in the darkness of her mind.

Dakhra was playing on the hopes of innocents who had not asked for this war, whose lives belonged to the Seraph and not power-hungry rulers. The thought burned inside her and touched the shard in Lynn's heart that connected her to Vedyr. Their Bond reacted, and Lynn used the surge of strength to leap onto a house, run along the roof, and jump over a narrow street to the top of the church.

The building was much smaller than the main Alterian cathedral, but it mimicked the opening in the ceiling that gave the Ever-Tree a window to the sky above. Lynn lay flat, peering down at the people gathered around the circular pews. The priest talked from under the tree, and normally wouldn't have been visible, but the leaves had fallen here too. Lynn caught glimpses of the man's white and silver robes and quick flashes of the ruin-stone around his neck.

His words drifted up to meet her. " . . . Seraph left us, saying She will return when we have proven ourselves worthy. But what does it truly mean to be worthy? Is the worthiness in our clothes? In our words? No, my faithful. True worth is within our hearts. That is something no one can take from you, even if your heart is stilled."

Lynn frowned. He hadn't said the words, but talking about stilled hearts was as good as telling these people they would be worthy in death.

"What you do. What you give to this world, to the people around you, matters more than any judgement. Your faith must be strong in life, but what is a life worth if it is lived in meekness and waste? Enemies have always surrounded us, but now is the time to show strength, to show the worth in your lives."

The anger that Lynn channeled to jump onto the building had her fingers gripping the edge of the opening. This man hid his preaching in vague words, but to those who were desperate and willing to see enemies anywhere, his veiled meaning would be clear.

Lynn backed off, keeping her anger as controlled as she could. She breathed in and out, in and out. There was proof enough. She wouldn't judge the man herself, but she couldn't let him continue his preaching for another night. She waited until his words ran out, tithes were paid and blessings given, and the faithful started trickling from the church. A few remained, though: two women and a man. They approached the priest and asked a question she couldn't make out.

If the priest answered them, it was too quiet for Lynn to hear, but after a moment, they followed him toward a door past the Ever-Tree. This was it; the chamber stood empty. Lynn checked that her mace and war-scythe were secure, then raised her hood and lowered herself through the hole, dangling with arms outstretched and body swinging.

She would need only one movement here. The time for stealth was gone. She was a Sentinel, and she had seen enough to judge these people. The priest was the inciter, but the other three had made their choice. She threw her legs back, then forward. once, twice, three times—then pulled in as much of Vedyr's strength as she could and launched herself forward, releasing the lip. She fell toward the wall that housed the door the priest had gone through. She knew what waited behind. Every church had a cleansing chamber at the back. Lynn put her shoulder forward as she met the wall. She probably wouldn't have managed the stunt in the Alterian cathedral, but she didn't expect the same solid construction here.

She blasted through the wall and sent the door flying off its hinges. The four figures stumbled to the floor. The priest and the other man held vials of red liquid in their hands. Lynn measured her strength, but not her speed. The man was desperately trying to uncork a vial, but Lynn pulled out her mace and knocked the visitors out with blows to the head, no harder than need be; they weren't soldiers. Her guess was that they were the ones who'd devolve into Madness and spread it through the streets. Reznik could deal with them now.

Lynn advanced on the priest, ripping the vials from his hand and smashing them on the wall. The man crawled back on his elbows but stopped when he saw Lynn's silver-burning eyes. "You-you can't! You have no idea how deep this goes. I know people. Powerful people in the Church! I can help you rise." His voice was tinged with desperation. He likely knew that Sentinels were allowed to kill, even within the holy city.

The man's words only flared Lynn's anger, but she could use this even without taking up his offer. "You were recruited from within?"

He nodded. "I saw no faces, but they have a web working in the shadows. The Church will fall. You can be one of those who rise above the rubble."

Lynn tapped his head with the butt of her mace, knocking him out. Her anger was rising, and the Bond was already pulling at her mind. She couldn't press it, not while the strain of the Questioning still lingered. Lynn's head pounded, but the desperation in the priest's voice still rang in her ears. "They have a web working in the shadows. The Church will fall." The Pontiff was right. It was impossible to know who to trust, but capturing wayward priests would only scratch the surface. She needed to find these people, infiltrate them. She was too recognizable, though. Especially after Durnn.

She'd need to find someone she could trust. From outside the Church.

The name that came to Lynn's mind was wrapped in guilt, but Ferrin had past ties that were too valuable to ignore. She'd considered training him, giving him the tools to protect himself, and it wasn't uncommon for Sentinels to take up wards in times like these. He couldn't be her ward, though. She'd have to find another Sentinel, perhaps one who appeared to be a rival.

The Church would accept Ferrin. His sister had been a priestess, his brother a Sentinel. That both had been killed could mark him as a target for these people in the shadows. If Lynn could find another gathering, one Ferrin could attend and where he could show resentment toward the Church . . . He could use his position as ward to entice these people, and that might lead him to the ones at the top. The only problem was that Ferrin didn't know about Alren.

Lynn knew what had to be done. If she were to count on Ferrin, there could be no secrets between them. It was time to tell him about his brother.

CHAPTER FIFTEEN

The Earth-Breakers believed they should control the First Tree, and for a while, they did. From it, all manner of earth-spawn were birthed, creatures that this land must never see again.

— Tales of the Hagun

A t least they didn't tie Nasha to a post this time. The Yltigg cell, if it could be called that, was dug into the ground—a pit with smooth, rounded stone walls and a cave-like depression breaking the circle. The alcove was deep enough to keep Nasha out of the blistering sun that seemed intent on scorching the Yltigg peak, but the shade came with a stench that she couldn't quite place —the sourness of what might have been rotten fruit, melded with the scent of the earth. The combination made it impossible to breathe comfortably, but that was the least of Nasha's troubles. She'd been betrayed; she was the peace offering all along.

Tomu had to be involved. Leku didn't have that kind of power and the Ronar warriors had done nothing to help her, but what about Mansa? He told her he'd send his hunters. Were they too outnumbered to act, or had he been part of the betrayal? Just when she'd told herself she could work with him . . .

The Ronar come first, always. Nasha had believed the words, believed the clan was the way forward, even after deceiving it to help Shai's family, but it seemed Tomu had proved himself a believer as well: sacrificing her as a peace offering to the Yltigg.

Nasha drove a fist into the wall and let out a frustrated yell. The clan had looked down on her all her life. She'd waded through the derision, done all she could to defend the clan and warn them of Zala's coming. This was how they repaid her.

She let the anger rise up her arm and struck the wall again, cracking the stone. "Bastards."

"Nasha?"

Her gaze flicked upward, as if the cloudless sky were speaking to her, but the voice was enough to direct her senses to the shots of emotion coming from Shai. It took Nasha a moment to place it, but Shai's voice wasn't coming from above. She searched the darkness in the alcove behind her and found a small crack in the wall that led to what looked like a second pit, similar to her own. It was dark, and she could see only slightly more than Shai's eyes, but knowing she was alive sent a ripple of warmth through Nasha's chest. She crept up to the opening. "Did they hurt you?" she asked.

"Does it matter?" The bitterness in Shai's words echoed through the pain of betrayal pulsing in Nasha's heart. She'd led the girl toward the clan, told her it was the only safe path. Now they'd both been discarded, shunned like the monsters in the tales.

"It matters."

"Why?"

"You know why, Shai. I'm taking care of you and your family. I promised your father." It went deeper than the promise. Nasha would have felt responsible for Shai even without the promise.

"Most people wouldn't clutch so tightly at a promise made to a dead man."

Nasha looked down, arms resting on her knees. "It's not only about the promise. Ife was the only person I ever knew who didn't see me as a monster or a tool. He risked his life to give you a better one, and I don't doubt he'd have done the same for me. It's more than just a promise. I'm proving he was right to believe in me, and I'm making his sacrifice and the life he lived matter by protecting what he gave it for, what he loved."

"I'm not like you, Nasha. I'm not a warden. I wasn't even part of the clan. The clan, the war—what does it matter? The Slopes will be the same. Whoever ends up on top will still step on us to climb higher, after whatever it is they want, while we can't even get a decent meal. We're nothing."

"That's what they want you to believe," Nasha said. "That's how they take the fight out of you and make you accept it. We have to fight, Shai."

"Not sure we can fight our way out of this one."

"So we give up?"

"All life that is wasted must be taken."

Nasha breathed deep. "Then don't waste it."

The silence remained, and Nasha peered through the crack to find Shai with silent tears on her cheeks. Shai noticed and wiped her face. "I hate those bastards."

Those bastards could be anyone, but Nasha found she couldn't disagree with any of the options that sprang to mind.

"I miss Uvo," Shai said, voice wavering. "I miss him not listening to me, his stubbornness. I miss the look on his face when I got back home with food."

Shai's emotions grasped deep into her, but Nasha was so used to suppressing emotions that comforting words for others were foreign. "We'll get through this."

Shai nodded, wiping tears from her cheeks, and turned away.

There was a long pause. Nasha couldn't hear Shai's sobs, but there was a tinge of grief riding the emptiness. "Maybe we should have followed Uvo and my mother to—"

"Don't," Nasha said. "We don't know who's listening."

Silence. Good. At least Shai still had hope for her family.

"We'll focus on getting out of here, Shai. Then we'll fix this."

Shai didn't answer. She might be shielding herself from hope, but Nasha couldn't give up. Not now. Not ever.

Was it pride that kept her going? Proving the clans wrong after she'd been discarded time and again? Nasha told herself she was better than that, but she wasn't sure it was true. Fear was the likelier option. She'd seen what Zala's taint could do, and she'd felt the darkness shifting inside her.

All her life, she'd told herself she wouldn't become the monster. Seeing what monsters looked like—trapped in their own rage and grief—was enough to fill Nasha with an overpowering dread. But there was more. That spark inside her that told Nasha if she could just get over one last hill, climb one last step, she'd be all right. She'd be in control. She'd know who she was. But there was always another hill, another step.

She let the thoughts churn in her mind until the sun had become the moon, and Shai's silence was joined by a soughing wind that sang cold over the opening of her pit. The edge was too far up to reach, the smooth stone walls impossible to climb. Maybe she could have dug into her curse, but she and Shai seemed to be imprisoned far enough from others that Nasha could find no strands of emotion to pull on. There was also the darkness that had reached into her in the tent. She didn't know what it was, but it felt dangerous enough that she only touched the edges of the curse in search of Shai's emotions.

"Shai?"

No answer. No emotion.

"Shai!" Louder now, a note of desperation bubbling up from her heart into the call.

Loose rocks tumbled into her pit, and Nasha shot to her feet. A shadow covered the moon. It stood on the lip of the pit above, hair falling over its face. Swaying with a rattling and chinking of stone. There was no gleam of moonlight on the whites of eyes, but a soft blue pulsed from the face. Not a face. The veil. The Yltigg speaker.

Nasha's thoughts shot back to the tent where she'd been subdued. The emotion had been pulled out of the tent, but it wasn't like the other times when she'd used it up. It had been closer to what happened with Razi, and Nasha saw the emotion sucked into the man's veil.

The speaker stood with his head down. Nasha couldn't tell if he was even looking at her. After a moment he sat, cross-legged and silent, hands on his knees. Nasha reached out for Shai's shooting emotion once more, but there was nothing. Maybe the speaker had pulled that away as well. "The girl has been moved in the interests of our privacy," he said. His voice was scratchy, as if he could only speak in whispers and was straining to be heard.

"You weren't here in the Proving." Nasha could have used whatever this syphon was to keep her curse under control back then.

"Changes have prompted my rise within the clan."

"Why are you here?"

"There is power within you. No person can throw off men like you did in the tent, Warden."

Nasha eyed the man with tight lips. There was no way of being sure how much he really knew about her or her curse. He could be gauging her, fishing for proof. Nasha sat back in the alcove. "I'm no warden. Never was."

The Roots had only used her. Mansa had been right about that. They'd blinded her with the title, the promise of a safe and comfortable life within the clan.

The man chuckled. "How would you prefer to be addressed?"

"You know who I am."

"You are a prisoner." His voice seemed to scratch more the louder he spoke. "To be taken to the arena tomorrow. I was sent here to give you a chance." He ran a hand over the stone veil that covered his face, and it pulsed with a soft blue light. It wasn't as strong as Razi, but she was sure now it was syphoning the sensations around it. "The veil has felt your power as it feels the words of the Earth. Zala's fingers run within you."

Nasha took a few more deep breaths. Did that veil give the man the power to recognize the emotions of others, like she did with her curse? "What do you know of it?" she asked.

"I know only what the Earth tells me."

175

Nasha shook her head in the shadows. The man was like Jabillo. All theatrics with nothing to show for it. "You know nothing then."

"Assuming one's knowledge is never a wise course of action, Warden."

"Stop calling me that!" It was almost a shout. Maybe it was her own frustration, or maybe the truth in the man's words was responsible for the rising heat in her blood, reminding her of her earlier thoughts. She'd held onto the title, trusted it and the clan as something she might be part of, help shape and be shaped by in turn. Instead, they'd thrown her away, discarded like the Slopers. Just one more worthless life in the eyes of the clan leaders. The speaker had asked how she wanted to be addressed, but the truth was, she didn't know.

The man seemed content to let Nasha work through her thoughts, but his silence was unsettling. He might have no answers, but something inside her drove a need to fill the darkness with something other than the wind. Perhaps she just didn't want to be alone with her thoughts. "Why are you here?" she asked.

"I told you. They're taking you to the arena."

"To be killed, to settle the fires of the Yltigg as retribution for the Proving."

"There is a belief that your blood will be enough to appease the dead goddess. Make right what was done wrong in the Proving. I, however, believe you can be of greater use."

The thought that Shai could be killed beside her sent a dagger through Nasha's heart. She'd promised Ife, given Landi and Uvo hope before sending them off to Azur. She couldn't let Shai be killed for nothing. "You want something from me."

The veil moved in what Nasha could only recognize as a nod in the moonlight. "You brought back the severed head of one of our touched. Meddling with the tainted is not the path the chief or the Yltigg expected to take, but, as I said, changes have created unique circumstances."

Nasha kept her gaze locked on the man as part of her mind searched for the truth in his words, but there was nothing in his emotions that she could pick up.

"You infected them?" Nasha's words sounded disgusted even to her ears.

"Oh, no." The speaker scoffed slightly. "But it would be foolish not to use what the Earth is providing. These folk have been touched by Zala and have offered themselves to the clan. There is no return for them. What I do is simply delay Zala's fury, so it may be unleashed on the correct opponent."

Nasha's breath came heavy as she realized his meaning. "You want to use me, make me into a monster."

"Monster is a curious name for it. I thought you disliked labels."

Nasha had never been one for the tales. She hated them, but the things she'd seen, the darkness she'd felt within, were enough to tell her that Zala was shifting under the Earth. And that tapping into whatever the dead goddess offered was too big a risk. "You think you can control it?" she asked. "This is greater than the clans or the Domain. Every time you meddle with it, you risk making Zala stronger. The Earth is offering you nothing. Zala is."

"All the more reason to understand it and use it against her. The veil feeds me the voice of the Earth, and it asks for all the help we can find."

"You're insane."

"Sanity is a matter of perspective. Many things are called insane until proven to be the salvation we seek. I am giving you the chance to be that. A savior."

"You want to make me into a monster, a weapon to be used against your enemies." Nasha saw what they'd done to Bahar, and the reminder of how Mansa had used her ripped at the inside of her chest. This was deeper than simply being used, though. If this man could truly see what stirred in Nasha, and wanted to push her to her limit, it would bring her closer to Zala. She'd risk becoming one of the tainted, and losing what little she knew about herself. Perhaps it was the fear taking her over again, but Nasha turned away.

"You have until morning to consider it, Warden."

The title sent angry waves through Nasha. It felt like he was intentionally trying to rile her, testing her limits, even if she hadn't agreed to his proposal.

"The chief believes blood is all that heals the Earth," the speaker said. "And that blood alone has kept Zala asleep and the clans alive."

"Blood hasn't been working."

The speaker chuckled once more. "Blood is what ties Zala to the darkness, and She will never lose her taste for it, but you have shown us something more. I believe not even you know what it is, but should we not explore and learn what it can do? There are few in the clans who would not jump at the chance to be seen as a hero."

It was Nasha's turn to scoff. She was almost sure she'd rather be called a monster than a hero. At least it would be sincere. "Why even give me a choice?"

"I do not wish to keep you caged. You have true potential, but you must believe in it. I cannot walk that path for you." The speaker stood. "Everyone's hero is someone else's monster. Perhaps you have chosen to believe the wrong side. Consider my offer." He left.

Nasha let the sound of the speaker's footsteps be taken by the wind while her thoughts stumbled over each other. Would he help her control her curse, or was he seeking to use her as another disposable weapon? She wasn't Ronar anymore, and she definitely wasn't Yltigg, but was a weapon all she was meant to be?

CHAPTER SIXTEEN

Betrayal is only a different kind of loyalty.

— Azuri saying

Adrian paused before the door to Lady Rhiall's chamber. He'd failed to gain an audience for the past week but had been told she'd be here. He'd spoken with Zarath and Bedak, but neither had been successful in breaching the Rhiall blockade of their family leader's room. Lady Zarath had told Adrian it was not uncommon for consuls to sequester themselves before a meeting like this, so as not to have their decisions influenced by the constant political maneuvering among the families. This was Rhiall's own form of politics, though. By isolating herself, she could claim she'd not been influenced by lesser families—using that as an influence of her own.

Adrian sighed as the guard shook his head at the familiar sight of him and Bac. If Bac intimidated the man, it didn't show in his tone. "She isn't here, Lord Light."

He wanted to tell the man he'd have his head once he was

Xakhar, but he feared the threat might reach Rhiall. He held his tongue. If Rhiall wouldn't see him before the meeting, he'd have to sway her while it happened. He couldn't risk leaving what he had to say in writing, and he didn't trust the guards to convey the message anyway. He could ask Zarath or Bedak again, but there was still something he didn't fully trust about them. It was like the whisper in his blood rose when he was around the pair. The feeling was probably just his own anxiety, but he needed a backup plan all the same.

He turned from the guard and walked down to one of the gardens. Bac was close but silent, leaving Adrian to his memories. The garden was far enough from the one Derren had died in but was still uncomfortable. Nightshade flowers grew here as well, and the sight of them was like needles in Adrian's skin. Reminders of how his friend had been taken from him.

He turned one of the blood mages' spheres in his hand. Kel Bradaz had taken his blood throughout the week, instructed Adrian in parts of the blood magic, and given him one of the copper spheres to be used as a test. It was the same design Bradaz had used to take Adrian's blood the first time, with retractable spikes that extended to pierce the hand that held it. Bradaz taught him signs to release a coppery mist after the sphere held his blood, hoping Adrian and Nasir could use ruin-stone to help in finding a cure to the Madness. They'd tried with a few madmen in the House of the Afterdark. The ruin-stone had given Adrian a measure of control for a time, but the Madness eventually won out as Adrian's energy was sapped. The sphere he held was a weaker version, though. Bradaz had tampered with it, hoping Adrian could build his resistance to where he would eventually be able to not only hold off the Madness, but cure it.

The visions of Myrra and Derren had been strong when he'd used the magic, but that took enough out of him that he knew he had to use it with caution. There was something constantly running through him, though. At first he thought it was the feeling of almost being with Myrra and Derren again, but then he realized it called to him even when they weren't there. Like an addiction; a pain that rose, asking to be bled.

He'd grab onto his pendant of the Bone when the call in his blood became stronger. It helped push the shadow away. Perhaps there was more to be explored in the interaction of ruin-stone with this blood magic.

Adrian had asked Nasir to get him more shards, and Adrian carried those with him now. But this was not the place to experiment. He was close, could almost feel the familiar scent of the Domain, different from the spice-ridden winds of Dar Drezji. He'd been away for some time, though. What kind of Domain would he return to? He turned to Bac. "Why do you want to go back?"

Bac frowned. "Where?"

"The Domain."

"This land is strange," Bac said.

"The Domain imprisoned you. Framed you, if you are to be believed."

Bac shrugged. "It's still my home. And you look like you want to change it."

Adrian paused. He'd never considered it change. All he wanted was to get justice for Myrra and Derren, have his worth recognized. "Is that a good thing?"

"It is if you win. Men like me aren't allowed close to men like you. We're not used to . . . decisions. I know how to survive. Better if it isn't in a cell with death waitin' for me at the gallows."

Adrian almost smiled at that. Bac had so little, Adrian barely had to offer him anything to ensure his loyalty. Just like the Church did with the blessings, promising to extend people's lives in return for their faith. Adrian shook his head. If the blood magic had taught him anything, it was that there truly was power in his blood. He'd never believed in the blessings, no matter how long he'd lived. He believed even less in them now.

He put away Kel Bradaz's sphere and was leaving the garden with Bac looming behind when Nasir found him. "You must come with me now, Lord Light."

The sight of the priest, just after being lost in memories of Derren, rekindled Adrian's anger. He had to remind himself of his lack of allies to remain civil. "What is it?" he asked.

"I've managed entry into the dungeons, but we must be brief."

Adrian nodded. Talking to Amal, the Khorfa boy who'd tried to take over his family's seat, had been Adrian's original plan when searching for allies. He still didn't trust the ones he had. Perhaps the boy's desperation would prove a better assurance.

He followed Nasir through the palace corridors to the stairs that led to the dungeons. The guards serving the Jurat had abandoned their posts, perhaps a result of something Nasir had done, but Adrian knew it wouldn't last.

The steps to the dungeons were a rough sandstone, and the heat rose as Adrian descended. Sweat snaked down his back, reminding him of Ultenvell when he'd gone down the steps to find Myrra's body, pacing to the rhythm of his pounding heart. The memory clamped a vise around his chest. It squeezed harder with every step.

They reached the bottom, and Adrian moved to the cell where Amal Ban Khorfa was held. He nodded to the jailer, chest still too heavy for words, especially foreign ones. He half expected defiance. Maybe the man would contest his presence here, but it seemed the only distinction he made was between those within and without the cells.

"Stay here," Adrian told Bac, and entered the cell.

The smell of shit and sweat had been bad outside, but it was almost unbearable within the cell. Adrian tried to breathe through it as best he could. The Khorfa boy sat with his back against the far wall of the rectangular chamber. His foot was chained to the wall, and his arms rested on his knees. His head was bowed, face covered in shadow. Whatever finery his clothes might have come here with was in tatters now. He seemed unperturbed by the smell, perhaps because he was the source of it.

"There is a saying in Azur," Amal said, without looking up. "Betrayal is only a different kind of loyalty... I hear the Xakhar is dead."

"And who told you that?"

"Such events cannot be kept secret, Lord Light. Even down here." He shifted his foot, rattling the chain. "When are you telling the jailer to release me?"

"It's not that simple."

"We've been successful. The Xakhar is gone. There's no reason to keep me here."

"Who is the bearded man who introduced us?" Adrian asked.

"I . . . don't know, and that's the truth."

"You offer me only your word as assurance?"

Amal looked up. An angry scar ran over the sun-tanned skin where his left eye should have been. "I've given much more than that. Release me."

"I told you. I can't do that yet."

"What?" Amal got to his feet, but the chain around his ankle kept him back. "Has my uncle gotten to you? The man is ancient. His thinking will only lead you astray!"

Adrian could certainly appreciate Amal's reservations about his uncle, and in a different time, he might have been more trusting, but there was little to be gained by releasing the boy without information. "There is some discussion as to my legitimacy for the position of Xakhar."

"You got in here easy enough."

"Getting in and getting out are two very different things. I need information to help me find the right allies. See it as something to guarantee that your loyalty is not taken as betrayal."

"I do not have what you seek. The man was cautious; he could serve any consul."

"I need to be certain I will not be stabbed in the back, Amal."

"There are no certainties in Azur, Lord Light. That is the best advice I can give you, even if it's easy to forget at times. I was certain you'd release me, yet here I stand in rags and chains and shit. Do not depend on others. I did and look where it landed me."

"If I manage your release, you would owe me your life."

"I would."

"I'll keep that in mind."

Amal sat back down. "I'll pray you don't find other loyalties that render me a traitor, then."

Adrian stepped toward the door. Maybe Amal was right. There

were no certainties in Azur. Adrian had seen enough to trust him on that. All he could do now was try to create his own.

———

Adrian took his time getting to the gathering chamber. He needed to be sure his thoughts were in order, or this could be the end of his desperate attempt to rebuild an army. These were dangerous waters, and he didn't expect to swim them unscathed, but he had to find a way to avoid striking the hidden rocks the consuls would no doubt place in his path.

He didn't doubt that Attar had been doing his work. There'd been no change with Jurat Faruq, but the old consul had connections among the Jurat order, and Adrian didn't expect Attar to give up on killing him.

Attar would have other allies as well. He'd probably convinced Erhul, the other merchant consul. And the Taraff spicer family would follow the Erhul. Both military families—army and navy—were undeclared. Maybe Khorfa would try to seize the throne, but Adrian doubted Mahir would let him. It didn't matter who had more troops, as neither had enough to take the throne by force. Adrian would have to focus on them and hope he could sway Lady Rhiall.

Adrian breathed deep. She'd come around. Bedak said so, and Lady Zarath had heard encouraging rumors as well. That was probably why they were on his side. Once Rhiall declared for him, others would follow. He paused before the doors of the dining room.

"Bac."

"Aye?"

Adrian almost chuckled. He'd hated the title of Lord Light when he received it, but the recognition had grown on him. Now Bac's lack of formality was almost refreshing. "There shouldn't be trouble, but if there is, I'll need you to follow my every word in there. No hesitation."

Bac nodded, and they walked inside.

The meeting was held in one of the palace dining rooms this

time. Three massive, curtained windows took up the left wall between copper marble pillars. A rug-like map of Azur hung on the opposite wall, with guards in colors of every consul standing before it. Adrian's steps echoed across the silent chamber as he approached the table. Bac stood by the door behind him.

Nasir stood to the other side of the guards, close to the windows, while the consuls sat around the great dining table. Rhiall sat at the far end; Lord Taraff and Lady Fakhina, leaders of the spicer families, to her right; Erhul, the merchant, to her left. Zarath and Bedak sat beside Erhul, facing old lady Yankah and Mahir, who led the navy. Adrian knew them all well enough now, but the woman sitting at the head of the wooden table was new. She was dressed in the black and grey silks of the Jurat. The air of superiority around her was unmistakable, and even Faruq had assumed a deferential posture. This was High Jurat Hasna. Faruq sat to her left and Attar to her right, a glint of victory in his eye.

The head Jurat would be a powerful voice. Adrian could only hope Rhiall would be enough to balance the scales if Attar had gotten to her.

Khorfa sat beside Attar, eyeing Adrian with a frown, but it was Hasna who spoke up. "Tardiness does not bode well for one who would seek to rule our nation, Lord Light."

"It is a foolish man who does not respect the proper time needed for a moment like this, Head Jurat," Adrian replied. "Rigidness is a dangerous trait in a ruler." He took a seat beside Lady Zarath and caught Mahir smirking on the other side of the table. A swayed vote, perhaps?

A bottle of shraz sat at the center of the table, and most consuls had glasses before them. The Head Jurat did not and seemed eager to get on with business. "Let us begin," Hasna said. "All those who wish to cast their names into consideration or defend a candidate may do so now."

Lord Erhul immediately stood. "Brothers. Sisters. Our nation has strayed too far from the path of past glories. Our previous line was not a strong one, and now has left us leaderless. I propose we choose one whose family has always held the tradition of strength, of justice. That is why it has kept the oldest seat on this council. They do not need a trade; their contribution to the nation comes from experience and wisdom. And it is in that wisdom that I ask you to recognize the correct choice and appoint Lord Sahim Attar as Xakhar."

"Your words might have made sense months ago," Lady Zarath said. "But I'm afraid these times require more than tradition. Our nation is under siege, and Prince Adrian is the one who has brought us the warning. He had convinced the Xakhar. He knows more about this enemy than any of us. We should trust him to lead."

Lord Attar scoffed. "You bring words of plagues on foreign shores as though it should be our concern. I hear Lenir made a show in our last meeting, but where has that led? What of the people? Do we see chaos taking the streets as he foretold?" Attar shook his head. "Your words ring hollow, as does the threat. I can only assume the beggar prince has you in his pocket somehow. I thought you'd be above a foreigner's pay, Isra."

Adrian gritted his teeth. Attar's words stung, perhaps because they held a sliver of truth. He'd been begging for his father's favor his whole life and had come here begging for an army. He pressed his teeth tighter, and the cuts along his arm flared. Kahlia's scratch on his face had nearly healed, but the spot still burned.

Zarath shook her head. "This plague is not held on foreign shores, Sahim." She looked at Lord Bedak, who stood and clapped his hands twice.

The doors opened and servants filed in.

Lord Taraff rolled his eyes. "This again?"

"We've had enough theatrics, Lenir," said Lady Fakhina. Rhiall did not react.

The servants came in pairs, each carrying a stretcher with a corpse on it. Four pairs made their way through the doors before Adrian noticed the marks around the eyes of the dead. The bodies were laid out on the dining room floor. All of them killed by the Madness.

Adrian gripped his ruin-stone pendant. No matter what Nasir

186

had done to it, in Adrian's mind, the pendant would always be Myrra's.

Attar watched, seeming unamused. "This proves nothing. Your family deals in secrets and assassins, Isra. You could have gotten these dead from Immeria or infected them yourself."

"Prince Niilar had the same markings," said Mahir. He wiped the sweat off his brow and dabbed at his multiple chins. He seemed less resistant to Adrian now. Maybe Bedak and Zarath had swayed him.

Taraff nodded. "He did, but he displayed no frenzy as the foreigner suggests."

Adrian cleared his throat. "That is because the blood mages of the Afterdark kept him under control. There are many with the condition in their cells." He looked to Lady Rhiall. It was time. "Including your son, Lady Rhiall. They are keeping his Madness at bay by using my blood."

A few of the consuls shifted in their seats. Lady Yankah had a disapproving frown on her face, but Mahir was intrigued enough to lean forward.

Adrian pushed on. "Which of your sons could be susceptible to this curse? How much are you willing to risk so that your notions of tradition are maintained? Yes, I'm a foreigner, but so is this plague, and I'm your best chance at beating it." He paused, looking over the consuls. "The Xakhar had chosen me. I was the one he saw fit to lead Azur. Even without this plague, your ruler chose me because the alliance of your forces with Othonea would make us the most fearsome nation in Avarin. You must see this."

There was silence as the consuls exchanged glances, weighed risks and gauged alliances. The silence held long enough for Hasna to rise. She placed both palms on the table. "If there are no others to speak, we will commence the vote."

Adrian let out a slow breath, the tingle rising in his blood. He could almost see the shape of Myrra in a shadowed corner, and the scars along his arm flared once more. There had been no retort from Attar, and the thoughtful pause by the others bode well. It was time. He would get his army.

Hasna raised a hand to signal the vote, but Bedak cleared his throat. Adrian's gaze flicked to him, and the tingle in his blood spiked, making his heart skip a beat. What was this? Now wasn't the time. The consuls were ready to vote for him.

"If I may, Head Jurat." Bedak didn't look at Adrian, but was focused on the consuls. "Prince Adrian is wise to talk of risks."

The words did nothing to settle Adrian's beating heart.

"There is power in his blood, power that has been confirmed by Kel Bradaz himself, but should we not be wary of that? Should all power be held by one man?"

"We've talked about this, Lenir," Mahir said. "We must have a Xakhar."

"We must have the position, yes. Without one, I fear we would bicker amongst ourselves until the entire nation of Azur stood still. But must the position be in the hands of one man?"

The fury rose in Adrian's blood as he realized what Bedak was doing. He'd been played. Bedak waved, and one of his guards moved forward. He had a thick beard and wore a turban. Adrian didn't recognize his face, but how would he? He'd only seen it covered. It was the man from the market, he was sure. The one who'd sent the assassin.

"This man approached me after the Xakhar's death," Bedak said. "He had interesting information about the Lord Light's involvement in the attempt on Kahlia's life." The consuls were all looking at Adrian now. "Let us not be hypocrites," Bedak continued. "None of us are above plotting."

There was a chuckle from Mahir, but Khorfa's gaze was piercing. Amal had attempted to wrangle control of the Khorfa from the man, and it seemed he wanted Adrian to pay for that as well.

"There is one way of reducing the risks, however," said Bedak. "We split the power. Lady Rhiall has proved to be the most neutral among us. She has met with no one, been influenced by no one. She must be part of the leadership."

There were no complaints, other than the raging scream at the back of Adrian's mind. His blood seemed to boil, and he leapt to his feet. But as he stood, so did Khorfa and both Jurats.

Rhiall did not stand. She looked calmly at Adrian. "Lord Bedak speaks the truth: none of us are above plotting. You have shown yourself capable enough of that, Lord Light, yet you are a tool, not a leader. Consuls, I propose joint leadership. Bedak has been a valuable partner and has shown the strength to wade through treachery and plots in the shadows. He has given us the best solution our nation can hope for, and the most stable." She gestured towards Attar. "Your efforts have not gone unnoticed, Sahim. You will join us, and we shall rule as a triumvirate."

There were nods and mumbles of agreement. Adrian shot a desperate look toward Zarath. She wore a rare expression of genuine confusion.

"The threat of this plague is real," Rhiall continued, "and that is why we need our troops to protect our borders. Prince Adrian will help us." It wasn't a question. "And in time, the ruling council will consider aiding the Domain."

Adrian's boiling blood rose, and the cuts in his arm burned so deeply, he was sure they'd opened up. Myrra's vision was staring at him from the other side of the room, her masked face as twisted as ever. Blood oozed from where the mangled skin was stitched together, but her words were clear in his mind. *You are stronger than you think. Help me.*

Derren was there too. Gasping, trying to breathe.

I've been running after the favor of others for too long.

"Enough!" Adrian bellowed. The anger in his voice made old Lady Yankah jump in her seat, and Khorfa draw his sword.

"Guards!" Rhiall cried, as if the vote had already been taken. Adrian knew they would obey.

Adrian turned to Bac. Nasir was hovering close to him, but Adrian knew they couldn't hold back the Azuri guards. His mind went back to Khet, when he was surrounded by hopelessness and Raklin was infecting his men. Respect isn't asked for or earned. Respect is taken. Enough. It was so easy to forget himself in this heathen land.

His hand dug into his pocket and closed around the sphere Kel Bradaz had given him. Nasir said the consuls were warded, but faith burned strongest in desperate times. Adrian closed his fingers around the sphere, and the spikes cut into his palm. He knew what to do.

He pulled the ball from his pocket and rolled it onto the table. It left a streak of his blood behind. And the reddish mist formed around it. Adrian drew the signs Kel Bradaz had taught him throughout the week.

Attar laughed. "This is your attempt? We're all warded." Neither of the other consuls seemed perturbed.

Blood holds ties. For once, he hoped his father was right.

The mist expanded, twisting around the room and clouding it in red. A few consuls began to shift, hands moving to pendants or wristbands or earrings, as if checking their wards. A flutter rose in Adrian's chest and turned into a glimmer of hope as Attar's grin became a cough. It spread. Slowly, consuls tried to rise. Some went for the device on the table but pulled their hands away as it sizzled and spluttered more coppery smoke into the room. Some were on the floor, taken by the coughing, while others ordered their guards to open the doors.

"Bar the exit," Adrian told Bac, and the man blocked it without hesitation.

A few guards might have tried to break the windows, but they were doubling over now and struggling to breathe. It reminded Adrian of Derren for a moment, but then he looked at the image of his old friend through the smoke. Derren had a satisfied look in his eye, as if every Azuri life taken fed his revenge.

I told you I'd make them pay, old friend. I wish you were here to see it.

I'm always with you, Adrian. Your light keeps me alive.

Adrian nodded and moved close to Nasir. "Ruin-stone?"

He was immune, but it was clear now that his blood was not safe to others. What Kel Bradaz's device poisoned them with was different, though. It had been weakened for Adrian to test his power. There would be no frenzy in the consuls or their guards. Only pain. Their bodies would contort and writhe, and then lay still. It seemed like as good a moment as any to test the effectiveness of the ruin-stone in protecting them.

Nasir already held a shard of his own, and he pulled out what could be a dozen more. He handed them to Adrian, who walked towards Bac and placed a shard in his hands. The big man had been holding his breath, and relief washed over him when he took the shard. He and Nasir breathed normally, and Adrian immediately felt the drain on his strength. It seemed to work, though. They were unaffected by the Madness in his blood. The Madness he'd infected himself with back in Khet to stop Raklin.

The first consul Adrian walked towards was Mahir. "You seem like a slimy bastard, but I'll need the ships. You understand a navy means nothing against my power, yes?"

Mahir nodded between gasps.

"Good." Adrian dropped a ruin-stone shard on the table close enough for the man to grab. Mahir's gasping decreased as soon as he grabbed the stone, and he breathed in deep, like a drowning man breaking through the surface. The strain of holding back the Madness rose and Adrian's muscles burned, but it was still enough to bear.

He moved on. "Lady Yankah, congratulations. You are now the sole supplier of weapons in Azur. Your competition might have a sour turn soon." He didn't wait for an answer.

Faruq had a desperate look in his eye, trying to crawl toward Adrian over Hasna's twisting body. The Madness was already taking hold of her. "You will serve me as Xakhar? Have the Jurat at my disposal?" Faruq nodded. "Say it."

"Y-Yes."

"Yes?"

"Y-yes, Lord Light." Adrian dropped a shard into Faruq's hand.

"Now. Does anyone wish to challenge my rule?"

Adrian was answered only with panicked coughs and gasps as people wheezed for air around him. He gave shards to Erhul, Taraff, and Fakhin. He'd need the merchant and the spicers. Five consuls left. The magic pulled harder at Adrian, but he kept his gaze locked on the image of Myrra. His muscles were tiring, but her face was changing, as if being stitched slowly together to resemble what it had in life. It still hurt seeing her like that, but Adrian had learned to recognize the pain and use it to power his blood magic. The Madness's anger pushed back, like it had with Rhiall's son in the house of the Afterdark, but Adrian fed his pain to the shards of ruin-stone. The pain fueled his magic, and the shards linking him to the consuls kept their Madness at bay.

Khorfa was next, but Adrian had no questions for him. "Seems like Amal will be taking over your family after all, Lord Khorfa." Khorfa struggled to resist, but there was little strength left in him as Adrian walked past.

Lady Zarath was trying to crawl to a window. Myrra walked past Adrian and knelt by the woman's side. Adrian followed slowly and crouched beside her. "Did you know?" he asked.

A gasp and bulging eyes were his only answer, but her eyes were filled with fear. The fear revealed the truth now plastered on her face: she'd been played, just as he had. She was ashamed, and would likely die before admitting it, but she hadn't known. Adrian had half a mind to let the Madness take her for her incompetence, but it would take time to reestablish her network of spies and assassins. Time he didn't have. He held up a shard. "No more secrets between us, Isra?"

She nodded, and he tossed her the last shard, feeling another string pull at the pain in his heart and tear along his skin. It almost felt good now, a testament to his power.

"Now, what to do with the new triumvirate?" he asked, watching Rhiall, Attar. and Bedak squirm on the floor beside their guards. The last had desperate eyes on Adrian, and Adrian held his gaze the longest. "You reached too high," Adrian said.

He wasn't even sure Bedak could hear him; he'd gone into a state of coughing that produced more and more blood. All three remaining consuls struggled with a few last breaths, then were still. Adrian had to hand it to Rhiall; the woman actually mustered a rage-filled glare. The rage in Adrian was stronger, though. He'd lost too much, and now was the time to get it back. He didn't spare the guards; he had no strength left for that. His breath was already growing heavy, and he must not appear weak. They must believe this was the least of what he could do.

"You have had a taste of the power in my blood," he said. "As Xakhar I will spare your lives as long as your loyalty is ensured. Any objections?"

The silence in the room was thicker than the coppery mist, which started to clear when Bac opened the door.

Show a man death and he will quail in his boots. Give him his life, and he will forever know who holds it.

"Excellent. Lord Mahir, ready your ships. We sail at once for the Domain."

CHAPTER SEVENTEEN

Reminder: Airship gas is to be kept at proper pressure and temperature in accordance with protocol. If you do not recall proper values, the manual is to be consulted. We shall not tolerate further accidents.

— Dakhran chief engineer's note

K admus headed back to his shop. The way grew more crowded as he went. The guards became fewer, their armor and weapons progressively lighter and less polished. If anything, it should have been the opposite, but the coin that paid the guard did not seem to find its way to the poorer areas of Pelaket.

The people didn't seem to mind the reduced patrols. Strange that within the walled, more protected part of the city, fear seemed to walk freely among the empty streets, while here, ignorance—or a lack of much to lose—had people going about their lives as if the Madness were just another daily risk.

The guards that were here tried to ensure that crowds broke up quickly, but Kadmus knew that was more for show than anything else. A single madman could rip through a street faster than most of its victims could react. There need not be a crowd to create danger. In fact, a crowd might slow such creatures down and aid the guards.

Kadmus avoided everyone he could and quickly found his way to the shop. He let out a sigh. The trip had taken too long; he couldn't afford to waste his time. He unlocked the door and pushed inside, ready to resume work on the cure. All was quiet when he entered, and he was down the stairs before he knew it, shoving open the door.

The silence stopped him in his tracks. The heavy oak door always kept most of the basement's sounds in the basement, but the madmen were rarely this quiet, even when dosed. The smell was new too, a sour scent of death that Kadmus had come to know. He shook his head and rushed from cage to cage, all three of the old ones. None of the infected were moving. The blackness had spread across their faces, and some had tried to claw their way out of the cages. They were all crumpled on the ground now. Dead.

He approached the final, more recent madman he'd captured with Grunt. This one had a cut along his abdomen and ribs. Claw marks. Self-inflicted, it seemed. He was bleeding out. He wasn't struggling, and the blackness around his eyes seemed to fade, as if the Madness were bleeding out of him through his wound. He'd lost too much blood already. Even if Kadmus could stitch up the body, he doubted the man's life could be preserved within it.

"Shit!" There was no one to scream at, but Kadmus's rage came at himself. He'd been failing for too long, and now he'd lost his subjects. Without infected blood, he couldn't test the cure.

"Shit!" He shouted it louder.

He grabbed an empty vial and approached the cage. Risks be damned, he couldn't lose it all. The madman was too weak to move, and Kadmus filled the vial with the man's blood, then another. There wasn't much left, and most of it was thick—some already crusting around the wound—but Kadmus managed four vials.

He looked down at them with heavy breaths. He wasn't himself, and even hope glimmered within his chest. It was enough to settle his thoughts a touch, but he still didn't understand what happened.

He'd tested his cures and been able to neutralize whatever affected blood tainted by the Madness—but it only worked on blood outside the body. The Madness seemed to renew itself in a host and find new strength to fight Kadmus's cures. This Madness was everything he hated. It was random.

Kadmus didn't know what to do with the vials. Would he try one last time? One last chance to save Nima? *Nima!*

He rushed up the steps, dread settling over the rage as his mind ran through the possibilities of what might have happened to her. Had she burned out like the madmen?

He burst through her door and found her twisting in pain under the covers. She still wasn't conscious, and the white veins in the ruin-stone he'd left around her were flaring up. He had to do something.

Kadmus pulled out another vial of the serum that had put her to sleep. Another of the type that would easily turn into poison if the wrong dose was administered. He didn't have time to hold back now. He couldn't lose Nima. He had to be better than his parents had been to him. He had to save her.

He held his daughter down. All the gentleness he'd treated her with was gone now. He needed strength to match the Madness. He jumped onto Nima, keeping her down with his weight, and held the sides of her jaw. If she were awake, empowered by the frenzy of the Madness, he wouldn't have managed, but as things were, he was able to open his daughter's mouth and administer half a vial of the serum.

She writhed for a few heart-stopping moments, then was still.

Kadmus pulled out all the ruin-stone shards he'd taken to heal Bahar and scattered them along Nima, touching them to her skin. The veins flared again, as if whatever was in them spoke to the Madness. Were the stones fighting the disease? Or was it just biding its time? If a Seraph did exist, Kadmus was sure She hated him.

He pushed up close to Nima, ear to her mouth and nose. She was breathing, but it was weak.

He breathed along with her. She'd almost died. He'd left her here to tend to the vanity of some bastard, and Nima had almost died. If he hadn't skirted the crowds, if he'd taken longer to descend from the upper city, if he'd stopped for supplies—the Madness would have taken her. His little girl, his life. More than his life. She was the only one he'd truly managed to love. She was what gave his life meaning, not a Seraph. He'd exchange countless years of his own for just a few more with her.

He would give her those years.

He looked down at the vials in his hand again. He couldn't risk squandering the blood—there was no knowing if the serums would keep Nima alive. Her breath was weak, and the increased dose was dangerously close to the limit a grown man could handle.

He walked from the room, an insane part of his mind almost wishing there were some deity he believed in, someone to pray to, who could remove the weight from his shoulders. But there wasn't. All he could do now was find Grunt.

Night had driven the people off the streets, and Kadmus was thankful for that. He kept to the shadows even so, making his way as fast as he could to the big man's house. He hated doing it this way—without a plan—but Nima's madness had pushed him toward an insanity of his own.

He stopped at Grunt's door and knocked. It was a small house, a single story pressed between two others, but no other lights on the street were on. He waited, allowing for a small measure of caution. He raised his hand to knock again when Grunt's surprised face peered through the crack in the door. "I thought we said no meeting in the open."

Kadmus was so used to the man being silent that his voice seemed foreign. "Something's happened. We need more."

Grunt stepped out, then closed the door halfway behind him so that only a weak stream of candlelight escaped. "I can't."

"What?"

"I'm sorry, Leech." That was what Grunt had called Kadmus in the past, as Kadmus had used leeches to heal Grunt's wife of more than one ailment.

"You call me that, forgetting where it came from," Kadmus said.

"I haven't forgotten, and I'm still grateful, for that and what you did for me in the shop. Truly. But staring death in the face only showed me that I can't do this anymore. I'll do anything for you, as long as it doesn't threaten my family."

Kadmus bit back his rising rage. This wasn't like him. Men who could create what he could should not be taken by emotion. But Nima was dying. Grunt didn't know about Nima. No one did, and Kadmus wasn't about to tell him. He'd betrayed Kadmus once already. Diffusing his anger allowed Kadmus' thoughts to fall into place. Grunt had said family, not wife.

"Your wife . . .?"

"Is with child." He almost coughed it; a strange kind of whisper, but Kadmus knew then this was an argument he couldn't win. He didn't comfort the man, or tell him it would be all right, or to count on him in the future. He simply turned his back and walked away.

He moved quickly down the street, still wary for Nima's condition, but the way was long enough to consider his options. The one that remained soon became clear. Kadmus had denied it, and was certain he should avoid Bahar, but the man's offer was the only thing that could provide Kadmus enough resources to keep working on a cure. He hated being tied to the man and having to do what he was about to do, but he couldn't capture madmen alone. And there was no cure without their blood.

Bahar said he needed to replicate the Madness, and he probably wanted to test it on some unfortunate citizen deemed unworthy by the Church. But Kadmus knew better than to simply hand over the Madness to Bahar. He'd need to work with the man, but he was not putting himself in Bahar's hands and would not rely on trust.

He pushed through the door of his store and rushed up to Nima's room. She was still, chest moving lightly up and down. Kadmus let out a trapped breath and made his way down toward the workshop. He couldn't reach out to Bahar empty-handed, but he needed to be sure that what he held in his hand was under his control.

CHAPTER EIGHTEEN

Apprentices are to be trained in arms and faith in equal measure. Sentinels must be more than weapons. It is the ultimate failure to be wielded by the hand of death. We control the enemy's weapon.

— *The Book of the Blade (restricted)*

Lynn's feet crunched the gravel of the barracks training yard, with Vedyr's shadow drifting above her. She was glad for the griffin's presence, a sliver of comfort in what would soon come. Not even the drifting scent from the mess hall was enough to distract her. In fact, it told Lynn where Ferrin would be.

A few gazes flicked her way when she walked in, and soldiers who'd fought with her nodded as Lynn walked by. Lynn focused on Ferrin, who sat with a few of the soldiers from his troop. He'd kept the lieutenant position and seemed to be doing a good job of it too.

Just as he's creeping out of his hole, you come to drag him back in, Cara said. There was some truth to it, and that was why Lynn hadn't told Ferrin about Alren. But she had to do this now.

She stopped at his table. "We need to talk in the map room." It was the best she could come up with; the other Legion soldiers would think they were talking tactics.

Ferrin took a sip of his stew and stood. There was no resistance in him, but he eyed the stew longingly for a moment. He followed Lynn from the hall and up the stairs that led to the large double-doored room, where a map of the Domain sat on a table longer than Lynn was tall.

Ferrin closed the door behind them. "What's so urgent? Is Dakhra advancing?"

"No," Lynn said. "I need your help."

Ferrin waited with the same puzzled expression.

"The Church needs your help." She breathed out slowly. "But for that, you need to be fully committed. Your past can't hold you back."

Hypocrite, Dentos said.

"Lynn . . . what's this about?"

"There's something I need to tell you about your brother. About who he was, and how he died."

Ferrin stiffened.

"You talked about him in the woods close to Durnn, said you didn't know much about how he went." No use holding back. "Your brother was a Sentinel, Ferrin, and I'm the one who killed him."

Ferrin stood there, his words robbed by the shock on his face. Lynn moved and he flinched, as if to escape. As if she'd brought him here to kill him as well. Lynn shook her head.

"I'm not a traitor. Your brother was trained with me; we grew in the order together. We were close, a couple of others as well. He was sent on a mission in Vizcarra with Roki, another of our brothers. When they returned, they were mad. They infected two others from our group."

Ferrin's expression was struggling now, his face fighting against the grief that he'd failed to keep back. "Why are you telling me this?" His voice was oddly calm.

"You've been carrying this burden for too long, trying to live up to what Alren meant to you, same as Morna. It's hard to let go, but if you don't focus on life—your life—death will drown you in grief. You need to allow yourself to get past them, to tell yourself it's all right."

"All right? How is any of this fucking all right? You're a Sentinel, you have all the power, and you killed my brother!"

"There was no other way, Ferrin. The Church . . ."

"The Church? Fuck the Church. Who decides on taking a life like that on a whim?"

"Believe me," Lynn's tone hardened. "Nothing happened on a whim. He was infected. You've seen this Madness. Do you know what damage a Sentinel could cause if taken by it? Be angry at me, hate me if you must, but know that not a day goes by that his voice and those of the others don't ring in my head. He was my brother, too."

Ferrin's tears were flowing now, and Lynn stepped toward him as he broke down and fell into a chair, sobbing. She let him exhale the weight of what he'd been carrying. Let him work through the pain.

"My family has dedicated itself to the Seraph," he said finally. "Why does She keep taking from us?"

"It's easy to hate what we know, what we can see, but this wasn't the Seraph, Ferrin, it was Dakhra. They're doing it again. All of it. That's why I need your help."

Ferrin didn't react, just sat there with drying tears and a numb expression. "Why didn't you tell me before?"

"Would you throw a stone at cracked glass? You were hurting, you'd lost Morna. Death is a strong enemy. We don't talk about it, so we don't give it more power, but I could see you were struggling. I'm doing this now to show you there are those who would side with death and spread it among the Domain. Make us kill our own. We have a chance to fight them, to beat this Madness once and for all."

Ferrin looked up, renewed tears clouding his eyes. "Did you keep any of the bodies?"

Lynn looked down. It hadn't been her decision, but guilt still grasped at her heart for doing it. She shook her head. "We had orders to burn them."

Ferrin got up and walked to the door. He paused, looking back over his shoulder. "I'm so tired. When does this end?"

Lynn understood. She'd felt the same when she swung the blade. Worse, even. "When we end it. No one else can do it for us."

Ferrin nodded slowly, then walked from the room. He left the door open, and the sound of people moving about the barracks mingled with the scent of the stew from the mess hall. Lynn had thought she might feel better after telling Ferrin, but now she feared that all she'd managed was to push him further into death's arms.

I can only give you the tools. The path must be carved by your own hands. Your own strength. Elwin's words. What Lynn hadn't understood as a child had become all too clear in the years since. She tapped a finger on the table. Elwin was right. She needed to give Ferrin time to heal the wound.

And if he doesn't? Alren said. What if this kills him, too?

Lynn didn't have an answer for that. Her attention was drawn by a presence at the door. It was Rel, frowning slightly. "Commander wants us in the mess hall," he said.

The mess hall had been cleared for the Sentinels, and just under three-score waited for Olem. They stood between rows of long tables at a straight angle to the high table at the far end of the room.

Lynn still wasn't comfortable among the Sentinels. She trusted her ability to fight any of them, and she doubted it would come to that, but there were still too many gazes on her. Most of them were Syphoners like her, but Lynn drifted close to Rel and Deria. Channelers had always been fewer in number among the Sentinels. They couldn't convert as much strength or speed from their griffins as a Syphoner could, but their ability to load ruin-stone with emotions was always valued. Channelers had to understand their Syphoners —a kind of bond of their own. Not the same as Lynn's Bond with Vedyr, but she found it drawing her to Rel amid her discomfort.

The new commander stepped into the room a few minutes late. He didn't command the shroud of silence that Leardin cast when entering a room. A few mumbles persisted even as Olem walked to the front of the standing Sentinels. He didn't have Leardin's height either, but the Sentinels eventually quieted down and sat on the long benches.

Olem had new armor, befitting his new station. He'd always been the lead forger among the Sentinels, blending powdered ruin-stone with steel, so the speed at which his armor had been fashioned was not surprising. He didn't look comfortable in it, though, and beads of sweat dotted on his bald pate.

Olem ran a hand along his short-cropped beard before beginning. "Sisters. Brothers. We have suffered blows like never before."

His tone caught Lynn by surprise. She'd expected him to assert his command, instill strength in the order. She looked at her fellow Sentinels. She wasn't the only one caught off-guard. His sincerity caught everyone's attention, and silence finally settled over the hall.

"Our enemy is strong. It would be foolish to think otherwise, but Sentinels are not chosen for strength alone. Our faith is stronger than any other's. We know who we are. We know what we do, and we know how to face any threat."

A dozen voices rose in agreement at that, but not many more. Ildred and Wyman's silence was especially notable to Lynn.

"Let the blows to our pride not be deep enough to affect our confidence. We are still Sentinels, and there is no finer title in Avarin."

A few bangs on the table this time, and more muted calls of support.

"An opportunity has presented itself. The enemy is on the move. They're bringing something across the Skygate. Something big. We're taking it down."

"What are they bringing?" Deria asked.

"We're not sure," Gwynne said. She'd always been the fastest of them and was probably the one who'd scouted the enemy this time. "I couldn't get close enough for details, but the airship heading our way is the largest I've ever seen."

"Supplies for more potions?" Wyman asked.

"Could be," Olem said. "It would explain why they haven't

moved out of Durnn yet."

Lynn almost raised her voice against that, but the Pontiff had made it clear that whatever Dakhra was trying to spread among the holy city was to be kept secret. No secret would be safe if shared among these numbers, even in a group as trustworthy as her Sentinel companions.

"What about their defenses at the Skygate?" Rel asked.

Brehnna nodded beside Rel. "They must have at least a dozen airships, and if we all attack, they'll know Alteria is unprotected. The airships in Durnn would advance."

"We have a plan for that," Olem said. "Ildred, you're putting a force together and flying to Durnn."

Ildred smirked, with a gleam of what could have been triumph in his eyes. Lynn couldn't hold back this time. "You're letting him attack Durnn?"

"No," Olem said. "It's only smoke. Ildred's force will have to be large enough to be convincing, to pull away the bulk of Dakhra's strength guarding the Skygate." He pointed at Ildred. "But you are not to engage. A threat is all we need. If we take the Skygate, we can block Dakhra's reinforcements. It would allow us to attack Durnn. You'll already be in position then."

Ildred eyed Olem for a while, but the commander was undisturbed. Ildred finally turned to Gwynne. "And Thain?"

"Nothing that I could see," Gwynne said.

Ildred turned a glare on Lynn. He seemed intent on reminding her of her plan to ask Dakhra for help. Thain hadn't returned, but Lynn didn't need Ildred to remind her it had been her plan. She had her voices for that.

"If Thain hasn't returned by now," Olem said, "he's either a prisoner or a fugitive. The best chance we can give him is to remove Dakhra's foothold in Durnn, so we can reduce their power and start cleansing the other nations.

"I'll lead the effort against the Skygate in four days. Rel, Deria, Mirek, Gwynne, and sub-commander Lynn will accompany me. The rest will be split among Ildred and protecting Alteria."

Olem said it so fluidly that Lynn almost didn't catch it, but gazes were already aimed in her direction—Ildred's the most heated. He shook his head but didn't move. Maybe curiosity had pinned him in his seat, or maybe he needed more information before acting.

"Sub-commander?" Lynn asked. It was probably a bad question, and one a leader shouldn't ask in front of new subordinates, but the surprise had mounted into words before she could hold them back.

"I wasn't asked when I was appointed either," Olem said. "Get ready."

A few of the Sentinels stirred, and Ildred rose and stalked out. Lynn knew she hadn't seen the end of this from him, but sometimes anger is too hot for words. She had a mounting anger of her own. She'd promised herself that she'd stop running, but being thrust into this new role without being asked had her gritting her teeth. Perhaps Olem had already known what her answer would be.

You're going to fail again, Roki said, laughing as usual.

Lynn tried to refocus on the attack at hand. "They still have the Madness, Olem. We can't jump in without a cure."

"They're giving us a window. We know about their weapons now and can avoid them. We're still Sentinels, Sub-commander. We can take them."

Lynn shook her head, but there was little she could do now. The Sentinels seemed to have taken Olem's answer as the end of the meeting and were already exiting the hall. Beside her, Rel had that slight grin poking through his beard. The knowing one that he always had after a victory.

"Don't," Lynn said.

Rel remained silent, but the grin said it all.

Lynn got up. There were still the True to deal with. The enemy was advancing from outside their borders, but Syvern was already working within their walls. She'd need Rel's help. She knew she could trust him, but he would be riding out with her. She couldn't press Ferrin, but at least the new title would give her some sway over the other Sentinels to take him up as ward.

She looked around at those who remained. Ildred had already left, but he wouldn't have been an option anyway. Brehnna was talking closely to Deria in a corner. Brehnna was the one who'd crept up behind her and put a knife to Lynn's throat only weeks ago. Lynn had thought she'd back Ildred, but she'd stayed out of it after Lynn had taken down the airship.

Lynn couldn't walk up to her now, but she'd find time before flying out. They still had a few days, and she needed to be prepared if Ferrin came around.

Lynn waited on Ferrin for two days, but there was no sign of him. She'd caught glimpses, but he was present only where necessary, and then retreated to his rooms. She was already considering alternatives. Perhaps Rel had someone he could trust to infiltrate the True. Lynn hadn't talked to Reznik; maybe one of his bishops could be an option, but it was impossible to be sure. The Pontiff had directed Lynn to one of the bishops, though. He suspected another priest was preaching for the True within Alteria. It would be the perfect opportunity for Ferrin to join the congregation and find a way into the True. If he ever talked to Lynn again, that is. She would have to go herself otherwise, and it wouldn't be an infiltration. Maybe this new traitor would have more information than the last.

Lynn stepped into the main hall of the barracks and breathed in the warm scent of meat and spices coming from the mess hall. She had to look twice to believe it was Ferrin standing in her path.

"I'll do it," he said. His tone didn't carry forgiveness. It was closer to obligation, and perhaps a desire for revenge. Lynn could only hope it was directed at Dakhra.

"You're sure?" She needed Ferrin and didn't expect him to be unburdened by doubt. But he couldn't be crippled by it. That would cost him his life.

"I'm not coming to you as a friend," he said, "but I'll do it."

Lynn nodded. At least he understood they needed to fight Dakhra.

"What do you need?" he asked.

Lynn regarded Ferrin for a moment. His gaze was pained, but

he tried to shroud it with a curtain of determination that seemed to fill him from head to toe.

Lynn jerked her head. "Come with me."

It was enough to bring Alren's voice creeping from the darkness. *You'd better not get him killed, coward.*

They walked past the training yard, picking up dull sparring blades on the way. They stopped in a small area behind the barracks, surrounded by tents. It wasn't uncommon for generals or captains to spar with their troops, and this wouldn't be a constant enough thing to spark suspicion.

Lynn leaned close to Ferrin. "Olem has named me sub-commander."

Ferrin nodded, as if this was to be expected. Or maybe he was past the point of caring.

"I've asked Brehnna to take you on as her ward. You will be trained to hold your own on the battlefield like no other soldier."

Ferrin's gaze flicked skyward to where Vedyr circled above, but Lynn shook her head. "You aren't being trained to become a Sentinel; I'm just giving you the tools you need so you don't have to depend on me." She was glad she could give him that. "You will learn to fight better than anyone you know, and you will be fearsome in your own right. But Sentinels are not made through weapons mastery alone."

Ferrin's gaze drifted back to the path ahead as he walked beside Lynn.

"There is a faction working for Dakhra within the Church," Lynn said. "They call themselves the True. They twist the scriptures, preach a new future, then offer the Madness as a means to reach it. The Pontiff is aware, as is High Bishop Reznik, but we cannot trust anyone else with this."

Ferrin gave her a slow nod, and Lynn lowered her voice even more. "I'm serious, Ferrin. Tell no one, not even Brehnna. I've made sure a few Sentinels know you are Alren's brother. The news should reach the True soon enough. It'll help when you try to join them. I've been informed of a priest who might be recruiting more people into the True."

She couldn't tell if Ferrin was offended, but he nodded. "You need me because I lost my family to the Church," he said. "Because I have every reason to be angry and betray them."

"Yes." Lynn wouldn't keep secrets from him anymore.

"And what if I am?"

"Then I guess I'll need to place the same faith in you that you did in me."

Ferrin might have scoffed slightly; Lynn couldn't be sure. "You're the one to train me, then?" he asked.

"Only this time. Brehnna will pick up from here. She's assured me she'll do all she can to whip you into shape."

They stopped before an open space.

"I've learned some things in the Legion," Ferrin said.

"It isn't nearly enough." Lynn threw him a practice blade. "Attack me."

Ferrin frowned. "Where's your weapon?"

"I don't need one. Attack me."

Ferrin drew the weapon and raised it tentatively. He stepped forward, still unsure, then dashed and tried a half-hearted stab. Lynn pushed the flat of his sword to one side, then drove a fist into his gut.

Ferrin doubled over and gave her a betrayed look. His eyes almost reminded her of the look Alren gave her before she swung the blade that took his life.

"If *that* is what the Legion is teaching you, we're all doomed," Lynn said. "You've fought the madmen. They will not hesitate. You can't either."

Ferrin rose with renewed determination. He tried an overhead strike, but Lynn jumped to the side and tagged him in the ribs with a fist. Ferrin's pride seemed to dull the pain, and he used the momentum of Lynn's blow to spin and slash at her own ribs. He'd gotten faster, and his footwork was good, but there was still much to learn. Lynn slapped the flat of his sword down and punched him in the gut again.

"Again," she said.

Ferrin might have held a glint of anger in his eyes. *Good. He'll need to learn how to use it to his advantage.* He drove his blade forward but expected Lynn's evasion. The strike was meant to show which side Lynn would step toward. He mirrored the movement, following Lynn as she stepped to her left, and aimed a punch at her jaw. It was a good move. One that would have caught a common opponent off-guard and probably taken them to the ground. But the madmen were not common.

Lynn pushed the dregs of anger she'd harbored from Alren's voice toward Vedyr and found the power of his beating wings. She used it to strengthen her muscles and move with increased speed. It was enough for her to duck Ferrin's strike and drive her fist into his gut yet again. She didn't put Vedyr's strength into the punch, though.

Coward. Alren said.

The pain in Ferrin's gaze was accompanied by incredulity now. He coughed, trying to regain his words. "You—you can't! How am I —bah! I should have expected this." He spat on the ground.

"Do you expect the madmen to hold back because you don't share their strength? Their speed? I could have hit you a lot harder than that." She offered him a hand. "Dakhra has created a disease that makes people mad in return for an advantage. It consumes them, and they accept it. That is the enemy we fight. Honor is a story told in times of peace. War is not fair."

Ferrin breathed hard a few times, then took Lynn's hand. His grip tightened on her forearm and he tried to pull her down, but Lynn used Vedyr's strength to stay on her feet and flip Ferrin over her head. To his credit, he didn't scream. He flew over her and fell on his back with a loud grunt that sent the air out of him.

"That's better," Lynn said. "At least you're listening."

Ferrin lay on his back, groaning. "You'll get used to the speed. It'll hurt, but it will show you your limits and, if you're smart, you'll learn how to stand your ground with the tools you have."

Ferrin rolled sideways and slowly got to his feet.

"Shed your pride," Lynn said. "It'll only weigh you down."

Ferrin retook his stance.

"Good. Again."

CHAPTER NINETEEN

Darkness sharpens cruel knives.

— Yltigg clan saying

The wood-and-rope ladder was waiting when Nasha awoke the next day—as were the Yltigg guards when she climbed out of the pit onto a narrow shelf that jutted out of the peak. The view looked over a tall, round arena on a shelf of its own. A mixture of stone and wood supported the stands, which rose in circular levels. Even from here, Nasha could still remember the sensation of fighting in the arena. The shouting Yltigg and their emotions. Would she survive it again? She didn't like her chances this time. This was an execution, not a proving.

The path down hugged the peak to the left and ended sharply to the right, but the wind didn't care. It ran up and down the trail, screaming past the half-dozen Yltigg who stood a few strides behind the speaker. Nasha took a moment to gain her bearings, squinting in the morning sunlight. The sun was still too weak to replenish the heat being snatched away by the angry wind. She shivered, but not from the cold.

"You've considered?" the speaker asked.

Nasha eyed him, then strode past toward the guards. She'd get Shai out of this, but she wouldn't let this man deliver her into Zala's hands. She froze when she saw the man at the edge of the group, holding up manacles. They were made of stone with pulsing blue veins. Ancestor-stone.

The speaker stepped up beside her. "Is there a problem, Warden?"

"You'll have one if you put that on me." It wasn't resistance, and Nasha didn't say it like a threat. She hadn't touched ancestor-stone even since her newfound grasp on her curse. There was no knowing what it would do with her.

"There is a certain order that must be upheld," the speaker said. "We cannot break the chain of command, I'm afraid." He gestured toward a nook lower down on the path that descended the peak. Roho waited for them inside, shielded from the wind.

Even from a distance, Nasha thought she could see his glare. She drew close to the speaker and lowered her voice. "I can't control it. I can't touch the stone."

The man's veil shifted in what could have meant a smile beneath. She hadn't confirmed suspicions of her curse, but it was clear he'd known. He wouldn't have made his offer the previous night otherwise. "So there is power in you," he said.

"Enough to kill everyone here if that stone touches my skin." She wouldn't have minded it, but Shai was bound only a few strides away, and she wouldn't risk the girl. Not again.

"There are moments when we must trust the Earth," the speaker said in his whispery voice, and beckoned to the guard with the manacles.

The guard stopped before Nasha. Two more stood at his side, ready to act if she resisted. Nasha watched them for a moment, but anything she thought to do would mean delving into her curse, stepping closer to Zala again—and she wasn't ready to gamble on that. It was probably what the speaker wanted, some kind of test, to push her toward accepting his offer. She was sure the darkness that was living inside her was Zala's, but was the same darkness held in the stone? She extended her senses toward it. Gently.

She was slammed with a mass of unrecognizable emotion that made her step back. She sucked in a breath, almost a gasp, closing herself off and trying to recompose her mind. The emotions lingered within her, but what she felt held none of Zala's darkness. Perhaps she'd become strong enough to control the touch of ancestor-stone. Perhaps this was the gamble she'd have to take. The other option would be attempting an escape. That would be taxing, and she knew she wouldn't manage without her curse, without toeing the line that led to the dead goddess. She put out her arms.

The man placed the manacles around Nasha's wrists and fastened each with a rounded length of metal that was hammered to bolt them shut. The impact jolted Nasha, rippling through her, and it didn't fade. Whatever the ancestor-stone manacles held, it was fast. It rushed furiously up her arm, sinking into her and moving like ice in her veins, cold down to the bone.

Nasha's fingers curled into fists, and she peered down at the manacles through burning eyes. An explosion of colors bled from the ancestor stone, writhing like snakes fighting to slither up her skin. Part of her mind tried to hold on to what she knew of herself —the awakened part that she'd found after the Proving. But it was losing ground. Nasha gritted her teeth and strained against the fear telling her to run, the anger telling her to fight, the unbound joy telling her to laugh, the grief telling her to break down where she stood. They all danced under her flesh, intermittent and tireless. She tried to take hold of them, but she couldn't focus, couldn't grasp at anything, and the harder she tried, the more that sensation grew at the back of her mind. Heavy, creeping up from the abyss within her like a thick mist that whispered through her skull. *Give in. Let me out.*

Her muscles began to shake, but the guards were already pulling her along, as if her display were some kind of attempt at escape. Nasha's feet scraped along the dusty path as she was led down. The shaking intensified. She held on as much as she ever had, but her control still wasn't enough. The anger broke through. Bastards.

Bastards. After all she'd done, they'd traded her away like an animal. The anger swirled up her throat and threatened to come out as a roar.

And then it was silenced.

She was still strained, but something had syphoned the boiling anger out of her. Nasha looked to the speaker, who wove some kind of sign in the air as he whispered through his veil. The veins in his ancestor-stone beads pulsed, almost in unison with the ones on her manacles, but as they did, the glow from the manacles slowly receded, as if whatever was in the ancestor-stone was being spent.

The speaker was helping her. Not like the anchors she'd used in the past so the emotions wouldn't sweep her away. The man, or more likely his veil, was sharing the load so the emotions wouldn't pull Nasha's consciousness down into the abyss where it was kept when the curse took hold. It was enough for her to carry on, but still not enough to trust him. She dragged her feet with her head bowed, swaying slightly and mindful of the sheer drop to her right.

She didn't look up at Shai, but the veil had given her enough to hold on to. She recognized Shai's shots of surprise as Nasha was pulled past with pulsing ancestor-stone bonds around her wrists. Shai was bound with ancestor-stone as well, and the surprise was colored with a tinge of disappointment. It seemed that even those who relied on Nasha saw her at least partly as the monster. Maybe Shai had hoped they'd use Nasha's curse to escape.

They paused before Roho, who glared at Nasha and then took the fore, leading the group down the path to the much wider shelf where the Yltigg arena sat. The march reminded Nasha of her trial with the Ronar, before she became warden. There were no curious eyes here, though. No Slopers hoping for support, or even angry clansfolk. The path was empty save for their group, but Nasha knew that chaos awaited in the arena.

She looked toward Shai on her left, then the speaker on her right, but both were silent. Stragglers populated the path ahead, and a rising din of voices set Nasha's heart beating faster. They stopped before the arena entrance, and the sensations streamed toward her like hungry tendrils eager to wrap themselves around her heart.

Impatience, anticipation, even joy. The ancestor-stone had become bearable, almost dulled, but now the emotions found the manacles around Nasha's wrists and dug through them—the stone acting as a window that buried them under Nasha's skin. She was past the prickling and blurring of her vision. Her eyes burned and her ears had begun to ring. The speaker's veil had been enough to hold off the effects of the ancestor-stone, but the torrent from the arena would eventually overwhelm her. The signs had already escalated. It wouldn't be long before her mind was pulled from her grasp. Would Zala be the one to take it?

She stepped under the gate and through a shadowed path under the stands, feet pounding above her. She stopped at the edge of the arena. Emotions streamed over the stone and wood construction, colors flooding the dry arena ground and ascending steps of shouting Yltigg.

Roho paused for a moment as the chief addressed the crowd. Nasha couldn't make out the words. Her focus was on keeping her mind to herself against the eagerness of the shouting Yltigg trying to wrangle it from her.

Shai touched Nasha's arm, and something shot through. A warmness that tried to override the whirl of excitement from the crowd. It was a soft hope, but it was familiar; something to hold on to as she was pushed into the arena on trembling legs. Nasha clung to the hope, and the pressure around her wrists eased a touch. It was as if the emotion within the ancestor-stone was being spent, and the growing emptiness of the stone fueled the shred of hope she'd taken from Shai.

The crowd roared as if Nasha and Shai were heroes come to save them. They weren't loved, but their end would be the same as most heroes. Dead in service to the clans.

The clamor was different from the Proving. These spectators expected death, but there was no doubt about which side would prevail. Her whole body was strained and shaking, and Nasha almost called out to the speaker for help, almost gave in to his offer. But even as she thought it, the darkness within her reared its head, grating against the hope Nasha clung to. It promised power, freedom, a chance to be a champion. But would she be a champion to the Earth—or to Zala, defiling all around her in exchange for the promise of power? Nasha bit down out of habit, perhaps expecting a peel of citrus to focus her senses, but there was nothing but the building hope and the veil to keep her grounded.

She looked to the top edge of the arena, the place where she'd gone over the side and fallen into the river after the Proving. There was no clear path of escape this time—the wood and stone steps seemed even more packed than before. Her gaze slid involuntarily to the speaker, but she forced it back down as she was placed on her knees beside Shai.

The Yltigg chief stood before them, holding two obsidian blades. It wasn't customary for the Yltigg to use obsidian; they didn't live on a mountain covered in it, as the Ronar did. Perhaps it was just part of the message to appease the crowd.

"Yltigg!" The arena quieted at the chief's call. "We bring you a promise today. A promise that has taken too long to be delivered."

Cheers rose at that, and Nasha bit down again, searching for Shai and letting out a muffled cry of pain herself. The ancestor-stone had emptied now, but the hope she'd allowed herself was joined by amplified emotion, channeled through her manacles. The stones picked up all that was thrown at Nasha and empowered it in a scorching stream of sensation. Her ears rang, her eyes burned and her vision began to grow white: her body's signs that the curse was escalating. She needed a way out. Now.

"The Ronar have betrayed us," the chief continued. "They have betrayed the peace of the clans, and Zala has taken notice. In our conflict, She has risen, and She seeks to spread Her touch among us. Fear not, however! We have made amends."

Nasha looked around. Swirls of color bled from the people, amplified in her brightening vision: orange streams of anticipation, angry red and a purple loathing. All were sucked into the ancestor-stone, running through Nasha and weighing her consciousness down, opening her up to the darkness within. It came in the form of a threatening rage, mindless and starved for emotion. It promised to take hold of Nasha and use her like Zala's puppet. She knew she couldn't avoid the curse entirely, but perhaps Shai's hope in her would be enough of a shield against Zala's hunger.

The chief was circling Shai and Nasha now, while still addressing the crowd. "No pain is greater than the loss of a son, of a brother. But we will repay that sacrifice with another. The Ronar have sent us their warden and her remaining initiate!"

Another roar rose from the crowd, and Nasha gritted her teeth as the ringing in her ears tried to drown it out. She was going to break. She was going to kill them all, even Shai.

"We will return these lives to the Earth. We will feed Zala the traitors who upset the balance of the clans, and we will make the Earth whole again!"

The chief slit his hand and walked in a wide circle, letting his blood fall to the ground. This was not a pact for peace, like the one he'd struck with Tomu before the Proving. He was tracing the symbol of unity. The one Jabillo had convinced the Ronar to paint on their flag of truce before Nasha rode towards the encampment with Leku.

Her whole body trembled in agony, every cry from the crowd a knife beneath her skin. She tried to stifle a cry, but it escaped loud enough for the chief to hear.

"Zala comes for Her blood!" He was done with the sign and raised the long obsidian blade. It gleamed in the sun as he looked down at Nasha. There was a certain relief to his gaze. Not only his gaze; relief oozed from him like a scent, ridden with a sour tinge of the grief for his lost son. It flowed through the ancestor-stone around Nasha's wrists, taking control until it made her almost glad it would soon be over. Her struggle, her pain.

Nasha closed her eyes, almost inviting the bite of the chief's blade. She'd said she'd get out of this. She'd always gotten out of it. But was this a hill too high to climb? Shai was shouting at her, the hope still wrapped around her words. "Nasha! If you're going to do something . . ."

The way the words hit her sparked something. They didn't shoot through like Shai's emotions usually did. They flowed. Shai's hope was pulled in by the ancestor-stone, empowered—and it renewed Nasha's own. The manacles reacted, their glow lighting up again.

It started slowly but soon crashed through. Nasha screamed as the burning intensified. She pulled it all in and let the emotions trample over each other: breathtaking exhilaration, trembling fear, searing anger, unyielding expectation, all rushing to take hold of her. But the hope kept her mind clear and the darkness at bay: a tether, like Mansa had tried with the anchors. A pulsing that came from the ancestor-stone, strong and constant. Her warning signs receded, as if the clarity of hope gave Nasha a new grip on her consciousness.

She shot to her feet, consuming the gathered emotions like she'd done in the past. Transforming them into strength. It was enough strength for her to pull her arms away and break the stone links of her manacles, still keeping the ancestor-stone bands around her wrists. As she used the strength, though, her heart faltered, as if the hope tethering her gave ground to Zala's darkness.

The Yltigg chief took a step back. The crowd's cheering became silence and gasps. The guards started toward her.

The silence was broken by a growl, followed by screams from the stands. People moved away, clearing a wide arc around a spot where one of the Yltigg spectators twisted and writhed. The same dark mist Nasha had seen on the other tainted man oozed out of him. It spoke to the darkness inside her, struggling to break through the barrier Nasha had created out of Shai's hope. Now her hope too.

The man stopped moving suddenly, then raised his head. His gaze fell on the arena, and he jumped in. He went for one of the guards, slashing long claws at his legs to bring the man down. Then he pounced on him, slashing his neck open with rabid ferocity. The tainted moved with blinding speed, arms rending the man beneath him with unnatural swiftness.

Nasha took a step back. The arena entrance was still blocked by Yltigg. Shai was scrambling away as well, half trying to get to her feet, half taken by desperation. Yltigg guards had closed in behind them, spears pointed at Nasha and Shai. Nasha's gaze moved wildly between them and the tainted man. There was a blackness around his eyes, and angry dark veins spread across his face. He locked gazes with her, and even from here, Nasha could see his frenzied gaze settling on her. He'd picked his next prey.

The frustration rose in her as a yell. All she wanted was to fight off these Yltigg, take Shai, and make a run for it. But she couldn't do that. Not with their numbers and this tainted man on her heels. Nasha charged at the tainted.

She sucked in the emotions to match his speed. The hope still tethered her, but the darkness was growing deeper, as if she were sinking into an ocean. Too deep and she wouldn't be able to break back over the surface. Fear rose up, but she used the spike it gave her to power her legs forward. She rushed at the man, the world slowing around her, no weapon other than bare hands and the strength she drew from the burning emotions.

She met the man with a fist to the chin, sending him flying back into the surrounding arena wall. It cracked behind him, splintering wood and chipping stone. Nasha didn't give him time to recover. She pulled on the lingering exhilaration from the crowd now as she rushed up and pummeled the earth-spawn into the wall. Face, torso, face. She punched as if he were the darkness within her given form, and she was driving it away. She would not become one of these tainted. She would not be Zala's champion.

A shroud fell over her mind, throwing her into a haze. A strange sensation, as if part of her was becoming hollow, parts of her that she'd always known: her memories, her name, all slowly drifting out of reach. Something else was trying to replace it—anger riddled with grief. It didn't come from the arena, but from within. Zala's darkness, trying to take hold. Nasha had been given enough signs from her curse to know what that meant. No matter the tether, she couldn't use her curse for long. Eventually, she would break.

Nasha let go of the power and stepped back. The man slid to the ground. He didn't move, but a weak breath still puffed from his lips. She remained vigilant, waiting for him to rise, but his breath faltered, and the blackness that had surrounded the skin of his eyes faded as he breathed out his last scrap of life.

There were too many questions surrounding Nasha, and none that she could answer now. Her mind told her to escape, but the Yltigg weren't moving on her. She immediately searched for Shai, reminded of the Yltigg warden who'd held Devu hostage in the Proving.

There was no blade at the girl's neck. The speaker stood beside the chief, leaning close to talk through the veil. Nasha's attention was pulled by the dying Yltigg guard. He was coughing up blood, but none of the others seemed intent on approaching. Perhaps meddling with the tainted had taught them that the illness was contagious.

The chief walked toward her with Roho in tow, and Nasha instinctively searched for whatever emotion still lingered. It had been dulled, shock and doubt taking over. Nasha was ready, but her shrouded consciousness kept her from reaching for the emotion. She breathed in and out, in and out. Slowly, the darkness receded, but it took her strength with it. She struggled to keep herself from swaying. The enhanced power from the ancestor-stone had given her more strength but also taken more of her away.

The chief paused before her, blade lowered. "It seems you have proven your life more valuable than your blood."

Nasha looked down at the tainted dead man, then back at the chief. Maybe it was fear that had kept her from accepting the speaker's offer, but Shai's hope had shown her that the darkness could be held at bay. Perhaps she could use her curse to fight it. Zala would not stop; She was coming and so was the Domain. Nasha didn't need a clan, but she was part of this battle. The clanlands couldn't be lost to either enemy. "Whatever you want from me," she said, her breath still heavy, "I'm doing it on my terms."

The chief nodded. "Follow me."

Roho had an incredulous look about him, but it seemed he knew better than to challenge the chief before the whole Yltigg clan. The stands had become near-silent, nothing but whispered words and weak sensations bleeding into the arena.

Nasha considered Ardin for a moment, then nodded toward the dying Yltigg guard. "You should burn him before he turns." The words came with an effort, but Shai was already beside her, helping Nasha stand straight as her body threatened to waver again.

The chief nodded and made for the arena entrance, commanding a guard before moving on. Nasha followed, with Shai helping her.

Everyone's monster is someone else's hero. Had she become that? Nasha balked at the notion. "Hero" was just another label from the tales, used by those in power to blind the people below. Same as warden.

If she had become a hero to the Yltigg, there was no cheering for it, but as she followed the chief from the arena, there were no protests either.

CHAPTER TWENTY

Griffin eggs have rarely been found in the wild. Griffins live for countless years, and the eggs conceived within the Sentinel order are similarly longevous, taking hundreds of years to hatch. One wonders if the process is natural or meant to be induced.

— The Study and History of Griffins, by Ander W. Demerith

Lynn had left Ferrin with Brehnna. She couldn't stay too close to him now without prompting suspicion. She told him which church to go to and trusted that his experience in the Legion and added training would be enough to protect him should things go awry. The Sentinels would fly off tomorrow, and Lynn wouldn't be here to watch over him. There was a final task before facing Dakhra, though, and every step up the barracks stairs sent a flutter of hope through Lynn's chest.

She'd left Rel to his own designs as he tried to come up with something similar to what Reznik had used in her Questioning. The Pontiff had told her the secrets of the Bone were to be kept with the

Bishops, but perhaps Rel could find something in the stone to help the Sentinels and their Bond. Perhaps they'd find a way to resist, if not cure, the Madness.

Rel pored over every book he could find, but the frown creasing his brow as Lynn walked in did not speak to much success. He sat at a rough wooden table, vials to one side, an open book to the other. Something had been burning, and there was the smell of something else, more acrid. Rel didn't look up.

"You've found something?" Lynn asked.

"Not sure."

"What do you mean?"

"You're the one who's going to tell me if you can use this." He held out a piece of ruin-stone.

Lynn turned it around in her hands. It didn't seem any different. "What did you do with it?"

"I brewed up something I found in the archives. Some Dakhran says it helped smooth the polishing process. All I did was make the concoction stronger."

Lynn kept turning the stone in her hand.

"I haven't polished it, just let it sit in the mixture long enough to see if anything is absorbed. Then I overloaded it."

"With anger?"

"And a bit of my frustration." Rel stood. "From what you told me, the burning when the stone touched your skin, the feeling you'd hollow out . . . it's as if the bishop bonded himself to you, like we do to the griffins."

"To me? That's impossible, Rel; my bond to Vedyr comes from the ruin-stone in our hearts. There aren't any more pieces of that stone. Reznik doesn't even know anger is the emotion I use with Vedyr."

"He's the master of secrets, Lynn. He could have found out. The Bond is only the first step, though. How he manipulates it is what you'll need to figure out. There was more you mentioned—the colors surrounding people like an aura? I couldn't find anything on those." He looked at her with a determined glint in his eye. "You can practice on me."

"No. You're the one who's been researching—"

"I'm not as strong as you, Lynn. Just be quick about it."

Lynn looked at the ruin-stone. "Rel, I don't even know how."

"Go on, we don't have time."

Lynn looked at him for a long moment, then twisted her mouth. "Sit down, then."

Rel sat and Lynn eyed the ruin-stone.

"Whatever you take from it," Rel said. "Don't push it toward Vedyr. Push it toward me."

Lynn nodded and grabbed the stone. She pressed her fingers slightly around it, then opened herself like she did with Vedyr. The flood was immediate. Almost too much. It burned through her like it had when Reznik was questioning her, starting at that same spot in her ribs, a feeling like she'd been bludgeoned. The instinct to direct it to Vedyr was strong, but Lynn couldn't imagine the torrent that she'd receive in return. She'd be hollowed out in an instant.

Focus.

The emotions in her were overflowing, threatening to take control of her consciousness. There was so much, it almost seemed like she could feel an emotion coming from outside her, maybe a touch of apprehension from Rel. It made her heart beat faster. She stretched an arm out to Rel, trembling with the effort, and touched the stone to his skin. His scream only lasted a moment before she was engulfed by her past.

She was in Gheria again. The same Vizcarran city she'd raided to track down Alren, Roki, Cara, and Dentos. The spear she'd hurled through the woman's chest in her vision with Reznik was still there, pinning the woman to the ground while a dark-skinned girl and another woman ran. The girl's eyes held a fear that seemed to bleed out of her in waves of dark green. Lynn regarded the girl like a predator might regard prey. There was no remorse in her heart, only the drive to cleanse the city. She picked up another spear, threw back her dirty-blond hair and looked sideways to Rel, expecting the shard of ruin-stone he always kept ready for her. His expression gave her pause, though. His eyes were focused, but his face showed flashes of something else. Pain, maybe. Lynn stepped toward him, half knowing it was a vision, but concerned all the same. She reached out a hand, and the vision was breached.

Gheria was pulled away, and she was suddenly standing on copper-shaded sand, below a roof held up by reddish sandstone. The image flashed and shifted into the dungeon she'd seen in her Questioning. Two silhouettes stood before her, but their shapes were blurred. There might have been the sound of a gear turning, but it was soon silenced, and Lynn was back in the chamber standing on reddish sand.

It was dark, and there was a small boy on his knees, weeping. Something was wrong with this darkness, unnatural. Lynn traced it to a dark aura pouring out of the boy. It moved along the ground like a fog. The boy looked at Lynn with nothing but rage, and the black started to turn red. "I'll kill you!" the boy yelled in Azuri. He rushed at her, and the red and black that was seeping from him coalesced into vines and shot at Lynn. She raised an arm, and the boy's vines wrapped around it. She could feel his rage and sorrow through the vines. It was so strong she couldn't move. The boy raised a knife—

"Lynn!" Deria was holding her arm and Rel was slumped in the chair, breathing heavily. "What in the Seraph's name are you doing?"

Lynn was breathing heavily too, almost as heavy as during the Questioning.

"We need to . . . do something," Rel said thorough gasps.

Deria looked at the ruin-stone in Lynn's hand, and then at the two of them. "Are you insane? What if it kills you?"

Deria strode to the window and pulled the curtains closed, as if someone might be watching. "Does Olem know?"

Lynn shook her head, already expecting more outrage, but Deria had always been too cautious to get things done. "He doesn't know, and we'll keep it that way." She was careful not to make it sound like a threat. Lynn had seen the way Deria looked at her after the battle in Durnn, and she hated it. It was like the gazes she received back in the prison at Sacantha: full of hope and awe.

At least you know you don't deserve it, Alren said.

"We will tell him when we're ready," Rel said. "For now, we stand on faith."

Lynn nodded. This was why Rel would have been a good choice as commander. He probably knew Deria had always leaned toward caution, but he also remembered that her faith was never among the strongest. Playing on it now was the perfect way to convince her.

Deria's gaze flitted between them for longer than Lynn would have liked. "If anything happens to either of you," Deria finally said, "I never saw this."

She left, and Rel stepped close to Lynn. "I thought I said not too long."

"I'm sorry, I had no control."

"Did it work?"

"I'm not sure what I saw, but I felt . . . I'm sorry, Rel. I wasn't supposed to see that. I'm sorry you lost—"

"Our past lives have been left behind for a reason, Lynn." He pulled out another chunk of ruin-stone. "Our pain defines who we are. It isn't comfortable, but it reminds you of what you need to hold on to. And to savor the good moments more often."

Lynn cocked her head. "Of all the things I missed when I left, being around you was at the top of the list."

Rel chuckled and tossed her the chunk of ruin-stone. "We should get ready to fly out."

Ildred flew out with a score of Sentinels and enough ground troops to pull away a large portion of the airships that guarded the Skygate. Gwynne had scouted ahead and reported three airships remaining. The Sentinels would have to split up into pairs, each targeting one airship. Rel and Lynn flew close to Olem and the others among the clouds. They'd fly higher than the airships and try to come down on them from above. The cloud cover would give them a moment's advantage. If they could take the ships down fast enough, it would give them time to close the Skygate before the Dakhran ship could get through.

Even through the clouds, the enormity of the gate was impossible to miss. The Skygate was built entirely of ruin-stone, from the ground to the peaks of the mountains forming the pass it blocked. Slab after slab of white-veined stone had been piled up to form what were essentially two doors with countless gears and massive internal mechanisms to operate the smaller slabs that opened at bottom and top. It had taken years to build, but that was King Iridan's demand of the Church before bringing Dakhra into the Domain. Lynn couldn't imagine how it was built. The Dakhrans were the ones known for their engineering, something they loved to flaunt with their airships—but it seemed the other Domain nations could perform similar feats when acting in concert.

The Skygate had held back any thought of invasion for a reason. The Dakhran vessels looked almost like a common ship that sailed on water, but there was no mast or sails. Their flight was powered by a core of ruin-stone. Even that had its limitations, though, and it did not give the ships enough power to fly over the gate. There was no getting the airships through the mountains that surrounded Dakhra, either—they were too tall, and the winds too treacherous. Even the most experienced Dakhran captains avoided that route. Trying to send an entire fleet through would be madness. The Dakhrans could try going over the Ulean Sea to the north, but that would mean they had to transport their troops on airships or by sea. The lack of ground troops to support the airships, and the threat of Sentinels bringing them down, had always been enough to hold Dakhra back. But Lynn wasn't sure of anything anymore. Still, she had to trust that closing the Skygate would be enough.

They broke off into three groups: Rel and Lynn, Mirek flying beside Gwynne, and Deria with Olem. He'd picked this unit well at least; Mirek and Rel were Channelers like himself and would make sure the Syphoners never ran out of ruin-stone.

The Dakhrans had been smart enough to come in daylight, and the clouds the Sentinels relied on for cover thinned as they drew near. The airships were on the Sacanthan side of the gate, and there was movement on their decks. Shadows scrambled across the decks and warning horns blared. They'd been spotted.

The ships differed from those that had invaded Durnn. They had more ballistae: one at the prow, one at the stern, and two more mounted along the sides. They had more men as well; a crew of about fifty that seemed ready, as if expecting an attack. And the gleam of sunlight on their arrows reflected off more than just steel.

"Brewer arrows!" Lynn shouted. She'd seen the explosive arrows in the past. Rel broke away toward the prow and Lynn flew upward, but the Dakhrans were already firing.

The initial volley seemed to be a decoy, though. The arrows quickly lost altitude and exploded in a wall of flame. Then a second volley was released, shot by bowmen with longer bows and aimed much higher, above Lynn's head. The arrows had nothing attached to their shafts, but a streak of reddish-orange liquid streamed behind them.

Lynn drew in a sharp breath at the sight. She'd be showered in the Madness if she didn't pick up speed.

She gripped a ruin-stone shard and pulled on the anger. It seared through her as she directed Vedyr up in a straight line. She gave him the anger, and each beat of his wings pummeled the air more powerfully. He flew up. Higher and higher, the wind howling past them, the shouting of issued commands growing more distant. Lynn put her head down and tugged on Vedyr just as an arrow cut through the air toward them. He changed his path, moving forward instead of up, avoiding the arrow and the potion shower at the last moment.

Lynn's heart thumped in concert with Vedyr's beating wings, and the smell of the explosion still lingered on the wind. She was directly over the airship now and pivoted Vedyr straight down toward the ship. Part of her wanted to search out Rel and the other Sentinels, but the continued shrieks and screams told her Dakhra's initial attempts to end the battle had failed. The Sentinels were engaged.

She glimpsed Rel below, but her focus was on the ballista trained up at her. The bolt was launched, but as Lynn pulled Vedyr sideways to evade it, a second volley of brewer's arrows flew, exploding to form a curtain of fire between Lynn and the ship.

Lynn didn't have to issue the command; Vedyr had understood her through the Bond. She dug up her rage for the invaders and directed it to him. Her eyes burned, and her muscles pulsed with his power. She stood on his back and launched off, arcing to one side of the explosion, while Vedyr cut to the other, both still heading down at the airship. They reached it together. Vedyr came down close to the prow with wings spread and claws that sank into a Dakhran soldier, then ripped through men whose yells of battle quickly became cries of pain. Lynn landed close to the stern with enough force to break the wood underneath her and send another handful of enemies screaming off the side with the impact.

The archers went for the swords at their hips, but Lynn already had her war-scythe and mace out. She slammed the mace across a soldier's chest, sending him flying into another with enough force to propel both into more archers behind. The enemy's numbers didn't dwindle, though, and Lynn was quickly surrounded again. She pulled on Vedyr's speed, stabbing and slashing at the enemies. Mace to the ribs, scythe through the chest, pull back, slash at a neck then pummel a face—all through grunts and screams, both hers and the enemy's. The movements came to her with little thought, and her opponents were slow, not taken by the Madness. She kept cutting like a sharp wind until she reached the end of the line, bringing the last man down with a stab to the gut.

Knowing Dakhra had soldiers who submitted to the Madness by choice almost dulled the bitter taste of death on her tongue. But it was still death. She'd never be comfortable with it.

Lynn looked down at the man she'd just taken down and pulled the war-scythe from his gut, but as she looked up, a dozen more archers were trained on her. They stood fifteen yards away, far enough to fire before she could reach them. Vedyr was at the prow. He slashed, sending another score flying, and used his beak to ravage those brave enough to stand before him. He leapt, beat his wings once to buffet the enemy below, then fell on them with beak and claw.

The men before Lynn didn't move, and even if she wanted to call Vedyr off, he wouldn't reach her in time. She pulled on his strength, preparing to leap over the inevitable volley, but before the archers could fire, the hull beside them burst into splinters as Rel and Ulenia rammed into it and pulled up, ripping a hole in the ship's side and taking out part of the deck. Some of the arrows were loosed, but they were off target and hit the ship, exploding and setting the wood aflame.

Vedyr sent the remaining enemies on the prow flying off the side or opened them with his claws. The smell of death flowed through Lynn, and her skin prickled with the numbness of it, but the battle wasn't over. The brief pause sent her mind teetering. She'd been using the Bond for too long.

Alren, Roki, Cara, Dentos. She could still remember them. Her mind was whole. She dug out a shard of ruin-stone and pulled on the anger inside. It fueled her Bond, but she could already feel the pressure in her head.

Maybe half a dozen enemies were left on deck, and they were growling at Lynn with bleeding hands, sharp claws and the Madness blackening the skin around their eyes. Two advanced on her with a speed that matched her own. The first one swiped diagonally at her shoulder, but she batted the claw away with her mace while pulling stronger on Vedyr's speed, then ducked the next man's horizontal strike. She rose with a swift slash of her scythe that cut his arm off. The one she'd batted away lunged at her, but Lynn pushed the armless madman into his path and then rolled away, letting the pouncing man's claws dig into the armless one's back.

There was a crash beside her as Ulenia landed with Rel on her back, stomping three madmen. Ulenia's claws rose and fell with vicious speed, piercing those she'd landed on. Rel jumped off and engaged with one of the remaining women, while the one who'd sunk his claws into his companion's back rushed at Lynn again. He seemed even faster than the others now, like he had something deeper burning inside of him. The way he ran suggested a sliver of consciousness, as if the attack was more controlled than what Lynn had seen from other madmen. He broke mid-rush, lowering his body and attacking Lynn with an upward slash. Lynn shifted one foot back, but the man had tremendous speed and his claws ripped a shred from her cloak and dug grooves in the side of her Sentinel Mantle.

The strike laced Lynn with a coldness she rarely experienced in battle. She'd taken her fair share of wounds, but even a scratch could infect her with the Madness.

Roki was laughing in her mind. *You are weak.*

Coward!

The voices did it. They made the fear running cold in her veins boil into anger. She pulled even more on Vedyr, feeling the strain on her mind as pieces of it drifted away toward Vedyr. Whatever consciousness told her to stop was overruled by her instinct to survive. She took Vedyr's strength and used it to push off her back foot and drive her war-scythe through the madman's heart as he turned for another attack. He fell, and the Sentinels were left alone on the burning ship.

Both of the other ships had fallen as well, one of them burning as it plummeted to the ground, the other with two griffins tearing it apart, similar to how Vedyr was digging toward the ruin-stone core at the stern. Lynn pulled him off; the fire would do its job soon enough. Lynn jumped on Vedyr and urged him toward the Skygate.

Vedyr touched down on the wide stone walkway carved from the mountain to the left of the Skygate, while Rel landed Ulenia on the opposite side. The walkway on each side led to a guard room that controlled half the door. The Sentinels jumped off their griffins and rushed in.

Lynn's head pounded with every step, and even if she could draw on more power from the shards, she knew too much of it would pull at her consciousness.

The crank that closed the top gate was heavy, four times her size and not meant for a single person, but Lynn was not alone.

Alren, Roki . . . Cara, Dentos. The thoughts came slower, but Lynn still had enough in her to take Vedyr's strength and turn the mechanism.

Rel seemed to be doing the same on the other side, and both ruin-stone doors started to close. Lynn looked through the window of the guard house, toward the Dakhran side of the mountains. The shadow of a massive Dakhran airship was approaching, but the gates were already close enough to being shut. They wouldn't get through. She kept watching the airship, expecting it to turn away. But it didn't.

The shadow was growing and growing. It wasn't only four times the size of a normal Dakhran airship; there was something else about it. A sheen reflected off its hull. Not only the hull. The whole ship was encased in metal. Even the deck was closed off, with only window-like openings for the ballistae, and slits along the sides for arrows. The Dakhrans had built an entire airship out of steel. It drew nearer and nearer until it was only a few feet from the gate. It was going to ram it. Lynn frowned. She'd never seen rams break ruin-stone. She doubted an airship could do it, even one this size.

Rel was already mounting Ulenia, and the shadows of the other Sentinels flew nearby.

"Olem!" Lynn shouted before rushing out and jumping onto Vedyr.

The other Sentinels hadn't seen this new airship, but Lynn and Rel mounting their griffins was enough for them to follow. Lynn pushed Vedyr up, close to the mountain wall that blurred as they rushed up and over. Lynn crested the wall just as a latch opened on the airship's prow, and nozzles sprayed some kind of smoking liquid on the ruin-stone. It seemed to do nothing at first, but then the ruin-stone began to change. The liquid glistened and hardened. It was freezing the stone. A ram came through from the middle of the airship's prow and battered at the Skygate. It cracked.

All six sentinels converged on the ship. Lynn considered going for the prow, but the nozzle that had sprayed the freezing liquid was turned toward them as they advanced, and she had to veer away.

Deria's griffin, Nerida, rushed past Lynn, going straight for the hull. A strange pulse coming from the ship gave Lynn pause. It hit her in that spot that was becoming common now. The one in her ribs that pulsed every time she was plunged into a vision. Maybe what she'd tried with Rel had lingered, but she couldn't abandon the Sentinels now.

Deria slammed her griffin into the ship, claws first, and Lynn followed in her wake, stretching out her scythe to cut at the steel. It barely breached the surface. Whatever alloy the Dakhrans had used seemed infused with ruin-stone, almost like the metal of her blade and mantle, but that wasn't all. Something ran along Lynn's blade and up her arm, pulsing in her ribs again—like a jolt of lightning threatening to freeze her in place. Lynn pulled back her blade as if stung, but there was no time to consider as a pained screech from above pulled her gaze.

Deria was still at the spot where she'd landed, but both she and Nerida were paralyzed. Stunned in place. Nerida couldn't remove her claws, and Deria had jumped off and was straining, feet glued to the metal hull, trying to break away from whatever held her.

Lynn urged Vedyr towards them, but all she could do was watch as a latch opened beside Deria, and a nozzle similar to the one that was freezing the gate spewed a reddish liquid onto the Sentinel.

"No!" Lynn shouted, but it was drowned out by Deria's screams.

More latches opened around Nerida. Spears poked at her legs, and blades tried to reach her underside. The griffin struggled, in desperation finding the strength to break free from whatever spell the airship's hull held, but her wing was pierced by a spear as she launched off the hull. She beat it with an effort as she retreated, flying back to the Skygate, and just reaching the walkway that flanked it.

Anger boiled in Lynn's veins, and she slammed her mace against the metal plates, but each blow threatened Lynn with the same jolt as the first one. She didn't know what this was, and risking Vedyr's life was foolishness. Mirek, Olem, and Gwynne had seen Nerida and Deria frozen to the ship. None touched the airship's hull after that, and their own blows proved as futile as Lynn's.

Deria had fallen off the ship. Rel had caught her, but the woman was shaking on Ulenia's back. There was another crash. Lynn looked back at the gate and saw the ram pull back and hit another section of frozen stone. It did more than crack this time. A thick chunk of ruin-stone broke and tumbled down.

Rel pulled up beside Lynn, but he had little hope in his eyes as he looked down at Deria. "We need to pull back. The gate won't hold."

Lynn gripped the ruin-stone Rel had worked on in Alteria. "We need to save Deria." Rel didn't argue.

More steel ships appeared on the horizon. They were smaller, but if the Sentinels couldn't break through their hulls, their size would be the least of it.

Lynn turned Vedyr, guiding him over the sieged gate and into the woods around Pehd Valley.

You've failed again, Alren whispered.

Just like you failed us, Dentos said.

Lynn gritted her teeth. She would not fail.

They found a clearing and landed, quickly pulling Deria off Ulenia, who kept her silver eyes locked on them. Nerida struggled to get close, but Vedyr was holding her down. She shrieked as Deria clutched her head, screaming.

Lynn wasted no time. She pulled out the ruin-stone Rel had tinkered with, while grasping another shard of ruin-stone and funneling its anger into the first. She didn't know what emotion Deria or her griffin shared in their Bond. The anger would have to do.

Lynn pushed the ruin-stone onto the bare skin of Deria's forehead. The woman screamed again. The skin around her eyes was darkening. Lynn's world darkened too, as she was pulled into her vision. Pehd Valley was fading, the Gherian city square coming up, surrounded by houses that looked translucent among the trees.

"Hold on," Lynn said through gritted teeth. She couldn't be pulled into her own vision now; she had to connect with Deria. The woman wasn't Rel, though, and Lynn had been away for so long she had little to go on. Deria would have to help.

"Use the stone," she told Deria. "Push the taint toward it." Lynn pulled on the anger herself, but the more anger she took, the more real Gheria became around her.

Some part of Deria must have listened to Lynn, because the square that was taking the trees shifted into a gloomy church hall. A young woman stood there, reading the texts. Her body was stiff, and the colored aura Lynn had seen in her visions was streaming out of Deria as well. The aura had a dark blue tint to it, with streaks of violet, and flowed slower. Lynn took a few steps closer and touched the woman's shoulder. She turned to Lynn with tears in her eyes. The blue lines coalesced around Lynn's hand and squeezed.

Lynn's chest tightened as if she were about to cry as well, but the sadness carried an undercurrent of shame that was so strong it fueled the familiar anger Lynn was accustomed to. The woman had lost someone and was ashamed to admit the pain. The woman laughed. A desperate, broken laugh.

"Deria, push it into the stone! You can beat this, don't let it take you!"

Lynn was screaming at Deria in the vision, but the woman's younger self only laughed harder. She threw her head back, and when she set her eyes on Lynn again, they were surrounded by pools of black.

The laughing stopped and a sudden sanity seemed to grip Deria. The woman in the vision aged slightly, taking on Deria's current appearance. The blue and violet lines that had gripped Lynn slackened for a moment, and Deria nodded. Lynn recognized the request.

"No, I can—"

Deria screamed. Feral now, and the colors streaming out of her turned a deep black. Lynn stepped back, but the scream was cut short and the vision faded. Her mind fell back into herself. Deria lay bleeding on the ground, chest pierced by Rel's spear, straight through the heart.

Lynn let out her own wordless shout. There were no words to encompass the frustration of her failure. Just like she had with Rel, she'd dug into Deria's past—but couldn't find the right strings to pull. She saw the Madness taking hold but was powerless to stop it. Lynn strode toward a tree and fueled her anger into a swing that unconsciously pulled on Vedyr. It cracked the trunk and sent the tree tipping to the ground, but the blow rippled through her and set her head to pounding.

"Shit!" Lynn screamed. A renewed fire filled her gut, but she let go of the Bond.

"We need to get out of here, Lynn." Rel's tone was wavering. His gaze set on the gate. It creaked and groaned, so loud it seemed the mountain itself would fall. Lynn looked up at it. Fissures had spread along the stone. There was another crack, loud as thunder, then another. At first, nothing changed, as if the moment was held frozen in time. Then the stone began to crumble. It started with a small piece, but the cracks spread like roots. More and more stones fell, each one crashing to the ground below. A slab as large as a house met the ground with the boom of a falling sky. Piece by piece, the Skygate was coming apart.

The Sentinels were retreating, their griffins helping Nerida along as she desperately sought Deria's body. The sight sent a painful stab through Lynn's heart. She turned to Rel. "Take her body."

Rel removed the spear and picked up Deria's lifeless body, her arms and legs sprawled like a puppet with cut strings. He placed it on Ulenia's back as Lynn strode back to Vedyr. She jumped on his back, too filled with frustration to form cohesive thoughts.

Rel took off and Lynn followed. She gave a final look at the ruined gate, just in time to see the Dakhran airship coming through.

CHAPTER TWENTY-ONE

Politics should never mar the Faith, yet know that politics cannot be overlooked if employed against it.

— *The Book of the Bone*

Adrian looked out over the ships floating on the glinting Ulean sea. He almost smiled at the sight of his renewed Legion ready to sail him home, but something held him back. The faces of the consuls flashed in his mind. Their desperate clinging to life. Would Jovu have done it this way? What would Ellana say? Even as he told himself they deserved it, the final question rose in his mind: Would Father had done it this way?

I'm not him.

Derren stood beside him. The apparition's face was still somewhat bloated, but not nearly as much as it had been when Adrian first laid eyes on it. Adrian didn't look for long.

You deny it, but you remind me too much of your father, lad. Derren repeated the words he'd told Adrian shortly before losing his life, when they'd been locked in the dungeons of Khet.

I'm not him, Adrian repeated to himself.

He turned toward Mahir, who looked over a score of ships gathered in the bay. The Azuri lacked ballistae—the Pontiff had always made it clear the Domain would consider their use an act of war after the Azuri invasion of Dakhra all those years ago—but Nasir brought word that Addo had taken Sacantha. The shore was protected by the stolen Sacanthan navy, and Addo had an airship.

The Azuri had massive siege weapons on the coast. The one Adrian stood beside resembled a wedge. It rose fifteen feet high, and its base seemed to descend into the earth itself. A huge spear protruded from one of its sides, aimed at an angle into the air. There were others littering the dockside, framed by the copper sands and morning sun in the distance. The spears could be angled to shoot at ships in the air or on the sea.

It was effective at protecting Azur against airship raids but could not be loaded on the ships.

"Admiral?"

"Yes, Lord Light."

"What are we waiting on?"

"Supplies are being loaded, Lord Light. Khorfa has his men waiting on your word. Do we have a destination yet?"

Adrian did not. He looked beyond Mahir to Amal ban Khorfa, who was talking to Nasir and Oma ban Zarath, Lady Zarath's eldest daughter. Lady Zarath would stay to make sure Azur remained under Adrian's control. A new ruler was never comfortable, but Zarath's network of information would take the city's pulse while her daughter led the assassins who went with Adrian.

Adrian had released the Khorfa boy from the dungeons, and his immediate command of the troops showed prior military experience that would be valuable in the battle to come. Adrian made him a general of the Legion. He felt sure the Legion itself would have no issue with that. Not that it would make any difference. He was Light, and his power had only grown—as had his army. He now commanded twenty thousand. Double what he had before.

I'm coming to show you, Father.

"I will have a destination soon, Mahir." He walked past the man and toward the gathered officers.

"We have a problem," Adrian said, approaching with Bac in tow. "We don't have ballistae and"—he looked to Oma—"they have an airship."

"Seems like we'll need to get a ballista then," Amal said. The one-eyed general lacked formality, as one might after going through what he had. Adrian perceived no lack of respect, though. Adrian was the one who had taken him from the sweat and shit of the dungeon. "You Domain folk are full of those, no?"

"It is not that simple," Nasir said. "The situation within the Domain is . . . unprecedented." He turned to Oma. "Maybe you can get your scouts to find the cities that are least affected? See if they can spare any?"

"I will not be begging for siege weapons, Nasir." Adrian said. He was done with that. He'd already proven himself, and looking over at the Azuri siege weapons sparked an idea. More of a memory, really. "Halsport has had them on their docks for a century. They feared Azuri raids. I was caught in one in the past." The memory of the Khetish port town burned through Adrian. He almost longed for the simpler time when he and Myrra still believed Dakhra and Othonea could be allies within the Domain. When Adrian believed he could fulfil his mother's vision of unity among Domain nations.

How far we've fallen.

"There will be no risk of Azuri attacks now," Adrian said. "They should have enough."

Amal and Nasir nodded. "A sound plan, Lord Light," said Nasir. "It pleases me to see we are not running headfirst into the enemy."

Adrian had already tried that and lost too many. The underlying truth in Nasir's words cut deep, though. Perhaps it was part of the training in blood magic, always reminding Adrian of painful events. Adrian let it run through him. The pain was like a companion now, almost a part of him and always calling for the images of Derren and Myrra.

"If it comes to running headfirst into the enemy," Adrian said, "we have him." He jerked his head toward Bac, who remained impassive. Adrian looked to Nasir. "Are the wards ready?" he asked.

Adrian had requested Nasir to procure ruin-stone wards from the blood mages. They would protect the soldiers against the Madness long enough to be killed before they turned, or to fight against the enemy. They'd turn eventually, but the added moments of sanity could determine a battle's outcome.

"The front lines will have them," Nasir said. "But I must preach caution, Lord Light. We don't know how this will affect you."

The pendants held Kel Bradaz's enchantments and a drop of Adrian's blood. They were untested, but Adrian couldn't stand down now. "My blood will be enough to give us a chance," Adrian said. "If the troops are infected, I'll hold off the Madness until they can be dealt with. Have I not shown you enough to have faith in my blood?"

"Of course, Lord Light." Nasir said.

"Good," he looked to Amal. "Be ready at first light."

Adrian's new fleet had made good time and now approached the Khetish port-town of Halsport. It looked still from a distance. The sun was setting, and shadows crept from alleyways to take hold of buildings and cobbled streets, but that seemed the extent of the place's movement. The mark in the sky was back above them here and larger than ever. It had grown to the size of two moons now. It hung low in the sky, which was probably why it couldn't be seen from Azur. Something flashed beside Adrian, and there was Derren, looking up at the sign. The image of the general was as sharp as Adrian had ever seen, but still held the red tint of blood.

Looks like she's coming back, eh? Derren said. *Can you feel her in your blood?*

Adrian paused. The whispers that had run through his veins did seem louder, and Derren's image was there even though he hadn't used the blood magic. Was this mark affecting Adrian? His blood?

He'd have to think about that later. Now he needed to find the ballistae.

Adrian tried to spot one of the siege weapons that had lined the docks in the past, but his ships were either too far from the docks, or he was looking at the wrong spot. They had over a score of ships, and even though they flew the silver-and-white colors of the Legion, Adrian still didn't trust the history between the Khetish and the Azuri—at least, not enough to approach with his full fleet.

"Take our boat close," he said. "Leave Mahir behind to command the rest." The command ship was large and held enough Azuri harpoon launchers to defend itself. He hoped they wouldn't have to use them—and that ballistae could be found near the ports, so loading would be swift, but his hopes were not high.

The town remained quiet as they approached. Adrian turned to Amal. "It shouldn't be this quiet. Something's not right here. Have the men search the docks, but keep most of them on board."

They docked, and Amal made a clicking sound with his tongue, as if dealing with a horse. A man appeared, and Amal relayed the order. He turned to Adrian. "I sent the ones who were most loyal to my dead uncle. I call them the dogs, so they remember their misplaced loyalty is what has them in this situation."

"Is it wise to keep men you can't trust?"

"As fodder." Amal smiled. "And to remind myself of the chains I broke. Old Lord Khorfa did not recognize my value, and so I will never recognize it in the men loyal to him." He walked off, and Adrian was left thinking about his father. Would he ever break the chains that kept Father from recognizing his worth? Or would he always be some boy who disappointed the old man by his mere presence? Father had told Adrian the Legion was nothing, and it had been for a time. No longer, though, and Father would recognize that one way or another.

Amal's men soon returned, reporting no ballistae on the docks, though they had found mounting brackets where ballistae had been removed. Adrian nodded. They'd head to Vernell, the small city that housed the palace overlooking Halsport. Governor Arnek probably still held it, and he'd likely pulled the ballistae back to defend the palace. Arnek had always been favorable to Adrian when Adrian spent time there; it should be easy enough to persuade him with a careful approach.

"Form a column," Adrian told Amal. "We're heading for the palace."

Amal didn't take long to set up the men. There were two hundred to escort Adrian and Nasir through the city and on to Vernell. Each soldier wore a ruin-stone pendant, as did Amal. The stones had darkened, like Adrian's, and the veins pulsed orange and red.

They disembarked and moved slowly across the quay. Adrian, Nasir, and Amal were surrounded by soldiers scanning all sides. Bac stayed close to Adrian as the soldiers searched for hidden horrors in the growing shadows of a dying afternoon.

The houses were low and packed together, mostly made from wood. They were clustered around the dock and the main street that sloped up toward the back of the town, where a gate opened onto the road to Vernell. Adrian kept the column on the cobbled main street, wary of the surrounding stillness. The Azuri were alert, and Adrian didn't sense the same fear he'd felt from the Legion after fighting the madmen. Maybe that was a good thing—and maybe not.

They'd passed through most of the town and were approaching the gate when Adrian heard the scream. A chill ran through him, but this was no ambush. Dakhra wouldn't have sent their forces all this way to greet him, and Addo was too much of a coward to part with his army. Adrian doubted either even knew he was here.

A score of madmen came running from a shadowed side-street. Whatever afflicted them didn't seem to consume them as it had Lindamm or the other Legion soldiers Raklin had tested. These seemed more sustained and focused on death.

The scream had come from an Azuri with a madman's claw in his chest. Adrian felt the tingling in his blood. It was weak, as promised, but it was there, pulling at his strength while trying to keep the Madness at bay.

The enemies rushed at the soldiers with greater speed than the

Azuri had probably ever seen. It caught them unprepared, and three more were injured before Adrian's unit had formed in the square and were stabbing spears and curved swords at the attackers. The Azuri used their numbers, penning the madmen in and stabbing with long spears, but the madmen showed no pain.

One of them jumped high and fell claw first onto an Azuri soldier, who screamed as the life was ripped out of him through a gash in his neck. Adrian felt the tingling in his blood again, but it left when the man's life was snuffed out. The soldiers around the madman stuck him with enough spears to pin him to the ground. Their companions sought to do likewise with the others.

Adrian drew his sword, and Nasir was weaving his fingers. A growl came from behind and Adrian turned with a chill running through his gut, expecting an attack. All he saw was Bac's form driving a fist into the madman's chin. The man skidded across the cobbles, and the Azuri soldiers were quick to end him with their spears.

Adrian looked around, but the surprise had passed and Amal's men had overwhelmed the enemy. Even with greater speed, frenzied strength, and immunity to pain, the madmen could not overcome vastly superior numbers.

Adrian considered Bac, remembering what he'd said in the gardens of the Azuri palace. He did know how to survive, and his loyalty seemed to be rooted in the belief that Adrian would guarantee his survival. Adrian nodded to Bac, then walked among the men, feeling the pull of one of the pendants that had resisted the Madness. He stopped before a soldier with a hand over his arm, breathing heavily. Those around him watched with uncertain gazes.

The man looked Adrian straight in the eye, without anger or defiance—almost as if he could sense what was trying to make its way through him. The tingling rose within Adrian, almost turning into pain. Even if he kept the Madness back, he knew it wouldn't be indefinite.

"Spears," Adrian said in Azuri. The soldiers didn't hesitate, and in a moment the injured man was surrounded by glinting steel spear points.

Adrian found the strings tugging at him. He closed his eyes. They were like black tendrils on a field of white, creeping toward him, tightening around his arms, and sending that tingle through his blood. Whispering to him. "Let me have him."

Adrian recalled the symbol Nasir had taught him in the binding. The circle with a horizontal line and two other lines that crossed the first at an angle. He opened his eyes and traced the air with it, then traced another pair of lines in the opposite direction. The symbol to sever the connection.

The injured soldier felt it then. The pain of the Madness. Adrian felt an echo of it as the man doubled over and twisted. It wasn't even a bad feeling anymore—more like his body craved the pain and the power it brought from the blood magic.

He issued the command, and the spears sank into the man just as the skin around his eyes turned black, and his head jerked up with a snarl.

Adrian breathed away the call of the blood magic. Myrra was there again, extending a hand, asking him to join her—but she stood over an abyss. It emanated a reddish glow like his blood coils, as if to promise power along with the comfort of being with Myrra. But it offered Adrian no confidence that he would escape the abyss. He walked on, leading the men away from the town and onto the road.

When they reached Vernell, they found two of the missing ballistae atop the gate, pointing down at them. The guards drew their weapons at the sight of Azuri coming up the road. It could be they were prepared for war. Or perhaps Domain folk would always draw steel on Azuri marching across their lands, even if they marched beneath the silver-and-white banner of the Legion.

Adrian turned to Amal. "Stay here. I'll talk to them."

Amal nodded, and Adrian advanced with Nasir and Bac in tow. The Vernell guard did not move from the gate.

"Have you not recognized the Legion banner?" Adrian called as he approached.

"World's gone mad," the guard said. "A lot of broken ones like that lying around."

Adrian stepped up to him. "Does it look like we're here to siege your walls?"

"No, but these things don't have to look like it, do they? You could be trying to sneak in, make easy work—"

"Soldier, is this how you treat the Light of the Legion?"

Adrian looked past the guard to what seemed to be a captain. The man stepped close and pulled the soldier back. "I'm sorry, Lord Light. I'm Captain Treene. I witnessed your liberation of Khet from the traitors who call themselves the True. We are grateful for it. Please follow me. Governor Arnek is unavailable, but Priestess Ellana will be pleased to meet you."

Adrian paused. He'd known Ellana would continue to serve the Church but had never expected to find her here. Had she known he was coming? No. More likely this was the farthest place from Father she could find.

Adrian signaled to Amal to join them, and the four marched through the city gates.

Vernell was nothing like Halsport. The housing here was richer, with bricks forming multi-storied buildings meant to hold either the Khetish nobility or merchants who'd made their wealth from the nearby port town. Even the shops looked cleaner and more expensive. The streets were almost as empty as Halsport, though. Fear seemed to have driven people indoors. It gave Adrian a strange sense of calm. At least there was less chance of madmen springing at them from a crowd.

It wasn't all that long since Adrian had been in Vernell. It was one of his and Myrra's favorite places in Khet, and being here without her felt wrong. He looked up at the darkening sky as they walked. That second ball of light was still strange, and Adrian found no comfort in it. Derren might have told him something about a text, maybe claimed it marked the Seraph's return, but Adrian knew better. She wasn't coming to save them.

They made their way quickly through the palace gates and followed Treene through the entrance hall. Father might have taken Khet as an Othonean province, but nothing had been done to change the colors or style of the palace. The rectangular entrance hall was twenty feet tall, its flat ceiling supported by pillars with woven lines of green, gold, and the gray of ruin-stone. Light played on the colors through large windows cut high in the walls on either side. Adrian used to love those colors, almost as if they represented his and Myrra's resistance to their fathers. The meaning was different now, bleaker. The colors seemed dead, like her mask.

I have my army. All I need are the ballistae to take the Sacanthan shores. He wasn't sure why he was being taken to Ellana, but maybe that was a good thing.

They pushed the doors open, but the chapel was empty. Treene marched straight through and toward a side door.

"She'll be in here, Lord Light."

Adrian nodded to the men following him. "Stay here." He opened the door and stepped inside. The room was small, with polished stone walls broken by a single thin window that looked almost like a scar running across the smooth surface. It reminded Adrian of his own scars, the deeper ones that didn't show.

Ellana sat behind a desk, bent over a stack of paper and riffling through the pages. She didn't look up as Adrian entered, and he waited patiently until she noticed him.

Her eyes widened when she did. "Brother?" She got up and rushed to him, embracing Adrian as if he were an answered prayer. The warmth was unexpected, but it felt good all the same. Like Adrian was back in the Othonean gardens with Ellana walking beside him. Safe, with no pain. "What are you doing here?" she asked.

"I could ask you the same thing. You've become a queen?"

"Arnek is sick. His faith has the palace guards answering to me."

Adrian frowned. "Sick?"

"It isn't the Madness as far as we know, but I'm not sure the people would make that distinction. We're keeping it quiet." Ellana stood, hands still close to the papers. "I thought you'd be on your way to see Father by now."

"Why?"

"He gave you Azur."

Adrian gritted his teeth. "He gave me nothing."

"What of the wedding? Was that not his doing?" Ellana's words seemed cautious, as if she wanted to reach out to him, but Father's memory loomed between them.

"No." Adrian had paid too high a price to let that be taken away. "The Xakhar and Princess Kahlia are dead."

That gave Ellana pause. "What are you trying to prove? This is not the moment for rashness, Adrian. Are the Azuri coming?"

Adrian couldn't blame her for not getting the news. The Domain was in too much chaos to turn its attention to foreign shores. "It's resolved. They follow me."

Ellana watched him for a long moment. "Has Father asked for something else?"

"I'm not here to talk about Father, or to argue, Ellana. I've rebuilt the Legion. Twenty thousand strong. I'm here to push Dakhra back."

"Twenty thousand Azuri? You've formed a Legion of heathens?"

Adrian breathed deep. "Heathens that will fight to protect the Domain from a nation you considered loyal months ago. It's not about faith, Ellana. I have the numbers, and they will fight. That's all that matters."

Ellana shook her head. "I'd love to agree with you, but the numbers will do nothing against their potions. It'll just turn more to their side." She looked down at the pages again.

"I have that under control."

Ellana's gaze shot up to him, and she tilted her head. "What?"

"I'm not letting Syvern take the Domain. He'll pay for every-thing he's done." *He'll pay for spreading this Madness.*

Adrian didn't know why or how Myrra had been affected, but knowing Syvern was to blame was enough. The thought dug its claws into Adrian, stabbing at his chest and making him clench his jaw. He was sure Ellana would notice the expression, but he didn't hold it back. *Let her judge me.*

"Adrian, you've seen this madness. You can't stop it."

"I can delay it." He pulled out his pendant. "I've learned things in Azur. More than Father would ever tell us. My blood—our blood —has power."

Ellana's eyes lingered on the black ruin-stone, pulsing orange and red through the cracks. "You've found a cure?"

"Not yet. But I think I can hold it back. Maybe long enough to win a fight." The pulling sensation of the man injured by the madman in Halsport swept over him, but it had been the first time. Adrian would learn to resist. He'd get over it, like he had everything else.

"The Seraph smiles upon you. You'll bring hope to—"

"I haven't come to bring hope to Vernell or to ward your men, Ellana. I've come to take siege weapons so we can take back Sacantha."

"What?" The coldness in Ellana's voice was almost like Father's.

"I'm striking a blow at Dakhra, taking away an ally, exposing the rear of their army so they can't move forward into the Domain."

"Adrian, you can't be serious! We need to focus on a cure. People will die inside the Domain!"

"And how long will it take to find a cure? Doesn't the Seraph watch for the worthy? Isn't She supposed to protect them?"

"She has faith in people like us, like you to do that! Can't you see? The message is clear!"

Adrian shook his head. "There is no message, Ellana."

She turned her back to him, looking out the thin window. "You're just like Father. You have the tools to make the Domain better, but you'll only use them for yourself."

"I'm—" Adrian shook his head, biting off the word. "I thought you'd understand, see what we're up against. I thought you'd believe in me!"

"I believe in doing the right thing, Adrian! We can't beat Dakhra without a cure, and clashing against them only heightens the risk."

Adrian was still shaking his head. She'd made up her mind. "We have the same blood. Perhaps yours will work as well." He took out the copper ball Kel Bradaz had used to quiet the Madness in the Rhiall boy. The same one Adrian had used to kill the consuls. "This holds enchantments from the Azuri blood priests. Feed it your blood and give it to the Priests of the Blood. It will as likely kill as it will heal, but I guess you'll have to have faith. In our blood, if nothing else."

Ellana glared at him. "You've changed."

"We all have. Maybe it's time you stopped trying to change me back. I was never happy with Father."

"You were happy with me," Ellana said. "Can't we still have that? Work together?"

Adrian placed the copper ball on the desk. "I can't stay." He paced toward the door. "I'll tell Treene to load the ballistae onto the ship. Don't stand in the way."

CHAPTER TWENTY-TWO

The Earth is more connected than we know, but time has a way of breaking things.

— Tales of the Hagun

Nasha's muscles complained as she strained to keep up with the chief, and Shai had to catch her more than once as she stumbled on the path up the mountain. They seemed to be heading toward the Yltigg village at the top, but the more they walked, the farther off it seemed. Nasha kept her head down, leaning on Shai when she needed to.

Chief Ardin strode up ahead. Nasha and Shai were led by Roho and surrounded by the chief's guard. The speaker walked beside them. His veil wasn't pulsing; nor were the ancestor-stone manacles around Nasha's wrists. They were still attached, the chain broken and dangling, but the ancestor-stone was dormant, absorbing nothing and having seemingly spent the emotions it had held.

They entered the town, but it was mostly empty. The houses

were rounder here, and built on the incline. The Yltigg seemed to use the peak itself in several places, carving entire chambers into the rock. Their deeper reaches were shrouded in darkness. Most of the people were still at the arena, dealing with the aftermath or slow to return to their homes. Nasha was glad for that. She'd had enough emotions to deal with; better to cut a straight path, without the pressure mounting. She looked at her dulled manacles again as they passed a stretch of tightly clustered roundhouses and approached the chief's hall, which stood on a flat patch of land near to the top.

The sensation of ancestor-stone touching her skin was still strange, but part of her was glad she understood some of how it worked. It was clear now that ancestor-stone was loaded with emotions, and that once any emotions had been fed to Nasha, the ancestor-stone channeled and heightened them all around.

The thought had Nasha wanting to remove the manacles, but there was still nothing, as if even in her depleted state her body had understood. She was learning to block the emotion, at least while surrounded by only a few of the Yltigg. The curse had done this before. Like a muscle straining, then growing after the pain she'd put it through. Becoming stronger and more controlled.

It's still a curse. She wouldn't stop reminding herself of that. No matter the tether she'd found in hope, or the control she thought she'd gained, Zala's presence was still there as well.

The chief flung the doors open, leaving Roho there and leading the speaker, Shai, and Nasha inside. The guards remained outside. The room was long and sparsely furnished, mostly built from brownish stone and what seemed to be dried mud. There were firepits here and there, none of them lit but all surrounded by benches. A dais at the far end held a high-backed chair. The chief strode through the chamber, ignoring the chair and taking a door on the back wall to its right. He left it open for them to follow.

Nasha and Shai walked out onto an open ledge. If the pit they'd thrown her into had been any indication, the wind here was supposed to howl louder than ever, but there was something to the placement of the trees that gave the place a sense of calm and quiet. The Yltigg had built what looked like a garden at the top of the peak. Trees surrounded the edges, taller than many Nasha had seen down below. They cast a cool shade over the bushes and grass that covered the soft earth. This was nothing like the dry, hard earth Nasha had trudged through on the way here. There were even flowers in different shades of yellows and oranges, purples and blues. At the garden's center was a slab of ancestor-stone twice as tall as Nasha. It was engraved with runes. They differed from the Ronar warding pillars, but the stone served the same purpose: a warding pillar to keep Zala in the ground. Maybe that was what gave the garden its bloom.

Nasha's stomach lurched as her gaze slid to the base of the pillar. It was dull, with black corruption inching up the stone, the pulsing cut off midway. It was the same as she'd seen in the Hagun village, only this pillar wasn't entirely taken yet.

"We do not have multiple wards like the Ronar." The Yltigg chief's tone was somber. "This one comes from the heart of our mines, and Zala has wrapped her fingers around it."

Nasha turned to the speaker. "Why would you use tainted? Why risk increasing Zala's power if she already corrupts your land?"

"The spread of her corrupted changes nothing," the speaker said. "We've been keeping an eye on it." The man gestured, directing Nasha's gaze to the trees that surrounded the pillar. More Yltigg stood guard there, all of them veiled like the speaker, though none of their veils used as much ancestor-stone as his.

"The Proving was meant to return life to the Earth. The blood was supposed to stop the rot," the chief said. "When the accord was broken, I grieved for my son, but I feared for the clan even more. Tomu left your ancestor-stone behind instead of leaving his life, but even if we could have understood the runes his daughter wove, we could not replicate her enchantments."

Nasha looked around but didn't see the Ronar Cradle that had been brought to the Proving.

The speaker's whispery voice seemed amused. "Your chief asked for it back, in return for you." Nasha couldn't tell what he really felt without seeing his face or reading emotions that were shielded by the veil. "We wanted your tivezzi, but no one seems to know where she is. We accepted you, thinking that perhaps Zala would be appeased with your blood since both you and your initiate were part of the disruption in the Proving."

"Then why spare us to show us this?" Shai's tone was sharp, and Nasha knew where that came from. She'd always hated being seen as just another worthless Sloper life to be sacrificed. Her temper was rising, working its way into Nasha through the curse.

The chief's tone was equally sharp. "Your warden has proven herself to be more useful than her spilled blood."

"I'm not the warden," Nasha said, "and Adda isn't my tivezzi. They'd call me an Earth-Breaker and kill me if they saw what I did in the arena."

The speaker and the chief chuckled between themselves. "Tomu has always been short-sighted," Chief Ardin said. "Jabillo too afraid in his interpretation of the tales. Ento here has a more . . . flexible way of seeing things."

"I did nothing," Nasha said. "All I did was kill the tainted."

"All you did?" Ardin said. "Zala gives her corrupted speed and strength. You are a formidable weap—"

"I'm no one's tool!" It was Nasha's turn to raise her voice now, but the chief only laughed.

"You cling too strongly to your labels. It's like you want them to define you."

Nasha glared at the man and balled her fists. "I was a hunter, thrice-striped. I did more than my part. I was named warden and beat you in the Proving. I am no one's weapon, and I'm more than just a name."

What exactly that was, Nasha couldn't say, but the chief didn't linger on it. He shook his head. "Your prowess in combat was not what saved you. You brought the stone back to life."

Nasha frowned. "What stone?"

"Your manacles," Speaker Ento said. "Whatever made the ancestor-stone pulse was pulled into you when we put them on. They dulled, but whatever you did relit them, and now you seem to have a measure of control."

"You knew what would happen?" Nasha couldn't hide the

surprise in her tone, and she could sense Shai's confusion behind her.

"These are desperate times," Ento said. "I wasn't sure, but after your display in the tent, we could leave no stone unturned. If you failed, Zala would have your blood at least."

Nasha was taken by anger again. They'd been using her from the start, just like Mansa. The speaker asked for her acceptance, and then forced her onto the path he desired.

"We are all tools," Ento said. "Be glad we do not hide how we intend to use you."

"I can't heal the stone," Nasha told them. "I'm not a tivezzi. Where's your stone weaver?"

"Taken," Ardin said.

"By who?" Shai asked.

"Zala," the chief said. "Our tivezzi was trying to stop the taint. I like to think it is her life that keeps it at bay. If not for that, we might be joining the Hagun in wandering the clanlands after a chance of survival."

"Is there no word of them?" Nasha asked. "Can they help?"

"We think they've gone east," Ento said. "But we cannot afford to send scouts after them. We don't know if they're even alive, and Zala is already trying to take our peak from us. After the Proving, we even tried taking the Domain man's blood. It worked for a while but wasn't enough."

"Bahar?"

The speaker nodded. "We would have drained him had it worked. The land was healed by his blood, but only temporarily. It seems Zala can only be appeased by the blood of the clans. The chief was adamant that I not kill the emissary, though. He will suffer more alive than dead for what he did."

"Well, it's turning back on you now," Nasha said. "He's bringing the Visslands onto us."

The chief nodded. "That is of little importance if there is no land to protect. You do not need to change the stone like a tivezzi. You've shown you can replenish it. Touch our pillar and heal it as you did the manacles."

"That's not how it works, and I've told you, I won't let you turn me into one of those beasts. I won't let Zala control me." She still had a promise to uphold.

"But . . . you are already tainted," Ento said.

"What?" Shai's voice was filled with surprise.

Nasha felt no surprise. She knew the darkness inside her was Zala's. "Do you see blackness around my eyes? You may call me tainted, as Jabillo would call me an Earth-Breaker. But I am neither."

She looked over to Shai. They'd escaped execution, but if the Domain ran over the clans, they'd be dead soon anyway. She still needed to make sure Landi and Uvo were safe as well, and that Razi was with them. Did she need the boy back? He'd syphoned the emotions into himself just as Ento did with his veil, but the effect was tenfold. Did he have the power to heal the stone?

If you do nothing, Zala wins. Nasha almost let out a hopeless laugh at the irony of the fact that she was the one that had to stop the dead goddess. She breathed it out instead and turned to the chief. "If I help you, it will be on my terms. I am not your weapon or your hero." She let out another breath. "And you'll need to find a way to push back the Domain."

The chief nodded. "They'll attack the Ronar first. We can use the time to heal the stone."

"We could use the Ronar," Ento said. "You have connections there still, on their Slopes, yes?"

"No," Nasha said. "Not anymore, it seems." They'd thrown her to the wolves.

"Mansa would listen to you," the chief said. "He was not involved in my negotiations with Tomu."

Nasha gritted her teeth. Mansa would probably have been the first to accept the trade, while making sure the Yltigg thought him uninvolved. She shook her head. She'd been defending the idea only a few days ago, but she couldn't fight beside the Ronar if they were as likely as the enemy to stab her. "I'm not sure I can."

"We'll have to," Ardin said. "Once the stone is healed, I will convince them of your worthiness. Restore your position."

Nasha had hated the title when it had been given to her, but in the face of all that had happened, it had become a haven—something familiar for her to hold on to. Maybe Ardin had been right about labels. A few weeks ago, she'd wanted to be defined by them; now she saw through the illusion. She was no warden and had no desire to become one again. "No. The past is done. We look forward. Talk to the Ronar if you must, but leave us out of it."

She looked over to Shai but could feel the girl's satisfaction even before their gazes met.

Ento appeared to smile under the veil, then pulled something from his tunic. A bundle that he slowly unwrapped before Nasha, finally revealing a shard of dull ancestor-stone: no pulse, and black corruption spreading over it like lichen. The cracks where veins should pulse blue were still clear, though.

"This is a shard from the Hagun warding pillar," Ento said. "It is dead, but the corruption is not."

Nasha eyed the stone and then the speaker. "Your veil tell you that as well?"

Ento nodded slowly. "You must use this stone. Understand the taint that has taken it, so you may fight the larger one that threatens our home." He pointed at the Yltigg ward.

He offered the stone to Nasha, but she didn't take it. Whatever she'd done in the arena wouldn't work unless she was immersed in emotion, and there wasn't nearly enough here. Ento stepped closer, but Nasha shook her head. "Your mines are the largest in the clan-lands, yes?"

The Yltigg nodded.

"Good. That's where we'll do it. Show me how deep they go."

CHAPTER TWENTY-THREE

The bottom of a fall is always safer than the top.

— *common saying in the Visslands*

K admus worked all through the night and was ready when
Bahar's man walked into his store early the next day. Bahar
had picked the afternoon the last time, but he'd said enough for
Kadmus to predict he'd want to change that. Bahar thought he was
strong enough to take the pain, and he likely thought an early start
would give him time to heal from one wound and have Kadmus
work on another the same day.

Kadmus might consider it if Bahar pushed him hard enough,
but he was hoping what he had to show the emissary would direct
his thoughts elsewhere. Kadmus had always steered clear of the
upper city's affairs, but that didn't mean he was ignorant of how
things worked. The council and Queen Lesraile had always followed
the Church's designations in days of the week. Each week started on
Reflection-day. Resolution-day came four days later and was tradi-

tionally kept as a day for important meetings to be held. Accordingly, the council held its meetings on Resolution-day. And that was today.

Kadmus made sure the vials he'd worked on all night were safely packed, then set out after the messenger to find Bahar. He'd already checked on Nima, trusting his prediction that the messenger would come early. His calculations were one of the few things he placed a slight trust in. Unlike people, they rarely let him down. And when they did, they could always be analyzed and a reason determined.

Leaving his daughter behind in the state she was in still tugged at him, but staying by her side without advancing toward a cure would do nothing to help. He'd monitored her breathing, and she'd been steady since the last dose of the serum. She was strong; she would hold until his return.

The man led Kadmus into the upper city. They climbed higher this time, two levels below the palace. The roads were emptier here and the houses larger, some of them resembling miniature keeps with low, rounded towers rising into conical roofs. It was oddly quieter up here, but silence was something Pelaket never truly knew. Not on the streets, at least.

The messenger paused before a manor that would have looked like a castle to the people in the lower city. Here, though, it seemed small, with not nearly as many levels as the surrounding buildings, and a low gate not half the size of its neighbors. Kadmus understood why Bahar might have picked it. The messenger opened a gate and gestured for Kadmus to step in but didn't move forward himself. Kadmus went through and strode up the wide walkway to the house. He opened the door without knocking.

The entrance hall was wide and tall, with a set of stairs that were almost as wide as the room, leading to a mezzanine. There were purposeless benches to the side of the stairway, facing doors that led to other parts of the house. He couldn't imagine anyone would remain seated for long with nothing before them but doors, but Bahar sat on one of them all the same. Waiting. His clothes were finer, with silk softening the hard look of his face. His hair was tidier as well, and he held a cane that ended in a ruin-stone handle.

The slow pulse of white was what drew Kadmus's eye to the man, otherwise he might have missed him amid the scale of the room.

"Your skill has proven to be quite proficient," Bahar said. He turned to Kadmus, the scar that had once seemed to be an extension of his mouth now smooth, the skin knitted into a semblance of normality even if there was still an angry red streak along his cheek. The other parts of his face were another matter. Scabs and thick scars still fought for space, an especially large one running across the left side of his forehead and around his eye.

Kadmus had no answer. Flattery gained him nothing, and he didn't need his pride boosted by Bahar.

"We will need to be quick today. You will work on what you can now, then I will leave you and return after the council."

Kadmus nodded. The clothes were enough of a giveaway, and even if Bahar was not officially part of the council, everyone knew his presence there would not be denied. Whether he would keep true to his word and bring Kadmus before them, though, remained to be seen.

"I've reconsidered," Kadmus said.

Bahar eyed him suspiciously, likely unsure whether Kadmus referred to the healing or to Bahar's offer.

"I will heal you, but you will take me with you to the council meeting."

"Will I now?" Bahar had the beginnings of a grin pulling at the side of his mouth.

Kadmus produced the vials he'd worked on all night. He'd give Bahar what he wanted, but Kadmus had added enough to it to maintain control. This was not the same Madness; it was not incurable. What he'd brought to show the council was a lot weaker than what afflicted people in the streets. Bahar might not enjoy having Kadmus control part of the process, but Kadmus was sure he could convince Bahar to move forward, whatever qualms the emissary might have.

"This is what you asked for," Kadmus said. "The Madness. Isolated so we can work on a cure."

Bahar didn't move for a long moment, watching Kadmus with

what seemed to be rising suspicion behind his eyes; then he stood, leaning on the cane and limping toward Kadmus. He stretched out a hand for the vial. "Let me see."

"Who will you test it on?" Kadmus asked.

Bahar withdrew the hand and snapped angry fingers. A servant walked into the room, followed by a pair of what looked to be house guards.

Bahar pointed at the bench he'd just risen from. "Sit."

The servant obeyed, and the guards stood to either side. He had a wary look in his eyes, but not enough to show defiance, or even enough fear to run.

Kadmus watched them all with newfound curiosity. Servants were hired from the lower city, promised blessings and ruin-stone. It seemed to be enough for them to accept orders without question.

Kadmus had never believed the Church's promises. Their extended life was hard to argue against, especially the Pontiff's centuries in power, but he would never allow himself to believe this was proof of the Seraph's existence. Kadmus had quickly seen through the Church's stories of Her, and had lived over sixty years himself, even if he looked little older than most men half his age.

Bahar reached his hand out again, with no give to his gaze. There was no negotiation to be had here. Kadmus handed him the vial.

Bahar limped toward the man, cane tapping on the marble floor. "Hold him."

The guards grabbed hold of the servant, who struggled now. The promise of an extended life seemed to wane quickly in the face of what was surely a threat to it. The guards held the man tight and forced open his jaw. His head was thrown back, but his gaze wildly sought Bahar's. There seemed to be an apology in the man's eyes, even if it was not accompanied by certainty.

Kadmus shook his head. Even now the man could not stand for himself, thinking he'd done some wrong and hoping someone would tell him what to do.

Bahar paused before the servant, took a long look at Kadmus, then emptied the vial down the man's throat. If the guards were uncomfortable with this, they hid it well, likely knowing any hesitation might see them on the bench next time. They held the man's mouth shut until he shuddered slightly. They stepped back as the shudder became a shake, and the man fell convulsing to the ground.

Bahar gave the man some space, watching the blackness spread around the man's eyes. Kadmus couldn't deny he was curious himself. He hadn't tested the concoction, but his calculations had rarely failed him before the Madness.

The guards drew swords, but Kadmus raised a hand. "That won't be necessary."

They ignored him until Bahar, after evaluating Kadmus, tapped his cane twice on the ground, calling them off. The man's convulsions reduced, then subsided. He was left on the floor, panting but sane.

Kadmus let out a breath that tasted of shame. He shouldn't have been holding it; he'd never doubted himself like this. His calculations had been correct; he'd created a weaker version of the Madness, one that wouldn't consume the test subjects. Still, it was the Madness. The disease that threatened to take Nima from him. Kadmus hated seeing the transformation.

Bahar had a glimmer of curiosity in his eyes, and Kadmus knew the question that would come. He shook his head. "It isn't a cure. I've made a version of it that can be experimented on but won't last long enough to be dangerous. With the council's resources, we should be able to use this to monitor the changes in the blood of the subjects. It should bring us closer to a cure."

Bahar's mind seemed to work behind his gaze. It wasn't what he'd expected, perhaps, but Kadmus had given him enough to take before the council.

Bahar finally nodded, waving a dismissive hand to the guards, who lifted the servant and dragged him away. Kadmus watched the man being dragged off, but there was no outrage in the man's stare, only a twisted sense of thankfulness. Were the people now so afraid they would thank the Seraph for a lesser evil, so long as it didn't take their life?

Bahar's gaze remained fixed on Kadmus. "Looks like you've found your way into the council meeting."

There was only one more level before the palace, and it barely seemed populated. Kadmus eventually spotted houses too large to be serious, and with far too many gardens and courtyards between them. It was clear this level was reserved for the council, and for them alone. The manors were far enough from the waterfalls that the sound was hardly an annoyance, and almost pleasant.

Bahar barely looked sideways as the carriage carried them along the sloping street. They traveled across long ramps that cut their way up the mountainside to the final tier—and the palace.

It was the top of the city, but this level stretched out into a plateau, with a mountain range looming to the left. A slow-flowing river cut its way down from the peaks, ending in a lake that extended to the cliff where the palace sat over the three waterfalls that were the symbol of the Visslands.

The palace of Pelaket was said to be unassailable by ground, and Kadmus could see why. No army could march on water, and the rising city levels built into the mountainside seemed an impossible obstacle.

They rode the carriage across a wide expanse with the lake to their right and the base of the mountains to their left. At the mouth of the valley where two peaks met was the final piece of the puzzle, the reason the palace would never fall, even if an army reached the top. A hundred-foot-high wall rose over the capital city of the Visslands, holding back an immense mass of water.

The dam was one of the main sources of the Visslands' power. They supplied many of the Domain nations with fresh water, which was itself reason for those nations to refrain from attack. If the flood gates were opened, they would hardly affect the palace or the upper city, but the effect on the outer city and the clanlands beyond would be immeasurable. The wall that covered the valley mouth was ten times wider than it was tall, with flood gates strategically placed facing away from the palace and upper city. The size of the whole thing was astounding, and not even Kadmus could calculate the volume held within.

The carriage stopped before a bridge-like walkway that led to the palace gates. The path was almost level with the lake. The surrounding water was a smooth mirror, reflecting the sky above. Bahar straightened his back and walked with his head held high, visibly trying to ignore his limp as he strode across the pristine stone path. The palace was tall and wide, crowned by a huge dome. The structure itself protruded over the edge, as if to challenge the drop. It held Kadmus's gaze as he walked the path, but even with the distracting grandeur of the palace, Kadmus read the discomfort in Bahar's gait. The emissary still tapped the cane on the stone, if at less regular intervals.

There was no challenge to their passage. The guards recognized either Bahar's face beneath the scars or the colors of his house.

The palace was filled with wide empty spaces, mostly wrought in blue and gray marble—the colors of Queen Lesraile. There were patches of ruin-stone here and there—which most royalty were prone to using as a display of power—and special care had been taken to make the ruin-stone stand out over the marble. The queen's status showed even in the stone walls of the palace.

The entrance hall had windows that let in the sound of the water, which rang slightly louder now, and stairs that led up to what Kadmus imagined were quieter levels. Bahar took the set of stairs closest to them, setting a brisk pace even though pain was painted on his face.

They walked to the end of a corridor and entered a chamber with a wide, open balcony. There was a curved table at the center of the chamber, forming a circle with an open area in the middle. The circle was unbroken, save an opening near the door. Bahar walked to the center of the circle, trailed by Kadmus.

A gray-haired, hook-nosed man looked directly at them, the distant roar of the falls audible through the balcony behind him. Statues of the six-winged Seraph flanked the balcony. The floor beneath them was transparent and showed the falling water below.

The statues stood defiantly on the glass over the waterfall, each one holding up one of the four Signs of the Seraph. A priest in silver and white stood before one of them, to the left of the man eyeing Bahar and Kadmus.

Kadmus kept his gaze away from the priest, forcing himself to mask his contempt. He imagined what the council must be thinking of them. A limper with half-healed scars and an unknown dweller of the lower city with even deeper scars on his face. Would they even listen?

There were ten seated at the table; they made up the Visslands' ruling council. A throne stood behind them, also on a glass floor, but Queen Lesraile did not sit upon it. No one did.

Kadmus recognized the gray-haired man. He'd never been close to him, but he'd heard enough descriptions and seen enough depictions to recognize the man as Lord Carswell. He was as close to being head of the council as anyone.

Kadmus eyed the councilor closely. He didn't look like a man who'd just lost his son, but then again, he couldn't. The boy had been lost in the clanlands, that much was clear, and the body could not be retrieved for a burning. That was as much a statement of unworthiness in the Seraph's eyes as anything.

"Welcome, emissary," Lord Carswell said. "We appreciate the respect for our time."

Bahar nodded to the councilor. "I bring an opportunity before the council. One that may resolve our problems with the clans."

There was no reply to this. The council either had tired of such openings or trusted Bahar enough to let him continue.

"We have suffered losses. Enough to let our enemies know that the Domain will not stand for them. There is turmoil within, and you have kept our borders safer than most nations against the Dakhran threat, but they are not our only enemy. The clans must be dealt with." He looked at the priest. "We are faithful to the Seraph and do not mourn or speak of the dead, but the clans are not faithful. They are enemies of the Seraph and challenge Her will." Bahar's gaze went back to Carswell, who seemed to be wrangling his expression under control. Kadmus kept his gaze on the man, intrigued by the internal struggle between loss and faith. "I am not here to argue the worthiness of the fallen. I am here to tell you that the clans have made their wish for war clear, and waiting for them to prepare only brings us more risk. We don't know what Dakhra is planning, and we cannot afford to wait on attack by two enemies. We have allies who are standing against Dakhra's advance. The Domain depends on us to stand against the clans."

"You need not convince us of this, emissary," said a woman with a stern expression.

"Of course, Councilwoman Vetta. What I have to show is something that will convince you to march now."

Kadmus could feel the frown creasing his brow. Bahar had promised to bring him before the council in hopes of researching the Madness and finding a cure, but the way he spoke now was closer to someone about to present a weapon. It hit Kadmus all at once. Bahar *was* about to present a weapon. The weapon Kadmus had built. Rage and relief fought their way through Kadmus, but he'd long since learned to suppress his emotions in situations like this. He needed his mind clear. Still, he was thankful for the relief brought by his foresight to build in something that would prevent his creation being used as a permanent plague.

Bahar turned to Kadmus and stretched out a hand, as he'd done in his home. Kadmus was not resistant this time. He simply handed over the vial. "This vial contains a plague similar to what Dakhra has created. They have proven themselves to be traitors of the Seraph, but we cannot fault their tactics. We will use this on the clans, plunge their lands into chaos and end the threat."

A man with a circlet of brown hair shook his head. "You can't be serious, Bahar. We're fighting this, and you want to spread it?"

Bahar turned a hard gaze on the man. "I have not come before you to waste the council's time, Councilman Gerret. This concoction is weaker, temporary. I have seen it myself and will perform a demonstration if necessary. All I ask is that you mobilize the troops and fund the research of my man here." He gestured at Kadmus, who wasn't sure how he felt about being called Bahar's man. "He created this and can further his research, perhaps even find a cure for Dakhra's plague."

There was a slight mumbling that joined the sound of the water-falls. Something caught Kadmus's attention in the words. Not only the words; the movements and gazes were riddled with unease. Gazes directed at Kadmus and Bahar, unconscious itches, hands moving to foreheads and necks. Kadmus's gaze shifted to the throne. Did the unease have to do with the queen's absence? Had she been infected? It did not take long for Carswell to raise a hand. "We would have a moment to discuss."

Bahar lowered his head and led Kadmus from the chamber.

Guards flanked them as they waited outside the doors. Bahar kept his gaze blank, but Kadmus knew he was in pain. He'd been standing for too long. It almost made Kadmus nervous, thinking about how long Bahar could manage if the council called for a prolonged discussion. Kadmus couldn't afford to leave without the council's support.

The door opened, and they returned to stand before the council, Bahar's cane tapping more heavily this time.

"This matter would require further discussion in normal times," Carswell said. "But the Domain has been invaded, and the council believes the risk of fighting two enemies at once is, as you say, too great. We will fund this research and ready a march within the week." Carswell gestured to his side. "High Priest Malit has been leading the Church's effort in search of a cure. He will accompany your man, and by the Seraph's grace, we will find an answer to Dakhra's threat."

Bahar bowed his head. "By the Seraph's grace."

He left with Kadmus in tow. Maybe he expected a protest, but there was none coming. Bahar could fight his war; Kadmus had what he needed to save Nima.

CHAPTER TWENTY-FOUR

Death shall not endure.

— Words of Cleansing

The griffins landed on the wide balcony of the cathedral tower, a long slab of stone built with the creatures in mind. Olem, Gwynne, and Mirek all jumped off and rushed into the tall chamber beyond, while Rel tended to Nerida, a now-riderless griffin. Lynn followed the others inside, with Deria in her arms.

The chamber was one of the ones used to house griffins in the cathedral. It had stalls all around the walls, but on a single level—unlike the tower in Durnn. Fifteen griffins could be housed there, but the cathedral had other such chambers, and this one was empty.

"We need the Pontiff," Olem said. "Let no one in." He rushed off through the double doors that led into the cathedral, while Gwynne and Mirek stood guard outside. Lynn was left with Deria in her arms and her voices laughing at her failure.

Nerida shrieked on the balcony, the pain still running through her as the shard of her heart in Deria's chest lay dead. Rel had a hard time keeping her down, but Ulenia helped.

Lynn didn't have to wait long on the Pontiff. There was the usual calmness about him. With all he'd seen, it would take more than a dead Sentinel to shake him, but there was something different in his gaze when it fell upon Deria's black-stained face.

Lynn waited with bated breath. He had the power to preserve her body, to be brought back when the Seraph returned. All he need do was declare her worthy.

"Does anyone else know?" he asked.

"No," Olem said. "We came straight to you."

"Good. Best not to strike a blow at the people's confidence in times like these. Prepare a cleansing, Commander. She is to be burned immediately. I will conduct the ceremony."

If there was any resistance in Olem, it wasn't mirrored in his words. "At once, High Pontiff." He saluted and opened the door for the others to follow. Outside, Rel had healed Nerida's wing, but she was struggling to get inside.

The Pontiff looked at her, and Olem paused at the door. "Should we tame her, High Pontiff?"

The Pontiff shook his head. "It has been long since we lost this many. There is a part I must play. I'll have the room, Commander. Sub-commander Lynn will aid me while you address the order, yes?"

Olem paused, likely thinking he should be the one to stay. The Pontiff seemed to understand. "My job here is of less importance. Sub-commander Lynn cannot address the Sentinels in your stead in this. You will tell them Deria was lost and ready a defense against this new weapon Dakhra brings toward us. We must protect the holy city."

Olem saluted again and left, but the Pontiff didn't turn from Nerida. "Place the body on the ground, my dear."

Lynn obeyed. Rel paced across the room, then signaled for Ulenia to release Nerida, and closed the doors as he left on the cathedral side. Ulenia lifted her claws and Nerida struggled to her feet, feline body dashing toward Deria, wings tucked close to her body.

The Pontiff did not interfere. He pulled out a shard of ruin-stone, similar to the one Lynn had driven into her own heart to bond with Vedyr. He placed it over Deria's dead heart. "The power held in a griffin's heart is limited," he said. "It will dissipate from a dead shard eventually, and can be reclaimed, but it is always better to extract what we can straight from the source."

The shard in his hands lit up, and the veins pulsed stronger, the white almost silver. He pulled it away, and Nerida's gaze followed. The griffin seemed to relax a touch, as if the pain had been removed from her.

"You have your talents," the Pontiff said to Lynn. "Mine is to help them forget what ails them." He glanced at Nerida. "Put death out of their minds. This shard will be given to another Sentinel in time." The Pontiff raised the stone. Nerida turned and dashed out the griffin-sized opening onto the balcony, then flew off. "She will return when another is trained and has the faith to perform the bonding ritual. Nerida will feel the beat of this new shard when it finds another rider's heart."

Lynn watched in awe. She'd known the Sentinels answered to the Pontiff, but not that he was the one responsible for their continuity.

"Why me?"

"What's that, my dear?"

Lynn put her words into place. "Why show me?"

He offered Lynn the shard, but she hesitated.

"You have been through a Questioning. That puts you in a position to choose a replacement who will be loyal to the Church."

"Does Olem know?"

"He will in time, but for now we must find one who will fight alongside us against Dakhra. Replacing the essence of a griffin's heart is a . . . longer process without the body, and we cannot afford to lose any more Sentinels."

"But . . . Sentinels are trained since childhood. How can we replace one now?"

"You are wise to consider that, my dear, but some risks must be taken in moments of desperation."

The Pontiff didn't look desperate, and his words didn't sound it either.

"Take your time if you must, sister, but know you have the Seraph's blessing to grow Her elite if need be."

He was still holding the shard out, and Lynn finally took it. She didn't want this kind of responsibility. She knew what happened to those apprentices who failed to connect with their griffins. Their pierced hearts would kill instead of empower them, their pledges rejected by the Seraph. She'd have to think about if and when she'd use the shard, but the Pontiff was right; they needed every Sentinel they could get.

The Pontiff gathered the Sentinels in one of the many cleansing chambers within the cathedral. It was large, like most of the cathedral—twenty strides across, and its walls twice as high. A cloister surrounded the chamber, slightly elevated over the central opening that housed the stone slab where Deria's body lay waiting. Only a slit of light entered from above. The Seraph's texts were carved through the walls, as usual. There was a musty stillness to the gloom, as if the smoke of past cleansings had lingered here, casting a thick veil over the darkness. Olem, Mirek, Gwynne, and Rel accompanied Lynn. All who were present needed to be there to see the body burning and be sure death would be cleansed from their minds, and Deria forgotten in time. It was not uncommon for Sentinels to be kept for revival by the Seraph, but the Pontiff's judgement had been swift, and Lynn still wondered if there was something he could hear that she could not. Perhaps the Seraph did speak directly to the man, even if he'd never said as much.

They'd still lost a Sentinel, though, and even if the Pontiff could retain the essence of the griffin's heart for Deria to be replaced, how many would they be able to replace if the Madness took them?

Burke stood by the Pontiff, as did Reznik. A Sentinel was still worth that, at least. The Church leaders would be here for her cleansing. Lynn's gaze lingered on Reznik, who stared back at her. She looked away. She hadn't approached the man, but it seemed he had some interest in her still. Had he not seen enough in the Questioning? The memory sent a chill up Lynn's spine. She focused on the Pontiff, who walked toward Deria's body with a torch in his hand. He paused before the body, torch raised. "The Seraph shows Her strength even in loss. We cleanse Her Domain so death will not endure."

"Death will not endure," the leaders echoed.

"Death will not endure," Lynn and the other Sentinels repeated.

The Pontiff placed the torch onto Deria's body until the flame caught, then stepped back into the cloister beside Olem.

It was a short ceremony—death should not be lingered upon—but none of them moved until the body had turned to ash, the smoke slowly escaping through a slit in the ceiling.

The Pontiff looked around, nodded slightly to Lynn, and left the chamber. The light as he opened the doors made her squint and cover her eyes. She moved to leave but found Reznik beside her.

"Your efforts are much appreciated, Sub-commander," Reznik said. "The one you sent me has been most fruitful in his information."

Lynn realized what Reznik meant. The priest she'd captured before leaving. So much had happened that she'd almost forgotten about the Pontiff's request to root out the True in the holy city. Lynn looked around, cautious of being overheard, but everyone else had filed out.

"You require something from me, yes?" Reznik asked.

"What?" Reznik was the Church's master of secrets, and his bishops were adept at extracting information, but there was no way he could know that she'd asked the Pontiff about learning the secrets of the Bone.

"Our time is limited, Sentinel. It would be wise to speak freely."

She thought back to the Pontiff and the trust he'd placed in her. His trust was founded in her loyalty to the Church, though, not to a single man. If Reznik gave her the opportunity to learn how to control ruin-stone so she could attack the Madness, she would not fail. This was a test of faith—in herself.

Heathen, Roki said. *The Pontiff will end you.*

Lynn breathed his words out of her mind and looked up at Reznik. "I need to learn how to manipulate ruin-stone. Like you did in my Questioning."

A pause. "Why?"

"I believe it is the answer to stopping the Madness."

"You believe you can heal it?" Something changed in the bishop's voice. He thought Lynn either too innocent or too foolish.

"I've seen madmen in control. They wore ruin-stone. Whatever the Dakhrans created, I'm sure ruin-stone is at the heart of it."

"Giving this to one who already holds power such as yours is not a simple matter, Sentinel. I doubt the Pontiff has signed off on this?"

"He hasn't." She couldn't lie, and doubted he'd fall for it if she tried.

"I need assurances, then."

"Of what?"

"Of your collaboration. If I create a monster, I must be sure it will be on my side."

He sees you for the monster you are, Roki said.

Lynn couldn't hold back a glare, but it was probably lost in the smoky gloom. He might have been right. Maybe she was a monster. "I am sworn to the Seraph and the Church. You have tested my loyalty and found me worthy."

"I asked the Pontiff's questions. What you propose is deeper than that. Intentions can change."

"You want to question me again?" It was almost a scoff. He couldn't be serious.

"I need to, if you are to be trusted."

Lynn hesitated. She didn't want to, but, as Elwin had always said, some things just need to be done, regardless of the wanting of them. She breathed out. "Is that all?"

"That is the first step. Consider it your initial instruction."

Lynn was silent for a long moment. "Where do I find you?"

The High Bishop smiled. "We begin now."

Lynn followed him out. She still needed to check on Ferrin, but the Legion wouldn't have been quiet if something had happened to him. Besides, Reznik didn't give her much of a choice. Better to fight the True with what he could teach.

CHAPTER TWENTY-FIVE

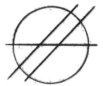

The pain of loss can only be quelled by the drowning of memory. Life is ever looking forward.

— The Book of the Blood

T he ballistae had been loaded onto the ships in good time. Six in all. Adrian wasn't sure it would be enough, but it was better than what he'd arrived with.

They'd been sailing for three days, enough to draw near the Sacanthan shore. Adrian had ordered the ships to be kept back, and they'd docked in a bay to wait for the cover of night. Oma's men had scouted ahead to avoid Addo's lookouts, but found none, so she sent them further on to check the enemy's defenses. Taking down an airship wouldn't be easy, and Adrian needed all the information he could get.

There was a presence beside him on the prow of the ship. He slid his gaze sideways to see Derren looking up at the mark in the sky. Adrian knew the image was a side effect of the blood magic, but the apparition seemed almost alive sometimes.

He followed Derren's gaze upward. Maybe the mark was connected to Derren's more frequent appearances. No one knew what it meant, but it was large enough now that Adrian had decided to keep an eye on it. Maybe it was some kind of Dakhran trick. Some new airship that shone bright so the faithful would focus on the Seraph instead of the invasion, thinking belief alone would save them. Adrian shook his head and closed his eyes, then opened them. Derren was still there.

I hadn't expected the more measured approach, Lord Light. Even in death, it seemed Derren clung to the title.

"Old way wasn't working," Adrian mumbled under his breath.

Aye. Derren chuckled. *You could say that.*

Silence hung between them for a long moment before Adrian turned to him again. "I'm sorry. For everything."

Derren only smiled at him, and Adrian blew out a heavy breath. This wasn't Derren. This was just some figment of Adrian's mind escaping the confines of the darkness that should have held it. A tainted memory that could only be cleansed by taking down Addo.

Steps creaked behind him as Mahir, Amal, Nasir, and Oma approached. Bac was always close, but he didn't bar the passage of Adrian's officers. Oma seemed agitated, and Amal's single eye was always darting up toward the clouds.

"What?" Adrian asked.

"The scouts have returned," Oma said. "There are two airships, not one."

"Six ballistae might not be enough," Amal said. "We need to turn back and find more."

Adrian shook his head. "We don't have more, and we can't delay." Addo was too close. Adrian wouldn't let the coward slip through his fingers again.

"Lord Light," Nasir started, but Adrian's mind was working up a plan. He raised a hand. "The fire you created when we were fighting the madmen in their camp," he said to Nasir. "Can you replicate that with my blood?"

"That was . . . situational, Lord Light. Circumstances must be correct, and a wave of flame large enough to consume the enemy ships would consume the host as well."

"The fire is persistent, yes?"

"Yes, but—"

"We don't need a wave. Once you've sparked the flame, it will spread." Adrian turned to Amal. "I agree. Ballista bolts alone won't bring down the airships, but fire will. Take my blood. Put enough onto the ballista bolts to ignite the tip and shoot them at the airships. You'll need to spread the fire then, Nasir."

The priest watched him with a calculating stare. "Lord Light, that and the wards on our men. If they attack with the Madness, the pain would be excruciating."

"I can take it." This was his sacrifice. He'd take it gladly to get closer to Addo.

"And if you can't? What then? The fire will fail, as will the wards, and the Madness will spread among us."

"Then I guess it's time for faith again, Nasir."

"Even if your plan is successful, how are we to reach the airships before they sink half our ships?"

"We'll break up our forces," Adrian said. "This is the largest ship we have. The harpoon throwers will sink Addo's fleet. Put fire to the harpoons as well. We'll bring attention to this ship, use it as a decoy so the airships are drawn in, then we move in with the second force. Our ships will attack them from the other side when the airships are dealt with."

"You'd risk sinking the command ship?" Mahir asked.

"The rest of our path is on land, Mahir. We won't need it. Nasir, can you create the fire?"

The priest bowed his head. "If you can take the pain, Lord Light."

"I'll lead the command ship," Mahir said.

"Even though we may lose it?" Adrian asked.

"That'll be even more reason. No one better to avoid that risk."

Adrian nodded. "Fair enough. Then ready the ships."

Amal, Oma and Mahir set off to prepare for the attack, but Nasir lingered.

"My mind is set on this, Nasir."

"And I do not wish to sway it, Lord Light. Yet it is my place as high priest of the Legion to remind you that we are back in the Domain. Loss of life should be measured even in war. There will be many lives on this ship. You will be using them all as bait."

Ellana's words drifted into Adrian's mind: *You're just like Father.* They joined the question he'd already asked himself: Was he becoming like Father? Should he not do what was necessary to rid the Domain of its enemies? *I'm not a child. I'm not your little brother; I'm the Light of the Legion, not Father's servant. Not yours either, Ellana.*

Adrian shook his head at Nasir. "Do you think the Domain or the Seraph cares about these lives? These are Azuri. They are not faithful to the Seraph."

"It's death all the same, Lord Light. And you must remember, it is not the Domain that will carry that weight. It is you. You have come far, proven your strength, but our greatest battles are always fought within ourselves. Your choices will define what emerges from within you."

"You're right. I choose not to let the Domain be limited by old texts and false notions of faith. Our enemy does not tie his hands, nor can we afford to if we want to beat them. We will break their blockade and take back Pyrran."

"As you command, Lord Light."

Nasir moved away, and Adrian looked to the setting sun. It was already over halfway into the horizon, but the Seraph's mark shone bright. A man of faith might have watched it and asked the Seraph for help—guidance, favor, maybe even ask Her to cloud the mark so that their approach could be veiled in the night. But Adrian was not that man, and he directed his focus to the call in his blood instead. A light thrum ran through him, and Derren was standing there again, Myrra too, with her ruined face.

You sure about this? Derren asked in a rasping voice.

Adrian nodded. "We all have our sacrifices."

Mahir had put together eight more vessels to accompany the command ship. Adrian and Nasir took one with a ballista and would stay on the backline. The siege engines were covered by thick tarps and the ships set off into the night, leaving a larger force of twenty ships waiting to engage after the airships had been dealt with.

Adrian's force slowly approached the pilfered Sacanthan fleet, with most of the soldiers scanning the skies in search of Dakhran airships. The clouds broke, and two became visible flying over the score of Sacanthan vessels: wooden hulls, no masts or wings or air-filled compartments. Each was kept aloft only by the power of its glowing, ruin-stone powered engine, light bleeding from the stern.

The waters were calm, and the Azuri ships were quiet. They'd been perfected for generations, descended from raiders whose success depended on the silence of their approach. The night provided cover, and there were no alarms or battle cries from the Sacanthan ships.

The galleon was in the center of the front line of five ships, all of them positioned sideways. Adrian was close enough to hear but not see Mahir. "Light the harpoons!" Adrian commanded in Azuri.

Fires breached the night—slowly at first, then spreading as more of the harpoon heads were put to flame. Enemy shadows moved across their own decks, brought alive by the fire of the Azuri ships, but Mahir gave them no time to prepare. He lowered an arm and the harpoons fired with loud whooshes, racing over the sea behind burning tips and smashing into the enemy vessels. The bolts ripped through wood in flaming streaks, sending up sprays, splinters, and the screams of enemy soldiers who were flung away. Two of the enemy ships caught fire, and frantic shadows ran along the deck to put it out. Other ships were cracked and seemed to be taking on water. Harpoons shot from four more of Adrian's ships, lighting up the enemy fleet that was only now moving.

Ships angled towards Adrian, revealing bronze-cast rams at their prows. Ten of them—half the enemy force. They cut through the smooth water, aiming to ram the wide side of Adrian's front line.

The ones who didn't head straight for the firing Azuri vessels were maneuvering around, trying to use their numbers to pen Adrian's ships in as the two airships went straight for the command ship. They'd taken the bait: the command ship was the largest of the fleet, and the most formidably armed.

Bac shifted beside Adrian, uncomfortable with the proximity of the airships perhaps, even on the back line, but the approaching airship was what Adrian had hoped for.

"Get ready," Adrian told Amal. The general shouted orders to the men on their smaller ship.

Adrian watched the boats cut a path toward them, trying to measure whether his ships could take the impact, but as his gaze moved from prow to prow, half of the enemy ships turned, and glinting arrow tips reflected off the fire-lit harpoons. The Madness.

"Take cover!" Adrian bellowed, but the arrows were already streaming through the air. "Amal, keep the men back! Don't hesitate, slay any who've been touched by the potions!"

Bac drew his blade beside Adrian and raised a shield overhead.

"Back!" Amal said, and drew his curved blade. "Raise your shields. Arrows from above!" He stepped back as the arrows fell onto the ships, even reaching Adrian's crew on the back line.

The tingle rose in his blood—a whisper at first, but rising. A sizeable contingent of his soldiers was warded. Their stones linked to Adrian, but there was no telling how long he'd be able to hold their sanity. The strain from his men's wards was dulled by Kel Bradaz's enchantments, which shouldered the load of the Madness, but there were thousands stinging at Adrian until every landed arrow cut down to the bone. The pain was not from the tips that pierced his men, but the Madness-infused potions that coated the arrows and the vials that exploded onto his troops, infecting them with the Dakhran plague.

Adrian's blood was fire, the pain twisting at his insides as he tried to hold on. He grabbed the railing, almost splintering the wood. Nasir was beside him, a hand on his shoulder, but he pushed the priest away.

We all have our sacrifices.

He squeezed his eyes shut, taking in the scent of burning ships. A loud crash pulled Adrian's eyes open as the other half of the charging ships rammed into Adrian's frontline. The enemy tried to gain space for another charge, but Mahir had ordered his troops to rope the enemy ships in. The Azuri had been ready with ropes and hooks and planks. They took on the blow, but Mahir boarded the enemy ships to avoid another strike.

"Damn it, Mahir!" Adrian shouted, but he knew he wouldn't be heard. The admiral had issued orders like an Azuri raider of the past, taking no account of the madmen who might lurk on the opposing ship. His men were engaged, curved blades slashing at Addo's forces. Shadows danced on the decks behind the flames, accompanied by screams and growls that crossed the sea. Adrian clenched his jaw and looked straight into the dark, watery abyss. Myrra was standing over it, staring back at him. Offering a hand. *Take it. Share your pain.*

Red lines coiled around her arm, but they were woven with darker lines that snaked up her body from the sea below. Her face was still mangled, and the aching in Adrian's chest grew stronger at the sight of it. Almost strong enough to make him take Myrra's hand, but something still held him back. Maybe something in Nasir's words, cautioning him about the magic and death. Or perhaps it was some underlying instinct, but Adrian did not reach out.

He looked up. The airships had men firing arrows at the Azuri on the decks. They had their own ballistae, but the airships were flying low so their weapons and archers could take better aim. They were close enough.

Adrian struggled against the pain, pulling the word from within. "Fire!" he managed to yell, but even as he did, burning ballista bolts were already flying upward from the Azuri ships.

Three found their target in the first airship, and Adrian caught Nasir's movements from the corner of his eye, weaving his signs to grow the fire. The flames leapt up the side of the airship, climbing it like hungry beasts. It burned at Adrian as well, all up his back, and then Myrra was there again.

Give me your pain, she said. *Let me use it.*

One last jolt of pain had Adrian's vision swimming, and he relented. He gave her his hand. Pain flooded through Adrian, tearing a blistering path over his arm and the back of his head as Myrra's tendrils wrapped around him. They burned to the bone, creeping over his face and settling around his eyes. Something in that pain directed him and led his gaze upward, to the fire on the airships. He could almost feel it, almost touch the fire with his fingertips, as if the blood that fueled their burning tied the flames to the burning within him. He felt the ties, like he'd felt the strings in the blood binding. He pushed the pain through the paths that linked him to the fire, and the flames roared across the airship. It turned away, but the fire had already taken most of it, forcing enemy soldiers to jump over the side. Adrian pushed more pain toward it with a howl and the ship became a ball of flame that plummeted toward the sea.

Battle cries rang in the distance, and Adrian turned to see the larger force of his ships rushing toward the Sacanthan fleet. They had their own rams mounted at the prow and slammed into the enemy, splintering wood and splitting the enemy's focus. Men fired arrows from both sides as the Legion boarded the enemy ships. Their foe seemed to be running out of the Madness. Perhaps Syvern had not given Addo enough for a large battle, and Addo had relied on the first wave of arrows to spread it. As the Legion advanced on enemy vessels, men leapt into the sea and swam toward shore.

Adrian's eyes still burned as he looked up at the second airship. It had turned away, fleeing or going after the larger Legion force that had just engaged the Sacanthan fleet. Adrian couldn't let it move away. The airship had taken a glancing shot, not enough for the flame to catch. The other bolt seemed to have missed, and the ballista-carrying ships were too far away to reload and take a second shot.

Screaming pulled Adrian's attention back to the ballista on his ship. It was unmanned, burning bolt waiting, while Madmen fought his new Legion all around it. He'd used his pain to fuel the fire, but that seemed to have breached some of the wards. The madmen moved with incredible speed, taking down Azuri left and right.

The man who was to fire the bolt had been impaled on the claws of an attacker, and the soldiers around him were transforming.

"To me!" Amal screamed. He raised his Azuri scimitar and dashed fearlessly at the closest madman.

"Together! Go for the head, swarm them, hit and run!" Amal's soldiers swarmed the madmen as he commanded, and Adrian found his moment.

"Cover me," he told Bac. He raised his sword, forced his way through the pain, and ran for the ballista behind Bac as the big man stabbed and kicked an infected Azuri from their path. Adrian slashed another who'd just turned, feeling the impact all up his arm. They pushed past a third who was clutching his head in pain—and reached the ballista. It was loaded and ready to fire.

Adrian let go of his sword and grabbed the ballista with both hands while Bac hacked and slashed behind him. Adrian swiveled the device upward, aimed, and let fly.

Adrian held his breath as the bolt cut the night, watching as it crashed through the outer hull and into the airship's heart. Nasir was already weaving his signs. The fire caught and Adrian fed it the pain, pulling more from Myrra. The flame spread, taking over the airship like a madness of its own, consuming its host.

Adrian watched as the airship plummeted into the sea in a burning, screaming mass of wood and soldiers. He gave one final glance at Myrra, not wanting to let go. He needed to see her face, needed her beside him, but his muscles were shaking, and the pain had already lightened his head. He released the power she'd been feeding him.

Adrian stumbled away from the ballista. Amal had swarmed enough of his men onto the maddened soldiers to deal with them, and the other ships on the back line had cleared the enemies and turned soldiers as well. It seemed Adrian's wards had been enough.

"Lord Light!" Amal shouted. "Do we signal a chase?"

The frontline ships were already turning toward the fleeing

Sacanthan fleet. Mahir would give his own command if Adrian did not.

"Stand down." It came out as a rasp at first. "Stand down." Amal heard him the second time and signaled to his men to relay the command. Adrian wouldn't risk chasing them blindly into a trap, and there was no need to expose the Legion to more of the Madness. Let Addo have what remained of his troops. Adrian would overpower him in Pyrran.

Adrian stepped across the deck, breathing hard as he looked over the burning wooden carcasses sinking into the Ulean. The path through the inlet that led to Pyrran was now open. Nasir drew close, offering support as Amal and Bac watched, but Adrian did not take the priest's arm. Myrra was beside him and held him up herself.

Her face seemed to have healed a touch, approaching what Adrian had known in life. Every step closer to Addo, to his vengeance, seemed to heal his memory of her.

Adrian hobbled to the edge of the ship and supported himself on the wooden railing. Cheering rose from the farthest ships, then caught like a flame itself as the frontline abandoned their intended chase and returned to the command ship instead. Men hit weapons against shields and wooden railings on Adrian's own ship, and Amal started the chant.

"Xakhar, Xakhar!"

Soon the crews of the other ships were chanting as well. It wasn't what he had in mind when he thought of proving himself to his father, or when he thought of being loved like Jovu. But he seemed to have sparked an old memory in the Azuri, one of conquest that had been stifled for a century by the Domain. He didn't deny the warmth of satisfaction spreading through him, but it was still too early to savor it. Addo still lived. It was time to take back Pyrran.

CHAPTER TWENTY-SIX

Wars are rarely born of logic, but there is unique opportunity for scientific advancement in the desperation of men fighting to protect all they hold dear.

— *Studies in Dakhran Alchemy*

K admus paused at the top of the stairs, clutching a vial with his latest cure. He tried to remember Nima as she had been. Laughing, meddling with ingredients, marveling as they changed colors. This time, it would work. He'd been tampering with this for a week. It had to work.

Bahar's focus had not been on a cure the past week. The armies were about to march, and he needed the weaponized Madness. The taste on Kadmus's tongue was as bitter as the scent of the brewing, but he'd done it. He'd finished brewing the potions without letting even High Priest Malit close to them. The help he accepted was from acolytes performing menial tasks—nothing that might reveal his secrets or allow anyone else to replicate his brew. He would not give another the ability to spread this curse.

He paced down the hall toward Nima's room, glad Bahar would soon be gone. He wondered for a moment what the Church would think of so many Domain lives being thrown into the jaws of war, but he knew the religion was for the faithful to follow and not the clergy. It was the tool of the Church, a lie to steer men into action. Their morals and scriptures were nothing but the shackles of old men trying to keep the people under control.

Kadmus focused on what was under his control. Nima would be healed. He put a hand on her door handle but was stopped by the bell that chimed every time the door to the shop opened. He spun round, frowning. He hadn't locked the door, but business had not been good since the conscription. Something about looming war had people staying indoors, perhaps finally recognizing the threats around and within their nation. The only logical conclusion was that whoever had walked into his shop worked for Bahar. Kadmus pocketed the vial and descended the steps.

He couldn't hide his surprise when he found Bahar himself standing before him. He was dressed in what seemed to be a travelling cloak, perhaps with armor underneath. Kadmus had kept up the healing sessions, and while he hadn't managed to get rid of all the scars, his face seemed to be regaining a semblance of normality. The limp was another story, though. Bahar had insisted that Kadmus focus on it, but he'd only managed a slight improvement. Some wounds were too deep to be fully healed, even if Kadmus brought back the pain of the moment they were inflicted.

Bahar still had his cane but leaned less heavily on it.

"I thought your man would come in the afternoon," Kadmus said.

"There will be no healing today. I've come to let you know of the march."

Every muscle in Kadmus turned to ice. His back stiffened, and he tried to tilt his head to hide the surprise. Surely he didn't mean for Kadmus to march; there were enough men in the newly conscripted army.

"You need something for the road?"

Bahar chuckled. "You're smarter than that, Kadmus. You're coming with me."

Kadmus had known it, but the words seemed to bring a cold reality with them. A reality that clawed at Kadmus's throat. He couldn't leave Nima alone, but he was sure Bahar would not let go of this. "Why?" was all he could offer.

"You'll continue the healing and oversee the storage of the potions. They'll be our best shot against the clans. I won't have the concoctions arriving powerless."

"I know nothing of marching. I can relay instructions to a priest. I'll only slow you down."

Bahar shook his head. "This isn't a request."

Kadmus's mind leapt at the possible excuses, but there were none he could come up with. Keeping up the resistance might prompt Bahar to suspect there was something stronger holding Kadmus back. He couldn't risk Nima, so he simply nodded. "When do we leave?"

"Tomorrow, at dawn, be at the west gate of the upper city."

Kadmus nodded again, and Bahar left without ceremony, his cane tapping lightly on the floorboards of Kadmus's shop. Kadmus's gaze fell back to the cure he'd taken from his pocket. If this worked, he might be able to use it to stay behind and gain the favor of a councilor, maybe even the queen. Her throne had been empty, after all, and if she was infected, Kadmus was sure she'd want to see the man who produced a cure.

He ascended the steps again, going straight for Nima's door this time. This would work. It had to.

He knelt beside Nima's bed and spread the ruin-stone out around her. There was a lot more now—Bahar had fulfilled his promise—and Kadmus put all he could in contact with his daughter's skin.

Her breathing hadn't changed much from the last time she'd convulsed. Kadmus took that as a good sign. Stability was preferable to degenerating health. He held the vial in his hand for a long while, almost afraid of using it. It sent a stab of shame through him, as if he were a boy again, skulking through the church grounds, praying for the Seraph's acceptance. Hoping an impossible hope that his parents had been mistaken and would come back for him.

He gritted his teeth, trying to grind away the fear. He'd come further than anyone would ever have given him credit for. He would be the one to cure this Madness. Kadmus removed the stopper and poured the liquid down Nima's throat.

She twitched, slowly, then again, then arched her back with a scream. It sent Kadmus sprawling back onto his backside, but he knew pain was part of healing. He scrambled back to her bedside, grabbing her hand and watching, hoping as his daughter fought the infection within her, body twisting against the pain.

She stopped suddenly. Too abrupt for Kadmus's confidence to be revived, but her breathing seemed stronger now. The darkness around her eyes persisted, but there were fewer blackened veins around them, and the stain on her skin was not as deep. He waited, still hoping the effects would work their way through her and remove the curse.

Kadmus sat by his daughter's bed until he lost track of time. The sun had set, and shadows crept through the room until they made it their own. Still he sat, waiting, but there was no change in her condition. The fear he'd been gritting between his teeth had turned to frustration, then anger, and in the dark, for the first time since he didn't know when, Kadmus wept.

He hadn't allowed himself tears since a child, a promise to himself about his own strength in the face of a world that tried to tell him he would never be good enough to be part of it. He had no control over the tears. He'd given it all he had, and still the Madness would not release its grasp on Nima. He'd have to leave, and the thought of leaving her behind was unbearable. No one even knew she existed, and he couldn't tell Bahar. It would only give the man more leverage over him. He couldn't run either. Kadmus needed the resources. Nima hadn't been cured, though he'd given her strength enough to keep the fickle flame of hope alive. He hated hope. Hope was only a step away from faith, and there was no certainty in that, but he'd failed to find certainty in his cures as well. It appeared he wouldn't be able to solve this alone.

He almost smiled at the irony, cold tears drying on his face. When life forced him to trust someone, it was with what was most precious to him. Kadmus stood, brushing Nima's hands with his, and slowly left the room. His faith in the Seraph had failed him as a child. His faith in himself failed him now. Was there even a way to defeat this enemy?

He shuffled down the corridor. Perhaps he wouldn't defeat it, but he was too stubborn to give up. He made his way out of the shop and went in search of Grunt.

The nighttime streets were empty, and Kadmus kept to the shadows more out of habit than conscious effort. He was still numb with the frustration of failure and the thought of having to trust Nima to someone else's care.

Kadmus knocked. Like last time, the man's surprise was plain on his face. There was something behind his stare, though, as if he noticed Kadmus was not his usual self. Perhaps Grunt saw the streaks of tears on Kadmus's face. "Come to convince me?" Grunt said.

Kadmus simply shook his head. "I've come to ask for a favor." The words were difficult to form, foreign. "It's the only one I'll ever ask of you, but it's the most important request I've ever made."

Grunt stepped out and closed the door a few more inches. "What's going on, Leech? You don't talk like this."

"Nima is alive."

Grunt's eyes widened, as if some part of him had unconsciously been picking up the details and was now putting them together. "You've been trying to heal her?"

Kadmus nodded. "She's stable, but the Madness is . . . persistent."

Grunt looked down, his expression taking on the shadows of the night around him. "What do you need?"

"Bahar is forcing me to march with him to the clanlands." Kadmus breathed deep. His mind was still trying to convince him of the insane possibility that he could solve this on his own, but his heart knew there was no other way. "I need you to look after her while I'm gone."

Grunt looked at Kadmus for a long time, then let out a breath of his own. "Of course, Leech. I'm not a brewer, though."

"I've prepared everything. The dosage is in each of these vials. One a day." Kadmus brought out a vial. "There's more in my shop. It'll be better if you bring her here. You won't need help carrying her, I suppose?"

The big man grunted, perhaps even chuckled.

"I'll take care of her, Kadmus. You can count on it."

That was the problem. He had to count on it.

"Should we fetch her now?" Grunt asked.

Kadmus nodded and turned to walk back to the store with Grunt in tow.

CHAPTER TWENTY-SEVEN

True power lies in faith, but what defines a faith as true, and what should we be willing to do to prove it to the Seraph?

— Alterian preacher

Reznik had given Lynn only a few hours of rest, and she'd been trapped in the visions of the second Questioning every time she closed her eyes. This Questioning was more thorough, as promised, but the scenes had been the same. Gheria still rose around her, and Alren, Roki, Cara, and Dentos were all there, questioning her loyalty and her resolve to swing the blade and end the Madness. It seemed Reznik wanted to be sure that Lynn would not hesitate to wield death when needed. Apparently, he was satisfied, and now walked before her with a sputtering torch, making his way through tight corridors in the bowels of the cathedral. She'd never been this deep and had to fight the trepidation her voices were trying to pull her into.

The corridors narrowed until they reached a stairwell, which descended in a curve that opened into a wide chamber. There were voices. Pale green light came from lanterns hanging over wooden doors with barred windows that lined both sides of the chamber. Cells.

"You brought me here so no one finds my body?" Lynn asked. Part of her was serious, her mind already searching for Vedyr.

Reznik eyed her. "Focus." He paced forward and stopped before a door that had no sound coming from behind. He took a key from his robe and opened the door, then stepped inside.

A man was bound to a chair, blindfolded and gagged.

"What is this?" Lynn asked.

"Our test subject."

"What?"

"He's a Dakhran scout, captured by the Domain. We'll be performing your training on him."

Lynn frowned in the half-lit cell. "This isn't . . ."

"Right? Nothing is right about war, Sentinel. This is what must be done." Reznik produced a shard of ruin-stone from his robe. "This stone has been softened. It will allow you to connect with him. You must understand the moment. Understand what he is feeling. You will be able to see his emotions."

Lynn felt her eyes widen. "The colors?"

The bishop might have frowned at her in the dark, but he didn't ask how she knew about the colors.

"Yes. Each is represented by a different color. You must connect to it, have it coalesce into something you can touch and then manipulate."

"And how will that cure the Madness?"

"We are all made of emotions. If you dig deep enough, they will lead you to a person's core, to what controls them, keeps them sane. Be careful, however. We are easy to break. Make sure you have your answers before that."

Lynn wasn't sure she understood all of it, but it seemed like enough to start. She paused before taking the stone from Reznik. "I assume this comes with a price?"

He looked at the prisoner, then back at her. "You will follow my commands. This is not a power I will let loose unchecked."

Lynn shook her head in the darkness. She couldn't just follow orders blindly. "I—"

"There is no negotiation in this, Sentinel. I am giving you the blade, and I will tell you when and how to swing it."

Like you swung it to take our heads, Dentos said.

He stretched out a vial to her. "Take this. It will help you connect to him."

Lynn hesitated. She knew that the moment she touched the stone to the prisoner, she'd be accepting Reznik's proposal and agreeing to be a tool for whatever it was that he desired. She'd been judged for leaving the Sentinels, but that was her choice. What Reznik proposed now could lead her down the same path that had made her take her companions' lives. Was this any different, or was it as unavoidable as the choice she'd made before?

Stop being a coward, Alren said.

The lives you take will be to save countless others, Dentos said. *There is no use in power if it isn't used.*

Lynn took a deep breath. She'd come back to defend the Domain, and this was the price. *No more running.* She took the vial and swallowed.

"Good." He placed the stone in Lynn's hand. "Touch it to his skin."

Lynn did as he said. She'd become so accustomed to the initial sensation that she could almost ignore the pulsing in her ribs now. All was dark for a moment, then the chamber was filled with light. She was under the shade of trees, marching with a ragged group of silent men. They neared the edge of the trees, and a road that led to a city. Lynn looked up, but that same vision from her initial Questioning invaded her own. The dungeon with two shaded men standing before her. One seemed to hold something that glinted. Glass or metal, maybe both. The other weaved something with his fingers. Some kind of thread or ribbon. Her ribs ached even more.

"Focus," a disembodied voice said. She was conscious enough

with the vision to recognize it as Reznik. Lynn gritted her teeth and felt her fingers tighten around something. It was the stone Reznik had given her. She focused on it, feeling its pull. Almost like her Bond with Vedyr. She was weakening as well, same as with the Bond.

She was thrust back to the group waiting by the trees. She looked to the distant city. It was Alteria.

Her breath caught. Dakhra's armies had reached the city undetected. She had to get out of this and warn the city. She tried releasing the stone, but her fingers wouldn't move. As when Reznik questioned her, she couldn't let go of whatever bond had formed between the prisoner and herself. She studied the men. One of them had waves of orange streaming off him.

Lynn stepped close. Reznik said she needed to connect to the man. She touched him, expecting him to turn and face her, but he didn't move. All she felt was anticipation. The nervousness as they watched Alteria for enemies. She was feeling what the man felt. Even in the vision, she still had the stone in her hand. She tried to touch it to the man, but nothing happened.

The image shifted. It was night now, and the man crept below the Alterian walls. He was hooded and had a partner, but the orange waves still surrounded him. Stronger now, and darker. She tried to touch the waves but couldn't grasp them. The whole ordeal made her feel insane. Here she was in a vision, grasping at colors without being able to tell truth from memory. Or who it belonged to.

The man moved on along the wall, and it seemed like every step drew from Lynn. Like the Bond was taking more every time. Unlike her Bond with Vedyr, this one gave nothing back. She followed as the men crouched at the edge of the wall while guards walked past. His companion slipped and sent loose stones rolling across the Alterian patrol's path.

The guard shouted to his companions, raising the alarm. The waves of orange around the men changed to green. It hit Lynn, and she recognized the fear, the utter terror of being caught. They were surrounded by the Alterian guard, and the intensity of the man's emotion pulled harder at Lynn. She started reciting her names. The safety net she always used with Vedyr. *Alren, Ro . . . ki.*

The names vanished. Her mind was faltering, pieces drifting into depths where memory could not reach. She had to do something, or she'd be lost, hollow. She grasped at the man, who backed away from the guards, his fear spiking. Streaks of red rage flashed through Lynn. She fought back, trying to hold on, but the fear and rage pulled harder as rough hands grasped the man's shoulder. Too hard for Lynn to hold on. The anger rose in him, overtaking the fear when he realized what awaited him.

The anger brought a clarity to Lynn. She knew the shape of it, the familiar heat she was used to pushing toward Vedyr. She stopped pulling against the emotion and opened herself to it instead.

The fear that flooded into her almost had her running. Her ears rang, her vision was blurred and tinted white—but something anchored her through it all. The ruin-stone in her hand was a tether between the vision and her body standing in the dungeon. She held onto it, embracing the fear and the anger. She felt close, like she could control it.

Then the prisoner pulled out a vial and downed the potion that sent him spiraling into madness.

Lynn screamed. She was too entrenched to differentiate between the man and herself. Her nails grew into claws, tearing at her fingertips. The man slashed at a guard, then another, and the tainted taste of death rode her tongue. Blood and rage.

"Now is the moment." Reznik's voice broke through the Madness of her vision. "Focus. Use the stone."

Lynn pressed her fingers tighter around the stone that still refused to fall from her grip. She was thankful for it now. It anchored her in the sea of overwhelming anger. She thought of Vedyr, of how she could use these emotions—but she still couldn't grasp them.

"Open your eyes."

Lynn didn't realize they'd been shut. She opened them. There were more waves now. The red and green of anger and fear was tainted with the black of what Lynn could only guess was the Madness. It had coalesced into strands that flailed about the maddened prisoner. She raised the stone, as if calling for the wayward strands. They moved toward it, coiling, tightening into a solid rope of emotion. She did what she'd always done as a Sentinel. Maybe this was why Reznik needed her. She could give and take emotion as she did with Vedyr. She pulled, trying to separate the anger and the fear from the darkness of the Madness, pulling the emotions into herself while avoiding the rest.

The rope resisted, so Lynn pulled harder still. Her ribs burned, and something snapped. The world flashed white, and she was thrust back into herself. She fell onto her hands and knees, panting, hair soaked in sweat that ran down her face and pooled on the cold stone floor.

She looked up at the prisoner. He wasn't moving. His hands had grown claws, and he'd chewed his way out of the cloth that gagged him. Her heart rose into her throat, and she looked to Reznik. "What happened?" It was almost a shout.

"You killed him."

"What?"

"I told you. We are fragile. You'll need to be more careful next time."

"He wasn't like that before I started."

Reznik raised an empty vial. "How do you think we experiment on a cure, Sentinel? We've taken enough vials from scouts like these. He needed to be infected."

"You gave it to him?" She wouldn't believe it. Reznik was one of the Church leaders, not some madman like Syvern.

Reznik shot her an amused gaze. "I thought you'd be accustomed to taking a life. Are the Sentinels not the judges who keep our lands clean?"

"We judge the unworthy, and we judge them consciously!"

"This man was already dead. What difference does it make who pulls the final strand of life from him?"

Lynn rose to her feet. She was exhausted, but she could feel the burning in her eyes, and saw the silver light up the dark chamber. It made every difference. She would not be betrayed into death's arms without even knowing it. "This was not what we agreed on."

"This was exactly what we agreed on." Reznik showed no fear. "You cannot expect to save people without sacrifice, Sentinel. If one as high in the ranks of the Sentinel order as you thinks that is the way of the world, then the Breath is truly lost."

He's right, you know, things aren't as black and white as you think, Alren said.

Shut up! Lynn screamed at him in her mind.

"I have showed you the path," said Reznik. "Now you must learn how to walk it." He walked around her to the door. "The Pontiff is no fool. You'll have to progress on your own for now. Each of these cells holds a prisoner and a vial. You'll need someone to help you administer it, but I'm sure you can manage. Find me when you've developed a . . . lighter touch." He opened the door and looked back at her. "Follow the lanterns. They'll lead you out. Remember the way so you can get back." Reznik closed the door behind him.

Lynn screamed out her frustration and slammed a fist into the floor, pulverizing the stone with Vedyr's strength. Death's voice was soft in her mind. *You can't run from me.*

Lynn knew it was true, but having it thrust unwillingly upon her left her feeling tainted. Vedyr had taken enough of her anger through the Bond—she released it and took a breath. The taste was bitter, but the voice in her mind was right. She'd promised to stop running, even from death. Still, she couldn't infect others just for practice. Was death necessary for life to endure? The question burned inside her, the words a splitting pain in her head. It couldn't be, not like this.

How many lives will you save for the cost of a few who are condemned? Alren asked. *They're prisoners. They're already dead. A Sentinel's duty is to weave death as their own.*

No. This was not the work of a Sentinel. Death was to be dealt only as a final resort. Killing bound prisoners was not the same thing, no matter how unworthy the Church deemed them.

Lynn stepped from the cell and found a single lantern illuminating the stairwell. She followed the lanterns up the stairs as Reznik had instructed and found her way back to ground level.

She passed the Ever-Tree, almost averting her gaze. If a leader of the Church like Reznik was telling her to sacrifice prisoners, what did that say about the Faith? And what of her own faith? Was she still following the right path? Was this what the Seraph wanted? She might be answering through the falling leaves of the Ever-Tree. Were they a reflection of her pain at seeing what Her Church was becoming?

The questions walked beside Lynn all the way to her room. She stepped in with little thought, but her hands flew to her weapons when she noticed a figure standing within.

Ferrin raised his hands but said nothing. He brought a finger to his lips. "Best be quiet. I've been approached."

"Do they have ears inside the cathedral?"

"I don't know." His tone was still hushed. "But they have people inside it."

"Did they give you a place?"

Ferrin nodded. "They're meeting tonight, in the catacombs of the crumbled church of the Bracken Quarter."

Lynn frowned. The broken church had been a wreck for years. The ruin-stone had been removed, but the building was kept as a reminder to the locals of what a lack of faith could do to them and their city. It was one of the few uprisings in Alterian history, and Lynn found a strange sense of irony in the location. As if the enemy was using the old uprising as the symbol for a new one. "Are you ready?" she asked.

Ferrin nodded.

"No matter your training, these people are unpredictable and you can't know what they'll do. You do nothing until I arrive, understand?"

Ferrin eyed her with a hardness in his gaze that she'd not seen before. "I'm not a child," he said.

"What you think of yourself changes nothing. They know you're a ward, and they're fanatics. There are no rules with them."

Ferrin sighed. "I won't start a fight."

"Good. I'll watch your back."

They left under cover of night. Lynn rode on Vedyr, flying over Ferrin as he made his way to the Bracken Quarter. The Seraph's mark shone high above Lynn, and she lingered on it for a moment. "Help me. I need your guidance to beat this thing."

She didn't expect an answer. Even if it seemed the Seraph spoke to the Pontiff, Lynn knew death's voice was likely the only one she'd ever hear. She kept her gaze on the mark, with something beating deep within her. She just wanted this to end.

Ferrin passed some kind of commotion on the streets, and Lynn was struck with memories of Durnn and Pyrran. People were pointing fingers below, and Lynn thought she saw a bottle fly into the crowd. Would it be blood-filled streets this time, or a crowd mobbing one of the more ragged-looking refugees?

She flew low, but patrols were breaking up whatever had started, and Ferrin had already skirted it. He strode down darker, emptier streets into the Bracken Quarter and paused where he'd been told to wait. Lynn flew high overhead on Vedyr, ready, but far enough away to seem like just another of the many Sentinels flying over the holy city in the night. It was galling to know these people thought they could act undetected with the full force of the Sentinels in Alteria. Well, not the full force—Ildred had taken a score with him to Durnn and still hadn't returned.

Lynn refocused on the streets below as Ferrin followed hooded men down alleyways toward the broken church. There were few, if any, patrols here, and the men walked quickly through the shadows and into the ruins. Lynn knew she couldn't fly Vedyr close, so she stroked his neck, brought him near a building in one of the neighboring quarters, and jumped off.

Vedyr eyed her with what could have been concern. She'd felt it at times through their Bond, but to see it in his gaze was new. Perhaps even the griffins were not immune to the chaos that enveloped the Domain. They weren't used to seeing Sentinels fall, either.

Lynn patted his neck and drew close. "I'll be fine. You'll know if I need you." She let the heat of his thick fur coat seep into her and touch her heart. Vedyr answered with a low rumble, perhaps slightly comforted, then took off.

She'd walked enough among shadows to know where to step without being seen, and soon she'd twisted her way through enough alleyways to be sure she wasn't being followed. She approached the broken church and found what seemed to be a small gap only partially covered with a slab of stone. A strong man would have had to drag it, probably alerting those within, but Lynn closed her eyes and gave Vedyr the outrage of having to chase down the enemy within Alteria. He returned his strength to her, and she lifted the slab and placed it aside.

The expression on the man's face within suggested he couldn't decide whether he was more surprised by Lynn lifting the slab on her own, or that someone was actually trying to break in. She dealt him a quick blow to the gut that sent him wheezing to the ground, unable to call for help. Then she knocked him out with another blow to the back of the head.

The light inside was sparse, but the stairwell leading down was well-tended, as if the place had been used for a long time. Lynn crept downward, scanning for more lookouts, but she found only shadows along her path. The steps led to a small, torchlit hall that ended at a door. The side wall had crumbled yet seemed stable enough for Lynn to climb. She couldn't go through the door without risk of being seen.

She crept up, keeping low until thin beams of light broke through the rocks where part of the chamber beyond had caved in. Lynn didn't move. There must have been a score inside, Ferrin among them. The chamber had been relieved of furniture, but for a statue of the six-winged Seraph in the middle. Red lines had been painted on Her hands, as if they were bleeding. A man stood below the statue, speaking softly. Lynn couldn't make out his words but recognized the vial he held in one hand.

The room grew silent, and Lynn got closer, trying to make out what was happening through gaps in the stone.

"No, wait!" Ferrin's voice.

Lynn didn't hesitate. She ripped away the loose rock with Vedyr's strength and jumped into the room, arms at the ready.

A man with a scar on the right side of his face stood facing her. The people around him wore hoods and mostly ragged cloaks. All bore some kind of makeshift weapon—lengths of metal and wood —and showed no fear. Ferrin was nearly cornered but used the moment to retreat to Lynn's side.

The scarred man stepped up to her, close enough to grab. "Hello, Sentinel. Have you come to kill us all?"

Something glimmered in his hand, and Lynn didn't hesitate. She grabbed the man by the scruff and threw him at the wall behind her, the stone cracking under his weight. None of the others moved. They simply watched Lynn as she turned to the slumped man.

Take him, Cara said.

Lynn moved to the scarred man. "You have spread death and Madness within the holy city; your life is forfeit to the Church. Tell me where to find your leaders and I may spare you for imprisonment."

The man laughed at her. "Don't you see? None of it matters. My leaders are the same as yours. We all follow the Seraph, but we are the True faithful to Her cause. You can kill me, but the Seraph will bring me back. This city is lost. She is coming." He laughed again, almost echoing Roki's maddening laugh in Lynn's mind. "These people have come to prove their faith. They know what to do. You cannot stop us. You can burn our bodies, but She will remake them, just like She did in the beginning. The Church does not hold us. The Seraph's time has come, and She will smite you down."

The man pulled out a sharp piece of metal and Lynn dashed forward, taking Vedyr's strength and feeling the burning in her eyes. She grabbed the man by the collar, but he didn't strike at her. He'd stuck the sharp metal into his neck, but still held a smile as blood welled in his mouth. Lynn jumped back as he coughed it out.

Bodies thudded behind her, and she turned to find the others repeating the man's action. The shock of realization glued her to the spot. She'd never seen anything like it. They were taking their own lives. Somehow, this man had convinced them that death was a haven, and the Seraph would save them. They were embracing death, certain of their worthiness even if the Church did not preserve their bodies.

The leader she'd dropped let out a strange gasp, and Lynn turned to see a reddish smoke drifting from his lolling jaw. She could feel her eyes widening. They weren't just killing themselves; they were trying to infect her with the Madness.

She grabbed Ferrin and bolted for the door, tearing it off its hinges and pulling him as they ran upward, away from the madmen below. She bounded up the steps, multiple at a time, holding the air in her lungs. The breath of fresh night air was almost a blessing in itself, but Lynn did not relax. "Did they get you?" she asked. "Did you breathe it in?"

Ferrin was panting as well, but he shook his head. "You were faster."

Lynn regained her breath and waited at the edge of the steps for a long time, but there was no movement. A cold fear took hold of Lynn's gut; she almost expected the Madness to creep up on her. What if Ferrin showed the signs? What if she turned? Would she take her life like the madmen below? Lynn held her spot, gaze shifting from the descending steps to Ferrin, but neither of them showed symptoms of turning.

She breathed out the tension, thoughts returning to what the heathen had said. He'd claimed the people were there to prove their faith. It seemed their notion of faith was giving their lives, hoping to infect a Sentinel with their Madness. A different kind of Madness at that. Lynn had never seen it turned into smoke, or stream from the mouths of the dead.

"Lynn?"

She turned to Ferrin, heart pounding. Had he been infected, after all? She stepped toward him, but his eyes were clear and he appeared normal. "What?"

"They were talking about something before you crashed in. They said they've rigged the walls. Not only the walls, the whole city. They have a brew. The same as the one in the arrows Dakhra uses. They're planning to set them off when the airships arrive. They wanted to give me a potion. They said it would ensure my loyalty. They have people ready to blow the walls, wanted me to be one of them."

"That's impossible!"

"Is it? They've infiltrated the city. They've convinced people to take their lives and call it faith. You said it yourself: they're unpredictable."

Lynn paced back and forth, shaking her head. She didn't want to believe it, but the risk was too great to ignore.

She grabbed the slab that had covered the entrance and slammed it back in place with a frustrated scream. "Have the Legion sweep the walls. Tell me if you find anything."

Ferrin nodded.

"We need to find the Pontiff," Lynn said. "This goes deeper than we thought."

CHAPTER TWENTY-EIGHT

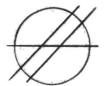

Pelaket might be called unassailable, but Pyrran is probably the hardest city in the Domain to siege—not because of its high walls, but because of its many routes for smuggling and escape.

— *Histories of the Domain*

The ship creaked and groaned as Adrian's Azuri fleet sailed through the inlet toward Pyrran. The Sacanthan capital loomed in the distant night, its three-hundred-foot-tall bridge linking the two sides of the city, sitting at the top of the sloping land to either side. Lights winked at him from both sides and throughout the sprawling city that had expanded down the slope to meet the water. More lights moved across the bridge, and through its arch at the very far end of the inlet waited the remains of the Sacanthan navy. It seemed Addo had abandoned a waterborne defense to focus on protecting Pyrran's walls.

The changing moonlight and shade summoned Derren and Myrra's visions as the ship passed through calm waters. It still hurt to look at their faces, even if they were less hacked up than the first time they'd appeared. It wasn't just pain working its way through Adrian. The anxious beating of his heart rose as they drew closer to the city.

Would killing Addo be enough to restore Myrra's memory? *It will. It has to be.*

But it wasn't only about Myrra, either. Now that he was back in the Domain, it was as if Father insisted on occupying the front of his mind. What would he think of all Adrian had accomplished? Would Adrian finally learn what Jovu had been doing in the clanlands? Did it have anything to do with the Dakhran invasion? No matter the questions, Adrian wouldn't grovel at Father's feet. He had an entire nation under his control now, and he would be respected. He would be accepted by his father as an equal.

Mahir had already started docking the fleet on one of the sandy banks where the land was accessible to the troops, just before it sloped up to Pyrran. Supplies were being unloaded further inland, to be followed by setting up camp.

Adrian disembarked and accompanied the men into trees that gave enough cover for camp. The sound of shouting and beating hammers soon rang out. Adrian's focus was on the city, though. The palace stood at a high point on Adrian's side of the bridge. Was Addo looking back at him? Or preparing to flee?

Leaves rustled behind him and Amal, Nasir, Mahir, and Oma parted bushes to meet him. Adrian still kept Bac close. He didn't need a bodyguard, but Bac had proven his worth time and again.

"Losses?" Adrian asked.

"Not many, Lord Light," Mahir said. "The plague took men on the ships by the hundreds, not thousands. We were able to stop it quickly thanks to your protection. We still stand at close to twenty thousand strong."

"We have enough for the siege then?"

Amal stepped forward, turning his scarred eyelid onto Adrian, then looking up at Pyrran. "It will be a challenge. A siege would require efforts on both land and sea. The bridge gives them the chance for escape to the other side."

"We have the men," Adrian said.

"We do, but we would need to sail an army across and surround them on both sides. Split our strength."

Adrian pursed his lips. Addo had holed himself up inside the hardest city in the Domain to siege. The coward was sure to have multiple paths of escape.

"We'd be spread too thin," Oma said. "Maybe a siege is not the best option."

"What else is there?" Mahir asked.

"We can storm the walls," Amal said, but Nasir was already stepping forward.

"We cannot force a solution where there is none, Lord Light. If we march south, we can aid in Alteria's defense. Dakhra has been occupying Durnn for some time, and we don't know when they'll march. The holy city is—"

"I'm not letting Addo sit here, Nasir. Retaking Sacantha will weaken Syvern. We'll be a looming threat if he advances, and I'm not letting Addo escape."

"The Sentinels are in Alteria."

Adrian gritted his teeth at the mention of Sentinels. Knowing Elwin had killed Myrra still stung, even if the Madness had been involved. "We can make do without them."

"There might be another way," Oma said.

They all turned to her.

"It is an old lesson that if you take away the head, the body will soon fall. Their head, Addo, is in the palace. Our scouts have reported as much for days now, yes?"

Oma didn't seem to expect an answer, but Nasir nodded.

"My mother's people have been in and out of your Domain cities for years. We know a path," Oma said. "If we can enter unnoticed and remove their leader, assassinate generals and captains in the barracks, then open the gates, we can destabilize them from within. An attack then will force surrender. Perhaps even the threat of attack."

Adrian considered the woman. He didn't fully trust any of his advisors yet; knowing Zarath had been spying on the Domain for years didn't help, but there could be something to this. An attack against the walls would send Addo to flight, and he would escape, but this might catch him unprepared. "How many would we sneak into the city?"

"We will split into groups," Oma said. "Create distractions, focus on the prime targets. Their bridge might provide easy escape in the event of a siege, but it also opens holes in their defenses. Walls cannot be built on water, Lord Light."

Adrian nodded slowly. This could work.

"Amal, your troops march close to the walls tomorrow when the sun sets. Stay out of arrow range, but show them we're here. Oma, get your assassins inside the city. Five-score should be a good start. Have them disrupt the city, open a gate, burn down an armory. And I want a group with me." He looked to Mahir. "You keep your ships ready. Make sure Addo doesn't escape on water if he sniffs something out."

"Why are we to keep assassins around you outside the city?" Oma asked.

"Not outside," Adrian said. "I'm going in."

You sure about this, lad? Derren's voice came from beside him, but Adrian did his best to ignore it.

Suit yourself, Derren said. *Just be careful with the priest, eh?*

Nasir eyed Adrian wearily, but Adrian's determination kept him silent.

"Lord Light," Oma said. "You are not an assassin. The chance of you being spotted is too big a risk."

"That's why we have the distractions. They'll pull focus from the enemy guard so I can sneak into the palace." Oma made to argue, but Adrian wouldn't have it. "Your assassins can deal with the rest, Oma. Addo is mine."

Amal and his men marched at nightfall. By now, they should be lined up before Pyrran. Oma's assassins were in the field, and her claim about little-known paths into the city seemed true enough.

The steady patrol lights on the bridge moved faster here and there, and confused orders rang out as enemy guards tried to pin down the commotion that Oma's infiltrated agents had begun to create.

Adrian waited with Oma and two other assassins. They kept to the shadows near the docks, where the city met the water. A wall surrounded the city, but the dock dominated the waterfront. Water lapped against stone quays, and a seaside walkway that should have been heavily patrolled stood empty.

Adrian eyed the assassins. Kiana and Joreh, Oma had called them. Both were lithe, with coppery brown skin and dark eyes. Kiana kept her hair under a cowl, while Joreh's hood covered a shaved head.

The smell of moss and seawater drifted up to meet Adrian. The scent brought back the battle at sea, and the burning pain that had run through him as he tried to keep the Madness at bay. He did his best to push it away for now, even if the pain called for him to open his wounds once more and see Myrra and Derren again.

Myrra's face had become clearer, more like herself and less of a mask, but it was still not whole. Adrian tried to piece it together, but the image eluded him.

I'm close. I'll have your back.

He almost felt a strange sense of gratitude toward Nasir for showing him the path of the blood magic, but Derren's dead eyes kept Adrian from truly accepting the priest. Adrian still needed Nasir, for now. The priest had made the necessary sacrifice; Adrian could understand that, and it was Adrian's own sacrifice to not act against Nasir. But he'd never forgive him. The priest's time would come.

A glint caught Adrian's eye, ahead on the sandy bank, beneath the three-hundred-foot-tall bridge. One of the assassins beside him, Kiana, seemed to have caught it as well. She turned to Oma and Joreh. "It's time."

Oma nodded but waited alongside Adrian as the assassins crept up the shore, hugging the seaside walkway with the bridge looming above them. They moved as if part of the darkness themselves. Oma had made Adrian leave his armor behind. He missed the weight of it, but he'd brought his sword, strapping it to his back to avoid impairing his movement.

"Follow in my steps," Oma said. She moved the same way as her assassins, pointing to where she placed her feet along the sandy bank so Adrian could follow.

Adrian trailed her as best he could, pausing when the group stopped to listen for patrols on the seaside walkway a few feet above. Adrian kept his head down and used his hands for support where Oma told him to until they came to a spot where the sand ended and the water grew deep.

A small guardhouse stood on the docks above them. Light still flickered within, but the body inside was slumped at an odd angle. Adrian squinted and saw blood smearing the stone. Perhaps that was the signal that had prompted them to move. Torchlight still moved along the bridge above and on the city walls behind the docks to Adrian's right.

Oma pointed, and Kiana crept straight into the water, and plunged down. Joreh followed, and so did Oma. They didn't wait or instruct Adrian; it was clear he should follow.

He paused, looking at the water. He'd always had trouble holding his breath, even when Jovu had made him do it—first as a game, then as training. "You never know when your armor will drag you down. You don't want to spend all that time sparring, just to be beaten by falling into a river, do you?"

Adrian had agreed, but he still hated the burning in his lungs. It seemed like nothing compared to the pain he'd experienced today. This pain meant something, though. It would end soon, and he'd have Myrra's untainted memory with him again.

The assassins had something pulsing lightly among the shadows under the bridge. Something for him to swim toward. Adrian grabbed the pendant around his neck, took a deep breath, and took the plunge. He swam until the pulsing light appeared before him, then broke the surface. He took a long gulp of air, as silently as he could, and joined the others beside a sewer grate. Another woman crouched in the shadows beside a door, at the base of a pillar that held up the bridge. Two dead guards lay beside her.

"We have little time," Kiana said. She pulled out a vial of dark green liquid and poured it onto the grid that barred the sewer. The liquid sizzled on contact with the metal. She poured it on the joints until the metal corroded and weakened. The assassins kept watch along the bank, while Oma stayed close to the door that led down from the bridge. There was no movement, and Kiana pulled away the sewer grate with little effort and less noise. She stepped inside, and Adrian followed.

The sewer drain opened into a more ample tunnel with a low vaulted ceiling and ankle-deep, dirty water. The smell was worse inside, but they crept along at a steady pace, eventually reaching a gated stairway leading upward. Kiana dropped more of her mixture on the gate lock and opened it carefully. Adrian paced up the steps behind her, heart thumping as they made their long way up to the city. He could have convinced himself his fear was born out of some misstep that would get them captured, but he knew the feeling too well to lie to himself. He was close, and it was always in moments like these that Addo found a way to slip through Adrian's grasp.

He almost jumped as the reddish outline of Derren walked up the steps beside him, face still swollen.

You nail that bastard down, eh lad?

Adrian nodded slightly, not wanting to reveal to the assassins what only he could see.

You make him regret all of it. All of it.

And then Derren was gone. There was no mention of Nasir. Maybe the apparition knew the priest would answer in time—or maybe Adrian was projecting the trust Derren had showed him in life, and none of it was real. He closed his eyes for a moment. The feeling was real; the pain when he saw Myrra, the fleeting wave of relief when her face became more like her own. That was the truth he'd cling to. Truth is not seen through the eyes, it is felt in the heart.

They climbed the steps until they came to a barred gate. Beyond it was a wide street at the base of the palace wall.

"Looks like it's royal shit we've been stepping in," Joreh said with a smirk. His voice was almost like a breeze, impossible for anyone to pick up beyond a few feet away. Adrian was sure he wouldn't be able to replicate it and kept his silence.

Kiana employed her potion on the gate. A sentry might later notice the damage with a close inspection, but if Adrian's plan worked, there would be no enemy sentries after this.

The city wasn't quiet. The time they'd taken to wade through the royal shit, as Joreh called it, had been enough for Oma's other assassins to pull the guards' attention away from the palace.

There would still be palace guards, and sentries atop the palace walls, but Adrian doubted Oma, Kiana, and Joreh would have much trouble dealing with them. He waited as Kiana stepped out, keeping to the shadows of empty streets. She glided close to the wall and watched the sentry moving. She let him pass a few times, probably studying the timing of his route to find the right time to climb.

She found her moment and threw a metal hook trailing thick hempen rope, then quickly scaled the wall. Joreh had broken off to the other side and was doing the same, while Oma waited with Adrian.

"Are you ready, Lord Light?"

Adrian nodded, watching the top of the wall as Kiana slit the guards' necks from behind. "You're lucky I'm not a religious man," Adrian said, "and don't restrain your killing."

Oma shook her head. "You are the one who came to us, Lord Light. This is war. Death is merely one of the players. If you refuse to acknowledge that, you are at a severe disadvantage."

Adrian wondered for a moment if that was the kind of disadvantage that had gotten Jovu killed. Had he tried to avoid killing? Had his beliefs killed him in the end?

Adrian shook away the thought. Of course not. He'd watched Jovu kill for more than a hundred years; it was likely Father's orders that killed him.

Both assassins had vanished from the wall-tops, but a side door was soon pushed open, and Oma pulled Adrian toward it.

They stepped into a courtyard at the rear of the palace, and Adrian caught a glimpse of Kiana squeezing through a second-story window. The walls looked impossibly high to scale, and the gardens too open to cross without being noticed, but Oma urged him on as if the palace were empty. There was no time for hesitation. Kiana left her rope dangling, and Adrian followed Oma toward it. Oma wrapped it around Adrian's waist and gave it a tug. "Hold on to it and place your feet on the building, as if you were walking on the ground." She pointed to the window. "Kiana will help you up."

It took Adrian a moment to trust in the steadiness of the rope, but he soon placed one foot on the wall before him, then another, and felt the pull as Kiana aided his ascent. He was inside in a moment, looking around a dark corridor.

"Addo has been reported to be in his chamber, Lord Light. Alone." Kiana whispered.

He nodded. Addo was truly a coward. The enemy army was at his gates and Addo cowered in the palace, ready to flee if things failed to go his way.

Adrian followed Kiana down a stone corridor toward the royal chamber. They paused at a corner. There were four guards standing at the doors of what had to be Addo's room. Who else would they be guarding?

Kiana pulled two small knives with large triangular heads and fell into a crouch. Her arm moved in a blur. A heartbeat later, two of the guards had knives in their necks. The other two had only a moment of surprise before knives flew from the other side of the corridor into their backs. Less precise than Kiana, perhaps, but Joreh and Oma were on the guards before they could cry out, slitting their throats and easing them to the floor.

Adrian approached Addo's door, heart beating faster than ever.

"We will take out the other leaders, Lord Light," Oma said, then moved off with her assassins behind her.

Adrian breathed deep. It was time to get his answers from Addo. He stepped inside with little care for silence. His sword remained sheathed; that would be too quick.

The large antechamber was decorated in Sacanthan blue and gray. An unused desk sat to Adrian's left, but Addo was sitting in a wide chair, looking out a tall glass-paned window with his back to the door. He turned with an irritated expression at the sound of the door, but his irritation soon turned to a look of dread when he saw Adrian in the doorway.

Adrian walked slowly. He wanted Addo to take it all in, to know from that very moment that there was no escape.

Addo jumped from his chair, already blubbering.

"Ad-Adrian . . . I . . ."

Adrian shook his head. "You'd best sit back down, Addo." He'd thought the anger would take him, but his tone was surprisingly calm. Firm.

Addo didn't obey. His gaze darted around the chamber, seeking.

Adrian only shook his head again. "There's no way out. It'll be quicker if you don't struggle."

"Help!" Addo yelled.

"They're all dead," Adrian said. "I saved you for last."

Addo bolted, fumbling at the window even though the fall would likely break bone. Adrian leapt forward and grabbed him by the scruff of the neck, throwing him to the floor. Addo got to his hands and feet and skittered away like a fleeing animal, but Adrian drew his sword and hit Addo on the back of the head with the pommel. Addo fell, face striking the floor. His movements became sluggish as he crawled away. Adrian grabbed him again and threw him against a wall. Addo slammed into it and crumpled down. He didn't pass out but didn't move away either.

Adrian used the sword to cut a thin line on his own palm and let the blood well up for a moment. His body welcomed the pain now, knowing it would bring Myrra's face with it. Adrian placed his sword on the desk and strode toward the former Khetish prince. "Fine, we'll do it this way."

Adrian pulled back Addo's head, just like Raklin had done to so many soldiers, and let his blood, tainted by Raklin's Madness, drop onto Addo's tongue. As soon as he was sure Addo had swallowed, he started moving his hands to perform the binding.

Addo groaned, but Adrian ignored it, weaving the signs Nasir and Kel Bradaz had taught him. His fingers moved calmly. Derren and Myrra were already in the room. Derren looked down on Addo with a frown that Adrian had seen him wear too many times. Myrra sat on the bed, hands folded on her lap. Her face was still a motley arrangement of stitched-together dead skin, a little smoother than before. Her pendant of the Bone grew hot against Adrian's chest as he looked at her.

Addo struggled as Adrian finished the signs, but there was nothing—no pain signaling the binding had worked. Had he done something wrong? He started weaving the signs again, but Addo was gaining consciousness now.

Good, he'll feel the pain.

It was Myrra's voice, broken as the words passed through the twisted lips of her mask. It tore at Adrian's heart, and the pain flared his magic, pushing him closer to the depths from which he drew it.

Addo looked at Adrian with defiance in his eyes. "You think you'll infect me? You think I haven't been protected? We are alike, Adrian. The taint will not affect our blood."

"We are nothing alike." Adrian finished the signs for a second time, but still his blood did not tingle or reach toward Addo. He pinned the man with a foot and looked at Myrra. She offered Adrian her hand, black veins swirling all around it, as when she'd offered it during the battle. Derren moved to one side, as if to give them more privacy. That same instinct that had initially prevented Adrian from taking Myrra's hand during the battle was only a whisper now. Myrra's image came from within him. That power was within him. He'd avoided it for too long. He needed it now. *We all have our sacrifices.*

Adrian took Myrra's hand, and the black maze of lines moved up his arm, every cut he'd inflicted on himself stinging to the bone. The skin around his eyes burned like it was on fire. So much pain— and so much power.

Myrra's face smoothed a fraction, and she smiled at him—the way Adrian had always remembered it. The way he'd struggled to remember after all that happened. She nodded, and Adrian grabbed onto the pain, the power—and directed it at Addo.

The threads that were invisible when performing the binding with Nasir were obvious now. Interwoven lines of black and red shot out and dug into Addo's skin. He screamed, and Adrian knew Addo felt the same pain that ran through him.

Addo coughed and struggled, but he was bound. The Madness ran in Addo's blood, and it called to Adrian: a wave of anger begging for release. A touch of it bled through, and Addo growled and strained but could not rise.

"It's hard to describe the pain," Adrian told Addo. "I never knew it could cut so deep, but you showed me that." He looked at Myrra and injected more of his power into Addo. Adrian's skin reacted. It burned and stung as if being peeled from his muscles. Addo howled, but Adrian accepted the pain. It was a price he would gladly pay to see Myrra's face become whole again.

"My father would tell me to thank you, Addo," he said. "He'd tell me pain makes a man stronger. But I know better than to thank a worm like you." Adrian moved a finger, pulling at the strings within Addo, and he screamed louder. "We are bonded now. That pain you feel is what you've put me through."

"Adrian, please." Addo said it with an effort, more gasps than proper words.

The burning on the skin around Adrian's eyes intensified and seemed to spread, but he didn't mind. It was just more pain, and he directed it at Addo. "Your pleading is wasted breath, Addo. If you tell me what I need to know, I'll consider lessening the pain."

"No, Adrian—"

"How long have you been in league with Syvern?"

"I-I reached out to him after my father was killed. It was a mistake, Adrian. Pl—Ah!"

"And what are you doing in Pyrran?"

"Syvern will bring down the Domain. Pyrran was my payment." Addo found enough strength for a light chuckle. "You can't stop him. Doesn't matter what you do to me, he's always been ahead."

Adrian closed his bloody hand around the ruin-stone of his pendant of the Bone. It sizzled and burned, and Addo jerked on the floor as the sensation was mirrored in him.

It seemed to put a spiteful anger within Addo. "I might be a coward, but I'm not blind like you. Myrra was the first. She started all this. That Sentinel you blamed, Elwin, all he did was his duty to the Domain. She infected him, and you infected her."

"Your lies won't get you out of this, Addo." Adrian was still calm, but something in the way Addo said it gave him pause. *Truth is felt in the heart.*

"I'm not lying," Addo said. "Syvern's target was you, but not even he knew what happened. You were supposed to be dead, and she was supposed to be alive. No one expected you to be resistant to it." Addo groaned again. "How does it feel? Knowing she died in your stead."

"No!" Adrian pushed all the hurt from Addo's words back at him, and he howled again. "Raklin's blood is what tainted me."

Addo shook his head.

"I've talked to Syvern's generals. His potion master. You were already tainted before Raklin. The Dakhrans have perfected the transmission of poison through touch."

Memories resurfaced of the amanthium Adrian had tried to infect Kahlia with.

"It could have been anyone in Khet," Addo said. "Anyone who had contact with your skin." His words came between heavy breaths. "You had it before you left."

"Liar! It's transmitted through blood, not touch."

Addo shook his head. "Not what they gave you. It was different, silent. Syvern wanted you to bring it back to your father."

Adrian's mind raced. He'd kissed Myrra before leaving. Kissed her with his bloody lip from sparring. No, it couldn't be.

Addo seemed to pick something up in Adrian's gaze and found the strength for a laugh. "Ah, you remember something. You're the one who passed it on to her." His laugh became a cough. "You think your father called you back by mistake? Did you think it coincidence that he convinced you to leave Myrra behind? You think he doesn't have spies? He knew Syvern was trying something. Maybe your brother knew it too."

"No!" Adrian bellowed. Myrra and Derren joined in his yell. The cracks on Myrra's face were coming back, looking more like the dead-skin mask. Adrian injected the agony into Addo again, making his limbs twist and his back arch.

It couldn't be. Myrra couldn't have been the first. Addo was trying to destabilize him . . . But even as Adrian tried to convince himself of the thought, he knew it was a hollow one. All the memories of her flooded back, and in his heart, he knew Addo was telling the truth. Myrra had been killed by the Madness, and Adrian was the one who had infected her.

"Why would Syvern risk Myrra?" Adrian struggled to keep his voice under control.

"It wasn't supposed to awaken," Addo said. "Something wasn't right, maybe with the transmission. That's why Syvern switched to the potions." Addo let out a pained breath. "More . . . reliable."

"Who infected me?" Adrian said through gritted teeth.

"I-I don't know— Ach, Adrian, I don't kn—" Addo howled on the floor.

"Tell me!"

"You think Syvern would tell me that? Ach, no, p-please."

Adrian breathed out. Transferring the pain to Addo did nothing to lessen his own this time. If anything, it amplified it, but Adrian didn't care. Addo wasn't lying about not knowing, but he would still suffer. Syvern would as well. Even Father had been a part of it in his own way.

Addo was still squirming. "You said you'd make it quick."

Adrian shook his head. "I lied."

———

Adrian had kept at it all night. It was almost like the last night before Derren was killed, but he wasn't planning anything throughout the night this time. He'd given Addo brief respites. Enough for him to cling to life so he would feel every excruciating moment Adrian could give him.

Derren and Myrra remained in the room with Adrian, but no matter how much he made Addo suffer, Myrra's face did not grow whole. It was better than before, but it was still tainted. Adrian knew why. Addo wasn't the only one responsible. Myrra's image wouldn't be restored until Syvern died.

The sun was rising. Adrian was used to the lack of sleep, but it was time to end it. His eyes still burned from tapping into his well of power, and the sensation didn't seem like it would go away this time. He got up from his chair and knelt beside Addo. The man's breath was slow and weak.

"You'll feel what she felt now," Adrian said. He let go of the incantation, and Addo's body sagged and was still for a long moment. Adrian took a step back and grabbed his sword from the table, holding it in front of him.

Whatever antidote Addo had taken had not been enough. Adrian had set the Madness free within Addo's veins. His body jolted, and he rose, taken by the frenzy. He snarled, but his body was contorting in pain. Rage soon won out over the agony and he pounced forward, but Adrian sank his sword deep into Addo's heart, impaling him like he had the woman who'd worn Myrra's dead-skinned mask.

Adrian fell to his knees, eyes burning, breathing deep. Myrra and Derren were gone, but he knew what to do. The Domain could not fall. He had to get to Syvern. He took a few more breaths, then got up and walked out.

Oma waited for him in the hallway. She took a step back when she saw Adrian.

"Lord Light, your eyes." She kept a hand on her knife, ready as if Adrian were about to become frenzied. "The skin is black around them."

"I have it under control, Oma. No need to worry. Is the city secure?"

The woman took a moment to compose herself, then finally released her blade. "It is, Lord Light. We took out their officers and opened the gates. There was little resistance in the chaos. Amal had no trouble orchestrating a surrender."

Adrian shook his head, and Derren did the same beside him. "Put all who followed Addo to the sword."

Oma paused. "All of them?"

"Yes. All of them."

"Lord Light, do you not prevent death in the Domain?"

"This enemy strikes at the core of our faith. They were calling themselves the True, thinking the Seraph is on their side. They do not deserve life. Will this be a problem?"

"No, Lord Light. I'll let Amal know."

"Good." Adrian strode down to the city gate with Oma and her assassins in tow. Nasir waited outside the city walls.

The blackness around Adrian's eyes didn't seem to bother Nasir as much as it had Oma. "I see the magic is taking its toll, my Lord Light."

"It'll fade." The pain hadn't faded, though.

"It might, as long as you stay away from it for some time. But some scars run too deep."

Adrian nodded. "I might have to live with it then."

We all have our sacrifices.

The Domain would not be sacrificed, though. He'd make sure Dakhra was defeated, but for that he needed more. "I need you to continue teaching me."

Nasir bowed his head. "As you command, Lord Light. We can do it on the way."

"Unload the ballistae from the ships, then. We march for Alteria."

CHAPTER TWENTY-NINE

Unity is only achieved through sacrifice.

— *Lothrak clan saying*

A slow blue light pulsed as Speaker Ento led Nasha through the Yltigg mines. If she'd been forced into an ancestor-stone mine a few weeks ago, she probably would have succumbed to the surrounding emotion, but all she felt now was something akin to the ponderous beating of a drum inside her head. It reminded Nasha of the way the emotions used to hit her, but this feeling was a lot more alien, and she still didn't feel confident touching the stones if she didn't have to. Still, like everything around her these past few days, her curse was changing, and the deeper it went, the more it showed her. It grew stronger with use, and she became better at controlling the emotion around it.

Nasha still didn't like the feeling. It didn't matter how strong her curse got; she was certain it came from Zala. Nasha's tether—that hope she'd found in Shai and grown in herself—would be more important than ever. She found herself clinging to it, silently praying to the Earth that she'd find enough hope in the ancestor-stones of these mines to use her curse to heal the Yltigg ward, while toeing the line around Zala once more.

Part of her questioned how she'd been cursed. She still had no recollection of her life before the clans, apart from what she'd seen in the vision during the Proving. A Domain city under siege, and herself as a child. Was it even her? Or was she looking out from the eyes of someone else?

She gazed at the chunks of stone that protruded from the muddy walls of the wide mine-tunnel. Maybe her answer lay within the stones' beating blue seams. She'd need to plunge into another vision to find out, but her focus was on healing the Yltigg pillar now.

Shai walked beside her, a frown on her brow, gaze flitting to Nasha and away. It gave Nasha pause, but Ento was too close for Nasha to delve into it with Shai. They walked through earth- and stone-coated tunnels. There were nooks where small groups of Yltigg used picks and hammers to free the ancestor-stone from the walls, but little movement beyond that. Perhaps the corruption of the pillar had driven the clansfolk away. Or perhaps there were no Slopers to throw in the mines here.

The ancestor-stone clusters grew in size and number as they made their way deeper into the mountain. Eventually, the snaking path led them to the mouth of a somewhat circular chamber with walls covered in ancestor-stone. Ento stepped in, but Nasha blocked Shai's path. The speaker turned his veiled face back at them, but Nasha didn't move.

"Wait inside, Speaker."

Ento watched them for a moment, then walked deeper into the chamber. Nasha pulled Shai aside. "What is it?" she asked. "I need you for this, Shai. I can't have you giving up while I'm in there."

Shai held Nasha's gaze. "The Yltigg are no different from the Ronar. All this, what we're doing. We're just doing it to be forgotten again. Traded away or killed when they don't need us anymore. Can't you see that?"

"We're not tied to them, Shai. We need to stop this corruption."

"So we can join their clan?" Shai's hands trembled slightly, and Nasha picked up on the anger. "They don't have slopes here, but I saw the faces on their miners. What the Ronar place above the mountain, the Yltigg place below. It's just a different name."

"You can't know that."

"I do. You weren't there, Nasha. You were part of the clan, a hunter. Thrice-striped, isn't that what you told Ardin? You were hunting meat for the clan while I was building rat-traps trying to get something for Uvo and my mother."

"I was getting food for you!"

Shai shook her head. "I refuse to let them trick us again. I'm not falling for any promises. Theirs or yours. Maybe the rot that's crawling out of the Earth is what the clans have been feeding it all these years."

"What about your family?"

"They're far, but they're safe. A lot safer than us, that's for sure."

"No one will survive if Zala escapes, Shai. She's the dead goddess. She won't stop with the clans. I know you don't trust them, but we're not doing this to join the Yltigg."

"What are we doing it for?"

To prove I'm not the monster from the tales. To quell this darkness trying to take hold of me. "We're doing it so your family has a safe home to return to. We're doing it because your father believed in me and asked me to look after you."

"The clans will never be safe, Nasha!"

"Then we'll change that, but first I need your help. I need you to trust me. To believe we can succeed. I need your hope."

Shai looked at her, still uncertain.

"We can't run from this, Shai. I'm not asking you to believe in the clans. I'm asking you to believe in me. We'll find a way."

Shai sighed and walked into the chamber. She'd given no confirmation, but she hadn't left either. For now, that would have to do.

This wasn't a natural formation. The mines had been a mixture of soil and hard rock, but here the walls and floor were covered in ancestor-stone. The Yltigg had built this. The pillar was only the tip. This was the true ward—what Nasha had to protect. She might have thought it luck that the taint had started on the pillar and left untouched what lay beneath, but the vibration of emotion coursing through her spoke otherwise. The taint needed to become stronger in order to breach this chamber.

Ento paused at the center and looked up. A tunnel, also lined with ancestor-stone, made its way through the ceiling toward the top of the peak. "This leads to our pillar. If the corruption descends into the heart of the mountain, we will be lost."

"Do you know what powers Zala's taint?" Nasha asked. Perhaps holding the taint at bay would be a start.

Ento shook his head. "We know blood keeps her fed, but Zala's true source of power has been speculation in many a tale."

Of course it has.

The speaker unwrapped the same dull ancestor-stone shard from the Hagun warding pillar, the one he'd shown her in the Yltigg high-garden. The stone was dead, but Zala's touch still writhed over its surface, a black corruption covering most of it. Healing this stone was the first step in understanding her enemy. It could be what she needed to cleanse the Yltigg ward as well.

Ento thrust the stone out toward her, waiting for Nasha to begin. She looked from Shai to the stone, her senses already casting about for the sensation she'd projected toward Nasha in the arena. Some echo of it rode Shai's underlying stream of emotion, but it was nowhere near as strong as it had been. Nasha kept it at the back of her mind and took the stone from Ento.

The dull ancestor-stone didn't flood her with emotion. It was like the manacles she still wore. Empty, but the taint riding the stone's surface was clear. It didn't burn through Nasha. It was more like a whisper, something smooth and quiet, probing at her consciousness, trying to find empty spaces to fill her with the same darkness that tried to take her mind when she used the curse.

It sent such a revulsion through Nasha that she almost dropped the stone, but this was part of what she needed to do. Still, the image of the clansmen taken by the taint turned the revulsion to cold dread. She gripped the stone tight, as if to strangle the sensation, and focused her mind on Shai's lingering thread of hope.

Shai regarded Nasha for a long moment, then took a few steps back to join Ento, who'd retreated to stand by the chamber entrance.

Nasha hesitated for a moment, one hand firmly gripping the shard, the other hovering over the ancestor-stone on the wall of the chamber.

There was enough in these stones to replicate the emotion from the Yltigg spectators in the arena, and likely more, as if the walls were the stands themselves, packed to double capacity. Every instinct told Nasha to pull her hand back. She gazed at Ento, who brushed a hand across the side of his veil. It was another line of defense, but it did little to bolster Nasha's confidence.

If you do nothing, Zala wins. It was still hard to believe she was the one who had to stop the dead goddess. She who'd always avoided the tales—but here she was, in a mine with the call of ancestor-stone thrumming through her chest. She closed her eyes and touched the stone.

The warning signs were immediate and loaded with an agony that tore its way through Nasha as if the stone had breathed a cold wind into her. Cutting a path under her skin, through her fingertips and up her arm, seeking her heart. Her ears rang; her vision blurred and became white. The ancestor-stone walls pummeled her with fear. Or maybe that was her own heart beating against the emotion shredding through her. The fear had her wanting to run, to hide in some shadowed corner. It was her consciousness that tried to escape. *No. No, no, no. Stop it. Run.* Nasha blinked. What was she doing? Why was she touching ancestor-stone? She couldn't touch ancestor-stone. She tried to remember, but there was only a hollow space where her thoughts should be. An anger crept up, trying to fill it, trying to move Nasha into action. A shot of hope pulled her consciousness back. Shai.

Nasha looked down at the blackness running along the stone in her hand. She needed to heal it, to push the corruption back.

Zala was tainting the anger inside Nasha, but Shai's thread of hope—that flutter just before a breaking storm—still tethered Nasha to reality. It told her she could get through it. Her whitening vision took on a tinge of yellowish green. It wasn't the deep green of fear; this was her hope, bleeding out into her body's warning signs. She focused on it, giving in to the belief that she could do this. The belief in herself, even if she'd lost all sense of what exactly she was supposed to be.

The pain dulled, but still throbbed—pumping through her in time with the blue pulse of the cave. The path the tainted anger cut toward her heart was blocked, its advance halted. The moment of respite gave Nasha enough clarity to spread her consciousness along the other strings of emotion, feeling for different patterns. Something to pull in and use to cleanse Zala's grasp from the Hagun stone. To breathe life back into it.

The world shifted as she reached out. She was in the Hagun village. The central pillar brimmed with life, its blue veins tracing a path along its length, and extending from the stone into the ground. Nasha could see their path clearly through the Earth, as if it were all ancestor-stone. The veins spread out like roots, but three spots coalesced into thicker coils that seemed to travel farther. They pulsed in unison, and with each one, Nasha's mind was pulled along one of the broader coils.

One.

The first beat sent her through the twisting vein within the darkness of the Earth, traveling a blinding path that flickered in every color of emotion: blues, greens, reds, oranges, yellows, and pinks. They lit up Nasha's darkness until the Ronar village flashed before her. She stood by the Ronar warding pillars, something familiar calling to her. From beneath the Earth, the coil of veins she'd traveled fed the power into the Ronar pillars, and they came from the Hagun. Nasha creased her brow, but before she could form a thought, another pulse pulled her consciousness away.

Two.

She was thrust into the Yltigg high-garden. The Yltigg pillar's light beat like a heart, veins extending all through the peak, three of them coalescing into wider braids like those of the Ronar and Hagun. Nasha could almost place it now, as if each beat held the same rhythm the Hagun and Ronar pillars had shown her. They powered the Yltigg ward, and it returned its own pulse.

Three.

Snow now, carried on a wind that Nasha could see but not feel. Another pillar—massive, twice the size of the others, but still connected. The blue veins traveled underneath the snow and filled the ward with life. It pulsed in unison with its siblings. Connected.

There had been mentions of unity in the tales, but this was more than a tale. The ancestor-stone shone bright, coursing with power from all four clans.

Something pulled at the back of her mind, and a burning spread up Nasha's back. She arched without thought, and grimaced. She'd lost sight of Zala, focused on the unseen connection between the clans. One that she'd never heard talked about.

The pain brought Nasha back to the Hagun village. It was no longer thriving. There were flames and soldiers. A battle. Hagun ran about while armored Domain men in blood-red and black tore through people and buildings alike. This was not a force for occupation; it was too small for that. Most were engaged, but small groups seemed to be breaking into homes. Nasha followed one and found them turning things over. They were searching for something.

Nasha stepped back out. The main clash was at the center of the village, where a raven-haired Domain man fought his way toward the Hagun warding pillar. Hagun warriors stood in his path. It was not a large Domain force, but it was enough to fight its way through a surprised group of Hagun, who'd never been the most militarily inclined clan.

The battle went by in flashes—Domain steel clashing with the stone-bladed axes and spears of the Hagun—until it ended with bodies all around the Hagun pillar. It had cracked—Nasha could not imagine how—but the cracks didn't pulse like the natural blue veins of the stone.

The Domain man approached, searching for something at the base of the pillar. Whatever he sought, he didn't find it before war horns sounded. Hagun reinforcements.

The Domain men retreated, but still the dark-haired man

searched the base of the pillar, while one of his officers—a bearded man with tangled hair—struggled to pull him away. When he finally did, it was too late. The spear had already come whistling through the air. It pierced his chest just as he turned to leave. The bearded officer pulled him away, and their images vanished like dust in the wind. The image was replaced by a vision of the aftermath.

Ash took over the Hagun village; the ground barren, the warding pillar lifeless and dull. Nasha stepped forward, but her mind brought her back to the Yltigg high-garden, where she stood before the warding pillar, covered with corruption. She stretched out her hand to touch the pillar, but something caught her attention. The lines connecting the pillars—the clans—were not whole. What had been a thick braid was now untangled, frayed, and broken. The light that had pulsed through them was no more.

Nasha reached for the broken lines, her hands ethereal, her skin burning. Her hands passed into the ground without resistance. She gritted her teeth and pulled more from the ancestor-stone mines. Determination was the first thread to answer, but it was soon joined by too many emotions to tell apart. In the vision, Nasha funneled them all into the veins of the Yltigg warding pillar.

Something complained. It could have been Zala's taint within her, trying to break free; she couldn't be sure. What was clear was her body's reaction. The ringing in her ears intensified; her vision—even in this vivid dream—began to blur and turn white. It was the same as before, but instead of a mounting pressure ready to break her consciousness and plunge her into uncontrollable emotion, she felt more pieces of her memory withering away. As if her mind were turning hollow, the barrier of hope cracking to let in touches of angry darkness.

She tightened her ethereal grip on the connection between the pillars and pushed the belief that she could heal Zala's corruption into the link. There was no reaction. The blackness at the base of the Yltigg pillar stood unaffected. Nasha pushed hard against it, but her vision grew brighter and her muscles wavered. The emotions cutting the path through her stung under her skin, but still she pushed. She would push Zala back and rid the Earth of this taint.

A voice called to Nasha. She couldn't pin down the direction, but her strength was close to its limit, and with every breath the voice grew more distant, until the vision itself began to crack.

"Nasha!"

The vision broke, but her mind was still in a haze. Her name came to her slowly. She recognized the voice that called to her, but not the face. Where was she again? She blinked once, twice, then things fell into place. Shai was on her hands and knees, breathing heavily.

"Nasha . . ." The word came wavering between breaths. Ento was sprawled out beside her, his ancestor-stone veil pulsing a deep blue. He coughed and rose slowly.

"What happened?" Nasha asked.

"You . . ." Shai was still struggling. "You pulled it all in."

"The emotion?"

"Everything."

Nasha looked around. "What do you mean, *everything?*"

"The stones started lighting up," Shai said, struggling to her feet. "The light faded, like it was draining out of them, and then the life drained out of us."

"Did you heal it?" Ento asked.

Nasha shook her head. "No. Zala's grip is strong. But I think I found something. The Hagun were attacked. Some kind of Domain army." Mansa had told her this. A prince from one of the Domain nations had led them, searching for sacred texts. That must have been the raven-haired man. "The pillars are all connected. The Hagun pillar was cracked in the battle. That opened the door for Zala to creep into the Yltigg pillar as well. Your tivezzi's sacrifice seemed to hold Zala back, but I don't know for how long."

"What are you saying?" Ento asked.

"I'm saying the pillars are in spots of convergence. Whatever the truth of the Tedros tales, the founders of the four clans knew where to place the pillars so that Zala would be kept away. The connection is broken. I couldn't pull enough strength to fix it." And she'd almost pulled the life out of Shai and Ento while trying. A cold dread crept up Nasha's back. This was why she'd been so resistant to this in the first place. She'd come too close to breaking, too close to Zala. The haze clouding her mind when the vision ended had been close enough to remind Nasha of when she'd broken and even forgotten her own name.

Hurried steps drew their attention to the entrance, where a Yltigg man paused to catch his breath. "Roho sends word, Speaker Ento. He requests your presence on the battlefield immediately."

"The battlefield?" Nasha asked.

"The Domain have invaded. They're trying to get into the mines."

Nasha's eyes widened. The Domain should have gone straight at the Ronar. Had Bahar done this, or was it connected to the other invading nation, the one that sought the texts from the Hagun? No, it had to be Bahar. Had Mansa's plan of blaming the Yltigg worked after all? Maybe he'd even directed the Domain here after Nasha was handed over. Whatever the reason, Nasha could see the truth now. None of the clans could fall.

"We can't lose the ancestor-stone," said Ento. "We'll need it to fight Zala."

"We can't lose our lives either," Shai said. "You need to talk to Roho. Set up a defense."

"There's no time," the messenger said. "Their attack has begun."

"Why would they come here?" Ento's tone suggested that answering the question might help convince the Domain to turn back, but there was no talking their way out of this, not with Bahar on the other side of the battle.

"Tomu showed me the ancestor-stones from the Ronar mines," Nasha said. "They were dull. Maybe the Domain found out as well. It doesn't matter. We'll help push them back and figure out a plan when we have space to breathe." They headed for the surface.

Moving toward the battle filled Nasha with a dread she thought she'd overcome, and her whole body started going numb. She'd fought in the Proving and avoided execution, but a large-scale battle was different from anything she'd ever faced. She'd crept around the Yltigg siege of the Ronar village but hadn't fought in it. Still, she understood enough from her vision to reignite her hope. If they could push the Domain back, there might be a chance to fight off Zala. She knew where to focus now. They'd need to unite the clans. It wasn't much of a plan just yet, but it was a start, and that was a lot more than she'd had a few days ago.

Nasha might not be sure about what she was meant to be, but delving into the vision, touching the connections between the pillars —those were things only she could do. And she would do them again, after pushing back the Domain.

She wanted to ask for help, perhaps utter a prayer to the Silent Earth. Perhaps even Zala would want the Domain to fail, so She could have their blood. Nasha kept her silence, though. Help had never answered her.

The sun's harsh rays greeted them as they approached the mine's entrance, and the silence of the ancestor-stone was broken by shouting and clashing weapons.

CHAPTER THIRTY

When Tedros set his borders against the Domain, he knew of their numbers and their steel, but they did not possess the favor of the Earth. The power within it is what fed Tedros's own.

— Tales of the Lothrak

The sun had just passed its zenith and glinted off the metal plates of the massed army. As much as Kadmus valued numbers, he'd barely given the army enough attention to form an estimate, but they seemed to be more numerous than the enemy. The defending clan's warriors stood at the mouth of a pass-like entrance that probably led to the ruin-stone mines Bahar was bent on seizing.

Bahar had sold the campaign to the council as necessary to defend their borders, but Kadmus had lied enough to recognize that as a falsehood. Perhaps he was here for the ruin-stone—and the council hoped to get more of it themselves—but revenge for his lost son seemed a likelier motive.

Kadmus watched from the safety of the trees, far behind the battle. The woods spread all around the plain where the armies readied themselves, and Kadmus's distance from the Domain back line held a relative promise of safety. His potions were stored on carts like the one he sat on now, keeping cool in the shade. All along the edge of the tree line, men tended to catapults, ready for Bahar's command to launch the potions.

Kadmus didn't want to move. His feet hurt. He'd been offered a horse, but that hadn't been much better and merely shifted the pain from his feet to his back and legs. He'd considered escape after the first few days, but where would he go? He'd be chased as a deserter, and he doubted he'd even find his way back to Nima. He was stuck here and would have to wait for the upcoming battle to be over before trying Bahar's patience by asking to return.

They'd marched for the better part of a week to reach the base of the Yltigg peak. Most Domain folk barely knew how many clans there were, but Kadmus had made a point of knowing which people neighbored his nation. The army had skirted the Ronar, which—according to Bahar—was the best course of action if they were to strike a blow the clans would feel. The Yltigg had the largest ruin-stone mines, and the Ronar had always been closer to the Domain in more than physical location. Kadmus doubted Bahar was looking toward negotiation, but taking this peak did seem a sound strategy. Not that Kadmus would know. He could respect the strategic aspect of a battle but had always shied away from the brutish clashing of arms.

There was little movement on the battlefield ahead, so Kadmus turned around and raised the tarp. He'd been brought to make sure the potions worked, after all. It took him a moment to notice it, but after a surprised breath, he picked up one of the vials and held it up for close inspection. The liquid inside it seemed to have separated. What had been a uniform mixture of bright orange was now split into a duller orange sitting on a section of coppery-red. Had the binding agent lost its potency? The elements would not have the desired effect separately.

I don't know what it'll do. Kadmus frowned. *I don't know what it'll do!*

Had it been the sun? Was it the constant jostling of the trip? There was no knowing whether the potions would work. Would Kadmus be punished? Would Bahar take matters back home and take his frustrations out on Grunt? On Nima?

He almost jumped when he saw Bahar entering the shade of the trees. The limp was reduced, but still present, and the scars on his face could be called markings now. Still, Kadmus had expected the man to be closer to the battle than the carts.

"Is the serum ready?" he asked.

Kadmus didn't flinch. He'd lied enough to know when the truth would be a problem. "Yes."

He wasn't sure, but his uncertainty would change nothing now.

"Good," Bahar said. "Wait for my word to load the catapults."

Bahar left, and after a few moments, Kadmus was hit with the sounds of battle breaking out on the plain before him.

Nasha squinted as they rushed from the Yltigg mines. Her eyes were still adjusting, but her ears were already picking up the sounds of battle. Steel clashed with stone, and the world was a blaze of white, slowly clearing to reveal Domain troops barreling against the Yltigg defensive force.

The Domain had not pushed into the pass leading to the Yltigg mountain village. They were heading for the ancestor-stone mines instead.

The entrance to the mines was a massive hole at the bottom of the mountain. The path before her ramped upwards, a valley-like pass sixty feet wide and flanked by rocky walls rising on either side. The walls ended in flat plateaus that protruded from the mountain's slope. Most of the Yltigg had gathered around the pass's mouth further ahead, while more stood on the plateaus above, hurling spears and slinging stones.

Rope ladders hung from the walls, giving access to the upper ground. Nasha found Roho walking atop one of the rocky shelves, and quickly climbed a stair to meet him.

She paused at the top, taking in the scene on the dusty plain below. Armored troops clashed with Yltigg, while more troops advanced in ordered ranks behind them. The Yltigg pushed back, desperately trying to guard the descending ramp into the mines. The screams of dying men rushed up to meet Nasha, followed by the smell of death, but that wasn't all. The emotions from the battle were a rising sea that threatened to pull Nasha into its depths. She focused her mind on the hope she'd found in her vision and strengthened it with the memory of the feeling she'd always received from Shai. Strangely, what hit her this time was the desperate hope Shai had felt in the Proving, the one she'd shot her way when Nasha was lost in her curse and attacked the girl. That memory might not be what defined Nasha, but it told her what she could never let herself become. It was enough to ground herself against the tide of screaming desperation from the battle, and step forward. Her own fear still loomed within, but she wouldn't run. She knew what had to be done to keep Zala imprisoned, and she knew of no one else who could do it.

The Yltigg were using the tight space of the pass to their advantage, holding off the greater Domain numbers with the aid of spears and stones launched from the cliff before Nasha. The Yltigg were barely holding, though, and the Domain appeared to have double their number to throw at the pass.

Nasha rushed toward Roho, with Shai and Ento behind her. Roho's eyes lit up at the sight of them. "We can't hold them. We need your help." He said it as if she owed him something.

Nasha was already struggling with the proximity of the battle's emotions, and her skin tingled with every step closer. "I'm only one person."

"You killed a tainted before the entire clan. Use your power."

Nasha looked from Roho to the struggling Yltigg. The way he ordered her grated against her pride, but in war every soldier is just another tool. At least he saw her as something more. "I can't hold them back alone."

Down below, a volley of arrows fell, pulling screams from the Yltigg on the frontline. The Yltigg responded with spears and stones, but Nasha could feel the fear from the Yltigg lines, bordering on terror. Not for their lives, but for their homes. These warriors wouldn't run, even when they knew the enemy was too powerful.

Nasha let her gaze follow the path toward the larger and narrower pass that led to the top of the Yltigg peak. The Domain did not approach it. It was much longer than the pass to the mines, and more advantageous to the Yltigg. Nasha wished Mansa were there. Only for a moment. He'd see something on the battlefield and steer the troops to their advantage, but she had nothing to give the Yltigg in that regard.

Nasha let out a long breath. She'd always told herself things would work out if she just got through what lay ahead. Imprisonment, trials, the Proving. Nothing seemed to be as large as this battle, though, and even if she clung to the belief within, the other, darker half inside her tried to taint that belief with doubt. Roho was betting on her curse, but Nasha knew better than to trust it. She had to bet on herself. "I'll do what I can to hold them back," she said.

Ento looked to Nasha. "If we turn them away, is there hope?"

Nasha nodded, certain. "I found something in the mines, a connection between the clans that runs deep within the Earth. We'll find a way to use it. Unity is the only path to reclaim the clanlands from our enemies." Another bout of pained screaming from the Yltigg sprouted an idea in Nasha's mind. She turned to Roho.

"Pull your men back. Make it look like we're losing ground."

Roho frowned at her. "We are losing ground!"

"Then lose it faster. I need them drawn in."

Roho's lack of answer was agreement enough, and he turned away to issue commands.

Ento's features were hidden, but Nasha thought she could feel the anxiousness coming from him, even through the veil—the emotion too strong for the artifact to keep back. Shai stood beside him. Nasha eyed them both.

"Stay close to me, both of you. You're my anchor."

Shai eyed her suspiciously for a moment.

"Zala will not stop," Nasha said. "The Domain will not stop."

"You're not going to drain me again, are you?"

"No," Nasha answered as firmly as she could, but she knew Shai didn't need a curse of her own to see that Nasha wasn't sure. Still, she stood there, ready at Nasha's side.

Is this who I am? Am I just using her like Mansa used me?

Roho knew what he was doing. His warriors had given ground, but only enough to seem like they were moving away from the range of the Domain's archers. Nasha couldn't rush down and advance on foot from behind them—there were too many men to push through. She had to drop into the battle and try to keep control. She could lose herself, but better to do so amid the enemy than her allies. Nasha walked past Yltigg stone-slingers as they hid behind rocks and reloaded. She kept her legs moving and her gaze on the troops trying to break through the mouth of the gorge-like pass below.

The prickling on her skin returned. It was almost like touching ancestor-stone. A mass of emotions stormed around her, all of them trying to flow into Nasha like water. She closed her eyes, recalling the sensation from the mines, feeling the flare of the manacles around her wrists. She opened her eyes, and the emotions had coalesced into swirling strands of color.

Nasha looked down at the ancestor-stone manacles, chains still dangling. The manacles quivered with power, already absorbing the abundance of fear, anger, surprise. So much more. They came along with a slight burning underneath her skin. No matter how much control she managed, using her curse would never be comfortable. She took a long breath and looked to Shai and Ento. "Stay in sight."

Then she sprinted straight for the edge, letting the anger, fear, and desperation from the fighting men beneath be sucked into her. She felt them run their course through her veins. Every inhale was loaded with power, and every exhale consumed the emotions and flooded Nasha with strength. Zala's envy raked at it, trying to touch the emotions with Her darkness. Nasha did all she could to avoid the dead goddess's touch by clinging onto that thread of hope that rode beneath it all. They had a path now; all that she had to do was fight back an army.

Nasha neared the edge that rose sixty feet above the battle. She'd balk at the height even if jumping into a lake or river. Leaping into an army of heavily armored Domain soldiers had her mind screaming insanity. But that didn't stop her. Nor did the icy sensation in her gut as she ran. *No, no, stop!*

But she leapt, sailing through the air high above the battle, a scream in her throat; half fear, half determination. A wish that she had not miscalculated the power beating deep in her chest. She fell with the wind matching her howl, the sounds below growing louder and louder, until she slammed into a Domain soldier close to the Yltigg line.

The impact sent the men around them flying but did not affect her body. She pulled out her obsidian knives, taken by the mad thrill of being alive after the fall, and advanced on the enemy.

The Domain soldiers were heavily armored, but Nasha had surprise on her side. She jumped forward, twisting surprise into speed within her, and found the crack between the chest and shoulder plates of a Domain man, sinking her knife downward into his heart. Nasha was close enough to see the man's eyes bulge in his helmet as the blood painted his lips. She'd moved too fast for him to react and plunged the knife too deep for him to survive. More surprise ran through her, but it burned as Zala tried to taint it with her touch. Hope and belief would only get Nasha so far. She had to pace herself.

The Domain soldiers were drawn to the spot Nasha cleared with her landing. Two more advanced on her, but she was already in position: parry-knife before her, striking knife ready to kill. The first came with his sword raised overhead, chest open, trusting his armor against the knives. Nasha pulled both arms back and met the man's chest with the sole of her boot, directing the strength from her curse into the kick. She was swimming in a sea of emotion and her curse was drinking it in. The impact crushed the man's breastplate, and he was launched backward into his companions.

The second soldier thrust his sword at her, but Nasha had already retaken her position. She parried his blade on hers, throwing her opponent's sword aside and leaving his neck exposed for her stab as the man was carried forward by the momentum of his attack. Nasha slid her striking blade into the side of the man's neck three times in quick succession, then pushed him back. A spike of fear hit Nasha before the man died, but it was sucked into her ancestor-stone wristbands, ready to be consumed by her curse. Deep within her, Zala reached for it, weighing on Nasha's mind. The dead goddess's touch escalated Nasha's warning signs, and the tingling on her skin became the blurring of her vision.

The large empty swathe around her was closing now, more soldiers drawing in, encouraged by numbers or unaware that death waited at Nasha's hands. The Yltigg had been encouraged as well, and they'd cut down the Domain troops behind Nasha to join her. These emotions were different, full of hope. It wasn't the same as hers or Shai's, but it was enough to keep her strong against the depths within her where Zala waited.

A renewed strength surged through her, but it came with a ringing in her ears. She was getting closer to her limit. Nasha peeked back at where she'd left Shai. The girl had vanished, but Nasha could still feel her shots of emotion. Too unstable to be coming from the back of the line. It reminded Nasha of the Proving. Shai had joined the battle.

Roho led the men, filling up the space around Nasha and urging them on. Nasha answered with a raw howl that challenged the ringing of steel and screams of the dying. The Yltigg did not have her power, but her display seemed to inspire them, and the fear in the Domain troops rose around her with each blow to the enemy. Even so, they kept coming.

Four men barreled forward, all attacking in unison, but Nasha had fought greater numbers in the Proving. She moved her leg to avoid an overhead mace-strike, while twisting her opposite shoulder away from a stab by a second man. She stabbed his ribs, the blow strong enough to launch him into the ranks behind. The third man went for her chest, but Nasha ducked and rose, driving the butt of her knife into the man's lower jaw. His head snapped back, and Nasha punched at his exposed neck in two quick movements. The man fell gasping, but the final opponent had abandoned his blade and barreled into Nasha, falling over her as she dropped with her back to the ground.

Nasha pulled harder at the sea of emotion around her, and it flowed through the ancestor-stone on her wrists and into her veins like a fire. Nasha slammed her forehead into the man's helmet. It should have shattered her bone, but instead it sent the man flying off her, with his helm crushed into the front of his skull.

Nasha jumped to her feet and found Shai beside her, panting. Her anger at Nasha from the mines seemed to still be present, but it looked like the girl was directing it at the enemy soldiers.

Nasha nodded and followed the advancing Yltigg. They might be able to protect the peak after all.

Kadmus remained with his potions, behind the Domain back line, but the screams and clashing troops were impossible to ignore. There were soldiers around him, caring for the potions and siege weapons on slightly elevated ground, but their gazes were as intent as Kadmus's on the battle below. Bahar's army had pushed the savages back, but the opponent had set loose some kind of insanity of their own. Kadmus thought it was the Madness at first; perhaps some of the Vissland soldiers had taken vials and used them on the enemy, but he'd quickly seen that the warrior was too controlled to be taken by the Madness. It was a woman from what he could see, and she fought like . . . a Sentinel?

Kadmus frowned, that familiar irritation at not knowing all the variables rising within him. The clans didn't have Sentinels, and if this woman was one, where was her griffin? Whatever she was, she was empowering the clansfolk to push the Vissland army back. The Yltigg had rallied around her now, and the Visslands were suffering heavy losses. Kadmus saw soldiers piling onto the woman, but they were sent flying like stones across the battlefield.

He was still trying to understand when the messenger arrived, taking a moment to catch his breath. "Commander Bahar . . . orders . . . immediate launch of the catapults."

The soldiers around Kadmus were moving even before he finished. Kadmus jumped off the cart and pocketed two of the vials.

He wasn't sure they'd work, but victory in battle mattered little to him. If they lost, they'd march back home. That seemed more likely than victory in his mind. Perhaps a more . . . patriotic man would have warned them that the serum might fail, but Kadmus simply watched as the catapults were loaded and pushed out from under the trees. The ropes were cut, and vials of coppery-red rained on the Yltigg.

The Yltigg had gained ground on the Domain, and enemy archers were firing into the warriors behind Nasha now. Roho turned to Nasha, maybe looking for an answer as to how they might stop the barrage, but Nasha's attention shifted to the sky as another volley flew at them. It wasn't arrows this time. The Domain had launched what seemed to be liquid-filled glass tubes from what must be catapults at the back of their line. She followed the glint of the copper-colored containers as they smashed open on the Yltigg just ahead of her. The impact sent some of them to the ground, while others were cut and bleeding.

Nasha stepped back, half expecting some explosion or fire-tipped arrows to fall on them, but it seemed like the Domain troops were stepping back as well. Roho had a look of triumph as he raised a fist and howled a battle cry, but it was answered by the growls of his own men.

The connection to Shai pulled at Nasha. The hope that tethered her was straining, as if Shai had wavered, and affected Nasha in turn. Deep inside, Zala stirred. Nasha thought she could almost hear a laugh in her mind. Shai was a few steps ahead, among Yltigg who were writhing and struggling on the ground. Some had already risen and turned on whoever was nearest. They were taken by the taint. Zala's taint.

No! It can't be! How?

A million answers jumbled incoherently together, and a chill that was stronger than any warning sign flooded through Nasha. She tasted the blood and smoke again. The taste of fear from when she'd been a child under the floorboards, as the Domain city she'd seen in her vision burned around her. Shai turned, facing Nasha. There was blackness around her eyes, and dark veins spread across her face.

NO!

Nasha always thought her promise to Ife would be the first thing she'd remember if she saw Shai in danger. But it wasn't. All Nasha could think of was how Shai had always believed. Even when she had a knife to her throat and Bahar's people were threatening to kill her, Shai had always believed in Nasha. That was why she was easy to pick out in an ocean of sensations—why the girl's hope, her faith, was the strongest tether Nasha could find against Zala's taint. Now that taint had taken over Shai, and as it spread, Nasha could feel her own barrier cracking. A splintering sensation ran across her skin, as if it was being sucked dry. A fire seared her mind, and pieces of it crumbled into the darkness like ash. The laughter Nasha thought she'd heard grew louder now, and stronger as her hope cracked and fell away at the sight of the infection spreading through Shai.

"NO!"

Instinct kicked in. Nasha latched onto Shai's emotion, her confused terror, and dug deep, reaching for the same darkness that she'd become familiar with now. It wasn't hard to find, and Nasha already knew what it wanted even before touching it.

All around her, Yltigg were being attacked by their own. They fought back as the Domain troops retreated and waited. Nasha's focus was on Shai, though. The darkness was an unquenchable void, similar to what she'd sensed in the Hagun ancestor-stone, but where the Hagun stone's taint was vast and entrenched, Shai's was still fighting for control. Nasha knew what to do. The darkness was hungry, and it would feed on Shai, consume her life. There was only one way to stop that.

She let go of the hope and lowered her barrier, freeing her own darkness. A fury ripped its way through Nasha, and for a moment she wanted to scream, to rage, to forget who she was and kill whatever was around her. If it hadn't been Shai, she probably would have given in—taken by the taint, transformed into an earth-spawn like the others. Instead, she held on, pulling in emotion from around her to fight the darkness, like she'd done in the mines. She wasn't sustaining a barrier, and there was no vision this time, but the sensation was the same: the darkness weighing on her, taking small pieces away. Where she'd come from, the name of their commander. Nasha focused on what she needed to know: The girl before her was Shai. Nasha had promised to protect her. Zala could not claim her.

Strands of blues, greens, oranges, pinks, and yellows all bled into Nasha through the dark mist that seemed to take the battlefield as the taint spread. Shai trembled, her consciousness seemingly split as she jerked her head from side to side, grabbing at it and screaming in pain. Nasha kept her focus, pulling in the power, the emotion from the Earth—and pushing it against the void within Shai.

Nasha's body burned like she was standing in a fire, but this was Shai. This was her promise. Pain would not stop her.

She pushed all the power from the gathered emotion toward Shai with a roar, but Zala pushed back, unbroken. There wasn't enough to destroy the taint, not even with all the emotion around her. The laughter was rising in Nasha's mind, but an idea came with it. She'd lived with the curse. Shai could still be saved if Nasha sealed it off. She dug deep, searching for the core of Shai's belief, a hope strong enough to fight the despair taking hold of her. Zala still blocked Nasha's path. She needed more to break through, and only one source would give her enough for that. She needed to consume the darkness, like she'd done in the Ronar lands before recognizing what it was and the dangers it held. It would strengthen Zala's hold over her, but this was Shai.

Nasha dug into the darkness, and what came back was raw and primal. Her feet became heavy, sinking into the hard ground, but still she took more. Her vision grew white, and Zala's power flowed like a wave that pulsed through her body and into the Earth.

Once.

Twice.

Three times.

The smell of fear and the taste of blood gave way to a rot of death as the Earth let out a resounding crack, as if splitting open for

Zala to claim Nasha as her prize. Her champion. The edges of Nasha's mind were frayed and shattering, but just as she thought it would slip from her grasp, she found the slow pulse of what she was looking for: the hope that flowed at the core of Shai's belief.

The Earth groaned under her feet, paying the price, but Nasha touched the stream of Shai's emotion and was taken by a memory of Ife, smiling as he embraced her. She saw it through Shai's eyes, her memory, but the feeling flooded through Nasha's body. The hope Ife always held for his family was mirrored in Shai, and it was on that strength that Nasha drew to seal away the corruption that threatened the girl. Slowly the darkness receded, and Nasha pushed harder and harder until the darkness within Shai was wrenched free and pushed into a pit as deep as the one Nasha held inside herself.

Nasha broke down and fell to her hands and knees. Her fingers sank into what looked like ash. Something pulled her up, but Nasha couldn't move her arms or defend herself.

She looked up, groggy. It could have been a vision; maybe she'd cracked again and was seeing things. Shai was holding her up, her mind seemingly whole, her touch filled with more than hope. Nasha clung to that faith. It was enough to lift the clouds from her eyes and the weight from her mind. Shai dragged her along, following the Yltigg as they stepped away from the tainted.

"It's infectious. We can't stay here!" Shai bellowed. Nasha couldn't see who the girl was screaming at. All she caught were glimpses.

Beast-like men pounced on the retreating Yltigg, blood splattering from the warriors around her. Roho swam into her vision for a moment, but Nasha could hardly think; it was all she could do was keep her legs moving as Shai dragged her along.

"Gather whatever ancestor-stone you can and inform the chief. We need to abandon the peaks." It sounded like Roho's voice, but he'd vanished from her sight already.

The Domain were not giving chase, but on the battlefield, the tainted ripped stragglers apart. The entire plain where they'd fought was ashen and cracked. Parts of it were sunken or split by faults.

"Did I do that?" she asked Shai. She knew the answer. She'd

taken the life from the Earth around her and broken it as far as her eyes could see.

"You healed me, you fought it." Shai dragged her along as they made their retreat into the mines.

Roho stepped up, helping pull her along now. "We'll follow the tunnels, come out on the other side. I've sent word to evacuate the peak."

"Where are we going?" Nasha asked.

"Somewhere to regroup, find allies."

Nasha nodded. Maybe she was too weak to argue, to tell him she'd best be left behind. She was the one who tainted the earth to save a single life. But another part reminded her that even with the unthinkable cost, she had saved Shai from Zala's taint, and it was the Domain that had tainted the girl in the first place.

Mansa was right. The Domain was toying with life, using Zala, maybe even worshiping her. Nasha had thought the enemies were separate, but they seemed to be the same.

A renewed determination burned within her. They couldn't protect the peak from the Domain—making a stand would only produce more tainted. They'd fight back, though. United. Mansa had been right about that as well. In the past, the Domain had demanded clan blood in the name of peace, but the clans would pay no longer.

Kadmus was still in shock as the savages retreated. The Vissland armies advanced with cries of victory, but all Kadmus could do was stare. Too much had happened too fast. The potions had worked. It wasn't only that this wasn't what he'd been expecting—the Madness hadn't faded. The priest had done something to the potion. Kadmus was sure of it. Blasted Church and its fake idealisms. They'd brewed the disease that would not let Nima go, and they'd done it with Kadmus's help.

Kadmus didn't know how. He'd only used the Church brewers as hired hands, monitoring the brewing of the Madness he'd devised, and he'd overseen it all the while. How could they have altered it?

If things had stopped there, maybe his mind would have found a path to move forward, but he'd watched the warrior, the one who fought like a Sentinel, heal another savage with nothing more—it seemed—than her will. Some would call that magic, as they did with the Sentinels, but Kadmus knew magic was only a word for the lazy to label what they didn't understand. There was an explanation for this, and suddenly, his mind knew the path to take. He would uncover what she'd done. Find the cure she'd used.

Kadmus had been dragged here, but he'd ironically found what he'd been searching for. Something he'd never find in his workshop or calculations. The path to heal Nima was now retreating with the Yltigg, and Kadmus had to get close to it. He had to infiltrate the clans.

He looked around. A plain stood between his current position and the Yltigg peak, but more forests beyond promised enough cover for Kadmus to find the clans without being spotted. All he needed to do was get past the guards who'd stayed behind to man the catapults.

Most of the soldiers were by the siege weapons—a score of strides away—cheering as infected clansmen tore at the enemy. Kadmus pressed his teeth hard. Their simple minds cheered on the very Madness that threatened to take their homes. He'd get past them and keep going until he'd put the battle far enough behind him to cross the plains undetected. Then he'd reach the cover of the trees beyond the Yltigg peak. He'd have to run. He couldn't risk losing the retreating clan.

There was only one man close to him, two carts down, also cheering. The plan was not without risk, but Nima was worth any risk. The soldier was distracted by the battle, but his cheering had subsided. It was enough. Kadmus grabbed one of the vials from his cart, jumped off, and crept behind the soldier. Kadmus had walked long enough in the shadows to know which movements would create enough noise to give him away. He crept right to the back of the soldier, then smashed the vial on his head. The man wore no helmet, and the potion soon drained down onto his face.

Kadmus took several steps back as the man turned in surprise, but the soldier couldn't keep the liquid out of his eyes and mouth. He gave an angry step toward Kadmus, but soon fell to the ground, starting to transform. He'd easily find the others by the catapults, and there would be a massacre. Enough to ensure Kadmus' escape in the chaos.

Even for Kadmus, this felt vile. Spreading the Madness while knowing there would be no cure went against every fiber in his being, but this was what Nima needed. She could not afford the shackles of Kadmus's conscience.

He removed his cloak and outer layer of robes. He'd worn them throughout the march, and they were recognizable. He threw them over the man.

Part of the plan was based on the hope that the madman would leave the bodies of the soldiers who'd stayed close to him too mangled to be recognized. The hope that now that Bahar had taken the Yltigg and brewed a weapon of his own, he would have no further need of Kadmus other than to heal his wounds. The hope that Bahar would think Kadmus dead among the bodies when he saw his cloak.

Kadmus hated relying on hope. Hope was brother to faith, and Kadmus had always known how fragile that was.

The growling began, and the claws cut their way out of the soldier's skin. The man's cry when hit by the potion had attracted a few other guards, but Kadmus retreated to the shadows of the trees behind them and ran in the opposite direction. Toward the catapults.

The men abandoned their posts in favor of the commotion, giving Kadmus the opening to run past the siege weapons and farther away from Bahar's army.

It was just another hope that he'd find the fleeing clansfolk—but that was the hope of seeing Nima open her eyes. It kept him running away from the army and everything he'd ever known.

CHAPTER THIRTY-ONE

And when She returns, the Body will come to Her, renewed in the strength of its faith.

— The Book of the Body

The True had not been lying. Ferrin hadn't waited for the dawn to round up a unit to check the walls, which found two spots where the Dakhran exploding potions had been stashed. They were in houses close to the walls, almost pressed up against them.

He brought Lynn in to see them, and the number of vials had filled her with dread. She was no brewer, but they seemed enough to level the entire block of houses at least. Certainly blast a hole in the wall.

The people had approached panic with the Legion knocking on doors and pushing into houses. A battle couldn't be fought like this. They couldn't hold Dakhra off their walls if they were fighting another enemy within. She needed to speak with the Pontiff.

She found him in his reflection chamber, where he seemed to

spend much of the night. Lynn hadn't requested an audience, but the Alterian guard still directed her to his private chapel. Lynn was seething the entire way. How had they sabotaged the city? How far did their reach go? Were Sentinels involved?

Two guards stood at the door to the Pontiff's reflection chamber, but Lynn's silver glare was enough for them to knock on the door, then open it.

The Pontiff looked up as if expecting her presence. "Close the door, if you will, my dear."

Lynn pushed the doors shut behind her. The room was dark, and like all reflection chambers, held the perforated walls that cast the Seraph's scriptures in light on the ground.

"You have a report?"

Lynn sighed. "The True are infiltrated deeper than we imagined. They saw me. Saw us coming." She still didn't know how to describe what they'd done. "I suspect they've known about the movements of the Church for a long time. They have people within the ranks."

"Did you trace them back to a leader?" His green eyes fixed on her own, seemingly intent, but his tone led Lynn to believe he knew exactly how deep the corruption ran.

"No, they . . . They believe they do not need the Church to be proclaimed worthy. They took their own lives but believe the Seraph will bring them back."

The Pontiff's expression was shadowed in gloom, but it seemed to shift away from its usual knowing calm. "Without a body?" he asked.

"They cite the texts. The Book of—"

"The Book of the Body describes the Seraph's creation of our kind. 'And when she returns, the Body will come to Her, renewed in the strength of its faith.'"

"Yes, High Pontiff."

The Pontiff sighed. "They are twisting the texts through interpretation."

"There is something else. More troubling," Lynn said. "None of them hesitated to take their lives, but after they did, a red smoke streamed from their mouths. They were trying to infect me, turn a Sentinel to Madness even in death. They've evolved their potions." Lynn struggled to keep her voice under control. "And those are not the only potions they're using. They're planning to aid Dakhra when they reach us. I had the Legion sweep a portion of the walls. They found explosive concoctions. Enough to level a hundred yards, maybe more."

This gave the Pontiff pause. "That changes things." He started pacing around the room. "You believe you can deal with this?" He was unnervingly calm. How could he not be rattled?

Lynn took a deep breath. No matter how deep her faith, lying would do them no good. "No. Not here."

The Pontiff stopped walking and turned to her. "Not here?"

If she were to cure the Madness, she'd need time to find a solution in what Reznik was teaching her, and even if she did, there was no fighting the threat of explosions that might happen anywhere in the city. Dakhra would be here soon, and it would be a war on two fronts.

"I fear the True are too entrenched within Alteria, High Pontiff. Even if Dakhra hasn't marched from Durnn yet, they are too close. We don't have the time or resources to be sure that all the explosive brews are found. We can't fight Dakhra and their new airship with the risk of our walls being crumbled from inside."

"What are you suggesting?"

"Syvern has been one step ahead because he knows what we'll do. He's been a ruler long enough to understand how the Church works, how the Sentinels and the Bone will try to fight back. We need time, and we need to set up a defense where he has a smaller presence. Where he doesn't threaten to bring down the walls before throwing a single soldier against them."

"Retreat?" To the Pontiff's credit, there was no disbelief in his voice. It was closer to curiosity, as if he'd consider a plan with merit.

Lynn pressed her teeth together. The last time she'd risked something like this, she'd brought Dakhra into the Domain. Now she was about to give them the holy city.

"I know how it sounds, but I see no alternative. Othonea has always harbored hatred for Dakhra, and Syvern's grasp won't reach that far."

The Pontiff appeared to think it over.

"We'd have more time," Lynn said. "Reznik might find a cure, and we would level the odds of battle. Alteria has stood for centuries, but we must show Syvern that Alteria is more than piled stones."

"There is power in stone, my dear," the Pontiff said. "Power that fuels a faith. We do not have monuments for nothing."

"And we will return to them once we've had enough time to prepare and fight the enemy on our terms."

"Evacuating an entire city is no simple matter. Especially this one. A marching army moves faster than refugees."

"I know. And I volunteer to stay here and hold them off until the faithful have fled. The Sentinels won't hold back their army, but we don't need to stand against them. There's plenty two-score Sentinels can do against marching men. We'll strike and pull back. Make it hard for them to advance."

The Pontiff considered, taking her in for a long moment. "An honorable proposal, Sub-commander, but I would rather have you and your order by my side. Ildred still holds his ground around Durnn, does he not?"

"He does, High Pontiff."

"Good. Have him carry out this plan of yours. Send one of your Sentinels to inform him. Hit and run. That should give us time to flee."

"High Pontiff, respectfully," Lynn said, unsure how to phrase things. She didn't want to disagree with the man, but attacking Dakhra on the road was one thing; attacking them within a city they'd fortified was entirely another. "The risk of losing our brothers and sisters is much greater if they move on Durnn. Dakhra has been in the city long enough to build up defenses."

The Pontiff paused next to her. "Sentinels are the greatest warriors in the world, Sub-commander. They are not to move on the city, merely delay Dakhra's departure so the people may have time to leave Alteria. I have faith they will find a successful course of action by the grace of the Seraph." He made to move past her but laid a light hand on her shoulder. "I'll order a retreat."

The time it took to get to Talnea did nothing to disperse Lynn's anger. The image of the scarred man sticking the makeshift knife in his neck, then oozing the Madness-infused smoke, burned at the back of her mind all the way. They were trying to take down Sentinels. The thought of using the Pontiff's shard occurred to Lynn, but she needed to be sure about the host. Picking someone who failed to establish the Bond would kill them instead of adding another Sentinel to their ranks.

She stood on the balcony of the Talnean cathedral with Rel beside her. They looked down at the chaos the city had become as refugees competed with citizens for space on the streets.

"It was the right thing to do," Rel said. "I'm glad the Pontiff saw you for what you are. Olem would never have taken this leap."

"Olem is the leader we need, Rel. The Pontiff is just using me because of the Questioning. He knows I'm loyal."

Rel grinned. "Didn't stop you, though. You did well."

"We still need to find a cure. There might not be explosive brews threatening the walls here, but we can't have our soldiers exposed when Dakhra arrives."

"We'll find a way to deal with them. Even without a cure."

Lynn looked up at the Seraph's mark, her anger at the True still hot. She'd told herself she wouldn't do it—and questioned Reznik's status as a Church leader for telling her to sacrifice prisoners to find a cure—but seeing the lengths their enemy went to in striking at the Faith had her reconsidering. *Show me the path.*

The Seraph was silent, but the decision was taking form in Lynn's mind. She had to be willing to go as far as the enemy to beat them. "I might need your help with something."

"Besides curing the Madness?" Rel asked.

"Might be tied."

Rel nodded, then followed Lynn back inside and out the door.

Her steps were a touch lighter, knowing the True would not have followed them here. Not yet, at least. But the weight of what she was about to do bore down on her.

This is what you are, Dentos said. *It's what you've always been.*

You never really knew me, Lynn answered, but it did little to lessen the weight on her shoulders.

They paced through shadowed corridors, reaching a set of stairs that led down to the cathedral dungeons. Rel tilted his head at her, but Lynn gave him a reassuring nod and started down. She reached a chamber similar to the one in the Alterian cathedral—most holy buildings were similar to the one in Alteria—and tried one of the doors. It was locked, so she tried another, then another. The fourth one opened, as if Reznik had prepared everything for her.

"What are we doing?" Rel asked.

Lynn eyed a man who sat blindfolded and gagged, chained to the chair. "We're finding a cure."

She paced toward a table where two vials had been laid out. One held the silvery liquid Reznik said would make it easier to connect to the prisoner; the other held the orange-red liquid of the Madness. Beside the vials lay four shards of pulsing ruin-stone.

The man in the chair struggled against his chains. He might have tried to say something, but the gag made it unintelligible. Lynn paid him little heed. One should not dwell on the dead.

Rel drew up beside her and sucked in a sharp breath. He never expressed surprise, but this was clearly more than he'd expected. "Is that?"

"It's the Madness. We have to infect him so I can attempt a cure. Reznik has shown me how, but there are things he can't do for me."

Rel was silent for a long while, then nodded.

"It's what must be done," Lynn told him. "It's why we're Sentinels. Our faith makes us stronger than death." Something inside her still asked if this kind of death was justified, but her focus had to be on life, and the cure that would preserve it.

"What do I do?" Rel asked.

"I'll take the silver one, then connect to him with the stone.

Once I do, you'll give him that one." Lynn pointed at the red-filled vial.

Rel nodded, and Lynn downed the silver liquid from the first vial, then grabbed the ruin-stone shard. It was hot to the touch, and whatever was in Reznik's concoction worked through Lynn as if heightening her senses. Her skin tingled, and the sour stench of the cell filled her nostrils to the point where she almost bolted from it. The world was fading, though, and it wasn't Gheria this time. It was the other vision, the one where the two men stood over her as if she was in a chair. Lynn couldn't move her arms, and something ran through her—something angry, trying to pull her mind away from her grasp and replace it with a mindless rage, a mind that knew nothing but death.

Lynn pressed the stone tighter. It still tethered her back to the cell, like last time. She pressed it against the prisoner's forehead.

The vision changed. Shifting from stone walls and the two men with shaded faces—one of them weaving red lines as if tangling threads—to Alteria.

She saw the prisoner walking in shadow. He wore a heavy ruin-stone pendant shaped in the sign of the Bone. Something steamed off the man, a green-tinged aura like those Lynn had seen in previous visions. He was afraid. Lynn got closer, instinct keeping her to the shadows even though she knew he was only a vision.

The man walked into a building, and Lynn's vision followed him inside the room. Four other men waited there, one of them a priest in silver and white. The room was filled with rubble and shadow. It might even have been one of the chambers in the broken church in Alteria.

The priest spoke to those gathered there. His words were unintelligible to Lynn, but she saw her prisoner's aura shift. The green took on tinges of orange anxiousness. The priest handed vials to the four men, and the fear spiked in the prisoner as he took it.

Lynn found herself shaking her head. This man wasn't Dakhran; he was doing this out of some misguided belief, but that still didn't make him worthy. Lynn pressed her fingers around the ruin-stone that still tethered her to the cell. For a moment, it brought her out of the vision. Rel was beside the prisoner, vial open, ready to infect him.

Lynn's mind refocused on the vision, and before she could hold it back, her hand touched the man through his aura of green and orange. The man unstoppered his vial and lifted it slowly to his mouth, but something pulled at Lynn. A mingling of desperation and hope—but also something more. That feeling reserved only for the closest in life. A brother, a spouse. A child. The man's emotions became clear to Lynn, as did the root of his fear. He thought he was protecting his family, doing something to end this war so they might be seen as worthy, even if he would not.

She still was unsure, and saw nothing to confirm it, but perhaps she was the judgment the Seraph had sent this man. She pulled the stone away from the man's forehead, breaking the vision and throwing out her hand before Rel dosed the prisoner with the Madness.

Rel gave her a puzzled look, and Lynn's voice was almost a whisper. "We can't infect him."

"He's the enemy, Lynn. Unworthy."

"This man was driven by desperation, thinking he'd protect his family. He's worthy to someone."

Lynn removed the man's blindfold, but not the cloth from his mouth. His eyes were wide, his whimpering constant.

"Listen to me," Lynn said.

The man struggled, but Lynn held him by the shoulders and shook him. "Listen to me!"

The prisoner's whimpering slowed, then stopped. "I'm putting you on the first cart out of this city. From there, you are to return to your family. If you involve yourself with the people that got you captured again, you won't get another chance. Do you understand?"

The man only blinked at her.

"Do you understand?"

He nodded. Tentatively, then more vigorously.

"Good. Lean forward." Lynn brought out her mace.

The man was slow but obeyed. She hit him on the back of the head and his body went limp. Passed out, but not dead.

"Lynn . . . Can we afford this? I understand your reservations, but this is the time to use death."

"I won't kill this man, Rel. Not like this."

"You think Dakhra wouldn't kill prisoners to get what they want? We need to cure it, Lynn; we need to fight them. The Seraph trusts us for this."

Lynn nodded. "She does, and that's why I won't do it. You said it before we came down here. We'll find a way."

"This is the way, Lynn. We won't get another shot at this."

Lynn sighed. It was off-putting to see Rel rattled, but the insanity they'd been living through was more than any of them had ever experienced. "I understand your concern, but you wanted me to lead, so you must trust me on this now."

Rel looked away. He showed no anger; that wasn't his way. "Faith is never easy, but I'll do as you ask."

"We'll find another way," she said. "Can you get him out of here?"

Rel nodded. "Of course, Sub-commander."

"Did you get something?" Ferrin asked.

He was walking close to Lynn down a crowded road. Refugees and Talneans fought for space with elbows and glares, but Lynn's mantle did a good job of opening up the way.

"No," Lynn answered. "We'll need to find another way to fight them."

Or you need to do your duty and find that cure! Dentos said.

Lynn couldn't kill that man. She'd seen where his intentions were rooted. There was no desire to tear down the Seraph or the Domain. The man was just desperate. How many more had succumbed to the True in that way? And how could she judge them?

Reznik had found it easy, but Lynn found herself questioning his staunchness again. Lives could not be discarded so easily, no matter the objective. She looked to Ferrin. "Why do you believe in me so much?"

Ferrin narrowed his eyes at her. "I choose to."

"That doesn't explain much."

"Of course it does. I choose to follow you, Lynn. I'm fine with that choice. I was angry when you told me about Alren, but I can live with knowing you did your best for him. That's all we can ever do, and what better person to believe in than someone you know will always do everything they can to protect those around them?"

Lynn was glad they were walking, because she had no answer. She'd been subjected to so much doubt from the Sentinels that Ferrin's belief, even after she hid Alren from him, was hard to deal with. She put her head down and continued toward the palace. He was right; it was a choice. She'd chosen not to kill the prisoner. Could she live with that? She'd made a similar choice with the girl in Pyrran after leaving the prison—the same girl who turned out to be infected by the Madness. The same girl who'd ravaged the faithful in the temple where Ferrin's sister had presided.

This is different. She'd done more than check the man's eyes. She'd seen his emotion, seen the desperation that drove him. It was, perhaps, the same kind of desperation that had led her father to kill Jeck and Pyth, Lynn's brothers that had returned infected from a campaign in Vizcarra. He'd been trying to protect her, same as the prisoner with his family. *This is right.* She could live with this.

Ferrin paused outside the palace gates. "Let me know what you decide, eh?"

Lynn nodded and strode in to meet Olem.

The main building of the palace was surrounded by towers with stained-glass depictions of the holy texts, each one leading into the next, telling a story for all who laid eyes upon it. The images seemed to be more focused on Othonean history than Lynn remembered; whether this was a reaction to the current state of the Faith or something more personal between King Iridan and the Pontiff, Lynn couldn't tell.

"You have a plan?" she asked Olem.

The commander shook his head. "No idea what the Pontiff is

up to, so we'll have to see if King Iridan has something up his sleeve."

Lynn doubted it, but Othonea's hate for Dakhra had been well documented. Maybe Olem had a point. Lynn bowed her head in thought as they walked on. Their Sentinel mantles were enough for them to enter the palace gates unquestioned, and guards escorted them down a long hall flanked with stained-glass panels. They depicted the Seraph on one knee, hand on the pommel of a sword stuck in the ground, a city burning behind her. Lynn looked at it for a moment. Was that the moment when the Seraph left them? There was sadness on Her face, but that could have been an Othonean interpretation.

Officers were filing into a room up ahead, while the Pontiff waited for the Sentinels at the doors. He led them in silently, with nothing to cloud his expression. His movements were as calm as ever, as if all he'd done until now, and all that came from the Madness, was happening exactly according to plan. Was that true, or was that the calmness required by the head of the Church?

King Iridan sat in a high-backed chair at the head of a rectangular table. A few Othonean officers sat stiffly at the table as well. General Burnham represented the Legion. They hadn't appointed a new Light of the Legion. There were rumors that the King's son, who'd been appointed by the Pontiff, had raised an army of foreigners and returned to the Domain. The Pontiff sat beside High Bishop Reznik and Chancellor Burke. He beckoned for Lynn to occupy the chair on his other side. Olem sat beside her.

The Othonean king's stare was cold and set straight ahead. The Pontiff wore a smile Lynn had almost become used to, but one that also seemed to set Iridan off. The king tapped a slow finger on the table.

"So, you've brought the snake to my doorstep," Iridan said. "Do you have a plan at least?"

"We are all in this together, Iridan," the High Pontiff said. "There are no closed doors within the Domain. Do you think if we held in Alteria it would be any different?"

"We have come to add our strength to yours, King Iridan,"

Burke said in a somewhat more respectful tone than the Pontiff. "The enemy is at all of our gates."

"How many Sentinels?" Iridan snapped at Olem.

"Almost two-score."

Iridan scoffed. "That's hardly enough."

"Would you prefer none?" Reznik asked.

"We have been dealing with Dakhra for years," said a mustached man in a tight red-and-black Othonean military suit. "We know how to fight them."

The Pontiff gave the room an amused smile. "Well, I'll just tell them to leave you to do the fighting then." He looked at Lynn with a glint in his eye, but she couldn't share the humor in a moment like this.

"The Sentinels will only become a liability if they are turned," Iridan said. "You bring us little worth, High Pontiff."

Lynn gritted her teeth. The man insulted the elite order of the Church as if none of them were there.

King Iridan shook his head. "You fill my streets with beggars, the army you bring is so green they barely know how to draw swords, let alone use the damn blades, and you plan to defend the city with what? Hope? Half the troops have no proper weapons!"

"I'm sure some of them can operate the forges if taught," Burke said. "We came here to gain time. Weapons can be made."

"Do your Sentinels not have their own manner of forging?" Iridan shot a quick look at Olem and Lynn.

Lynn held back a glare, but the talk of forging pulled back the burning city depicted on the stained-glass Lynn had seen on the way here. It set Lynn's mind to work and dredged up an idea from the shattered depths of her mind. The king was right. They did forge weapons, but they added ruin-stone into the mix. That was it.

Burke was rubbing his hands over the table's smooth wooden surface. "The Body of the Seraph is represented by her faithful. They must work as one to—"

"Forging weapons alone won't work," Lynn said. "And neither will waiting for Dakhra to arrive." Her words silenced the room.

"We waited in Durnn. It isn't the way. We don't have a cure yet, so we need to stop them from infecting us."

"And how do you propose that?" Iridan had a contemptuous curl to his lip.

"We burn their potions."

The king laughed openly now. "Do you even know where the potions are stocked? And how will you deal with their new airship? You failed to stop it once already."

Lynn frowned at him.

"You thought I wouldn't know?" Iridan looked away, but Lynn's focus was as much on the Church council as the king now.

"We weren't prepared," Olem said.

"We couldn't break through the defenses of their airships because they know us," Lynn said. "And they know the weapons we have."

"What makes it work this time?" Burke asked.

"We won't get close. We'll evolve our weapons the same way they evolved theirs." She set her gaze on Iridan. "You have ballistae, correct?"

Iridan shrugged slightly. "As did the Skygate."

"We'll forge new bolts, coated in ruin-stone. They'll crack through the Dakhran plating and expose the ships, so we can bring down any that protect the enemy camp. Then we find the potions."

Iridan eyed her for a long moment. "You are asking me to risk my resources and the lives of my men on an untested theory. Do you even know where the potions are? If they'll burn?"

"We have tested them," Reznik said. "They will burn. And a touch of faith in the Church's master of secrets would go a long way, Iridan." Reznik seemed to share the Pontiff's low level of respect for the kings, but that seemed to be his way with most of the people around him. "My bishops have gathered enough separate reports to be sure. The airship they brought in is housing the potions, but not all of them. They're kept on all of the plated ships. Dakhra is sure we cannot breach the plating."

"And if we don't," Lynn said, "they will drop the Madness onto your city from the sky. And where will your men and your resources be then?"

The king was silent.

"There is no other option. We defeat the airships or we die. We have ruin-stone infused blades that cut through their protective plates, which is how we know that ruin-stone ballistae will do the same. That's not the problem."

The king was interested now. "What is?"

"We had to attack the ships ourselves. Direct contact. They coated the hulls with something that paralyzed us. The griffins too. It all seemed connected through the plates. If the ballistae can tear holes in the hull, we can do the rest."

Roki laughed. *You'll only lead more of them to their deaths.*

Olem cleared his throat. "All we need are men to transport and operate the ballistae alongside the Legion." Lynn was thankful he'd understood the plan. "And protect the siege weapons while we burn the potions and take down the ships."

"That is quite the expense of ruin-stone," Iridan said. His officers nodded along.

Lynn knew she was glaring at the king, but she couldn't hold it back. "And what of the expense of life?"

Iridan scowled. "I am sure your faith in the Seraph will be enough to show you the worthy who must be protected, yes?"

Lynn had her hands closed into fists, but the Pontiff touched a light hand on her arm. "We will obtain the ruin-stone ourselves, Iridan. Have the forges ready." It was not a request.

Iridan gave a curt nod, then rose and made for the door, followed by the others. The Pontiff's hand weighed a little heavier on Lynn's arm. "Please remain."

She didn't move, and neither did Olem.

"This is a bold plan," the Pontiff said when they were alone. "Are you sure?"

Lynn knew where the question came from. Her plan had failed once before.

You'll fail again, Cara whispered.

"I am," Olem said.

"It is what must be done," Lynn said. "There is no other way." She would not take more lives in order to find a cure. That would make her no better than the cult that encouraged people to embrace death.

"There *are* other ways, my dear," the Pontiff said. "But the one you propose might cost the fewest lives. Is there anything else?"

Lynn struggled to keep her expression unchanged. She couldn't tell him about Reznik or the prisoners waiting to be killed. "No, High Pontiff."

Olem rose. "We will see this through."

"Excellent," said the Pontiff. "May the Seraph watch over us all. By the Breath and the Body, the Blood and the Bone."

Lynn nodded. "The Breath and the Body, the Blood and the Bone."

CHAPTER THIRTY-TWO

Little is known outside the Church of the process of bonding a Sentinel to their griffin. However, past researchers have documented that young griffins have an outer protective ruin-stone layer over their ruin-stone hearts, which they shed in adulthood. The discarded shards are said to be pieces of their very hearts.

— *The Study and History of Griffins,* by Ander W. Demerith

Adrian's march toward Alteria was not a common one. The Legion had forerunners, but they had to spread them wide and employ constant checkpoints to avoid ambushes. The threat was lessened now that Addo was dead and Pyrran back in Domain hands, but chaos still ruled the Domain. Adrian refused to let his guard down.

Derren and Myrra were his constant companions, their reddish outlines walking beside him. They'd smiled when Adrian issued the command to kill all of Addo's followers in Pyrran and watched beside him as he oversaw their execution. In a different time, the people would have been afraid, but the Domain had never really frowned on the execution of prisoners—and the times had people shedding their masks of hypocrisy. Bac seemed to balk at the killings, but that seemed tied more to his past as a prisoner of the very place in which the madmen were killed—the prison of Dalhold —than to the deaths themselves. Nasir himself did not protest, and Adrian knew why.

He'd always seen the Faith for what it was: a tool of self-preservation. The chosen were kept, the unfortunate discarded. At least Syvern had brought that to light. Perhaps these people calling themselves the True could have something to their preaching. Or, more likely, they were just another group seeking to exploit those around them.

The growing mark in the sky was worrying, though. Some now said it was the sign of the Promised Dawn, that the Seraph Herself was returning. Adrian doubted it. If She was watching, She didn't seem to be picking sides. Maybe the Promised Dawn would come, and Adrian would meet Mother again, but until then, he knew the path. Derren had told Adrian to have faith in himself, and that was what he'd follow.

Queen Niria of Sacantha had reestablished control of Pyrran, and the Legion went on its way toward Alteria. Adrian's thoughts had been on Father, though, and what Addo had said. The coward was a sneaky bastard, but he wasn't lying. Adrian could sense it when he was bonded to Addo. Syvern was behind this, and he'd answer for that. But if Father had truly known Syvern was planning something and convinced Adrian to leave Myrra behind, then he was as guilty of her death as Syvern.

Your father sucks the life out of us all. Derren said, trudging beside as Adrian rode atop a horse. It was the same thought Adrian had when he'd seen Derren's face light up after Adrian dragged him from Father's service and into the Legion. Would Derren have been that happy if he knew what awaited him?

They stopped in one of the Sacanthan towns, occupying the deserted inns and houses around the central town square. The inhabitants had fled toward the perceived safety of larger cities like Pyrran and Pehd and had yet to return. A few of the original citizens might have remained, but without the town guard or even basic trade for food, they'd likely have been forced out as well.

Adrian settled into a house close to where the troops gathered. He'd left Bac at the door but called the man in now.

"You've proven your worth," Adrian said.

"Church might disagree."

Adrian chuckled. "You do know I am Light of the Legion, yes? When you fight for me, you fight for the Church."

Bac scoffed. "Don't see no priests steppin' in front of those madmen."

Adrian couldn't hold back the smile. The bluntness didn't offend him. "You're right. But there is still more fighting to be done, and as I said, you have proven yourself valuable. What do you want?"

"What does any man want? A quiet house in the country. Safety. No more fightin'."

Adrian paused. "I called you in here to promote you."

"More fightin' then?" Bac didn't say it like he was complaining.

"The Domain responds to titles. I'm assigning you as my personal guard. If anyone asks, you can tell them you are a High Guard of the Legion."

"That title exists?"

Adrian smirked. "It does now. We beat Dakhra back, then you'll get your safety."

Bac nodded. "Aye." He walked out with little change in his gait, but Adrian let himself believe he'd helped the man, even if Bac did not understand it. The title would keep him safe from future imprisonment when they were done with all this.

Bac soon opened the door again, but it was to let Nasir in this time. Adrian had been expecting the priest and followed him upstairs and into one of the empty rooms, ready for instruction.

"What I taught you in Azur was a simple binding," Nasir said. "What Kel Bradaz began went down the path of the magic's true power. It comes from pain but is centered around control, both yours and your target's. What you have managed is impressive, but you will need to find new control over yourself if you are to shield the troops for longer or seek to control those you've bound with your blood."

"You can control a person's actions?"

"If circumstances are favorable, yes, my Lord Light."

Adrian frowned.

"You are in no danger of me attempting that on you, if that's what you're thinking." Nasir said.

Adrian held Nasir's gaze, still wary.

"You are safe from others," Nasir continued, "but you will always be vulnerable to yourself." He set a stern look on Adrian. "You have scratched the surface of this. The way you held the men on the ships and your prodding at Addo Brandt were a start."

Adrian felt his frown deepening, but Nasir was the one who awakened Adrian's blood, and he must have felt it when Adrian crossed over that barrier at Myrra's urging. Or maybe he'd assumed it because of the permanent shadow around Adrian's eyes.

"What you did on the ships was dangerous. I gave you an outlet through the fire, but that will not always be the case."

"What happens if I don't have an outlet?"

"Enough pain will always break a man, Lord Light. The effects can be . . . varied. Men have lost their minds. Others were so fully consumed by the pain, it took their lives. The markings around your eyes are a warning. An outlet can work to direct the pain away, but shielding your own vulnerabilities is the only way to keep it in for longer—to use the power before it drains your strength away. You must find something to hold on to. Something that tethers you to who you are, so that what you seek to control does not control you."

Adrian looked to the far end of the room, where Myrra watched beside Derren, her broken face staring in silence. "I have that."

"Good. Remember the shape of it, the emotion that it provokes within, and the shape of the pain. That will be your light in the darkness."

Adrian regarded Myrra. There was anger there, a constant burning—but it was nothing compared to the clamping around his heart. He'd become so accustomed to it, he'd learned to dull the pain, but it was clear to him now. This wasn't like the burning that washed over his skin, or the tingling in his blood that turned into stinging cuts down to the bone. This was deeper and held his heart in place, as if he'd be dead without her. It was what drove his vengeance—his need to see Myrra's face whole. "I'm ready."

Nasir nodded and led Adrian to another room. A man was bound there, gagged and blindfolded, his hands behind his back. He was one of the prisoners Adrian had taken from Addo's troops. He knew he'd need someone to practice on, after all.

The man lay on his side on the floor. He struggled against his bonds at the sound of Adrian and Nasir entering the room, but the coarse rope that bound him held tight. There was little furniture in the room; a bed and nightstand, but nothing around the bound man on the other side of the chamber. It was dark, moonbeams the only source of light. Those and the Seraph's mark in the night sky.

Nasir gave Adrian the ruin-stone knife he'd used in Azur, and Adrian slit a shallow cut along his forearm. He pulled down the man's gag and let his blood trickle into his mouth.

Adrian stepped back. He traced the signs of the binding, but Nasir was showing him new ones as well. Vertical and horizontal lines crossing, circles and swirls. Adrian didn't know what they meant, but with every sign the prickling on his skin grew more intense, until it became the pain he'd come to expect. It went deeper this time, pulling the strength from deep within him and coming back up as threads of glowing red that shot from his fingers and sank into the man on the floor, who began to growl with the Madness. The growl hit Adrian differently than before. He always thought it was Raklin who'd tainted his blood, but Addo's words had him thinking of Myrra, and the guilt of that memory rose within him.

"You must do more than hold it back, Lord Light. Control the Madness. Subdue it."

Adrian looked to Myrra. She glowed almost as brightly as the strands coming from his fingers. She smiled at him, but it brought him no warmth, only more of that clamping around his heart. This pain was his, and it was easily distinguishable from the anger that burned through the man.

Adrian tried to wrap his consciousness around it and hold on to the man's anger, control it, but every time he tried to grasp the anger, it bled away. Adrian's breath grew faster, deeper. The blood magic was taking its toll, but Myrra only grew brighter. He wanted this, needed it to be close to her. The world around him faded, and his eyes burned, but he didn't care. He'd live with her in his pain, so long as he lived with her. Adrian stepped toward Myrra, ready to take the power she offered. He would deny it no longer. He would control it. She touched him, and lines of black shot from her hand and up his arm. The clamping faded, and the burning around his eyes intensified, as if he'd taken the man's fire—the fire of the Madness itself—into him.

Another step, and Myrra vanished.

Adrian spun around, looking to Nasir. "What happened?"

"You lost yourself, Lord Light. Forgot what pain belonged to you and what was his. I had to cut it off."

"No. I've done this before. With Addo!"

Nasir nodded. "And the marks on you face are clear. If you do not control this power, this grief, it will control you. Your approach must be measured, Lord Light."

Adrian looked down at the prisoner; he was motionless, limbs twisted against the rope that still held him fast. Dead. He looked back at the priest. There could be no measured approach. Nasir didn't understand. Myrra was part of him. She was all he valued, the only thing that gave him worth. He wouldn't give up on her. Not now that he was so close. He had to have faith in himself. Only a drop of Adrian's blood and a touch of his power had killed the prisoner, but Adrian had resisted that power. "Running is not the way, Nasir. I can control it. I—"

There was a loud knock on the door, followed by shouting outside. Not shouting; rather, someone calling out for him. Adrian looked through the window at the empty square, eyes still burning. There was no battle, no sign of invasion. Instead, Amal stood at the door while Bac called up to the window.

"One o' the generals!"

Adrian let out a breath and made his way downstairs to open the door. "What?"

Bac stepped out of the way. Amal paused for a moment at the sight of Adrian, his gaze lingering on Adrian's face. The burning around Adrian's eyes persisted, and he knew the blackness around them must have been renewed with his recent efforts. "The scouts have returned," Amal said after composing himself. "Dakhra is moving."

"Toward Alteria?"

"No, Lord Light. The Pontiff has pulled back. The Alterians have retreated to the Othonean capital."

Talnea? The thought that Father would provide safe haven was absurd. "Get Oma and Mahir, then meet me here."

Amal nodded and set off to fetch the other generals. Nasir appeared soon after with a puzzled look. Adrian probably had as many questions as Nasir, but the generals soon arrived. Everyone sat around a table in the dining room.

"They've got a new weapon," Oma said. "An airship. It's . . . shielded."

"Shielded?" Nasir asked.

"Yes, the scouts say a huge one is reported to have brought down the Skygate after fighting off Sentinels."

Fighting off Sentinels? If Syvern had that kind of weapon, Adrian couldn't imagine how they'd beat it.

"Can we cut their path?" Amal asked.

"We might be able to reach them," Mahir said, "but if these airships resist our ballistae, there's little we can do." Adrian had expected more sourness between the rival families. Both had at times taken control of the military, but it seemed that betraying Lord Khorfa had put Amal on good terms with Mahir.

Adrian sighed. "How far ahead are the Dakhrans?"

"Enough to arrive in Talnea before us," Oma said.

"We must be cautious, Lord Light," Nasir said. "The Pontiff would not abandon Alteria lightly. Our numbers will mean little if they are turned."

Adrian nodded. He'd not run blind into the night again. "We

march for Talnea, then. If the Pontiff would not abandon Alteria lightly, as you say, they must have a plan. We'll join our numbers to theirs. Ready the Legion, generals. We leave at once."

The generals nodded and filed out, Nasir behind them.

"Nasir?" Adrian said.

The priest turned.

"The instruction doesn't stop, and you won't hold me back again."

Nasir bowed his head before leaving. Adrian breathed out. It was finally time to meet Father again. He hoped that bringing a renewed Legion in aid of Talnea would be enough.

CHAPTER THIRTY-THREE

My hair will grow, and touch the Earth, and that is when it shall judge my worth.

— *Tales of the Hagun*

If the Yltigg chief had been resistant to retreat, he hadn't shown it. The mass of clansfolk moving away from the peak hadn't taken much in their rush to escape the Domain, but there were enough ancestor-stone-filled carts to give Nasha a glimmer of hope. Ento had emptied the stores, but the ancestor-stone alone would do nothing to fight Zala. They needed allies, needed to gather more warriors to fight the Domain.

The Yltigg lands had never been lush with trees, and Nasha and the others had been trekking over bracken-covered plains for what seemed an eternity. The Yltigg kept their gazes fixed ahead mostly, with occasional nervous backward glances. Warriors brought up the rear, alert for Domain followers, but Bahar seemed to be content with the peak—and mines—for now. The glances always lingered on Nasha. They shifted from searching for enemies to watching her as the clan trudged past large swathes of ashen ground.

No matter how many of the enemy Nasha had killed, what spread was word of what she'd done at the end to save Shai. She walked beside the girl now, with two Yltigg warriors close behind. "How are you feeling?" Nasha asked.

Shai had been quiet since they left, but the sudden exhilaration told Nasha that she'd been dreading the moment when Nasha finally asked about it. Shai glanced at the warriors, then back to Nasha. "I'm good. You healed me."

Nasha shook her head and pulled Shai aside, letting the Yltigg walk on. "You can tell me the truth, Shai. I didn't take anything from you. It's still there. It's just sealed away, and I don't know for how long."

Shai gave her a slight smile, but it was loaded with sadness. "I know. I can feel it."

"Can you feel the emotion around you?"

Shai shook her head and looked away. "No, but there's . . . something else inside me. A pressure in my chest, as if something wants to break free. I know it can't. I felt the rage, the burning in my chest when they threw that potion onto us." Shai looked at Nasha, anger blooming now. "What is this, Nasha? What is the Domain doing? How can they control Zala's taint?"

"I don't know." And she didn't. Nasha searched for words, but there was little else she found to offer Shai. They rejoined the line. Shai looked up ahead and frowned. Nasha caught the glimpse of a Yltigg woman looking back at them, then quickly looking away.

"You see the way they look at us?" Shai said. "I know what it means. We're still just Slopers to them."

"They're afraid." *Rotting Earth, I'm afraid.*

Nasha had seen the land. It was almost like what she'd seen in the Hagun village, and she knew she'd done it here. She'd killed the land. The plain that held the battle had become blackened and ashen. She looked down, moving her mouth even before the quiet words left her lips. "I'm becoming the monster."

Shai was walking close enough to hear. She halted, looking

Nasha up and down, as if those were not the words she'd expected to hear. Even with her mind driven to abandon the clans and try their chances elsewhere, Shai was still counting on Nasha.

It was easier to have faith in others and put your responsibility on their shoulders. True fear lived in the doubt of not knowing whether you're enough, if you'll succeed.

Nasha half wished it was Mansa standing before her. He'd always quelled her fears in the past . . . but it had all been rooted in lies. *Shai relies on me as I rely on her. We need unity to defeat Zala.*

"It can't be us against everyone forever, Shai. Things are changing."

Shai nodded. "I know, but why does it have to be us? You promised my father you'd keep us safe, but does it have to be here? The clans won't save us. Let Zala have them."

"I told you in the mines, Shai. She won't stop with the clans. If we do nothing, then the world will die. Zala will break it piece by piece. You think I like the clan leaders? I was thrown away too, and they're still trying to use me, but what's happening is too big for us to build a haven only for ourselves. The dead goddess marked me. Marked us. I don't know why She did, but we can't let Her win."

Shai chuckled, but there was no mirth in it. "I thought you hated the tales."

"This isn't about liking the tales, or even believing what happened in the past. This is about dealing with what's happening now."

Shai eyed the Yltigg warily. "What now?"

They'd marched up to a line of trees—a small patch of forest with thin trunks widely spaced. There were enough of them to shelter the clan from the sun. Ardin and the Yltigg officers had already found a place in their shade.

"We bring them to our side. We control what happens, not them."

"They're still the leaders."

"But they need what I have." Nasha knew she was more than a tool, but she needed to use her own tools for once.

"I understand why you hate the tales," Shai said. "Whatever

stories may be told about all this won't be worth it. As bad as it was, all I want is to be back home, safe. We'll never get back to that."

Nasha pursed her lips. "Maybe that isn't something to look back on. Maybe it's something we need to build. The clans might not be the way, but I'm glad you're with me."

"Didn't give me much of a choice, did you?" Shai's tone wasn't angry, but it spiked Nasha's guilt all the same.

"I'm sorry," Nasha said. "I didn't know it would come to this, but I couldn't leave you behind."

Nasha looked away, but what hit her from Shai was closer to trust than the sense of betrayal. It was as if she understood Nasha's intent, and even if she'd been infected, understood Nasha's sacrifice in getting closer to the dead goddess so she could heal her. Shai smiled. "No regrets, eh? Let's build what we want to return to."

Nasha held Shai's gaze for a moment, seeing Ife's reflection in her. He'd taught his daughter well. Even with all they'd been through, Shai accepted Nasha, just like her father had. The uncertainty Nasha had felt from her in the mines still tinged Shai's emotions, but the anger was gone. They were together in this, and the feeling renewed Nasha's will to rebuild all they'd lost. Shai had always been her haven against the curse. Nasha would build Shai and her family their own haven. Nasha nodded with renewed warmth in her chest and made her way through the thin trees and mumbling Yltigg to the leaders.

Chief Ardin and Roho stood talking between themselves. Ento stood a few paces away, silent. No whispering in the chief's ear this time, and no warriors standing guard around them. Perhaps the men they could spare were looking after the people, to make sure none were tainted.

Roho eyed her with care as Nasha walked into their clearing. Ardin watched for a while as well, then signaled. Guards Nasha hadn't noticed stepped from behind trees. They blocked Nasha's exit as well as the space between her and the Yltigg officers.

Nasha shook her head. She thought the Yltigg wouldn't judge her curse as the Ronar had. Fear, maybe Shai's, tried to grip at

Nasha, drying her throat and quickening her heart, but she wouldn't run.

"Are we doing this again?" Nasha asked. "You think you have enough men?"

"A precaution," Roho said. "One does not invite in a wolf without holding the knife to strike it down."

"So is that what I am? A wild beast? Have I not walked with you from the battle? Have I attacked any of the Yltigg?"

"You broke the Earth, and the Ronar have betrayed us once already." Roho never seemed to accept her as part of the Yltigg plan. Desperation had changed him in the battle, and he'd followed her, but what she'd done at the end seemed to have lost his respect.

Nasha chuckled. "I'm not sure Tomu would call me Ronar, and I did what was necessary to save who I could. You fought by my side, Roho. Is this all that's worth?"

She didn't expect them to accept her, but she couldn't let her words to Shai about unity ring hollow. She hated this, but she couldn't abandon them.

Roho didn't answer, but Ento stepped closer. "Can you do it again?"

"What?" Nasha frowned, but perhaps she should have expected it. Ento had been throwing the tainted at the Ronar to create chaos just a few days before. "Did you not see what the Domain did? How can you think using this curse is a good idea?"

"We saw what happened to our warriors as well," Roho said. "And to her." He jerked his head at Shai. "You healed her."

"I didn't. I sealed it away. Zala is still there."

"I don't want to use it," Ento said. "But what you did might be the only thing we can present to convince the other clans."

Nasha frowned. They were scared of her, but it seemed she'd been right. Their need was stronger than their fear. It was different from being treated like a tool or a weapon. At least their fear spoke to her having a choice, rather than being under their control.

"The other clans?" Shai asked.

Ento nodded behind his veil. "You said you saw something in the vision?"

"Once the Hagun fell," Nasha said, "the taint started to spread. I couldn't take enough to heal the Yltigg pillar. I felt it pulling from the Ronar, but the Hagun and Lothrak stones were cut off."

"That means . . ." Shai didn't have to say it.

"We need to rekindle the Lothrak and Hagun warding stones," Chief Ardin said.

"The Domain has too many men," Roho said. "They'll be watching the roads and the woods. We can't turn back to Ronar, and the Lothrak mountains are too far south. We need to find somewhere safe for the clan."

Roho looked toward the chief, but Ento was already shaking his head.

"There is nowhere we can stay. Your scouts reported the spreading plague for weeks. We've seen it, walked by rotting land."

Nasha had only one option in her mind, and a sour taste in her mouth even before she uttered the words. "We need Mansa. The Ronar have kept their pillars untainted. The stone-shapers will need to find a way to rekindle the Hagun stone. The Yltigg can stay in their abandoned village." She could only hope Adda hadn't been the one responsible for keeping Zala at bay.

"The Ronar will never work with us," Roho said. "Not after all that's happened. The memory of battle losses is still too fresh."

"And the risk of running into the Domain is too great," Ardin said. "We can't risk our people like that. We don't even know they'll have a place to stay."

"Then take them with us," Nasha said. "We need to find the Lothrak."

Ardin considered, but Nasha was sure it was the best option. Well, maybe not the best, but it did seem the only one. The Domain was behind them, the taint was spreading, and the Yltigg had nowhere to stay. The Lothrak mountains had always been known for their snows, but winter was not upon them. Taking an entire clan into the freezing mountains was a risk, but it was the only option that held the promise of survival.

Ardin watched Nasha, narrowing his eyes. "Looks like the Lothrak are our only choice."

"The Ronar still won't work with us," Roho said. "What good is reviving only one of the pillars?"

"Mansa is a practical man," Ento said. "He'll listen to us,"

"He'll listen to me," Nasha said.

"None of the Ronar have your gift," Ento said. "You are the only one who can do this."

Nasha shook her head. Adda had shown a similar power. Perhaps she'd found others like Nasha and hidden them among the stone-shapers.

"Send a runner," Nasha said. "We can't wait for Mansa, but he's been a hunter all his life. He should take a few days to reach us, but we can set up a spot without stopping the march. I'll show him how I did it, and he'll instruct the stone-shapers so they can try to revive the Hagun pillar."

It was a risk, but this was a war with Zala Herself, and some battles must be fought on uncertain ground. Nasha had tried to sound confident, but the truth was she didn't even know if Mansa had been part of the betrayal. Heading to the Lothrak didn't help either, and a bitterness still rode her tongue. Her own Proving had been against the Lothrak—before she became a hunter, before the Ronar accepted her, at least in word, as part of the clan. That was the first time she'd lost herself and killed without having control of her body.

Ento, Roho, and Shai seemed to agree with the plan, and their gazes moved to Chief Ardin. He shifted on his feet behind a line of warriors that still looked tensely at Nasha. It took him a moment, but he finally nodded. "We talk to Mansa, and head for the Lothrak."

Roho had sent messengers to get word to Mansa. Nasha kept marching with the Yltigg for three days until a morning runner told her that Mansa was ready to meet.

Nasha broke off from the Yltigg—their march was slow and she'd catch up to them—and followed the messenger to the place

Mansa had chosen. The land been taken more and more by Zala's corruption the farther they got from the Yltigg peak and its protective pillar. But Mansa had found a spot that still resisted Zala's touch.

It was the entrance to an abandoned mine, in the woods that spread for leagues from the foot of the Lothrak mountains. It was private enough and easy for Nasha to escape if Mansa had received orders from Tomu to finish her. She hated to think of him like that, like Bahar. They'd been the only ones she trusted for a long time, but that time would never return.

Nasha went over the escape routes. Would Mansa have hunters waiting in the shadows? Would she have to kill him like she'd killed Chatta? All she could do was hope it wouldn't come to that.

A river found its way to the mouth of the mine, which descended almost vertically into the ground. The flow formed a gentle waterfall as it poured over the edge into the abandoned cave. The greenery was thick, with trees and lichen-covered rocks all around. A huge boulder, at least four times as tall as Nasha, sat to one side of the mine's entrance, fully taken by moss.

The image brought a slight warmth to her chest. Not all the world was dying, and places like these were just another reason to fight Zala.

Nasha caught a slight stir behind the boulder of the mine entrance. It sent her hands rushing to the knives at her hips.

Mansa stepped out from behind the rock. Alone.

A dash of frustration crept up on Nasha, creasing her brow into a frown. Even after diving into her curse, risking Zala's grasp, and gaining more power, Mansa had still managed to veil himself from her.

Mansa saw it on her face. "Still couldn't notice me, eh?"

Part of Nasha was taken aback by Mansa's lack of surprise in finding she was alive. Or maybe it was a compliment.

Nasha circled him, hands still close to her blades. Mansa didn't move. He kept his gaze on her and nodded. "I understand. I'd be on edge as well."

"On edge?" Nasha's voice was louder than she'd intended.

Maybe this hadn't been a good idea. "All you've been doing from the start is using me, Mansa! You let them trade me away, gambled my life. Again!"

"You can't expect people to protect you, Nasha. You have to do that yourself." There was a spike of irritation from him now. The emotion bludgeoned Nasha.

"I don't expect people to protect me. I expected you to help me!"

Mansa shook his head, moving around the boulder. The irritation that had come from him shifted to something deeper, like a painful root finding its way through Nasha's heart. Different from his normally blunt emotional pattern.

"I'm not the one to protect you," he said. "I never promised that." His tone was dry, but there was a sadness to his words—one that Nasha had never seemed to recognize, as if it had always been hidden somehow. Perhaps the curse was showing her new things after all.

Nasha held Mansa's hard gaze and stopped pacing. "Did you know Tomu was giving me up? Don't lie to me. I'll know."

Mansa didn't flinch. "No." He started to move closer. "I know who you are, and I know what you're capable of. Do you think I'd send you off to the Yltigg to be sacrificed on the implication of some ancient tale? This isn't about liking you. It's common sense, Nasha."

Nasha breathed out. At least he was being sincere about it. He'd manipulated her, but he was right. He knew what she was capable of. He wouldn't throw that away, if only because he sought to make use of her. She nodded. "You're not killing me, then."

"Depends." He grinned now. "Will you try to kill me?"

Nasha didn't smile back, but let the tension out of her chest and sat on a lichen-covered rock beside the slow-flowing stream. "Things have changed."

"They have. It'll take some time to convince Tomu to take you back, but you're free of the Yltigg now. This was our plan. We'll let the Domain deal with them, and I'll convince Tomu we need to strike at The Visslands."

"What? We can't do that."

"We can. Our troops will stay behind to guard the Ronar lands. You can lead the attack on the Visslands. With your gift, we can strike at the heart of Pelaket. If we put the capital into chaos, they'll pull back."

"It would never be that easy, and we can't let the Domain keep the Yltigg peak. We can't let any of the clans fall."

"The Yltigg are not our concern, Nasha. We have a chance here. We can bring the Domain down without putting the Ronar on the front lines."

Nasha shook her head. Words would not be enough to convince him. "Something happened with the Yltigg. With my curse."

Mansa raised an eyebrow as Nasha pulled a bundle from her vest. She unwrapped it, revealing the small shard of ancestor-stone. "My curse is changing." Nasha grabbed the stone, trying not to absorb the emotion coiling inside it, and sank it into the soft Earth beside her. "Did you bring what Ento asked?"

"Ancestor-stone doesn't affect you anymore?"

"It does. Just . . . less." She wouldn't tell him about Zala's darkness writhing inside her. She might have in the past, but that trust wasn't there anymore.

"The stone, Mansa."

Mansa paused for a moment, then pulled out a small shard of ancestor-stone.

"Put it into the ground." Nasha didn't want to touch it. Didn't want Mansa to think she was tampering with it somehow. Mansa placed the stone in the ground, then stepped back.

"That one is from the Ronar pillars. This one is from the Yltigg."

Nasha touched the Yltigg shard, letting the emotion flow from the stone into her. It would have plunged her into a fury in the past, but she could control it now, especially after the battle. It was almost like a thread, a small one, and Nasha let it flow through her. Deep inside, though, Zala stirred as if what Nasha had fed Her during the battle had been only the first step down a long road She expected Nasha to follow. Nasha frowned as she tried to block out the darkness, but it was hard, and her body's warning signs surfaced in the form of a burning across her skin and blurring at the edge of her vision.

Nasha kept her grip on the Yltigg shard and pulled at the thread of emotion. The sensation was mirrored in Mansa's stone. The shards had connected themselves under the Earth, and the emotions flowed through the connection.

Both stones flickered.

"The pillars are connected." She closed her fingers tighter around the shard and tugged at the thread again. Both stones flickered again. She looked up at Mansa, then pulled the emotion out of the stones, still without touching the Ronar shard, dulling their glow. "If one stone is taken by Zala, the others grow weaker. If one dies," she gestured toward the shards, "so do the others. It doesn't matter how much Domain blood you feed the Earth. It will be for nothing if the clans don't fight together."

Nasha pushed the emotion back into the stones and stepped back, eyeing Mansa as he looked from the stones to her. "It was hard for me, too. All I wanted was to kill Tomu, end the Ronar after what you did to me. But here I am. Besides . . . there's something else."

Mansa gave her a curious look.

"The Domain is using the taint. You were right about that. Bahar is leading them, but if the council in the Visslands allowed this, it's clear they'd let the clans kill each other to get what they want. We will fight the Domain, but we need to do it together. All of the clans as one."

Mansa slowly began to nod. "The Yltigg are willing to fight alongside the Ronar?"

"They are."

"And the Hagun?"

"That's why I need you. We don't know how long the warding pillars will stand against Zala. We're heading to the Lothrak— there's no time to head back to Hagun to heal their pillar. You need to do that."

"Me? You seem to be missing the fact that I am not gifted like you." He paced under the trees and breathed deep. Nasha took in the smell as well: wet earth that permeated the woods.

"You aren't cursed, and believe me, it's a curse, but the stone-shapers have kept the Ronar warding pillars alive. Certainly, Adda found people with power. People like me."

"You think they can do it? They aren't as strong as you."

"Take all of them to the Hagun village. Tell them to seek out the connection within the earth. The strands that lead to the pillars of the other clans. They'll know what to do."

"Are you sure about this?"

"No, but what other option do we have?"

Mansa eyed her for a long while, no sound other than the babbling stream beside them. "And the Domain?"

"We'll get help from the Lothrak, then go after them. You were right about the Domain prince. He was in the Hagun village after a text. The Hagun stone cracked after their battle."

Nasha felt Mansa's rage even before the fire touched his eyes.

"I'll get what I can to help." His tone was firm, angry.

"We need Tomu to rally the Ronar. We need to stand against the Domain as you wanted and push them out of the clanlands."

"It won't be easy getting him to agree without you there to show him what you just did to the stones."

"Put them in the hands of one of Adda's stone-weavers. Tell him she's dead, and that I know where Razi is if need be. Let him call me an Earth-Breaker. He's already discarded me once."

Mansa eyed her with the old grin creeping back onto his face. His emotions were stable enough to tell Nasha he wouldn't ask where Razi was. There was no anticipation, or even curiosity. He knew Nasha would never tell him.

"It looks like I managed to teach you something, at least," he said. "I'll talk to him." He stepped close and put a hand on Nasha's shoulder. "I'm proud of you. Proud of what you've become."

Nasha turned her back to him and headed back to her horse. Weeks ago, she'd have relished the words. Now, she couldn't bring herself to even return Mansa's smile. His emotions had touched her heart once, like a father's words might touch a daughter, but that

390

piece of her was now broken and discarded. "I wish things could have been different," she said over her shoulder.

"We'll march together once more, Nasha."

Nasha allowed part of herself to believe there was truth in that. It was a slim hope, just like the one they had of winning the coming battle against Zala and the Domain, but she'd learned to cling to hope. It might have been all that was left between them.

CHAPTER THIRTY-FOUR

When the clans were split, Tedros' wisdom was slowly lost. We roam our lands as separate bands, to hopefully learn what he had to teach.

— Tales of the Lothrak

The Yltigg had set up camp in the forest that led to the base of the Lothrak mountains. There was movement when Nasha returned. Not the normal movement of people going about their tasks; warriors were gathered around the chief, and some seemed on edge as Nasha arrived. Their emotions didn't lie either. Something had happened.

Nasha rushed through, the curiosity of the Yltigg brushing past her, perhaps feeding her own, but it was more than curiosity. Perhaps Zala had heard her talk to Mansa somehow. Perhaps she was trying to stop them from reaching the Lothrak.

Nasha pushed the thought away as she walked toward the source of commotion, but there was still something nagging at her. The emotions were all around, and she'd grown used to them. The manacles around her wrists even helped absorb some of them, and Nasha's body had found a way to keep the emotions at bay, but there was something different this time. Like her body was telling her to avoid the crowd. She stayed away from all she could and joined the small group around the Yltigg leaders.

They stood around a bound and kneeling man, but Nasha found no discomfort coming from him. All he emanated was calculated attention, his gaze moving among the gathered clansfolk. It froze when he saw Nasha. Something spiked in his emotion, but it was closer to triumph than anything resembling fear. He recognized her.

". . . isn't here, you'll have to talk to—"

"Here she is." The man spoke as if he had a plan and had known it would work all along. Even his appearance seemed calculated. His hair was thinning and combed back, but sat perfectly in place, as if it would bring him some kind of disadvantage otherwise. His nose was thin and his eyes precise and focused on Nasha, unmoving, as if any deviation might cost him more than he was willing to pay. What pulled Nasha's attention were the scars, though. They crisscrossed the sides of his face, as if he'd been cut along the cheeks multiple times. Four or five smaller ones on the left side, a big one taking up most of the right.

He kept his head down, maybe feigning weakness, but Nasha was alert. Too much confidence can hinder a man, but just enough is dangerous. It makes men believe they can succeed, no matter the odds. Even if this man was trying to hide it, Nasha could feel the confidence through her curse.

"What's this?" Nasha asked.

Roho had his back to her but turned at her approach. "This man says he's looking for the one who fought like a Sentinel in the battle. I told him we have none of those butchers among us."

Nasha paused. She hadn't even considered comparing herself to the Domain griffin riders. There were none of the beasts among the clans, and she'd only heard them talked about by Mansa and Bahar. Still, she couldn't deny her curse had given her enough power to sway the tide of battle—just as the Sentinels were said to do.

Don't be a fool. It's just another tale. What you have is a curse. They control their power. You're fighting to survive yours.

"Did you find him trying to break in?" Nasha asked. She couldn't imagine what the man wanted. Maybe he was a spy.

"He turned himself in," Shai said. "Walked into the camp claiming he had information on the taint."

"That's what you clansfolk call it?" The man spoke the tongue common to the clans, but it was rough. "I'll talk with that one. The rest of you can wait."

Shai scowled at the man, and Roho scoffed. Ento watched silently, the opposite of what one might expect from a man with the title of speaker.

The chief looked at Nasha, and then his leaders. "We have little time for this. Deal with him, kill him if you must. We move on."

Nasha considered for a moment, then nodded. The man seemed to be going out of his way to avoid being seen as a threat. He was either a bigger threat than any of them thought, or he was telling the truth. Neither option was comforting. Every man held a threat of some kind, even if it wasn't apparent.

Roho raised the prisoner to his feet, then pulled on the rope that bound his wrists. The man stumbled forward. Roho thrust the rope into Nasha's hands, then strode after the departing Yltigg leaders. Shai waited beside Nasha.

"Come on," Nasha said to her and the prisoner, then walked away from the crowd.

They stopped in a cluster of trees far enough from the Yltigg that their emotions were only a light drum on Nasha's senses, like the slow patter of rain that was starting to fall through the canopy. "Go ahead."

The man looked at Shai, then Nasha. "You healed her. You stopped the Madness."

"Madness?"

"You called it the taint."

The man had an arrogant grin that sent a spike of fury through Nasha. She eyed him with a clenched jaw. "Is that all?"

"I need to know how."

Nasha scoffed and turned away. These Domain folk charged into their lands, and this man expected her to help? She pulled out her obsidian striking knife and put it in Shai's hand. "Deal with him." She was sure Shai would have no problem returning the man to the Earth, but she wanted the girl to remember how it felt to kill. It would also show Nasha if what she'd trapped inside Shai would stir.

There was a brief shot of something that could have been resistance, but Shai eyed Nasha firmly and gripped the knife.

Nothing came from the man, as if he thought this was all a display or didn't mind having his life taken from him. "You don't think I'd come here empty-handed, do you?"

Shai stepped forward, ignoring the words. Nasha looked back over her shoulder.

"The Madness. This taint, it doesn't come from your goddess or the Earth, as you call it. It's made by the hands of men."

Nasha turned to the man, and her movement gave Shai pause. The man could be lying, and probably was. There was no way that whatever affected her—her curse—had been constructed. "You don't know what you're talking about."

The man was trying to manipulate her, but this wasn't like talking to Mansa. There was a coldness in him, as if all that was happening around him didn't matter. He didn't need to hide his emotions, because he seemed truly indifferent to everything other than his objective, whatever that was.

"You know I do. How do you think the Domain infected your people?"

"You could have captured the tainted, used their blood," Shai said.

The man shook his head. "We'd need too many of your tainted to be able to weaponize it. I know this was made, because I've made a version of it myself."

The anger shooting through Nasha was her own, and it touched some subconscious truth she recognized in the man. Maybe it was something in his underlying coldness, or perhaps he was angry at the admittance as well.

It made no sense. How had someone put this curse on her? Her visions had taken her to a Domain city. Was that where she'd lived as a child? Had something been done to her? What about Adda and the others?

Nasha shook her head. "That's impossible. I'm done with you."

"In my pocket." The man raised his voice for the first time. "I have a vial. You can test it."

"There's no one to test it on." Shai gave a step forward, raising the knife.

"Test it on me." The man's voice was calm again. "You can heal me like you did her." He jerked his head towards Shai.

Nasha eyed the man for a long time. His unwavering confidence in his words was off-putting. His faith in Nasha's ability to heal him, more so. There was sense to it, in a strange way. Why would he walk into their camp? Why would he try to talk to her? He wanted something, that much was clear, but his willingness to risk so much compelled Nasha to step forward and search his pocket for the vial. She pulled out a thin glass tube with the coppery-orange mixture that had been launched at the Yltigg during the battle.

The sight of it sent anger creeping up Nasha's chest again, but she swallowed it back down as she felt Zala's claws reaching for it. "I didn't heal her. I only sealed it away."

Shai's confusion at Nasha's apparent trust was piercing, leaving behind a lingering sense of betrayal. Shai had always been quick to assume betrayal; she probably felt like she'd been betrayed by everyone her entire life. Even so, if there was truth to this man's words, perhaps he could help her cure Shai. It wasn't a betrayal, even if it looked like one to the girl.

There was a touch of hurt in Shai's eyes, but Nasha focused on the man before her. "Whatever you claim to have made, it isn't the same. There are others like me. Too many for the Domain to have affected."

The man chuckled. "Isn't that the thing about a plague? All you need is one host, and it can change and spread on its own. Almost as if it were . . . alive."

Nasha eyed the man for a long time. Only his fingers moved, as if the binding was uncomfortable, but he didn't want to waste energy trying to break free.

"What do you want?" Nasha asked.

"To understand how you do it. To use you to create a cure for this Madness."

"I'm not your tool, and the Domain has just spread more of this taint among my people. You expect me to help you?"

"Oh no. There is no help involved. This is a negotiation. I am here out of my own volition." He looked down at his hands. "My current circumstance changes nothing. You have something I need. I'm sure I can offer you something in return."

"Who do you need to heal?" Shai asked, and Nasha found herself nodding along. It made sense. No one goes to such lengths if there isn't something personal involved. Mansa had always said self-interest was the most trustworthy of motivations.

"I am a Priest of the Blood in the Church of the Seraph. The faithful come to me—"

"Don't lie." Nasha could feel the shift in the man's words, the cold detachment gone in light of the current subject. "You have someone close. Important to you."

The man eyed them both with irritation cracking his gaze and his emotions all at once. "If you haven't healed the girl, as you say, I can help. We can make a cure."

"I thought you said there was no help involved," Shai said.

"Huh. Smart girl. Seems like there might be some. You don't need to believe me, and I lied about being a priest, but I didn't lie about making this Madness, and I was against the use of it as a weapon. Even outside the Domain."

Nasha paused. If this man was smart enough to weaponize the taint, she needed to be careful. Giving him information was as good as giving blades to a warrior. "What are you called?"

"Kadmus."

"You were working with Bahar?" Nasha hadn't wanted to ask it, but the words were out before she could stop herself.

The man narrowed his eyes and gave her a slight nod. "He was the one leading the campaign, yes."

"You will tell us all he's done until now, and what he plans to do."

"What I knew has already been carried out. He had me with him for the battle. I left him to find you."

Nasha eyed the man for a long moment. Perhaps he could be of use. "You stay bound and in my sight at all times. We will tell you what you need to know as it becomes necessary. If I see you are trying to manipulate us or communicate with the Domain in any way . . ." She looked over to Shai. "She'll use the knife."

Shai already had a scowl, but the man betrayed nothing. He had receded back into the cold shell of indifference that surrounded his emotions.

Shai pulled the man along as they made their way back to the Yltigg, who'd already marched on. The clan moved slowly, and it would get colder as they approached the Lothrak lands.

"Keep an eye on him," Nasha said. "Get Ento or Roho to help you if you need it. Oh, and Kadmus?" The man looked at Nasha. "Not a word about having created the potion." Nasha hadn't wanted to tell the man this, but it was clear he'd noticed an advantage. This was leverage, but if the Yltigg started seeing her as made by the Domain, they might question things they didn't have the time or focus to answer. Kadmus nodded to her, quick and determined, as if the leverage she'd given him was payment enough for his silence. At least for now.

Nasha looked down at the vial in her hand. The more she searched for answers, the more questions she had. Could she use this to understand the corruption taking the pillars? Or maybe it was what Nasha needed to understand what the darkness inside her truly was.

CHAPTER THIRTY-FIVE

Their stone hearts beat as one with wings
To face the threats the enemy brings
Do not fear the darkened sun
For their shadows mean that we have won.

—*war poem* by Ketie the Grinning Bard

The Pontiff was true to his word, and King Iridan lit the forges. Olem had always been the most skilled of the ruin-stone workers among the Sentinels, and his role as commander didn't keep him from the fires. Production went well, and huge boltheads of metal infused with powdered ruin-stone were mounted on the ballistae.

Lynn had checked them early on but now made her way through crowded streets toward the barracks, hoping to find Ferrin before they set off. She moved past the gates, across the training yard, and into the mess hall.

Some of the soldiers seemed to gaze at Lynn in awe, but Deria's face crept into her mind and set her stomach churning. Perhaps the upcoming battle was bringing up her guilt again. Elwin, Cedd, Deria, Leardin . . . The Madness had taken too many Sentinels. It was the only thing she'd known to kill so many in so little time.

You've forgotten about us already? Cara said.

Lynn shook her head. She hadn't forgotten. Maybe she would when she finally found a cure.

Ferrin wasn't in the mess hall, but that was a good sign. Lynn had found a private place for their practice within the Othonean barracks. He was probably there.

She paced through a back door, avoiding the gazes that followed her. The path behind the mess hall led to the armory, but Lynn made her way around the building and into a patch of beaten earth surrounded by trees. Ferrin was there, sitting on a rock. The image brought back the memory of when she'd found Elwin before his last moments. Sitting on a rock, head down. It gave her pause, and Vedyr seemed to notice. He'd been flying overhead, and recognized the empty space as an opportunity to land and pace nearby. Stroking the griffin loosened the tug at her heart caused by Elwin's face.

He's in Durnn. He'll be brought back.

At least you saved one of us, Dentos said.

Ferrin was sweating like he'd been at it for the better part of the morning. "You'll have to give me a moment," he said.

Lynn could sense something riding on his tone. He'd been colder since she'd told him about Alren, but this seemed different. Ildred's force was supposed to have arrived by now as well. "What happened? Did you cross paths with Ildred and the others?"

Ferrin shook his head. "No sign of them."

Lynn frowned, but Ferrin was focused on something else. "Dakhra," he said. "They're . . . they're spreading the Madness. We left scouts behind to report on their advance, and they saw it happen. Dakhra is taking people prisoner, infecting them even if they don't resist. The scouts got those who believed in them out before Dakhra arrived, but some trusted the war would pass them by if they just stayed in their homes."

Lynn's mind jumped to the man she'd released from the dungeons, and an anger roiled her gut more with each of Ferrin's words. The looks from the soldiers in the mess hall hadn't been awe. They were just a different kind of fear. Ildred's absence was concerning, but Dakhra infecting civilians that offered no resistance was too much. She funneled her rage into her fist and slammed it into a tree, splitting the trunk in half. "Bastards."

Ferrin looked up at the mark in the sky. "Why doesn't She stop them?"

"It's not the Seraph's job to stop them, Ferrin. We're the ones who drove Her away by acting exactly like we are now. We need to prove ourselves to Her."

Ferrin looked at her for a long moment. "It's hard to let go of Alren. It's hard to trust you, even though I know you had no choice."

"I'd bring him back if I could," Lynn said.

"I know, but you followed the orders that were given to you. What if they told you to kill me?"

"That was a long time ago. Things have changed. I've changed."

Ferrin looked away with a mirthless smile. "You were right. These people have no rules. I can't help it. I'm terrified, Lynn."

Lynn nodded. "I know. We all are."

Ferrin chuckled. "You're a Sentinel. What can you be scared about?"

"Failing. Losing the ones I'm supposed to protect. Having all the death around me be for nothing." *Learning I'm not good enough to wear this mantle.* Lynn stepped up to him. "You can't prevent fear, but you can't let it control you. That's what Dakhra wants."

Ferrin stood. "This plan of yours. You think it'll work?"

"If we can burn enough, they won't be able to restock quickly. They'll have to turn back or attack Talnea without the potions." Lynn stretched out a hand and clasped Ferrin's forearm. "Go get your unit ready. We're marching tonight."

Ferrin nodded, then set off to get the troops in line.

———

The Legion marched out of Talnea with the setting sun. Dakhra had been advancing and would be close enough for Lynn to find them that night. The Sentinels had prepared themselves, and each carried a torch to be lit when they found the potions.

"This better work," Rel said. "They'll be at our walls tomorrow."

"It will," Lynn said. They hadn't mounted their griffins yet, but she wouldn't leave them behind after what happened to Leardin. Even with their size, the griffins could handle stealth. They were part feline, after all. The army marched as separate units. The Legion's defeat under the command of King Iridan's son had taught them about strolling in the dark where madmen might be lurking in the trees. They split up into smaller groups, each pulling a ballista on wheels.

Ferrin was in Lynn's group, but she'd spread the Sentinels out. The Dakhran camp would be immense. The seven thousand that had beset Durnn had been joined by more and now numbered close to forty thousand men.

Ten of the almost two-score Sentinels who remained had stayed behind with the Pontiff. A score and eight had come with Lynn. They were the ones who'd have to face a camp of forty thousand, find whatever stashes of the potion they could, and burn them.

You're just leading them to their deaths like you led us, Alren said.

Lynn shook her head as if in answer. They'd strike and fall back, as they had in Pehd Valley. No Sentinels would have to die, and the Legion had orders to hold the initial waves, then retreat.

Dakhra had set up camp with a tall cliff at their backs, but their army was large and filled the entire clearing at the base. They sprawled over the open ground and up to the trees where Lynn and the Legion crept in silence.

An airship circled above the Dakhran camp. It flew low, as if patrolling the trees and daring the Domain to draw near.

"What do you think?" Ferrin asked one of the men pushing the ballista. Lynn watched nearby.

"They're low. Makes for a harder angle, trees might get in the way. We should get closer."

"Not too much," Lynn said. "If we get spotted, we lose the surprise, and they'll likely know we're after the potions. There's no other reason to leave our walls."

"A shot from here would be a risk, general," the soldier said.

Ferrin stepped close to the man. "Can you make it?"

"If the timing's right, but the others would need to fire at the right time as well."

"They know not to go any farther," Lynn said. "Olem made it clear to the other Sentinels. We shoot them from here. Ferrin, get the lantern-men to send over the signs when the time comes. You make the call. We'll set off as soon as the bolts pull the plating away." Rel mounted Ulenia, and Lynn fixed her eyes on the Seraph's mark in the sky.

Help me. Please.

The airship approached, its shadow darkening the night into a void that encroached on them like a creeping beast. This one was smaller than the airship that had taken down the Skygate—thirty yards from prow to stern, like the typical Dakhran airship. The metal plating all around it was the same as on its larger brother, covering the hull and upper deck, and lending a rounded shape to what would normally be the flat top-deck where Sentinels could have landed and fought. As the airship drew near, orders were relayed to the other groups, and the man commanding the ballista took his place.

The siege engine held a huge bolt, tipped with ruin-stone and attached to a thick rope. When it landed, gears would coil back the rope and hopefully strip away the metal plating from the airship. Lynn and a few of the other Syphoners would take the ships down, while the Channelers would search for the potions.

The soldier manning the ballista held one hand out toward the lantern-bearer, palm upward so the messenger would wait. His eyes tracked the airship's course. Once, twice, three times around the camp. When the ship approached a fourth time, the shooter balled his hand into a fist.

The lantern-bearer shifted the paddles on his lantern, sending varying light signals through the trees to another man nearby. The lanterns had been designed for stealth, and their bearer trained in angling the light signals so they could not be seen nearby or from above. Commands were relayed, always over short distances so as not to alert the Dakhrans, until all groups knew they could take the shot. The shooter let the bolt fly. Lynn held her breath as it went, following the trajectory of the bolt with the trailing rope behind. It cut through moonlight and the shadow of the airship and dug into its side, piercing one of the metal plates.

More bolts hit the airship from other positions in the trees around the Dakhran camp, holding the ship in place. The shooter turned the handle to pull the rope back. It tightened and then creaked, but the plating on the ship held fast. This was it. Deria had been paralyzed when she touched the plate, but Lynn was hoping whatever had done that wouldn't travel the length of the rope.

She pushed the shooter aside and dug up all the anger and frustration that had built up since she faced the True in Alteria. She barely even needed the voices to fuel her anger, and with Vedyr this close, the Bond was a surge that nearly overwhelmed her.

She took hold of the gear and turned, straining the rope even more. A piece of it started to fray, close to the gear, but slowly the bolt pried the metal plate off the airship. Lynn fueled Vedyr's strength into her arms. She turned again, and the plate came loose, almost throwing Lynn on her back when the tension released.

The ship groaned like a trapped beast as other bolts stripped away more plates, which fell crashing into the trees and the camp below. Soon enough, holes were opened, exposing a wooden hull beneath the plating.

Lynn raised her war-scythe with a roar, jumped onto Vedyr, and pushed off the ground, flying straight at the exposed airship. Other Sentinels did the same, while another group headed for the camp to find the potions in the airships that were still on the ground.

Vedyr beat powerful wings, and Lynn steered him so she could look for an opening in the plating, a hole that showed her the deck of the ship. None were big enough for Vedyr, but she could fit through. A large plate that had curved vertically around half the ship had been stripped free. It was still too thin to fly Vedyr through, but Lynn could fall into it from above and land on the deck.

"Follow Ulenia, head for the camp," Lynn said to the griffin, then jumped off. The wind cut at her, whistling through the tight gaps in her mantle and drying her eyes. She'd become used to leaping off Vedyr, but knowing she couldn't touch the metal plates sent a chill through her, as if the wind itself was cutting down her spine. She pressed her arms close to her body, shifted sideways and fell through the gap, avoiding the metal plates and spinning her body to land with a crack on the deck.

She rose with scythe in one hand, mace in the other, ready to fight off scores of madmen, but there were barely more than half a dozen Dakhran soldiers, all scrambling to man weapons and turn them on the other Sentinels. Some took notice of Lynn, but she wouldn't give them time to reach for their Madness potions. She tugged on the Bond, feeding Vedyr more anger and using his speed to dash across the deck at the first enemy. The Bond pulled back, threatening to take pieces from Lynn's mind. The strain of her manipulation over the past few days weighed on her, and even with ruin-stone at hand, she knew she wouldn't have much time. Her mind went to her names.

Alren. She reached the enemy and stabbed him through the gut, then kicked him away.

Roki. She jumped and fell upon another man with her mace before he could fire his ballista.

Dentos. Lynn smashed the empty ballista, then moved on to the group of five remaining men. They'd banded together in hopes of stopping her but only made themselves an easy target.

Cara. Lynn leaped, then directed Vedyr's strength into her legs, weighing them down so she'd fall with her knee into the face of the first man, crushing his nose. The force of her blow pushed him onto his companion standing behind, and Lynn slashed across the chests of two others before touching the ground. That left a single man standing, while the other survivor struggled to disentangle himself from his crushed-nose companion.

407

The Bond pressed around her mind, and Lynn's head lightened. She released her hold on the magic a touch, but her eyes still burned as she looked at the trembling man.

Give him to me. The voice of death. Lynn could not have mercy with these people; they were the enemy, but something in the voice gave her pause.

The man dropped his weapon and raised his hands. "I-I surrender."

You do not have time to take prisoners. Give him to me.

Lynn pointed her scythe at him. "Below deck. How many?"

"F-five." The man struggled to get the words past his trembling lips. "Don't kill me."

There was a loud groan of metal as another plate was pulled back. It opened a hole large enough for a griffin, and it wasn't long until two flew through with Sentinels on their backs. Gwynne and Brehnna.

"No. Please," the man said, staring at the griffins. Lynn grabbed him by the scruff of his leather armor. "Where are you stocking the potions?" She pulled on her Bond, knowing her eyes would flare silver.

"Belowdecks. They use them on the sprayers."

"Lead the way." She pointed him toward the stairs that led belowdecks.

Brehnna and Gwynne made quick work of whatever other men survived, then followed Lynn.

Shouting came from the darkness beyond the stairs as men tried to defend the camp from above. The man before Lynn stepped cautiously down the steps and across a shadowed corridor that led into the wide belly of the ship. Lynn followed until the remaining enemies came into view. There were two on each weapon: keg-like tanks fitted with hoses that led to nozzles. The nozzles sprayed the potion out through narrow holes in the airship's hull, trying to catch Sentinels who flew near.

The man before Lynn stepped past a doorway and was stabbed in the side from the shadows by a companion who lay in wait. The

Dakhran froze as he realized he'd stabbed his own man. A heartbeat later, Gwynne's javelin was in his throat.

The Dakhrans manning the sprayers turned to the Sentinels, but Brehnna and Gwynne advanced with spear and sword, slashing them down before they could move. The Sentinels turned back to Lynn, whose eyes were on the man bleeding out before her. It was almost like the vision. She could almost see the waves of fear coming off him, taste the bitterness of it. He eyed her, coughing blood, and Lynn dug her scythe into his heart to end his pain. Taking these soldiers down had hardly been a challenge. Was Dakhra so sure of its power that it undermanned its patrol ships?

She looked past the Sentinels in the gloom of the airship and approached the stock of metal kegs at the far end. Maybe close to a hundred. She pulled on Vedyr and cranked open a lid with little effort. Reddish liquid sloshed inside. The Madness.

The Sentinels ripped off the tops of the metal kegs until all were exposed. Lynn turned to Gwynne, who was ready with the small torch they'd brought for this. She gave it to Lynn, who put fire to the wooden hull. It caught and started to creep along the airship. "Let's go," Lynn said.

They rushed back up. Gwynne and Brehnna jumped onto their griffins and flew off toward the camp. Lynn dug into her Bond and called to Vedyr, who took only a moment to arrive. Lynn jumped up through the hole using his strength and landed on his back.

She steered him toward the camp that housed the forty thousand Dakhran troops. It was massive, stretching almost as far as the eye could see. Trees framed the edges, and the tents were pushed up against the low, stony cliff. Lynn flew lower, searching for movement from Ferrin's group amid the Legion troops at the edges of the Dakhran camp. She couldn't pick out individual soldiers, but she knew where the group was supposed to be. They weren't meant to venture too close. The plan was to stay at the edges, pull the Dakhrans away from the center where they'd likely be keeping their stashes, then run away. She thought she saw Ferrin's unit manning the ballista again.

Olem and Rel were close, holding the mass off the Legion troops.

Lynn steered Vedyr down toward them. Vedyr ripped through the air, diving so fast a silver streak burning the air around them was visible. He crashed into the madmen, crushing them beneath the weight of his claws. The impact sent others around them flying, but the growls and rage-filled howls soon drew near again.

Lynn jumped off, spinning with mace and scythe in her hands. She pulled on Vedyr's strength and fell in a whirlwind of steel, battering and slashing the madmen away. "In the airship hulls!" she shouted. "Go!"

Rel speared a madman and swung the body in an arc to clear enough space to let him jump on Ulenia, then launched into the air. Olem took off as well, but the madmen seemed to have focused on Vedyr. Lynn let Roki's question rise to the front of her mind now. *Are you sure?* She rushed towards Vedyr, letting the rage flow through her and become one with his own. The griffin screeched and swung his ruin-stone-tipped tail, hitting a madman in the ribs and sweeping away two more. They were fast, and showed no pain, but Vedyr was three times their size, and the power of his strikes did not allow them to close in.

Lynn jumped over the tail and swung her mace through the skull of a madman who was going for Vedyr's side. Three more came at her, almost matching her speed, with many more behind. Too many.

We need to fly.

Vedyr understood the thought. He jumped into the air and fell, sinking his claws into multiple enemies. The impact toppled others around them, and it was enough for Lynn to jump on his back and take off.

Fires were going up all through the camp. Rel and Olem seemed to have gotten the word to the other Sentinels. All around, silver streaks crashed into airships like glowing boulders falling from the sky, and Sentinels and griffins ripped at the plates with ruin-stone-infused weapons and claws. Lynn couldn't count how many airships were being invaded, but there were enough fires going up from ships to give her a glimmer of hope.

It seemed like whatever ruin-stone the Dakhrans used to power the airship was the same one responsible for charging its paralyzing plates. The Sentinels had no problem breaking through the powered-down airships on the ground.

Still, the Dakhrans now knew the airships were the targets. Lines of madmen streamed toward the Sentinels like water flowing toward a fall, and some airships had already taken flight. There weren't enough ballistae to keep them all on the ground.

Lynn watched as one fired a ballista bolt at one of the Legion troops on the edge of the camp. It landed with an explosion, forming a crater in the ground and throwing Legion men screaming into the trees.

The Dakhrans were using brewer bolts, carrying the explosive concoction they'd developed a century ago.

The airships taking flight and the exploding bolts were enough to tell the Legion it was time to retreat. The true battle was still to come. Lynn could only hope they'd raided enough potion stashes to give them a chance to hold.

The beating of wings pulled Lynn's attention, and Rel flew close to her with a slumped Olem before him. The commander's eyes burned silver, and his griffin flew beside him. Parts of Olem's mantle and hair were charred.

"We have to go. Now!" Rel shouted. "Olem's been hit."

"With the explosion?"

"With the Madness. We have to heal him, Lynn."

Cold fingers strangled Lynn's words. Maybe it was death's hands clutching at her neck. Her skin prickled all over. "We need to find Reznik."

Lynn turned Vedyr toward Talnea. Reznik would help, but the Bishops of the Bone hadn't managed to cure the Madness either, no matter their skill in manipulating ruin-stone nor how much help they had from the Priests of the Blood. She was the one who would have to do this.

CHAPTER THIRTY-SIX

Hide too long in the shadows, and you'll be blinded by the light.

— *Alterian proverb*

"Keep your Bond burning," Lynn said.

Olem was barely conscious, but the silver didn't fade from his eyes.

The Bishops of the Bone had quarters in the Othonean cathedral on the wing opposite the Sentinels, but there were no landing spots for those rooms. Lynn and Rel flew their griffins toward a room at the top of a tower. It was one of the cleansing rooms, with a large stone slab where they could hold Olem down. Lynn jumped through the window with little effort and helped pull Olem inside. Rel soon followed, leaving the griffins to circle the tower.

Lynn put Olem down on the stone slab. "Keep an eye on him. I'll go fetch Reznik."

Rel nodded, pulled out a pouch of ruin-stone, and turned to Olem. Lynn made her way to where she imagined Reznik's room would be but found the man turning a corner before she could reach the door. He put a finger to his lips and walked up to her. "I saw your griffins," he whispered.

Lynn nodded and pulled him along at a run, heading back to the cleansing room at the top of the tower.

Olem was struggling when they walked in, Rel trying to hold him down.

Reznik needed no explanation. "You need to connect to him. Now." He gave her a shard of ruin-stone and a vial of silver liquid like the one he'd given her in the Alterian dungeons. "I'll help you where I can."

Lynn had already known this was what she would have to do. Perhaps the Bishops of the Bone could not take on the weight of a Sentinel Bond, or maybe their connection was limited. The reason didn't matter now. She had to focus. There was no room for failure.

You had your chance on the prisoner, but you let that enemy go, and now you've killed your commander, Alren said.

Lynn downed the vial as if to drown his voice, took the ruin-stone, and stepped up beside Rel. Olem was arching his back, a black shade spreading around his eyes. "Keep him quiet," she told Rel, then pushed the ruin-stone onto Olem's forehead.

The commander's muffled scream lasted only for a moment before Lynn was plunged into a vision of a burning city. It was the Dakhran capital city of Erez. It rose in circular levels, each one with gates and walls to protect the level above. The topmost level housed the Dakhran palace, which looked more like a fortress ready for war. What looked like airships of an older design were half-sunk in the bay, while another lay burning in the lower city, which was overrun with Azuri raiders. Lynn looked around. She'd heard of this battle. It took place a hundred years ago—the last time the Azuri invaded Immeria, when Dakhra wasn't even part of the Domain. Olem arrived on his griffin, crashing into waves of Azuri, who seemed almost as frantic as the madmen. Something was off, though. There was no fear coming from Olem. Instead, he was surrounded in an aura of dark orange, streaked with yellow. Lynn raised her hand and found it held the ruin-stone, even in the vision. The emotions coalesced toward it, knotting into lines that Lynn could grab hold of. Perhaps her familiarity with the commander would allow her to save him. There were lines spreading out from Olem towards his griffin as well. It was a torrent of concentrated emotion: the Bond.

Olem struck down the Azuri raiders with ease, throwing one into another while his griffin cut them with claw and beak. It gave her an idea, and she raised the ruin-stone higher, trying to coalesce Olem's emotions into a Bond of their own. It worked. She had connected with him, a Bond flowing from Olem to the stone in the vine-like coils that had sprouted from Rel in her previous vision. Lynn pulled at one of the vines with her other hand, but it was almost as if this distracted Olem.

Lynn froze. It couldn't be. This was a vision. There was no way of affecting Olem's past. He turned to her and looked into her eyes, almost as if his past-self saw Lynn's projection. The distraction pulled him away from the battle, and an Azuri spear poked at Olem's ribs. Lynn felt it cut her own ribs—that same spot that always pulsed in her visions. Olem pulled back, bleeding, but the blood wasn't red. It oozed dark and thick, a black that spread across his skin and crept up the coil of orange and yellow emotion Lynn had grabbed on to.

Lynn gritted her teeth. She'd felt it. A mixture of vigilance and optimism during the battle. The orange and yellow represented the confidence of a warrior who had never been defeated. She clung to the feeling, pulling at it. It was stronger than that of the prisoners she'd worked on in Alteria. Fuller. Was this what was needed? Were only Sentinels redeemable from the Madness?

Perhaps if you had tried more on different subjects, Cara said, embodied in the vision.

Lynn pulled a little harder, but the taint clung to Olem's emotion like a cold bitterness riding his staunchness. The vision flickered as the taint consumed more of the coil, making its way toward the stone in Lynn's hand.

Then the link was cut.

Lynn was sent crashing back into her body, blinking wildly as she tried to make sense of things. Rel had been knocked out, bleeding from a head wound, his body splayed beside the slab where Olem lay. There was a knife in Olem's heart. What? Had she lost him? Had Rel been forced to kill Olem? Who had knocked him out?

Lynn searched for Reznik and found only a bloody hand grabbing at her arm to restrain her. She reached out to Vedyr, but before she could grab onto the Bond, she felt the coldness of ruin-stone on the back of her neck, and all fell into darkness.

———————

Lynn blinked herself awake. She was bound to a chair, but there was nothing binding her. Her back hurt and the energy had fled her body. She looked down, squinting through unfocused vision and a pounding headache. There was some kind of manipulated ruin-stone strapped to her wrist. She reached out for Vedyr, looking to use his strength to rip the arm off the chair and finish Reznik. It could only be him; there had been no one else in the room with them. Lynn grasped at Vedyr, but she received nothing.

Reznik stood before her, watching her struggle.

"You've allied with Dakhra?" Lynn's words were quiet, angry.

Reznik laughed. "Don't be a fool."

"Then what do you think this will bring you?"

"What I think is not important. What is important is what you will do."

Lynn struggled again but still got no strength. "Where's Rel?"

"He will be fine. As long as you cooperate."

"In what?" Lynn said over the laughing in her mind.

Reznik smiled at her. "In making me Pontiff."

"What? You can't be . . . Dakhra is invading the Domain and you're letting politics threaten its safety?"

"On the contrary. I am striving for the Domain's safety. The Pontiff was short-sighted and is failing to deal with the threat. I suppose I have you to thank for that. You helped bring Dakhra in. Showed how loose the Pontiff's hold has been. I could never have imagined losing the holy city, yet here we are, like beggars in a court of arrogant, faithless lords. These rulers are not the ones to lead the Domain, though the Pontiff has insisted on putting up with them."

Lynn eyed the man. His words seemed sincere, but that didn't change what he was willing to sacrifice, all the lives he deemed unworthy without a second thought. The rage flowing in her was too much to keep in, and without Vedyr to channel it to, it came out in a frustrated yell. "You need me," she said. "You can't heal the Madness, can you? You need someone who can take the strain it puts on you. Someone who can give and take from it. Someone with a Bond."

"There are other Sentinels."

Lynn narrowed her eyes at him. "But how many can manipulate the ruin-stone like me? You're using me to prove you can heal the Madness and convince the clergy when the time comes. I won't help you."

Reznik sighed. "How dull a long life becomes when there are no more surprises." He paced with his hands behind his back. "Your words are as I predicted, but make no mistake, you will help me. You will kill the Pontiff."

"You are the only one I'll kill, traitor." Lynn struggled again but still couldn't move. "What have you done to me?"

Reznik raised a vial filled with silver liquid. The one that allowed her to form the connections when manipulating the ruin-stone.

"I'll admit I gave you the final dose just now, but you've been doing it to yourself. You might be feeling weak."

"You've poisoned me?"

"Oh, more than that." He smiled at her. "Your friend is in the cell beside us."

I told you. You're going to get them killed, Alren said.

"It is up to you to decide his fate."

Lynn spat at the ground. "Have you any knowledge of the Bond? You can't poison a Sentinel."

Reznik chuckled. "While we could not cure the Madness, we did manage to produce something . . . similar. You've been taking regular doses." He lifted the same vial he'd given Lynn before her training—the one he'd told her would help her connection. "We hold a cure for this, of course, but your time may be limited."

Lynn bellowed at Reznik from the depths of her being. The Pontiff might have had his faults during the years, and Lynn might have questioned the Church, but Reznik showed a deeper corruption. He had no regard for life or for the Seraph. How was this different from the True taking their lives in the broken church? Lynn's eyes widened. "The True inside Alteria aren't the same that follow Dakhra. You command them."

Reznik chuckled. "Partly. Dakhra would have infiltrated the city anyway; best to have some of them answering to me, even if they don't know I'm the one they answer to. The Madness we provide is one we can control, though."

"You're killing people just to weaken belief in the Pontiff?"

"I'm doing it to save the Domain. The Seraph knows Her own, Sentinel. She will pick the worthy among Her new faithful."

"And those people who tried to kill me? The explosives on the walls? The airborne Madness?"

"The attempt on your life was not my doing. They might have known who your ward was, but ambitions are not always easy to keep under control. As for the explosives . . . I knew about some, but not all. As I said, my measure of control over the True is not absolute, but one must work in uncertainty and chaos if they are to sow the seeds of dissent. I must admit, though, you were helpful in uncovering that plan."

Lynn struggled again, her rage empowering her to shift the chair, but she managed little else.

"Your struggling will only take more of your time. And that is not a commodity you currently have." He pulled out another vial filled with silver liquid. "This is a dose that will keep you sane. For a time. You will get it when you've agreed to cooperate. Now . . ." Reznik moved his fingers, as if weaving invisible threads, and what held her to the chair was released. "You are free to decide."

Lynn tried to leap to her feet but fell forward onto the cold stone floor of the cell. She coughed and looked up at Reznik, instinctively reaching for the Bond and letting her eyes burn silver.

Reznik smiled. "Attack me if you must, but you'll only be hurting yourself. And your friend." He turned his back to her and raised the antidote vial over his shoulder. "Or you can take this and do as I say. You will be kept in a position of power when I am Pontiff. Close to me, of course."

Lynn slammed a fist onto the ground. She was weak, but the Bond still gave her enough power to crack the stone. It also burned through her faster than she'd ever felt. Her voices became louder and her mind felt brittle, as if ready to shatter and lose hold of who she was. She couldn't fight Dakhra in this state, or Reznik either. If she resisted, she'd only be widening the split within the Church. She stood and took the vial.

"Ah, clear thoughts have prevailed. Good. The Pontiff will be awaiting a report. We will go to him and offer a plan to fight Dakhra."

"What kind of plan?"

"The kind that opens the path for me. And you will be the hand that opens it."

"You want me to kill Sentinels?"

"I want you to do as you're told. I know you're training a ward, even if you have him under your sisters. Do not think my reach extends only to you. There are more concentrated doses of our concoction. Ones that work faster than what flows in your veins."

Lynn gritted her teeth, but the thought of Ferrin held her anger back. She'd trained him to protect himself, but this was something she could never have prepared him for.

Reznik stepped toward the door and paused. "You will come with me now, and you will support me before the Pontiff. Do not forget, Sentinel. You do not answer to the Seraph or the Domain. You answer to me. You will always answer to me."

———

There was still a light pulse in Lynn's muscles as she followed Reznik to the chamber where the Pontiff and King Iridan waited. Lynn's time with Reznik had been enough for the Legion to return, and the leaders of the Domain were already waiting in the conference chamber. Rel walked beside her with questions hiding behind his gaze, but whatever Reznik had said or done to him had been enough to hold them back.

Heads turned toward them as Lynn, Rel, and Reznik entered. Chancellor Burke stood by the rectangular table with a noticeable eagerness about him, while the Pontiff stood by the window with the same calmness he always seemed to bear, as if all was happening according to plan.

The Othonean king was not calm, pacing back and forth. There had been reports of the Legion coming from the north with renewed numbers, but if rumors were to be believed, the king would never be caught pacing in nervousness for his son's safety.

The occupants of the room remained where they were, formality overridden by circumstance.

"High Pontiff," Lynn said, bowing her head. Her throat was still raw from the rage-filled howls she'd given Reznik.

"And?" King Iridan said. "Did you burn them?"

"We did," Lynn answered. "We took enough of them down to even the odds, but not prevent the battle."

"So they'll be coming, then?" Chancellor Burke asked, wiping the sweat from his brow.

"Was there ever any doubt?" Iridan said, the contempt in his tone clear. "We've armed the ballistae with your ruin-stone bolts. Our walls will not fall."

Reznik cleared his throat. "They are still forty-thousand strong, King Iridan, and we have five. The walls can only be held against numbers like that for so long."

"I thought you a man of faith, Reznik," said the king. "Have you given up already?"

"We need to call for help," Chancellor Burke said. "Your son is said to have landed in the north—"

"My son is not trustworthy, Chancellor. We will fight with what we have."

The Pontiff stepped from the window and spoke softly. "Your

son is the Light of the Legion, Iridan," he said. "If he is marching here with an army at his back, he is what we have."

"I will not let our plan hinge on waiting for that boy."

The Pontiff smiled, as if talking to a child. "You won't have to." He looked at Lynn. "Where is Olem?"

Time to lie for your new master, coward. Alren said.

Lynn looked down. The words crept up her gut and burned on her tongue, but Rel's and Ferrin's lives were at stake. "Fallen in battle, High Pontiff. Blindsided by brewer arrows, then . . . infected."

Rel didn't contest her lack of detail or her statement that Olem fell in battle instead of being stabbed in the heart by the High Bishop.

The Pontiff looked between them, gauging the moment, then nodded. "You, as his sub-commander, will take up the commander's mantle for now."

"I hope to prove myself worthy, High Pontiff."

Hypocrite, Dentos said. He was right, but Reznik was watching.

Lynn knew there could be no other words, but the memory of her dead brothers rose in her mind again. Here she was, at the front of the Sentinels. She was no commander; death still walked in her wake.

You'll kill them all, Dentos said.

King Iridan turned to Lynn. "You can begin showing your worth to the Domain in this battle, Sentinel. Who will be commanding the walls?"

"I will," Lynn said. She looked briefly at Rel. "I appoint Rel as my second."

"A good leader to go against the airships while we push the ground forces back," Reznik said. "They have greater numbers, but we have kept the Madness under control in the city, and our troops will not be taken by surprise this time."

"Are these airships not . . . protected against Sentinels?" Chancellor Burke said. They were, and the only reason Lynn's raid on the camp had worked was that they'd taken the airships on the ground and by surprise. She shot a quick look at Reznik, but the man did not return her gaze.

"We cannot let fear govern us, Chancellor Burke," Lynn said. "Dakhra has been using it as a weapon since the beginning of this. We will place ballistae so that they may remove the airship's protection and allow it to be brought down by the Sentinels."

The Chancellor nodded, but the Pontiff held Lynn's gaze for a long moment. He betrayed no sign of what thoughts might brew in his mind, and Lynn did her best to mirror his lack of expression. He nodded and looked to Iridan. "We will hold Dakhra off the walls, bring the airships down, and hopefully, the Light of the Legion will arrive in time to aid us."

"Don't hold your breath," Iridan said.

The Pontiff ignored him and made for the door, but stopped at Lynn's side and put a hand on her shoulder. "I believe in you, Commander Lynn. We will restore the faith Dakhra has robbed from the Domain."

He could have said it loud enough for the entire room to hear, but the way his eyes were focused, it seemed like he had said it just to her.

"Yes, High Pontiff," Lynn said.

He left the room, followed by the rest of the Church council and the Othonean king. Rel remained.

"What did he threaten you with?" Rel asked.

Lynn sighed and closed her eyes. "So you know he's sending you on a suicide mission?"

"Doesn't have to be." Rel grinned at her.

"Stop, Rel. We have no time for this. Reznik has spies everywhere. We have to assume he's listening to our every word, but if I don't follow through . . ."

"He kills Ferrin."

"And you."

Rel walked to the window and looked out at the night sky. "All of us knew the risks when we became Sentinels, Lynn."

Lynn chuckled. A dry, humorless chuckle. "Seems like whatever I do, I always end up killing my brothers."

"You can't protect everyone, Lynn. I've told you that."

Rel turned back to her, and Lynn took a step closer to the window. "I need you to survive, Rel. All of you. Ildred and the others are still missing. So is Thain . . . The Domain cannot survive without the Sentinels."

"We'll find a way, Lynn. You just keep firing those ballistae."

Lynn nodded. "I will."

CHAPTER THIRTY-SEVEN

Beware the Sentinel's gaze, flashing ever bright.
A silver in the darkness, to dispel death's creeping
  blight.

— *Othonean nursery rhyme*

Adrian was sure Dakhra knew he was coming. He'd kept his scouts wide, reporting regularly, but there was no threat of madmen on the road. Father was still on Adrian's mind all the way. He'd try to keep his thoughts away from the old man, but they seemed to seek him out like water through a crack. Addo's words always came with the image of Father's face: "You think he called you back by mistake?"

Adrian tried to push them out of his mind and moved on. They stopped before a bridge that spanned a wide chasm. Two hundred strides across at least, and wide enough for a score of men abreast. The bridge was the last crossing before Talnea, but Adrian held his troops back. Mist rolled over the bridge, obscuring the path on the other side.

"Oma, send scouts past the bridge," he said. "We'll cross when they return. Amal, send men to protect them and be quick about it."

The generals nodded and went off to issue commands to their captains. The scouts set out soon after, and Adrian waited, heartbeat rising in his chest. It was still the middle of the afternoon, but the mist on the bridge rose above it, blocking their view of the sky. The last time he'd sent troops forward blindly was in the forest where they'd been set upon by madmen. He had made sure to stay away from the trees this time and had more than enough scouts among the woods flanking his army to feel confident against ambush.

There was an expectant silence as the Legion waited for the scouts and soldiers to return, but agitated noises soon rang from the mist, and what seemed like wind buffeted the stillness around them. Adrian shot a look at Nasir, then gripped his sword tight. A great shadow descended on the edge of the bridge, close to his men. Shouts rang out in preparation. Maybe his men thought it was the new Dakhran airship, but it wasn't large enough for that if reports had been accurate. The beating of wings made the griffin apparent. Not just one, but several of the winged beasts with Sentinels on their backs. They landed in streaks of silver, shaking the bridge and cracking the rock beneath them. Their impact dispersed the mist, and Adrian could see more descending now, landing on the ground behind the Legion. A group touched down a few strides behind Adrian, and a female Sentinel jumped off. She seemed flustered, unlike what Adrian had seen of Sentinels in the past. "Where is the Light?" she yelled.

Adrian hesitated, the memory of Elwin drifting into his mind and anger rising within him. Whatever this woman wanted, he would not give it to her. Elwin had been the one to take Myrra's life, and he was still part of Adrian's revenge.

"Where is he?" the woman boomed.

None answered, but soon Adrian stepped toward her. "I am the Light."

The woman held his gaze for a moment, perhaps evaluating the dark patches around his eyes. "Lord Light, you need to come with me."

Before Adrian could ask, the woman was striding away. He still wasn't inclined to help, but he followed her and could feel Bac and Nasir's presences behind him.

They reached the griffins, and the mind-haze that surrounded them greeted Adrian, but it was different this time. He was aware of it, but it didn't seem to pull at him like it had in the past. Myrra's pendant grew hot against his skin. Maybe his ward went beyond blood. The beasts parted to let them through, and Adrian and Nasir halted behind the woman, standing over a wounded Sentinel.

"He is our leader," the woman said. "Injured saving two of our brethren."

"I thought Leardin had perished," Nasir said from behind.

"This is Ildred. He leads our unit. We were charged with a distraction in Durnn, but we saw an opportunity and sieged the Sentinel tower in an attempt to take it back. The bastards had it laced with explosive concoctions mixed with the plague."

Adrian looked down at the man. The skin around the Sentinel's eyes was going dark, like he'd seen in the madmen. The veins on his face were also dark, and there were cuts all along the right side, as if made by shards of glass.

"What do you expect me to do?" Adrian asked.

"He asked to be brought to you, Lord Light. There have been whispers of what happened in Khet since you left. The symptoms are the same. This Dakhran plague has him in its grip. You're immune to it and have been fighting with soldiers who resist it as well."

"You're wagering the life of your brother on a rumor?"

"Better than leaving him to die." The woman clenched her jaw but seemed to hold back in the face of desperate need.

Adrian regarded the woman and the griffins for a long moment. Any of them would probably have killed Myrra without a second thought. That was what Sentinels did. This man did not deserve his help, even if he thought he could save him. "I can't help you."

"A few drops, Lord Light. That is all I ask. We have healers among us."

Adrian shook his head. "My blood throws people into this Madness; it doesn't heal them. I'm sorry, Sentinel, but I am not your answer." He wasn't really sorry, but no need to start a fight with this group. Elwin was the one he wanted.

The woman's eyes flashed silver for a moment, and she seemed to strain to keep herself calm. She could kill Adrian, or somehow force him to help, but it seemed his title was enough to deter her. He almost laughed. For once, faith had shielded him, even if it wasn't his own.

"Dakhra must pay," she said.

Adrian could understand the anger at Dakhra, but the Sentinels were no better. They'd killed Myrra, but Adrian would not let that happen to her memory.

The woman stepped closer. "My Lord Light, this is more than just a life. This is what will determine our victory. The Church has blind leaders pulling us all into Dakhra's grip. It was the Pontiff who let it get this far. We need Ildred if we are to reestablish an order that can fight this enemy."

Adrian looked up at a massive black griffin, intent on Ildred's condition. Its eyes were silver and moved to Adrian with a weighty gaze. Adrian didn't flinch. He knew he could not show it fear.

Myrra stepped close to him, breaking Adrian's stare from the beast. *Maybe we can use them to get to Elwin.* Adrian paused. It made sense. If he was to find the man, he could start by gaining this group's trust. He looked back at the woman. "I cannot guarantee he will live, and it will probably hurt like nothing he's ever felt before."

The woman nodded. "Where do we take him?"

Adrian turned to Bac. "Set up a tent and bring him inside." Bac set off to relay the order.

A tent was set up in moments, and the soldiers cleared a path as the Sentinels followed Adrian and Nasir toward it. Curious gazes followed him, but Adrian did not return them.

Nasir stepped in after the guards, carrying Ildred. The woman made to follow them inside, but Adrian held her back. "You stay with him." Adrian jerked his head to Bac, who remained expressionless. The woman paused, gauging Adrian, then nodded.

Adrian turned to Bac. "Make sure no one comes in."

"Aye."

A wide table had been left empty inside, and the guards placed Ildred on it before leaving Adrian and Nasir alone with the Sentinel.

Adrian shot a look at the priest. "You cannot hold me back like you did in the village."

Nasir nodded. "I will do what I can to guide you, Lord Light. You will need this." He handed Adrian a shard of ruin-stone. "The Sentinels have them in their hearts. They plunge it in as a sign of faith when they bond with their griffins; it's what allows them to connect. This one is like your ward; he will be bonded to you once you control what is within him."

Adrian took the stone and looked at Ildred for a long moment. The man was groggy, his eyes burning silver, but he seemed to have enough consciousness to know this was his only chance at life. Adrian slit the inside of his forearm and let his blood fall into the Sentinel's mouth. The man was silent for a moment, then began to writhe, his back arching, then straightening. His irises burned more intensely, almost white.

"Control him, Lord Light!"

Adrian was already motioning with the signs of the blood magic, and the burning around his eyes intensified. Myrra was there, a conduit between Adrian and the depths of his power, pulling it out of the darkness in the burning black lines that took hold of Adrian's skin more and more. Adrian took the burning and felt the pressing grief in his heart. He held onto it. The pain felt good. Felt right.

Adrian's fingers moved furiously, weaving invisible lines until thin red ribbons entwined with the blackness and sprouted from his fingertips. They came from Ildred's chest as well, ridden by another black weave. Adrian knew it was the Madness. It was up to him to control it with the power in his blood. The ribbons met midway, and Ildred quieted as soon as they did.

The black lines tried to push up along Adrian's arm, to unite with the Madness already in Adrian's blood and overwhelm him with it. Nasir grabbed a shard of ruin-stone, reciting his own blood incantation, one hand on Ildred's shoulder. It slowed the Madness but didn't stop it.

Adrian almost let it through. It promised him a path that led to unending power, and the speed and strength he'd seen in the madmen. He watched the black lines climb slowly back up his arm. He could control it.

Myrra's voice whispered in his ear: *You are stronger than you think.*

He wanted to believe her, and almost pulled the Madness into himself just to prove his strength. But as the thought rose, Nasir caught his eye as if feeling the intent, and shook his head. Adrian looked to Myrra again. The image of her torn face brought back the pain, along with that clamping around his heart. He grabbed onto it, grounding himself in all he still needed to do to rebuild her memory.

He exhaled, and the black twisting lines of the Madness receded a touch. Adrian pushed them back, the weaving of his fingers making the blood ribbons coil in the air. The pain around his heart grew, but it wasn't the only pain. The deep stabs from his cuts sliced into him, spreading the burning on his skin. This was not his pain, it was the Sentinel's, coming from the Madness. It ran over Adrian like a vicious animal, sinking its claws into Adrian's skin, threatening to pull his consciousness away. Adrian gritted his teeth, his mind pushing through the cutting pain to focus on that deep sadness in his heart. He grabbed onto it, separated it from the Sentinel's pain, and pushed the Madness back.

The Madness resisted, like a wall that Adrian wasn't strong enough to break. He pulled at the abyss of power, but even through Myrra it wasn't enough. Something else pulled at his mind, not from within the tent. It came from outside and above. Adrian found the shape of it, found the power within, and drew it into himself. He tried again, and the wall of darkness began to crack. The black threads retreated, moving down the red lines that bonded Adrian to Ildred, and coalesced into a dark pool on the right side of the Sentinel's chest.

"Now," Nasir said. "Contain it."

Adrian dug the ruin-stone shard into the dark pool on Ildred's chest and let out a long breath. The burning around his eyes spiked, then slowly receded. He stopped moving his hands. The blood-tie vanished, and the room was still for a long moment.

Adrian and Nasir looked down at Ildred, who groaned but did not snarl like the madmen. He shifted, then blinked up at them.

Adrian gave it another moment, hand close to his pommel. If a Sentinel were taken by the Madness, his only chance would be to strike Ildred before he could move. But there were no sudden movements. Ildred sat up and was still for a while.

"Your faith has been rewarded, Sentinel," Nasir said. "The Lord Light proves himself stronger than this plague of death."

Adrian watched Ildred, wordless. There was still a thrum riding his veins, and he could feel the pool of darkness coiling within Ildred, but something inside Adrian seemed stronger. There was something calling to him from the Sentinel. Not only that, but the power from outside called to him again, high above. His mind made the connection. The mark in the sky.

Had it elevated his power? Was the Seraph truly returning? Whatever it was, the taint seemed under control, for now at least.

Ildred got to his feet, and the first thing that caught Adrian's attention was the ruin-stone in his chest. There was a small piece of it protruding from the skin, and the veins pulsed black instead of white, as if it were struggling to control the Madness.

"This is uncharted territory, my Lord Light," Nasir said. He had a soft smile on his lips. "We have kept it at bay, but the ritual must be repeated regularly if we are to be sure. The current stone"—he pointed at the small tip protruding from Ildred's chest—"discarded. Every week should make us safe."

Adrian nodded. It would be good practice. He looked into the Sentinel's eyes. They were surrounded by black, like Adrian's. It sent a chill through him, but now was not the time for his faith to waver. His blood would remain strong. He was not subject to this Madness; he was its ruler.

"Where is Elwin?" Adrian asked.

The Sentinel paused, and for a moment it was as if Adrian could feel his intent, like another whisper running through his blood. Another moment of hesitation, and Adrian found himself willing the Sentinel to speak. It was almost an instinct, but Ildred spoke.

"Dead." Ildred's eyes widened a touch and Adrian could feel his own doing the same. It was mixed with rising frustration. Elwin couldn't be dead; Adrian had promised to kill him.

His thoughts were cut off as the expression on Ildred's face shifted into a frown, and his eyes lit up in silver, but Adrian's instinct had him cut that off as well. The Sentinel took a step back.

"I will not harm you, Sentinel," Adrian said. "But you must understand I have given you your life, and as such, I hold it." It was the same thought he'd had after dealing with the traitors in Khet, but he never thought he'd see it embodied so literally. "It is a small price for your sanity. I feel the same pain as you, and I am the one keeping it from taking hold of your mind. You will serve the Legion, and you will serve me."

Ildred looked at him for a long moment. There was something behind his silver eyes that told Adrian he didn't agree, but after a time, he nodded. "As long as we cleanse the Domain. And the Church of its weakness."

Adrian's heart beat a touch faster. Myrra and Derren were beside him, looking over the Sentinel. Elwin was dead, that part of Adrian's vengeance robbed, but he had his own Sentinel now and enough followers for Adrian to feel confident he would not be threatened again. He held Myrra's gaze, and the cracks seemed to become shallower, if not whole. "We march to Talnea."

CHAPTER THIRTY-EIGHT

The Lothrak face hardship in separate tribes, so that each part may come together to form a stronger clan. The challenge does not matter. The Lothrak will endure.

— *Tales of the Lothrak*

I t took the Yltigg a few days to get through the forest that spanned the Lothrak foothills. Eventually, the trees became sparser and opened up into a white expanse of uneven, snow-covered ground. The winds picked up as they left the cover of the trees, and a curtain of white surrounded them, tugging at cloaks in search of bare skin.

"The snows aren't supposed to be this bad," Roho said. There was no explanation, but they'd passed by enough corruption and crumbling land in the woods to know the clan couldn't settle in the wilds. They needed the protection of a pillar. They walked in a column, their sight limited to no more than twenty strides—less now that night had fallen.

"Help!" The voice came from up ahead.

Nasha had hung back with Shai, five strides or so from the back of the column. She'd seen the old man stumbling along for the better part of the morning. He'd been helped by a younger woman, but now he'd collapsed. The calls for help traveled up the line until a healer drew close, but Nasha knew this was likely just another life given to Zala.

The old and the wounded were the first to feel the impact of the Lothrak lands. Not all of them survived. All four clans had always valued strength. Weakness was to be culled, and lives returned to the Earth. Nasha hadn't heard Ento speak of this since she'd arrived, but if Zala's rise had changed things, it wasn't enough to let the weak or the dying slow the Yltigg's journey. The column kept moving.

Kadmus walked closer to the column, Roho's guards watching him. He hadn't been a problem, though the coldness of his emotions didn't translate into comfort in the icy mountains. The last time Nasha had seen him, his pale skin was so red it seemed bruised by the buffeted air, and his face was cut in places, perhaps by shards picked up by the wind. Or perhaps it was Zala's fury at him for tampering with Her power.

It was still hard to believe he'd created that taint, but Nasha knew there was still more to find from this man. She'd seen herself as a child in her visions, and she'd been living in a Domain city. If the Domain had done something to her, had it done the same to the clanlands? Was Zala true, or just made up to keep the clans under control? Just another Domain resource, as Mansa had always said?

Nasha sighed and pushed through the rushing curtain of snow around them. There were more boulders here. Larger ones too, all of them covered in white. Nasha kept her torch up, as if the flames would drive the snow away, but all they did was cast shadows on the rocks.

One of the boulders seemed to move, but Nasha blinked it away, cursing her mind for jumping at shadows. Then it happened again. She paused and shot a hand out for Shai to stop. They stood beside one of the larger boulders, big enough to give them cover should any of the Lothrak tribes attack.

"What?" Shai asked, almost shouting against the howling wind.

"There's something out there."

"It's only shadows, Na—"

Something pounced from behind the boulder: a beast with feline claws. Shai rolled to one side, Nasha the other. Part of her was almost thankful it wasn't one of the tainted, but there was no time to process the thought. She turned to find the snow-cat rounding on her. It was twice her size, with white-gray fur and fangs protruding from upper and lower jaws.

Nasha gripped her knives, her hunter's instincts returning. She'd fought off her share of mountain cats for the Ronar, competing with them for prey, but the Ronar lands had been hunted enough for predators to know the Ronar were not food. It seemed the same could not be said of the Lothrak mountains.

Shai ran at the snow-cat from behind before Nasha could shout out for her to stop. The creature was immense but still moved with dangerous speed and had an incredible sense of its surroundings. It turned on Shai as it heard the girl rushing toward its back, but that gave Nasha a moment to strike. She dashed at it, shouting "Duck!" to Shai.

Hope was all the guarantee Nasha had, but Shai turned her incoming strike into a slide and slipped beneath the creature's swiping paw. Nasha was on it then, slashing furiously at the creature's side, but it was like trying to cut stone. The creature's thick hide coated even thicker cords of muscle too hard for Nasha's obsidian blade. Her instinct kicked in, searching for the strength she'd taken from emotions, but she was too far from the Yltigg column to take anything from them. All that she found was Zala waiting within, an anger anxious to be let out.

Nasha retracted her mind, slashed again and jumped back just as the creature turned on her, already raking the spot where she'd stood. The beast was faster than she'd expected, though, and leapt as soon as it realized it had missed. All Nasha could do was grab onto her striking knife and plunge it upward as a mass of muscle and fur fell over her. Her knife found purchase under the beast's jaw, but it didn't sink deep, and the cat was driven to a relentless rage. It tried to bite at Nasha's head, but she dodged while struggling to keep a desperate grip on her knife and direct the sharp teeth away.

Shai was screaming behind them but seemed unable to cut the beast either. Nasha pulled on Shai's determination and let her curse build it into enough strength to keep her knife stuck under the beast's jaw. She tried to push the knife deeper, but even with the ancestor-stone manacles empowering Shai's emotion, it wasn't enough. She needed more. The beast lifted its claw, ready to end her, and Nasha could hold back no longer.

She pulled on the darkness inside her, taking Zala's strength and anger. It rose like a wave that clouded Nasha's mind and came out as a half-desperate, half-triumphant roar. It could have been a growl, like the ones from the tainted, but the haze wasn't strong enough to take Nasha's consciousness away. She still knew her name and what she needed to do.

The wave of power flooded Nasha's muscles enough to push the knife deeper into the creature's jaw, driving upward until it broke the impossibly hard muscle and found something softer underneath. Her hand sank into the creature's head as the tip of the knife broke up through the bone of its skull. The snow-cat's eyes rolled back, and it fell over Nasha, heavy and limp.

She scrambled to get out from under it, but the beast was heavy, and death had weighed its muscles down. Nasha was pinned, but she wouldn't touch the darkness for more strength. Her eyes were still burning, and the ice around her was melting.

A slight drumming trembled the ground beneath her, and Nasha's movements became more desperate. This was not the thrum of emotion. Something was coming. Voices soon followed the vibration running through the land, and a hand finally pulled Nasha free of the snow-cat's corpse. She rolled, then quickly got to her feet. Shai had pulled her out, and her gaze lingered on the spot where Nasha had been. The ice had melted, and the ground below was dark and ashen. Nasha eyed it, her head pounding. *Whenever I use Zala's power, I break another piece of the Earth.* Whatever she'd used had taken a toll on her muscles as well, and her thoughts seemed to come slower than before. She looked back at Shai, expecting some reaction of blame or fear, but the girl had her focus on the figures approaching through the snow.

Nasha turned from Shai and was met with whinnying and the hard gazes of mounted men. Ento, Roho, and Chief Ardin walked before them, all at spearpoint. The wind still blew up snow, and the Yltigg clansmen were a dark mass against the white. Nasha could only imagine how many Lothrak there had to be to keep them subdued while their leaders were being marched with weapons at their backs. But the Lothrak didn't gather; they were nomadic. Perhaps they'd used the terrain to sneak up on the Yltigg, like the beast that had stalked Nasha and Shai.

A dozen Lothrak rode long-furred mountain horses with curled horns on their heads. The beasts were almost twice the size of common horses, and the deep snow didn't seem to slow them.

The emotions hit her again, but Nasha kept them at bay, the recent use of her curse already straining her muscles. Her feet sank slightly, their heat melting the snow beneath them. Her instinct reached out to another memory, a more recent one, when Landi held Shai in her arms. Nasha had been filled with hope then, when she thought Shai and her family would be safe. She grabbed onto the feeling and pushed Zala back down.

The Lothrak held torches high, their fires blazing defiantly against the wind. A few men paused at the sight of the dead snow-cat, serrated knives in hand. Nasha tightened her grip on her own knives. The Lothrak gave her a wide berth, clearly heading for the creature.

The nomadic mountain-clan was said to not waste much. They couldn't afford it, and the snow and wind were enough to tell Nasha why. The Yltigg leaders were kept out of earshot while four horsemen advanced. One of them took the fore.

"You trespass on our lands," he said. He had skin darker than any of the Yltigg or Ronar, and long hair in braids. "Your leaders say we should talk to you."

437

"They aren't my leaders," Nasha said. "And we are here with a message."

"With the entire clan?"

"The Domain has invaded the clanlands. The Yltigg have come to offer help in return for shelter." Nasha knew better than to ask. A clan come begging would be turned away by the hard ice-folk in the space of a breath.

"And how is a Domain invasion our concern? They cannot brave the ice, same as you."

Nasha looked back at the snow-cat. "That's my kill your men are taking."

"It's our land."

"It won't be for long if you don't listen to me. The Domain is intent on sweeping us away. They want the ancestor-stone, and they are not the only ones." Nasha paused. Perhaps the Lothrak would find it absurd, but there was no other way to put it. "Zala comes for us as well, and the Domain are using Her taint as a weapon."

She expected a laugh, maybe resistance, but the man remained stoic, perhaps searching Nasha's gaze for the truth. He drew his beast close enough for Nasha to recognize his frown as he circled her. "And what would you know about Zala's taint?"

What do I know of Her taint?

Nasha let the emotions in. The ancestor-stone around her wrists flared, sending the burning over her skin again. It was almost comfortable in the gelid wind. The mass of lines streaking from the Lothrak riders filled her world with reds and greens and yellows. Dark blues that could be seen even in the night. She fixed her gaze on the man circling her on the mountain-horse. The beast's smoking breath clouded the threads of emotion around her, but she found the one coming from the man. An underlying anxiousness, uncertainty. It told Nasha enough. The Lothrak had not been immune to Zala's touch.

Nasha let his anxiety spike her heartbeat. Zala reached for the emotion, but Nasha blocked her this time, using the thread of hope from her memory of Shai's family to ground herself against Zala's mindless anger.

The anxiety powered Nasha, and she leaped over the huge mount, tackling the man off its back. The surprise hit her over the other emotions, but Nasha let it flood into her and flow away. She fell over the man, both of them going to the ground as the mount reared. The ice melted away where her hand touched it and she kept the man pinned with an arm over his chest.

Most clans would have seen the attack as an affront to their sovereignty within their lands, but Nasha still remembered her Proving, how the Lothrak valued strength above all else. It was the only thing that kept them alive in the cold of the mountains.

"I brought down that beast single-handed, and the Yltigg are right. You should listen to me. You'll need my strength to fight what's coming." If the other Lothrak riders stirred, it didn't register in their emotions.

The man grinned and gave her a curt nod. Nasha removed her arm from his chest and got up. He followed, calming his mount and climbing on its back. The others simply waited, whether out of respect for Nasha or the man she'd just attacked, was impossible to tell.

He rode back to the other Lothrak, and they spoke among themselves for a moment, then turned back to Nasha and the Yltigg leaders.

"Follow us and keep up."

They rode into the mountains through an opening Nasha and the Yltigg would probably have missed on their own. What looked to be a narrow entrance opened up into a vast cave. Nasha half expected to find a settlement, but was greeted only by torches lining a circular wall that led into tunnels on both sides.

The Lothrak and their mountain-horses took the tunnel to the right, the scavengers following with the snow-cat's remains, the Yltigg clan shuffling after. In the closed mountain tunnel, the noises of struggling people were louder, and the sour smell of the travelling clan was overbearing, but neither was as bad as their emotions.

Nasha didn't like it, and she quickened her pace to get as far from the crowd as she could.

"I thought they were nomads," Shai said, almost running to keep up.

Nasha nodded. She'd not been shown this place during her Proving, and wasn't even sure she'd been brought close to it. Perhaps this Lothrak gathering was just another product of what the clans were facing.

Soon the tunnel broadened and sloped upward, leading to a wide circle akin to a shallow basin sitting under an open sky. The space before them was vast, with tamer winds and a certain shelter afforded by a range of encircling mountains. Hovels had been carved into the sides of the mountains surrounding the three-hundred-foot basin, fires reflecting off the faces of their occupants. Tents had been pitched in the middle of the opening.

The man with the deep-dark skin and braids dismounted, and gave his horse to another, who led it off with the others. The scavengers who'd been working on Nasha's kill dragged it across the open space and into a larger passage that seemed to lead to a second basin.

One of the Lothrak directed the Yltigg toward one of the larger carved out spaces in the mountainside. The man who'd spoken to Nasha jerked his head for her to follow. Chief Ardin and the Yltigg leaders stepped after Nasha, as did Shai.

They walked under lightly falling snow with barely a breeze; the high mountains all around blunting the wind's teeth. It was a comfort Nasha had not thought she'd appreciate, but days in the cutting wind made this place feel like a haven. Beside her, men and women challenged each other in rings, perhaps jumping on the opportunity to fight rival factions of the nomadic clan that rarely gathered.

Nasha's group followed the passage where the snow-cat's body had been taken, into a tighter circle with only a few nooks in the wall. The new basin had an almost chamber-like quality, but with a cloudy sky for a roof. A massive pillar stood at the center: ancestor-stone, with runes carved into it, like the ones from the other clans. This one was twice the size of the others, four times larger than Nasha—and emitted a blue pulse that bathed the stone walls of the circle around them. At the base of the pillar, the ground was black and rotten.

Lothrak shamans stood around the pillar, some whispering, some chanting. Most of them with bowed heads; one of them touching the stone. The man leading the Yltigg walked around the shamans and up to a tall Lothrak in the nook behind the pillar. This new man towered over the chanting men, but still was nothing compared to the ancestor-stone ward. Nasha waited until they were beckoned by the tall man to join him on the benches around the firepit in his alcove. There was no throne or ornamentation. This was not a place meant to receive visitors, and had not been built to impress or demonstrate superiority.

Beside the alcove, the scavengers had strung up the snow-cat's corpse and were carving away the thick muscle. Nasha's gaze lingered on them for a moment. They had wooden pails to collect the blood, and the fur was being removed with care. She even saw a man taking the eyes, and cradling them like they were something precious.

The Lothrak man looked to the chief. "Bathel tells me you brought your entire clan, Ardin." He was as thin as he was tall, but lean muscle rippling in the firelight showed power without the need for size. Like most Lothrak, his face wore a heavy beard. Unlike his companions, though, his head was bald.

The Yltigg chief took a seat at the Lothrak man's gesture. The others, including Nasha, remained standing.

"And you have gathered all the tribes," Ardin said. "Perhaps our situations are not that different, Ishu. Your lands are troubled as well?"

"Every time has its own troubles, Ardin, but I gather you have not come here to discuss the Lothrak."

"You speak for the Lothrak?"

"In this gathering, yes." He eyed Nasha for a moment. "Bathel also tells me you brought that Relka down by yourself. Many a

Lothrak warrior have strived for this and been lost. The cats don't even leave the bones behind."

He didn't say it with flattery. More like this had been the first payment in a negotiation that seemed to be underway. Nasha simply nodded, but directed the focus to the matter at hand. "Your stone is dying, and the Domain is coming."

Bathel, the man who'd led them here, chuckled, seeming relaxed within the protection of the mountain. "I already told you, they won't get past the snows."

"How long are you willing to gamble on that? The other clans keep the Domain occupied, and the Domain stay on their side of the border as long as we're killing ourselves for them, but what do you think will happen once they've expanded to your doorstep? Once the ancestor-stone has been mined?"

Bathel made to answer, but the tall man Ardin had called Ishu silenced him with a slight movement of his fingers. "We recognize the threat," he said, "but we cannot simply share strength with nothing in return."

Nasha turned to the pillar, then back to Ishu. "How long has the corruption been rising in it?"

The man frowned at her. "What makes you think it wasn't always like that?"

"You may be isolated, but the clans cannot survive this way," Ento said. There was still wind, but his whispery voice seemed to carry in the alcove. "The pillars are connected."

Nasha nodded. "This started what? Four score days ago, perhaps more? That was when the Hagun pillar fell. The blood has kept Zala fed, but the pillars are what have kept her sealed. Once the first fell, it weakened the others."

Ishu's gaze was locked on Nasha. "A good one you've had join your leaders, Ardin."

"She is not Yltigg," Ardin said. "But she has helped us, nonetheless."

Even Roho was nodding along. "She has shown strength."

Ishu's gaze had not left Nasha. His eyes narrowed, as if recognizing something. "You are the one from the Proving. The one Mansa was hiding."

A burning crept up Nasha's throat. This man knew of her? Her hands moved, instinctively nearing her blades, but Ishu only chuckled. "You think we do not recognize the touched? Look behind you. They are what keeps our pillar alive."

Nasha turned to the shamans, her eyes widening. These people were like her? Some were trembling, others had fallen to the ground and were still in the snow. None of them were taken by the taint, however. Had the Lothrak found a way to stop Zala from taking hold?

Ishu gave her little time for questions. "You come bearing a warning, but with no request?"

"We need allies," Ardin said. "We need to take back our peak and push Zala back into the Earth."

"And how do you intend to fight Zala?" Bathel asked.

Roho looked to Nasha, as if awaiting some display, but she barely returned the gaze, focusing instead on the Lothrak leader.

Ishu considered her for a long moment. "Show us this power then. If you can heal Zala's taint from the ward, we will consider your request."

"We need more than your consideration," Nasha said. "If I heal it, then you agree."

Ishu cocked his head, but soon gave her a slight nod.

Nasha looked at the pillar and the men around it. She hadn't healed the Yltigg ward and had barely contained the taint within Shai. The Lothrak seemed to have men holding it at bay, though; perhaps they were the key to this. There was something else as well. The Domain prisoner, Kadmus. He'd tampered with the taint and made it into a weapon, if he was to be believed. He might hold information about it as well. "Give me a day and let me talk to your shamans."

"They do not speak to outsiders," Ishu said. "But you may watch them and seek whatever will help you in this."

Nasha nodded. That was probably as much of a concession as she'd get from a Lothrak leader.

"Bathel will show you to your resting chambers. Your clan may remain for now, Ardin. Accommodations are temporary, and will hold no luxury, but it is better than the wind, eh?" The man chuckled, but Ardin only nodded. He gave Nasha a weary look, probably weighed by the same thoughts she had, knowing she hadn't managed to heal the Yltigg stone.

It will be different this time. I will find what I need.

She repeated the thought to herself, as if that would help make it true, but the nervous thrum running through her remained. Perhaps it came from the chief, or Shai.

They left Ishu in his hovel and started making their way back. Nasha focused on the shaman closest to her, but there was nothing. No emotion. Now that she thought of it, the entire crater had been devoid of it since they entered. She frowned and shot a look at Shai, but the girl was not the one who would help her now.

"Get Kadmus."

CHAPTER THIRTY-NINE

*I am the Sentinel who keeps Her faith. I am the blade
that cleanses the land. I am the gaze that burns
the night away.*
*I pledge my life to the Seraph's name. May the stone
that beats in my heart show me Her path.*
By the Breath and the Body, the Blood and the Bone.

— *The Book of the Breath*

Lynn sat on Vedyr's back, perched above one of the flat turrets on the walls of Talnea. She hadn't counted how many airships they'd destroyed in their raid, but too many still filled the late afternoon sky. Orange was shifting to pink as the sun set, silhouetting the two-score airships that hovered above the forty thousand Dakhran troops lined up in the fields before the Othonean capital.

Her turret was roughly halfway along the wall, standing guard over the main gate they needed to defend. Before it, the five thousand soldiers of the Legion stood at the base of the walls. They'd let the madmen and their ladders reach the walls of Durnn, trusting the sturdiness of ruin-stone, and it still hadn't been enough. The Talnean walls were not made of ruin-stone. The Legion could not give Dakhra easy quarter. They'd count on the support of the Othonean and Legion archers and ballistae atop the walls, who would not be overrun by madmen coming up ladders this time. The Domain force was much smaller, but Lynn now commanded close to thirty Sentinels. The thought roiled her gut. She wasn't meant to be commander, but they were counting on her nonetheless. Reznik had forced Rel and another dozen to be assigned to attack the ships, even if they couldn't touch the metal plating, but the rest would be the shield that kept back the wave of Madness from the Legion.

Lynn looked toward the far west side of the wall, where Rel waited with his dozen. She wished she could go with them, but Reznik's orders had been clear, as was his threat to Rel's and Ferrin's lives. His own version of the Madness ran through Lynn, and he'd given it to Rel as well. The antidote he'd given them was temporary, and Lynn was sure she'd need more soon after the battle.

It's happening again, Roki said. *They're trusting you and you're going to kill them.* His words echoed in her mind, fueling Lynn's anger. She was ready, and so was Vedyr.

The Dakhran airships advanced in an almost circular formation. The largest of the airships—the wide, whalelike, metal-plated one that had come through the Skygate—sailed at the formation's center. The commander's ship, most likely. It was almost a hundred yards long, more than double the others, which spanned forty yards from stern to prow.

The Dakhran war-drums beat a steady rhythm, urging the Dakhran troops on under the same banner that had been displayed at Durnn: a hand with red lines running through it. The bloody hand of madmen who'd shattered their vials and had claws growing from their fingernails. They were accompanied by the purple and black banners of Dakhra this time. The troops were slow at first, marching steadily toward the walls. Then a horn sounded. Even from this distance, Lynn could see the orange gleam of the setting sun shining off vials as the Dakhrans gulped them down and began to shift. Odd movements from this distance, but unmistakable growls soon took the battlefield, and the enemy charged. Even in a frenzy, the Dakhrans seemed to have tailored their Madness so that their troops knew their enemy.

The Othonean archers had already loaded their bows and fired the first volley. Waves of steel-tipped shafts fell onto the fields below, piercing the enemy's advancing front line, but they did little to slow the inexorable numbers coming from behind. Some of the madmen ran straight through the barrage, their bodies riddled with arrows but their faces showing no pain.

Lynn turned to Gotzon, one of the Legion captains. "Command the ballistae. Shoot as soon as the airships are in reach. The Sentinels need the support." It was the best she could do for her brothers and sisters.

Lynn raised her weapon and howled a rage-filled battle cry, urging Vedyr into the sky. The Sentinels she commanded took off with her, from intervals along the wall to left and right. Lynn was one with Vedyr, his strength brimming through her, powering her muscles like a fire eager for freedom. She let Vedyr flap once, twice, then grabbed her weapons, fixed them into a polearm, and leapt off his back just as the line of snarling madmen closed in a few feet from the Legion. She fell with Vedyr's weight, ripping a silver streak in the air around her, eyes burning. She smashed into the Dakhran frontline mace-first, pounding the ground hard enough to form a shallow crater and launching madmen back in a half-circle before her. Vedyr crashed in a moment later, sending more Dakhrans flying back, then pounced forward and bludgeoned enemies away with a sweep of his ruin-stone tail.

Sentinels repeated Lynn's motion, crashing into the Dakhran army all along the line, opening wide circular swathes on the battle-field. Ferrin's unit was behind Lynn, and their battle cries rose to meet the madmen's growling. They used the moment of advantage provided by the Sentinels to meet the broken enemy charge, but the Dakhrans showed no fear. They had the numbers, and more and more madmen advanced. Some madmen were almost as fast as

Lynn. Others leapt over the frontline and made for the back of the Domain army to the sound of surprised gasps and screams. The press of battle helped balance out the speed, though, and Lynn kept slashing.

Ferrin drew in close to Lynn. The space she'd opened before her was already reduced to a few feet, and two madmen came for her at once. Lynn stabbed the scythe-side of her polearm through one's chest and swung the mace end into the other. He flew into the mass of enemies, but another madman leaped at her from behind the frontline. She pulled the scythe end of her polearm back, still with the impaled madman, and swung the body at the incoming enemy. It hit him midair, and Lynn's opponent reached her spinning at an awkward angle, head exposed. She separated her mace and scythe and bludgeoned the madman's head, sending his limp body back into the crowd.

Vedyr was doing his own damage. His claws, beak, and tail all had enough reach to keep the patch of battlefield before Lynn emptier than the rest. Lynn pushed into a space beside him. She swung her mace in an upward motion at a madman trying to get at Vedyr's side, then slashed her scythe sideways, taking the leg off another. Their snarls were filled with anger, not pain, but Lynn already expected this by now.

Something jumped onto Lynn's back, rabid. She swung an arm back, half instinct, half desperation, as the madman's claws cut strands of her hair. She wasn't sure how they missed her neck, but she felt them sink into the cloak and metal of her mantle, starting at the shoulder and cutting down the back of her armor.

A moment later, the pressure was gone from her back and Lynn turned to find Ferrin shouldering the madman away. She dashed at the enemy and swung her scythe, but this one had enough speed to evade her. Ferrin fell in, trying to foresee the madman's next attack. He sank his sword into the madman's shoulder, but it stuck there, and the madman didn't flinch before swiping at Ferrin.

The attack was stopped by Vedyr's beak digging into the madman and wrenching him away. The griffin snapped his beak shut, severing the body and flinging away the half that remained.

Another wave of arrows flew, giving them some breathing room, but even as a line of madmen fell, another took its place. Dakhra had the numbers. More Sentinels were needed to hold them back.

Lynn looked up. There were shrieks and screams from above, griffins trying and failing to breach the metal hulls and flying away as the Dakhrans tried to spray the Sentinels with the Madness potion. They slowed the airships' advance, but the ships were drawing closer to the Domain army.

Lynn took a few steps back and turned to the walls. "Where are the ballistae?" No bolts had been fired. "Ballistae!" she bellowed. "The airships!" But Gotzon had them firing down at the Dakhran troops instead. He'd ignored her orders, and Lynn didn't have to find Reznik or any of his bishops atop the walls to know this was his doing.

The airships had their own bolts. They were in range now and firing into the Domain defenders. Lynn watched a bolt as it descended and exploded into the Legion a hundred yards from where she stood. It sent men flying and opened a gap for the madmen to advance. More bolts fired from the command ship. They opened holes in the Legion, followed by desperate screams as soldiers and the area around them were consumed by flames.

Lynn looked back up at the Sentinels. They were trying to strike at the ballistae, but the gaps where the bolts came through the metal plating were too small, and the armored ships would hold the Sentinels and their griffins in place if they landed on them. They couldn't touch the airships without the support of the Domain's own ballistae. Reznik would let them be fired eventually—there was no point in losing the battle—but Lynn knew the bolts wouldn't be aimed upward before enough Sentinels had been lost. Reznik wanted to thin the order so he'd have less resistance when he overthrew the Pontiff.

Fucking bastard!

They're all going to die because of you, Cara said.

No. She would not kill her brothers. Not again. Lynn had been so focused on not fearing Dakhra that she'd let herself be taken by the fear of losing those closest to her. Rel had told her she couldn't protect them all. He was right.

The shadows of the airships drew closer, the setting sun giving way to night, as if Dakhra brought darkness with it.

That feeling hit Lynn in the ribs again. It was the same one she felt when she'd first touched the airship at the Skygate. It was stronger now, pulsing from that same airship at the center of the formation. She looked back to Ferrin. "I need you to hold. We need to take down the airships."

"Go!" he said.

Lynn mustered all the anger she could and took Vedyr's strength. Her muscles throbbed, but there was something beneath the power. A burn running through her, as if trying to hold her back. Her head lightened, her ears rang, and her vision blurred for a moment. Reznik's madness. Lynn roared, fueling her rage even more, the lightheadedness fogging her mind as she used more of the Bond and stepped closer to the hollowed-out state that would end her.

Alren, Roki, Cara, Den . . . tos. She reached out, seeking Vedyr, but what she found was the pulsing coming from the ship. Lynn looked up at it, and for a moment she could see the lines in a myriad of colors streaming from it, just like she'd seen in her visions. That was her target. Vedyr took off. Lynn fixed her weapon into a polearm and jumped, as if taking off herself. She fell onto Vedyr's back midair, one hand grasping her polearm, the other digging for the pouch of ruin-stone. She found one of the ones Reznik used in his manipulation and closed a fist around it, trusting it would lead her to the source of streaming emotions from the command ship.

The outer airships were engaged with the Sentinels, and Vedyr broke straight through. He flew under the big ship, following Lynn's directions as the stone in her hand guided her to the source of the pulse.

Get close, she told Vedyr, and the griffin led her around and over the mid-section of the hull. She had a mad thought in mind, hoping it would be enough to breach the hull. Rel had loaded ruin-stone with anger for her in the past, and what came from this ship was clearly a mass of emotions. Lynn touched the stone to a metal plate slightly above the airship's midsection and far from any visible sprayers. She was flooded with fear, anxiety, and the sense of betrayal as soon as the stone touched the metal. It almost overpowered her. Her mind screamed *Flee! Flee! Flee!* and her quickened breath echoed the suggestion. It was the sense of betrayal that kept her grounded, though, as if what was in the ship was being forced to do this against its will. Some of it bled through the Bond, and Vedyr almost balked at the unfamiliar strains that were not the anger he was accustomed to. Lynn held on, keeping the stone in place, as if connecting to the airship itself, hoping it would absorb enough without freezing them in place.

The surge from the metal plating pressed at her ribs, harder and harder, almost suffocating her, but she could move. She kept the stone on the plating and dug the scythe side of her weapon into the metal plate. It would have frozen her if not for the stone, but all Lynn felt was a jolt as she cut a gash in the airship's armor. The scythe's tip was slightly hooked—enough that she could dig it into the metal and slash a diagonal line across the plating. It creaked, and Lynn used Vedyr.

Alren . . . Ro . . .

It was too much. Her mind was wavering, almost losing itself. She could hardly push a thought through, but her arms already knew what to do. She kept slashing until a small gap became a hole that grew larger as Lynn slashed and pulled the metal apart. The fear and anxiety coiling around her were released, but the sense of betrayal remained, almost calling to her from deep within herself. Lynn could trace it to the source.

She peered through the hole, measuring her movement. It was big enough for her to move through and angled so that she could use the fall through to reach her target belowdecks. She jumped off Vedyr and through the metal shell of the airship, picking up speed as she fell toward the wooden hull within. She aimed straight for the source of the emotion-waves and crashed through into a dark room. Greenish light pulsed inside. There were no guards, but there was something in the center. A figure sitting in a chair. A man, shirtless, with his head down and what looked like tubes spouting from his back.

Lynn stepped closer and the spot on her ribs pressed tight again, almost like being hit by a mace. Almost like when she'd first reached Durnn and was hit by . . .

Recognition flooded into Lynn as the man in the chair lifted his head. Thain sat there with an empty gaze, but his eyes still burned silver. The spot that had been pressing at her ribs made sense all of a sudden. He might have been calling to her, or maybe it was a warning, but it was clear Dakhra had done something to him. The emotion bled out of him and almost filled the room. It went through the airship walls, creating a network that Lynn was sure reached the other ships. It was what coated their metal armor and would over-load any Sentinel that touched it, freezing them as it had Deria. And it had a Sentinel—Thain—powering it all. Lynn understood the previous feeling of betrayal.

She stepped closer. Thain gripped the arm of the chair he was strapped to. "I'm sorry," he said, his voice little more than a whisper. "I didn't want this, they . . ." The strength left him and his head fell.

Lynn rushed to his side, pulled out another of Reznik's ruin-stone shards and pressed it to Thain's skin without hesitation.

The vision took her. She knew it. It was the vision that had been trying to break in every time she dug into the manipulation the bishops had taught her. The dungeon walls were rough stone, there were dripping sounds in the distance, and moonlight shone in through bars above. There were mechanisms on tables all around, and the doors seemed to be worked by gears. A Dakhran dungeon. She looked down, but her hands were not her own. They were Thain's.

Something pulled at his back. Lynn shifted, moving Thain within the vision, but something held his body close, strapped to the chair. The two silhouettes she'd seen in previous visions were clearer now. Two men. One drew closer, with a wide glass tube ending in a long, needle-like metal tip. It was filled with a yellowish liquid, unlike the reddish orange of the Madness.

Lynn let out a relieved breath, but Thain tensed in the vision instead of relaxing. He was injected, and the Dakhran potion ripped through him, pulling under his skin as if trying to detach it from his muscles. Lynn felt it all. He burned all over and under his skin.

The other recited something in a foreign tongue. Azuri, perhaps. Too muffled in the vision to make out through the ringing in Thain's ears. The reciting man lifted two fingers, and the glimpses Lynn had through Thain's vision caught red lines streaming from them. They looked like blood, sewn into ribbons and reaching toward him.

They coiled around his arm, cutting a path across his already burning skin up to his elbow. The lines stopped. His eyes were open now, fixed on the red lines.

Thain tried to speak in the vision but was gagged. The lines dug in and he screamed from deep within—so deep that Lynn felt it in the darkness of her mind, echoing against her voices. The burning within Thain started coalescing into thicker paths that ran all through him and Lynn at once. The heat reached out for something outside Thain's body. Something calling for it within the dungeon chamber.

Lynn was still in the vision, but she gazed through her own eyes now. Thain was seated before her, the man with the injection and the Azuri with cuts along his arms focused on Thain. She found what the burning in Thain sought. Huge chunks of ruin-stone hung around him. They had been worked into something that Lynn could recognize for its power, if not for its appearance. These were airship cores, what the Dakhrans used to give them flight. Each had a metal plate covering half of it. The lines of Thain's emotion were visible in a tangle of colors. Lynn wasn't sure they were even his own emotions. They reached for the ruin-stone, finding the metal places and spreading, coating them in red, pink, purple, green, and blue lines.

The Azuri man followed them with his gaze, letting them weave around the plates for a long moment. He finally turned to his companion. "Tell Commander Alaya we are ready."

The other man walked out. Thain still hurt, and Lynn was engulfed by his pain. Her eyes stung, as if the silver that burned in Thain's eyes and was mirrored in her own was drying up her face, cracking her skin as if to pull it away. It was unbearable, but the Azuri held him like a puppet, powering the stones, holding his consciousness through some kind of heathen Azuri blood-tie. Even in the vision, Lynn still had ruin-stone in her hand, and she pushed it to Thain's skin, seeking to find whatever ran through him and release it.

Nothing. She pushed harder, but her hand bounced off, ricocheting from the concentrated emotion. She couldn't find a link to him, couldn't break through.

You know what to do. It was death's voice in her mind, cold as always.

Lynn tried again, but was thrown back this time, breaking the vision as she was pushed away from Thain, struggling to stay on her feet. The airship's hold was still empty and dark, but for the greenish light around where Thain sat. Lynn's head pounded, but her gaze fell on the tubes inserted in his back. The same yellow liquid from the vision. The Azuri mage wasn't here, but he must have been close enough to keep the connection of his blood-tie going.

Lynn knew what this was. Thain was nothing more than a relay for whatever twisted magic the Azuri was performing. Dakhra was using him for his Sentinel resilience, the same way Reznik thought to use Lynn to cure the Madness.

Release him, death whispered.

Lynn looked out of the hole she'd come in through. The Sentinels had not managed to break the other ships, and the Dakhran vessels were still advancing. They'd soon be close enough to drop flaming barrels on the Legion soldiers like they had in Durnn.

Lynn strode towards Thain and ripped the tubes from his back. He slumped in the chair, and she pushed the ruin-stone onto him again but suffered the same whiplash as before. There was too much of the Dakhran venom running through him even without the tubes, it seemed. Lynn couldn't pull him free from the vision he'd been trapped in.

You know what you need to do.

The voices laughed, but there was something different within Lynn this time. The taste of death was still repulsive, but she'd felt Thain's pain. Felt his silent plea for release from his endless prison.

To wield the enemy's weapon is to control the enemy. Elwin's words. Words she'd lived by for years—until the blade she'd been trained to use had taken her friends and opened a deep gash in her heart. Lynn felt the scar pulse with every comment, every slight from Roki and Cara. She knew the wound would never truly heal, but what she needed now was clear. She'd been instructed to kill her companions in the past, but the decision now before her was her own. Thain would have asked for it if he could. Was that blasphemy? Or did death hold a touch of mercy in its bony fingers?

She looked out through the hole again, this time at the Seraph's mark in the sky. "Seraph, guide my hand."

She sank her blade into the back of Thain's neck, the same place she'd stabbed Elwin. The man went limp, and the waves of color Lynn had seen streaming from him rippled and moved faster, as if a boulder had been dropped into a still pond. They moved outward, but disintegrated from within, from the core where Thain lay dead.

The airship shuddered, and Lynn knew the barrier was down. She rushed toward the hole. Behind her, a door crashed open and guards rushed in, followed by the Azuri man she'd seen in the vision. He began to weave his fingers as the guards dashed forward. Much as Lynn wanted to kill the man, she knew she had to leave. There were too many to fight within the ship, and it would be foolish to face the Azuri mage without knowing the extent of his power. She could wind up like Thain, used against her own people. Her mission was to defend the walls of Talnea and push the Dakhrans back.

Lynn jumped through the opening and fell onto Vedyr's back, the soft, familiar feel of his feathers offering comfort after the vision's ordeal. She flew toward the Sentinels, leaving the command ship behind.

The outer airships still used the sprayers, aiming at the Sentinels. But something had changed. Their armor plates held no further danger, and the griffins seemed to sense it. Lynn flew to the nearest group of Sentinels, yelling to be heard. "The armor's power is gone! Attack the ships!"

The riders turned their beasts and attacked from above, where the sprayers could not reach. Sentinels set upon the ships, landing on top, their griffins ripping off the plates so they could get inside. The Sentinels spread out in twos and threes, each after an airship to bring down. Lynn joined Rel, but even as they mounted their attack, shadows appeared on the horizon: more airships.

"We can't take all of them," Rel said.

Lynn gritted her teeth, her rage at Thain's fate still pulsing through her. Vedyr felt it as well. "We fight. To the end if need be. We protect the Domain."

Lynn raised her weapon and howled, and Vedyr shrieked in concert.

"Focus on the command ship," Lynn said. She raised her scythe and pushed Vedyr on.

The Bond had taken from her, as had Reznik's concoction, but the airships were exposed now, and she couldn't give Dakhra the chance to regroup and rebuild. She flew past the top of the command airship, slashing her scythe into the ruin-stone infused metal plates. They were resistant, but her blade was stronger.

More and more Sentinels joined her, tearing at the metal until the entire protective hull began to fall away. Smaller vessels flew off from the main airship, some taken down by the Sentinels—but their focus remained on the command ship.

The airship underneath the discarded hull was massive and filled with troops. The Dakhrans clumped together, ready to fight for their lives, but a woman in glinting armor stepped before them with arms raised. She held a sword in one hand and climbed the steps of the deck so all could see. She dropped her sword. "I am Commander Alaya of the Dakhran air-fleet. We surrender this ship."

A thrill ran through Lynn, and she hoped that taking the main ship would weaken Dakhra enough for them to turn back. "Take them in," Lynn said to the Sentinels around her, "then pull the airship apart. I don't want it—"

A silver-and-red streak screamed past and hit Alaya, flinging her onto the ship's siderail. Lynn recognized the griffin, a massive black-feathered beast. Ildred rode its back. He was not the same as she'd last seen him. His veins were bulged, and painted red lines streaked his face. His eyes were wild, with a blackness spreading around them.

He jumped off his griffin and took the woman by the head, digging his fingers into her hair and raising her with one hand, while his beast dared any to approach.

Lynn and Vedyr were there in a heartbeat. Lynn jumped over Ildred's griffin, while Vedyr stood ready if Lynn was attacked.

Ildred held the woman over the side of the ship with one hand and turned to Lynn. "Hello again."

"Bring her back onto the ship, Ildred. That is a command."

He laughed. "You? Commander? Is this how far the Church has fallen in my absence?"

"Please," the woman hanging over the edge said. "I'm not her. I'm a decoy."

Ildred turned back to the woman. "I know." He let go, and she fell screaming. More of Ildred's Sentinels came down onto the ship among the enemy soldiers—half of the score who'd followed him to Durnn. Some of their griffins dug claws and beaks into the enemies around them. They corralled the Dakhrans into the far end of the ship.

"Ildred, you will follow my commands or be deemed a traitor in the eyes of the Pontiff."

Ildred smiled. "Things will change, Lynn. I do hope you stick around to see it." He mounted his griffin and took off. Lynn followed his path with her gaze and caught movement cresting the hills at the edge of the battle. A new army was charging at Dakhra. This had to be Iridan's son—the Light of the Legion. His force was large enough to send a thrill of victory through Lynn. Combined with the Sentinels, it would push the madmen back. Above his army, though, another force of Sentinels flew. The remaining who'd been with Ildred in Durnn.

Lynn's gaze moved back to where she'd left the Legion, and Ferrin. A strange feeling pulled at her, one she couldn't fully explain. She mounted Vedyr and returned to the base of the walls of Talnea, but her heart was taken by ice as she approached. It took her a moment to recognize it, but there was a circle closing in on soldiers who were turning into madmen. The Legion were striking them down before they turned, and at the center of the turning soldiers was Ferrin.

Vedyr landed with enough force to push back the soldiers, and Lynn was at his side without the need for thought. He'd fallen to the ground, a gash at his side. He'd been cut. The Madness would take him.

No! Not again. Not again.

You thought you'd overcome me? Death laughed in her mind. *I am in everything you touch.*

"No!" Lynn bellowed, and her rage pushed back anyone still attempting to get close to Ferrin. She wouldn't let him go.

"What happened?" she shouted. "How?"

"The archers, ge-general," one of the soldiers said. "They aimed away from us. We got overwhelmed."

Anger and regret flooded through Lynn all at once, adding to the Madness brewing within her. Reznik had done this. He'd steered the archers away, probably because she'd attacked the airship and prevented her Sentinel brothers and sisters from being killed. This was his retribution. Lynn let out a wordless scream and pounded the mud beside Ferrin. He answered with a pained scream of his own that brought tears to Lynn's eyes.

No. There had to be . . .

The thought came to her in the chaos, cutting through the clamor of voices and laughter within her. She dug into her pouch of ruin-stone and pulled out the one she'd been holding back. The shard the Pontiff had given her after he'd taken the essence of Deria's griffin into it. It had the power to make a Sentinel—or kill the host if they failed to connect to the griffin.

Lynn couldn't know if it would work, but death already had its hands wrapped around Ferrin's neck.

I am the Sentinel who keeps Her faith. I am the blade that cleanses the land. I am the gaze that burns the night away.

Lynn took out the shard of ruin-stone and plunged it into Ferrin's heart.

CHAPTER FORTY

Blood holds ties.

— *Othonean royal family saying*

Dakhra was broken and retreating. Adrian could have gotten Ildred and the Sentinels to give chase, but there would be time for that. It seemed Ildred's old companions took exception to his way of doing things, but, if the Sentinel had been correct, that was just a weakness in the Church that needed to be fixed. Adrian would talk to the Pontiff, but he needed to see Father first. It was finally time for him to stand as his father's equal and to find out what his involvement in Myrra's murder may have been.

Adrian was calling it that now. A murder. Syvern might not have aimed at Myrra, but the blow had landed on the Dakhran king's daughter. His intention did not matter to Adrian, only the result.

Adrian lifted his cowl and paced up the Talnean streets with Nasir, Bac, and Ildred behind him. Derren and Myrra were here too. The Legion generals had been left to clean up the battlefield with their troops, but Adrian didn't need them to paint an imposing figure to his father. He was sure the old man had seen his arrival and how the Legion had prompted the retreat of the Dakhran airships' second wave.

There had been whispers among the Sentinels that Ildred's power had grown after Adrian's ritual. Many claimed it was the mark in the sky, that it was coming closer and the Seraph was empowering her elite. Adrian never dwelled on the unproven ramblings of religious fanatics, but this was different. He'd felt it as well. Felt the power coming from above, as if the mark had in fact given him the power he needed to keep Ildred's madness under control.

A religious man might have said the Seraph was coming to stand beside Her champion, but Adrian knew better. The Seraph had rewarded years of faith by allowing Dakhra to advance into the Domain and spread its Madness. Adrian wouldn't fall into that trap.

He looked to Myrra and Derren as they walked beside him. Their heads were slightly bowed, and they were smiling. They were in his blood, and that was what he could count on. The extent to which he could count on his blood ties with Father was what remained to be seen.

Two men rushed past with another on a stretcher. Adrian couldn't tell in the darkness if the man was infected, but the city was alive with soldiers. There didn't seem to be many infected left, but even as Adrian made his way to the palace, he passed another group hurriedly carrying corpses, as if the sight of them was still a blasphemous act, even after the battle.

For a moment, Adrian considered helping, trying to cure the infected, but he knew it would be too much. Ildred had put enough of a strain on him. Even with more training, he wouldn't be able to do it alone. And even if he did manage to hold the Madness at bay, it was only temporary. Perhaps Nasir's rituals would help, but it could be only with a certain few, not an entire army.

This will end now.

Adrian had told Ildred to bring him Alaya, but she'd left a decoy and escaped. It didn't matter. They'd shown Dakhra that Talnea would not be taken. The remaining Sentinels managed to take the command ship. Syvern would not escape for long. Adrian still needed to talk to Father, though. He couldn't march against Syvern with Father hatching his own plots or trying to maneuver Adrian as he had in the past.

The palace stood proud over Talnea. The squared towers with their stained-glass depictions of the Seraph were illuminated from behind, the images glowing in the night. They made Adrian's thoughts drift to Mother. He hadn't dwelled on her for years, especially after Myrra, and Adrian knew Mother would one day be brought back. With everything that had happened, though, he could only hope the Pontiff had brought her body with him.

Even with his face obscured by his cowl, the guards at the palace gate saluted as Adrian walked past. His armor was enough to identify his rank. That might be what they respected, but he didn't mind. Adrian didn't need to hold their love as Jovu had; all he needed was their respect. And as he paced through the palace, it was clear he had that. Or their fear. Either would do.

Adrian made his way past the long hall with its stained-glass depictions of the Seraph on either side. The one with Her kneeling before the burning city was easy to remember, but he paused to look at it all the same. The Seraph, a six-winged woman, was on one knee, clutching the pommel of Her sword, which had been stuck in the ground. A city burned behind Her. It reminded Adrian of the forest where he'd lost the Legion for the first time. The Seraph had only watched then as well, not lifting Her sword. Mother had always talked about this image. How we must have faith but cannot expect the Seraph to move us if we will not step down the path ourselves. He'd done that, and Father would give him the recognition he deserved.

Adrian paused before two guards at the doors of the throne room. "My father?"

"In the conference chamber, Prince Adrian. He's expecting you."

Adrian nodded and climbed the steps. Nasir, Bac, and Ildred

followed, but his focus was on Myrra now. It was the same path he'd taken with her before Jovu's burning. He'd been going down the steps, toward the temple where Jovu was to be burned, discussing what could have caused his brother to get himself killed in the clanlands. It was fitting, perhaps, that she walked beside him now, even if in a different form.

We'll find out what he was after.

Myrra nodded to him and smiled. It was enough to fill Adrian with confidence as he paused before the conference room door. There were no guards before it, and the door stood slightly ajar.

"Wait here," he told the men behind him, then stepped inside.

Father had his back to the door, looking out the same window Adrian had gazed through so many times while seeking to avoid the bickering of the king's officers.

Father turned as he stepped in, but Adrian did not remove his cowl. A slight frown creased Father's brow. "Something to hide, son?"

Son? Not boy? Had he finally broken Father's icy carapace? Adrian took a deep breath. "A lot has happened, Father. There have been . . . sacrifices I had to be willing to make." Adrian removed his hood and stared, waiting for a reaction, but the old man looked at him as if nothing had changed.

"It seems you've learned to strive for your answers, Adrian."

Adrian frowned. The lack of aggression in his father's tone was almost off-putting. "It's been a while since I remember you treating me like this."

"How?"

"With respect."

"I give you what you have earned, son. Othonea has many enemies hidden in plain sight. So far, you've not proven to be one of them."

"You will answer me then? You will tell me what game you have been playing with the Pontiff, why you need me to be Xakhar, and what Jovu died for?" Adrian held back the final question, the one Myrra was begging him to ask.

Father regarded Adrian for a long moment. His eyes were the same pale blue, his hair the same pale blond, but his expression lacked its usual pale coldness. "The Pontiff," he said, "has always been the ruling force of the Domain. We accepted this, and played nice because he knew Othonea was the greatest of the Domain nations. He knew he needed us, and we needed him for the blessings. But no one can accept living in chains, Adrian, even if they're long and slack. Make no mistake, the Pontiff has held chains around the necks of every Domain ruler, even under his guise of friendship."

"Is it not the Seraph who keeps him there?"

"He claims to know Her, to bridge the Domain and Her will, but that is an assumption based on faith, and we cannot accept it so easily. He feeds us scraps, like keeping your mother preserved. I was foolish enough to be blinded by that for a time, grateful even, but the truth cannot remain hidden for long. It was just another shackle to bend Othonea to his will. I had Jovu search out priests. Ones we could trust, who would benefit from a change in Church leadership."

Adrian narrowed his eyes. "There are none who would challenge the Pontiff in the Church. Not like this."

"We did not search within the Church. The disgraced might be forgotten by those who wish to remain in the Church's favor, but they have their uses. We found men willing to help. They led us to old texts, hidden among the clans."

"The clans? Why would the Pontiff hide anything there? Why not keep it close?" Adrian was asking the questions, but a fire was rumbling in his chest. More politics, more maneuvering. Jovu had sacrificed himself so Father could gain more power.

"Who would think to look among them? Keeping them within the Church would require the Pontiff to trust others within the Domain, but the clans are exiles. They were born of those who didn't trust the Faith or weren't interested in it when the Domain was created. The Pontiff has reached for Azur in the past as well. That's why I needed you as Xakhar: to take it away from him."

"What did the texts say?" Adrian asked through gritted teeth. He doubted any answer could be worth his brother's life.

Father gazed back out the window. "The Hagun got to Jovu before he could find them. The Pontiff could have been involved, but I can't be sure."

Adrian took an angry step forward. That was why Jovu hadn't been preserved; the Pontiff had seen Father's play. "So you sacrificed Jovu and risked Mother for nothing? For more . . . power?" Adrian almost spat the word.

"This is about the survival of our nation. My father built Othonea's greatness by wrangling it from the hands of thieves and traitors like Syvern. I thought you'd seen enough to understand that by now."

"Do we not live countless years, Father? Jovu is dead because you couldn't accept Dakhra as part of the Domain!"

"Syvern has always wished to bring us down! Is this invasion, this Madness, not proof enough?"

"And so you try to take control of the Domain to fight him? This isn't about survival, it's about you holding the power, you being the god."

Father shook his head. "I knew you weren't ready." The coldness had returned to his tone.

Adrian stepped forward. "And Myrra?" He held back the rage-filled tears, born from knowing his brother had died for Father's lust for power. The burning around his eyes felt as strong as ever.

"What about her?"

"You told me to leave her behind. You said she wouldn't be safe here."

"How is that relevant?"

"Was it true, or did you need her dead to break the alliance between Dakhra and Khet?"

Father opened his mouth, but Adrian cut him off. "Don't lie to me."

"You said you had your sacrifices. I thought you understood. I was clearly mistaken."

Adrian's blood tingled, but Father's words were too vague for him to form a conclusion. "Tell me what happened."

"Syvern wishes to end our line, Adrian. He's been trying for over a century. I knew he'd try something with you when his troops moved into Khet." Father paced away from the window. "Our conversation after Jovu's cleansing was enlightening. I thought you were willing to do what it took for Othonea to prevail. You saw Khet for what it was: a weakness to be removed."

"I wanted them as allies!"

Father shook his head. "Allies require maintenance. Dakhra was allied with Khet, and still I exploited that. This immunity in your blood. You think it's some gift bestowed by the Seraph?" Father scoffed. "I gave that to you, boy. Dakhra has been dabbling in poisons for centuries. Do you think I would leave my children exposed?"

Whatever Father had done, Adrian knew it hadn't been for Adrian's own wellbeing. He was simply covering another weakness. That was all Adrian was to him: a weakness. "You have a cure, then? To this Madness?"

"No. What was done to you, Jovu, and Ellana took years, and was not directed. We have a resistance in our veins, but the Priests of the Blood have been unable to make it into a cure the host can survive. Not all can hold the power in our blood."

"Why didn't you tell me?"

"Do you think if Syvern's daughter knew, she would not tell him? You trusted that Dakhran too much."

Adrian's blood felt cold in his veins, telling him what his heart—and Myrra—wanted him to do. "So you left me there long enough to see if Syvern would infect me? I was just another play, another piece on the board?" Adrian paused. "How did you know? How did you know he had a plague?"

"Things like these do not happen without testing, boy. Syvern had shown his hand years before. Infected Sentinels with it. That's when you were warded. He thought we wouldn't know, but his arrogance betrayed him, and I was ready."

"I was bait." Adrian shook his head. "If he tried to infect me, and I resisted, there was a chance I would pass it on to his daughter."

Father let out a sharp breath through his nose. "Syvern's moment of hesitation—was all that was needed. He didn't know if Khet or the Church had betrayed him. Didn't know what killed his daughter. He removed Dakhra's support from Khet."

"And then you moved in."

"We removed the threat of Dakhra from our backs. Whatever reaction they had doesn't matter. You pushed them back. And look where you are now!"

Adrian stepped up to his father—close enough to touch. Father eyed him, unflinching. The old man was to blame, just as much as Syvern or Elwin. He'd known Syvern would try something and not told Adrian. He'd delayed Adrian's return so Adrian would be a risk to Myrra. Father had killed Myrra.

Adrian let the anger rise in him, bubbling up until the tingling in his blood burned and the pressure in his chest seemed like it would stop his heart. There was something else beneath it, though; that thrum in his blood. Not only his blood; he could recognize the thrum calling to him from his father's blood as well.

"You killed her," Adrian said.

Father scoffed. "The only reason you're alive is because of me, boy. What will it take for you to understand? To be grateful?"

Adrian nodded. The anger in him was hot, but his words were cold. "Perhaps I should be grateful. All I've ever wanted was for you to look at me like you looked at Jovu, even Ellana. I've proven my worth time and again, but I'll always be nothing to you."

Father shook his head. "There's no need to be dramatic. Othonea needs you to follow my instruction."

"No."

"No? You think your title, this Legion, changes anything? You still answer to me, boy!" Father's voice was rising. Adrian took it as a good sign.

"You were always right, Father. Blood does hold ties."

Father frowned at him, but Adrian could already feel the burning around his eyes intensifying. Myrra had both hands on

Adrian's shoulders. Father might claim to have given Adrian his power, but Adrian had grown it with Myrra's help. The abyss that held it flowed into Adrian through Myrra, and his hands moved with the signs of the blood magic. He didn't need to make Father drink his blood. They shared the same bond, the same ties.

"What is this? Some heathen—"

Father's words were choked in his throat as Adrian constricted it. He could see what Nasir meant now, how he could control those tied to him. It was harder with Ildred, more distant—but the bonds between him and his father made it easy.

Father fell to the ground, gasping and clutching his throat.

"You may have warded yourself against Dakhran poison," Adrian said, "but I can reach into our ties. You always thought me nothing, but I've become so much more than you could have imagined."

The old man tried to grasp at Adrian's boots. His eyes bulged. He might have been apologetic, but there was nothing he could offer that would make Adrian stop. Myrra stepped to Adrian's side, her face growing smoother, almost normal. She had believed in him, and in his power.

"It is time for a new ruler to guide Othonea to greatness, Father."

Father would not be preserved. He wouldn't even get a private burning like Jovu. He would burn among the unworthy, his ashes indistinguishable from the ashes of those he'd looked down upon his entire life. The pain of Father's constricting throat was hard to separate from Adrian's own pain. Their connection was too strong. It almost sent a pang of guilt through him, and for a moment, Ellana rose in his mind. "You're just like Father," she said.

You're not like him, Myrra said. *You are better.*

Adrian directed the pain toward Father's eyes, painting them and the surrounding skin an Othonean red so deep, it became black. His father didn't have the Madness, but everyone would believe he did.

Adrian moved his fingers, weaving the red and black ribbons of blood until he had an invisible hand on father's throat. He squeezed slowly, letting the king feel every moment of it. Letting him try to wheeze out the pain. The cuts in Adrian's arm flared, and he sent that pain running through Father as well. The old man contorted on the floor without enough breath even to scream. All that came out was a final rasp before Adrian crushed his father's throat.

Adrian let him lay there for a long while. He let the burning around his own eyes sink in. The pain was a sign of progress. Myrra's face was still scarred, but no longer resembled an amalgamation of stitched skin. Adrian was one step closer to bringing her back—in his memory, at least. Derren's face resembled his usual self as well, as if killing Father had removed a weight from the old general's expression, even after death.

Adrian looked out the window at the bustling soldiers, still running through the streets and shouting commands on the walls, trying to take control of the chaos after the battle. His gaze moved upward toward the mark in the sky. It was higher and larger than ever before. Father was gone, but he'd been right about one thing. Allies required maintenance. Mother had wanted Dakhra as an ally, but they would never be that. Adrian would end them. That would be a good lesson to others thinking to oppose him.

He was more than the Light now. He was Xakhar, and he would be king of the most powerful nation in the Domain. The Pontiff would not stop him from claiming Othonea, no matter what the Church said about breaking ties with one's family. He'd use Ildred and his Sentinels to make sure of it if need be.

Syvern's death would be the final step to guarantee the Domain's victory. The final step to make Myrra whole. Perhaps that would bring the Promised Dawn. Perhaps that was why that mark had appeared in the sky. The Seraph was watching, as She did in the stained glass: Her sword stuck in the ground—waiting for Adrian to truly unite the Domain, Azur, even the clans. Maybe he was Her champion after all.

He stepped out, looking at Ildred, then Nasir. Bac stood a few steps away. "The king was afflicted by the Madness, a Dakhran potion smuggled in by assassins and hidden in his wine. No one is to have access to the body. It is to be cleansed immediately under your authority."

Nasir eyed him, clearly aware that Adrian was feeding him words to be spoken to others, rather than the truth. He nodded.

"Good," Adrian said. "Have them ring the bells for a new king."

CHAPTER FORTY-ONE

The First Tree holds the power that feeds life to the Earth and must be fed life in turn. Many have sought the path to it, seeking wisdom or healing, but not all can stand the power it offers.

— Tales of the Ronar

It was the girl who came for Kadmus. Shai, he'd heard them call her. They'd left him in one of the hovels. It was sheltered from the wind but didn't do much for warmth, and no one had bothered to light the small firepit within before tying him to a metal ring on the wall.

Shai had no words for him. All she did was grunt and push her short, shaggy hair out of her face before untying him from the metal ring on the wall. Kadmus didn't mind the silence, and the girl was confident enough that resisting seemed inefficient at best. The result would be the same. He paced behind her through open snow-covered patches and tunnel-like passageways until they came to a chamber where the Sentinel-like warrior—Nasha—waited.

Kadmus still couldn't place it. The Sentinels drew their power from their griffins, but this woman didn't seem to be bonded with one. The ruin-stone from the clans was the raw kind as well, less pure. Could anyone draw power from the raw stones? Was that a path to curing the Madness?

His questions were overtaken by thoughts of Nima as he stepped into the room. His parents would have prayed to the Seraph and asked for a miracle, but Kadmus knew better. He would not place the life of his daughter in the hands of the Seraph. He'd get what he needed from this woman and find the cure, no matter the cost.

The firepit was lit in this chamber, but the opening in the wall, supposed to serve as a window, let a cold wind inside. It made the flames dance, casting shadows along the stone. Kadmus had never been afraid of shadows; he'd stood within them far too long for that.

"You said you created the taint," Nasha said.

Good; she believed him. That was the first step in earning her trust. Kadmus nodded, thoughts still focused on Nima.

"I need you to tell me all you know."

Kadmus shrugged. "Would you understand the components? The fractions, the temperatures? The equipment?"

The woman clenched her jaw. "Where did you start?"

"What do you need this for?" If she was trying to heal the girl, Kadmus had to know.

"That is not your concern."

"That is very much my concern, and you will tell me if you wish to have my knowledge."

Nasha eyed him, head tilted, gaze darting from Shai to Kadmus. "What was your relationship with Bahar?"

Kadmus let the slightest frown touch his brow, hoping it was concealed by the shadows. "A professional one." That relationship had been severed, but the woman didn't need to know that.

Nasha stood and drew close to him. "You are very far from the Domain, priest. Death isn't measured here, and I'll keep you alive only as long as you make yourself worthy."

"I'm no priest, and are we not past this crude display of dominance?" Kadmus raised his bound hands. "Are we not far enough from the border? Where would I go? Even you clansfolk seemed lost in the snow-wind."

Nasha eyed him for a long moment, then nodded to Shai, who stepped before Kadmus with a long stone knife. His heart wanted to leap at the threat of crude weaponry, but he kept his mind on Nima to bolster his courage. The girl aimed the tip of the knife at Kadmus's heart for a moment, as if to warn him what would happen if he attempted escape, but Kadmus kept his gaze locked on hers with what he hoped was a cool stare. The girl finally cut his bonds and stepped back.

"Ah, decency prevails," Kadmus said as he rubbed his chafed wrists.

"Get on with it," Nasha said. The woman was irritated, but it seemed her natural state.

"I started with ruin-stone," he said. "You have a different name for it. Ancestor-stone. We take the raw thing, pulsing blue, then polish it until it shines silver and the veins are white. It becomes easier to mold that way, and more stable for the Church to use."

"Use?"

"The Sentinels draw power from it. Other factions use the power within as well."

"So it can be used to heal?"

Kadmus nodded. "Wounds mostly. The Madness that runs within is another matter. I tried crushing the stone, feeding the powder to the afflicted, but it didn't help. Mixing it in all manner of concoctions also proved unsuccessful, I'm afraid. The only thing that slows the effects is having it touch the skin. That's as far as I got."

Nasha seemed to think on this, as if noticing something she didn't—or couldn't—put into words. "And then you decided to make it into a weapon to attack the clans?"

Kadmus shook his head. It still hurt to remember, to know he'd been manipulated. "Bahar did." His words were curt and sour. "I was against it."

He couldn't tell how, but after a moment of consideration, Nasha seemed satisfied enough. Maybe she even believed him.

"Seems like we have a common enemy," Shai said.

"Perhaps." He had to hold back a scoff. The notion of allies and enemies was so . . . primitive. All that existed were actions, and his were fully dedicated to saving Nima. "Why do you need my knowledge?" he asked again.

"The Earth cannot contain Zala," Nasha said. "We need to heal the warding pillar. If your ruin-stone is enough to keep this corruption at bay, then we might have a chance. Can you transform our ancestor-stone?"

"I can, but it's not that simple. The results are . . ." Kadmus breathed deep. He hated the word. "Random. Having it close to the skin works on some, not all."

"Some is better than what I have now. How long will it take?"

Kadmus took a moment to consider. There seemed to be no benefit in lying about it. "If you get your clansfolk to help with the polishing, I can prepare enough stone within two days."

Polishing ruin-stone had been part of his training as a failed Priest of the Blood. He'd hated every moment, but he needed to see what this woman could do with polished stone. The lack of tonics to break down the stone would make it harder, but not impossible. He was sure he'd still be able to bring the power within the stone to the surface.

"You have until tomorrow," Nasha said.

Maybe she expected a disagreement, but Kadmus only bowed his head. "Then I'll need a lot of clansfolk doing the polishing."

Nasha nodded. "Get to work."

Ento gathered men to treat the ancestor-stone with little complaint, and the polishing was done. They'd marched the clan to the edge of the world, and it seemed there were few options for the Yltigg other than doing as Nasha wished. It still felt odd having their trust—or, at the very least, being their only option, but that was better than being seen as a disposable weapon. The thought rekindled Nasha's hope. Shai thought they'd be abandoned as soon as Nasha finished healing the pillar, but Nasha would make sure that this time, she was in control.

Ento sat with her in the hovel, both waiting to be summoned by the Lothrak. There would likely be others with Ishu, but Nasha didn't mind the crowds anymore. What worried her was how this new stone would affect her curse. She wasn't sure she could trust Kadmus, but knowing that he did not agree with Bahar gave her a sliver of solace at least. If his story was even true, that is. There were also the matters of these Sentinels he'd mentioned and the way the Domain used the treated ancestor-stone to fuel their warriors and priests. Nasha had heard of the griffin-riding warriors, but she'd never seen one. Until now, she'd thought them just another tale, something the clans used to keep their people away from the Domain. Now this man was comparing her to one. Nasha shook her head, making Ento turn his veiled face her way. "All we've found are more questions," she said.

"There is a lot to be learned from new questions," Ento said. "But we have found answers as well. The Lothrak shamans display powers that would have had them killed, were they Ronar or Yltigg."

Nasha nodded. It was another sliver of hope. There were others like Adda, like Razi, like her. She didn't know what kind of curse lived within the Lothrak, or if it had come from the Domain, but it seemed to be under control here. Taught, even, like warriors, hunters, stone-shapers, and speakers. Would she have found a different life, had Mansa left her to the Lothrak? Did he even know about their ways? He probably did but took her back to use as his tool.

Nasha's insides flared with the thought. She got up and strode toward the door. "I'm done waiting. Let's get our answers. But Ento —" She eyed the man as best she could through the veil. "If I lose control, you use that veil to pull me back. If it doesn't work, kill me. I won't be Zala's puppet." She would not become the monster.

Ento nodded and followed her out.

The shallow basin-like space that housed the Lothrak warding pillar was filled with moonlight, and the shamans were still gathered around the ward. The basin walls let in only a light breeze, but Nasha's insides were a roil. Shai had joined them in the tunnels, and Nasha sought her out now, reaching for the hope, for the belief that they'd get through this. What she found was mostly expectation, but a thin line of faith ran beneath it. The feeling warmed Nasha a touch, reminding her of all she'd been through with Shai to stay alive. She held onto it and stepped forward.

The nook was full now, with at least a dozen Lothrak leaders, including Ishu. All wore stone amulets engraved with runes, identifying their bands within the Lothrak clan. Chief Ardin and Roho were inside as well, with a handful of Yltigg close by. Nasha didn't search for their emotions, but the curiosity was strong enough to hit her just the same. They hadn't sent for her but didn't contest her arrival either. Ishu rose and stepped forward at the sight of her, the others looking on. "You are ready to convince us?" Ishu asked.

Nasha nodded. It was the most confident nod she could muster, even if it didn't feel that way.

"The shamans are at your disposal." He waved a dismissive hand, then paced back to the benches to watch with the other tribal leaders. Nasha eyed them for a moment, then turned back to the pillar. Shai stayed close, as did Ento.

She took a deep breath and closed her eyes. The darkness inside her beckoned to be set free, to be given reign of Nasha's mind—as if it could feel the corruption's attempt to creep into the pillar. Nasha focused on the hope and added her own to keep her mind strong against Zala. Focused.

She had grown stronger. She would beat this corruption.

There might have been the remnants of a laugh at the back of her mind, but Nasha breathed it out with all the rest, opened her eyes and gestured to Kadmus, who brought her the bangles of ancestor-stone that had once been her manacles. The stone was so polished it almost shone silver in the night, and its veins pulsed white instead of blue. Nasha nodded to him, and he fastened the bands around her wrists.

The ancestor-stone sank its teeth into Nasha like the first time she'd touched it, burrowing deep and sending strands of hot and cold in a twisting dance beneath her skin. It was stronger than she was used to. The stone pulled her in, embracing her in its vastness. The breeze seemed to carry vicious knives that cut her deep, even through thick clothes. Nasha gritted her teeth and pressed her eyes shut, but there was more than physical sensation. The stone was loaded with every kind of emotion. The heat of rage fought the bitterness of envy and the deep-rooted sorrow of grief. Each emotion had a different shape, one hotter, the other sharper, one slow and patient, as if to sneak up on her when she didn't expect it. Nasha didn't resist them. Her eyes filled with tears that were angry and sad, perhaps even a touch joyful. They enticed Zala, and Nasha could already feel the pressure in her mind, pulling at the hope she clung to.

She opened her eyes, and the world burst with color. There were the streaks coming from the ancestor-stone around her wrists, but the emotions were visible from everyone around her as well. They seemed stronger, amplified by the polished ancestor-stone.

Nasha's vision blurred as she strained against the taint. She knew this. Her body had always given her the same signs as the threat escalated. The ringing in her ears would be next, followed by the whitening of her vision, and then Zala would take her.

At the back of her mind, the familiar sound of her voice repeated the promise she'd made to Ife. That gave her a thin tether to the world, a hope that she could see this through. It filled Nasha with enough confidence to reach out and touch the warding pillar.

Nasha tried to relax her muscles. She couldn't consume the emotions funneling into her through the ancestor-stone bangles. She directed the stream toward the pillar instead. It lit up. The blue pulsed stronger, the corruption responding to Nasha's own darkness. She let her consciousness ride the emotions through the pillar, rushing through the stone until they slammed into the rot within. It was like a wall, pushing back, and eager to consume Nasha's sensations.

The shamans around Nasha stirred, as if feeling the flow of emotion. Her mind called out to them, seeking the connection to the Earth, to more emotion. They answered, drawing closer, not needing to touch Nasha to funnel their strength into her and into the pillar.

They seemed to take the anger from Nasha and spread it among them so the power of Zala's corrupted rage was blunted. This was why Nasha hadn't felt emotions when she first saw them. They were taking it all into themselves, like Ento's veil. Like Razi had in the past. Nasha used Zala's reduced presence to push her curse further. She focused on the memory of Shai's embrace with Landi and Uvo, and on the moment when she'd accepted the girl into the Ronar. They grounded Nasha and controlled the ringing in her ears enough for her to remember why she was doing this. To remember the person she was. She was not the monster and would not let the darkness within consume her. She pushed harder, but a fog seemed to settle within the crater, then blur everything around her as the world faded away.

Kadmus felt his eyes widening as his muscles weakened. Nasha had her palm pressed to the side of the pillar, but the blackness creeping up the base hadn't shifted. The air around him had, however, and the sky seemed to darken, as if Nasha were pulling the light of the world into herself. It was dark, but the ice around her seemed to grow gray and even black beneath her feet.

The wind blew through him, brushing against his cloak with fingers that pulled more and more strength from his body. He steadied himself on a low rock, hand trembling, barely strong enough to grip the stone. His breathing became ragged—deep but inefficient.

Kadmus took a step back. Whatever Nasha was doing still had no effect on the pillar's corruption, but it weakened him enough that he knew he shouldn't approach. He gripped the ruin-stone shard around his neck. It wasn't a religious gesture—the ruin-stone had always aided in healing—and Kadmus hoped to get some shielding against the torrent created by the clanswoman pulling at the life all around the crater.

A few more steps back and the pressure around him eased a touch. Kadmus breathed deep, as if he'd been holding his breath for too long and was about to suffocate. The air seared his lungs, but it brought back his strength and enough of his wits for his mind to search the area around him. The people closer to Nasha seemed to be struggling the most, but the girl and the veiled man looked less affected. Perhaps the Madness had given the girl some kind of resistance, but what protected the veiled man was clear. The ruin-stone pulsed in a deeper blue, and the shade of gray from the stones on his veil seemed darker. The stones pulsed in unison with the white veins on Nasha's wrists, and it gave Kadmus the makings of an idea. What Nasha was doing had his mind in a haze, but even in the fog of his thoughts, what he needed to do began to take shape.

Nasha plunged into the vision, like she had in the Yltigg Proving. This was different, however. Controlled. She was in the village, in the body of a child. Herself, years ago. She knew this somehow. There were other children, all of them in a dark room, lined up against a wall. In the center stood a tree with red and orange petals, the colors clear even in the darkness. The petals were still, the only movement coming from a man in white and silver robes who paced before the tree. He wore signs around his neck, like Kadmus's polished ancestor-stone, and she'd talked to Kadmus enough to realize the man in the vision was a Domain priest. He had a slight hunch, thin lips, and a bald pate that reflected what little light breached the chamber. In the darkness behind the tree, something silver glowed, but Nasha couldn't quite make it out. She tried to step closer, but a chain around her ankle tightened and held her back. She looked sideways to the other children. They were all chained.

She tried to move, to struggle against the fetters, but there was no release.

The silver glow shifted behind the tree, growing a touch larger, and a voice came from the darkness. Nasha couldn't make out the words. A language she had trouble understanding, perhaps.

481

The man before the tree unchained one of the boys and pulled him to stand under the boughs. The child struggled, but the man held him fast. He dropped a thick liquid into the boy's mouth, and the struggling intensified. The boy writhed and screamed as if something were burning through him, then fell still.

Some of the children were crying, others silent, likely taken by hopelessness. It was a strange feeling. Even through all the desperation echoing around the chamber, things seemed quiet. It took a long moment for Nasha to realize that something was missing, and only after a while did she realize it was the emotion that had always been fed to her.

The vision tugged at Nasha's mind and the room shifted slightly, as if time had passed. It was quieter. Fewer children remained—the silent ones. Nasha's arm was being pulled by the priest who'd been taking the children. He placed her before the tree, close enough to reveal what had been glowing silver in the darkness. Two eyes. A man's eyes, but there was a low rumble behind him. Something shifted in the shadows and a new pair of silver eyes lit up—larger, bright enough to show the markings of the head of the griffin they belonged to.

Feathers ruffled in the shadows, and Nasha took a step back. Even if she'd not been in a child's body, the creature would have been terrifying. The priest held her tight before him, while the man with glowing silver eyes stepped forward. His hand was bleeding, the blood dripping slowly from what seemed to be a self-inflicted cut on his palm.

The clergyman pulled out two vials. One held a dark mixture. The other was empty. He dipped it into the pool at the base of the tree to collect the sap, then mixed the contents of the vials into a single one and handed it to the Sentinel. The child version of Nasha might not have known what the man was, but Nasha still held enough control over the vision to know a Sentinel.

He stepped into the dim light, and Nasha's breath caught. There was a blackness around his eyes. Zala's taint ran through him, and the questions ran through Nasha. Were the Sentinels earthspawn? The heirs of the Earth-Breakers who'd nearly destroyed the

Silent Earth? Were the tales true? It reminded her of her own dark-ness. The spreading corruption across the ground after she'd healed Shai. After she'd touched the taint to kill the snow-cat.

The Sentinel took the concoction from the Domain priest, mixed it with his blood, then forced Nasha's mouth open.

They made sure she swallowed it, then watched. Nasha waited, the child sending streaks of fear through her, waiting for the pain to begin and her body to twist and jolt like the boy had. But all that came was a piercing shriek from outside the chamber. The men scrambled, but before the Sentinel could mount his griffin, the wall the children were chained to exploded into rubble as another massive griffin burst through.

Nasha thought she saw streaks of long, dirty-blonde hair on the rider who'd broken through the wall, but glimpses of the woman were all she caught as she was thrown off her feet. The child fell through darkness, and Nasha was returned to her body outside of the vision, as if she'd crashed into it.

Threads of emotion were swirling around the Lothrak basin, but she could trace them to their source now. It was as if the vision had unlocked something. As if the potion the Domain priest had given her in the vision had now awakened, granting Nasha more control. She grabbed at the threads. One by one, she took them from the people around her. The thread she held the tightest was Shai's hope.

The emotion coalesced around her manacles, then surged through her, amplified by the polished ancestor-stone that pulsed a burning bright white. It seared her skin, but Nasha had already paved the path toward the corruption within the pillar. She pushed the hope past the hungering pit where Zala waited within her and into the Lothrak ward. She let it pull at her strength and pushed hard against the corruption.

The pillar responded, lighting up in a vibrant blue that glowed almost like a beacon in the dark basin of the Lothrak. And still the corruption did not recede. A mad thought ran through Nasha; maybe it was fueled by the hope, or maybe it was the thought that fueled her hope—but something in Zala's resistance told Nasha that the harder she pushed, the more the dead goddess would hold.

Nasha had emptied herself of emotion, channeling it into the pillar. She didn't need to push. She needed to pull.

Nasha spread her fingers across the ward and reached out her mind to the darkness inside, pulling it into her. The ancestor-stone bracelets around her wrists worked the same way they had the first time, like windows that let in Zala's taint. The corruption did not come easily. It clung to the pillar, but Nasha pulled it in like a long breath, focusing on all she'd been through and everything she'd done to find her place among the Ronar. All she'd sacrificed to get through the Proving, and all she was doing now to keep Zala from taking over the clanlands. And through it all, Nasha saw the thread that pulled it all together, that pulled her together: her own belief. She'd always believed. Even through the curse, the betrayals, the pain of losing what she'd thought her life would be, Nasha always knew she'd get through it. Knew she was different. She didn't belong to the old world, but everything she'd done was clear before her now. They were the steps in building a world where she would belong. That was what fueled her hope, and why she couldn't let Zala win. She would not let Zala use her to tear down what her heart knew she must create.

The belief was like a flame burning inside of her, strong, persistent, and ready to face whatever fate was to come. Nasha became that flame, and as the darkness ran through her, she knew who she was. And with that thought, Nasha pulled the darkness from the pillar and sealed it inside herself.

The corruption fought back, using the emotions Nasha had taken in, trying to break free. The ringing in Nasha's ears was almost like the splitting shriek of the griffin in the vision. Her whole body was burning, her head pounding as she tried to deal with anger, fear, anxiousness, delight. Every one of them a string—and every one strangling her.

Breathe. Br . . .eathe. Nasha. Don't forget who you are.

The memories flashed in her mind again, and Nasha found the hope in her heart. She pulled on it, even as the corruption tried to use the emotions in the pillar to keep her tied to it, to pull her mind into nothingness and make her Zala's puppet.

You aren't a puppet. You aren't a tool!

Nasha howled against the twisting sensations and wrenched her hand away from the pillar. She stumbled back, breathing hard against the sound of the howling wind that seemed to have picked up. The scent of burning wood and the taste of coppery blood washed over her. Her arms wanted to move, to be taken by the dead goddess's strings, but Nasha resisted. Something touched her, and before Nasha could stop herself, she lashed out with incredible speed. Her hand grasped at stones that were too hard to crush, but her fingers closed around Ento's veil and pulled, tearing strings from it and scattering stones on the snow. The touch of the veil sucked the fire out of Nasha. Ento fell with the veil, and Nasha stumbled back, looking around aimlessly. Kadmus was gripping at something around his chest, but still on his feet.

She took another step back and noticed the pillar. It pulsed a deep blue—no more blackness around it. Nasha's mind was heavy, close to passing out. She blinked, and the weight of her mind shifted the world into a vision.

It wasn't a memory this time. Instead, she was in the Yltigg gardens, looking out through the ancestor-stone warding pillar.

Bahar stood beside it, talking to a man in silver and white.

". . . people sent to Azur. I want the boy and the two Slopers who sailed with him found."

Another man brought something to Bahar—a stone slab, inscribed with what looked to be one of the clan's tales. The words flashed before Nasha, floating in the air. It spoke of the First Tree and of Tedros. Nasha was still trying to make sense of it as the vision was cut off, and she was plunged into darkness.

Kadmus saw Nasha fall, but he had work to do before tending to her. The clansfolk around him were either dead or passed out. The leaders in the hovel were bent over, coughing, or still backing away. This was his chance. He rushed to the veiled man sprawled on the ground. His chest moved slightly, enough for Kadmus to know he needed to move quickly.

Some of the veil's stones were scattered around him, but they still pulsed with a power that Kadmus recognized. He couldn't have known this would happen, but seeing the stone triggered something inside him. Perhaps it was his training as a Priest of the Blood that allowed him to recognize the power in the stones. They were ruin-stone, but they held more power than any Kadmus had ever seen. There was nothing like them in the Domain, polished or raw. Nothing as strong.

He bent down and took four stones that had broken from the veil. The larger ones. He wrapped them carefully and stashed them in his robe, as if they held Nima's life itself. They might as well have. He'd seen what Nasha could do. She'd healed the corruption from the pillar, and the stones had absorbed her power. That would be what saved Nima, and what allowed him to create a cure. Nasha's power had been enough to cure the pillar. These stones would cure his daughter.

He turned to Nasha. She would still do more for him alive than dead. He dug for a vial in his robes—one of the ones he'd brought on the campaign with him. It was meant for himself if he was forced to fight, but he emptied the liquid into Nasha's mouth now, and after a moment, her still chest moved slightly. Up and down. Just enough to show her breathing was steady and receding from the brink of death.

Nasha opened her eyes to find shadows dancing on a rough stone ceiling. She tried to get up, but her entire body protested. It almost refused to move, as if she'd lost control of her muscles to her curse. Slowly, she lifted an arm, then shifted a leg, and soon she was on her feet. She half expected a voice to come from the shadows running around the small circular chamber, but there was nothing beyond the rough-hewn slab they'd laid her on. The entrance had been covered with a heavy cloth. When it shifted, she thought it shadow-play until Shai walked in.

Nasha took a moment. The memories were still flooding back to her. She'd seen it clearly enough that she understood them this time. The vision she'd been flung into when she cracked in the Yltigg Proving had shown her a burning city, Sentinels flying above it and purging all within. Now she understood why. There were other Sentinels there. Tainted. They'd been working with priests. On children. On her. The other Sentinels were destroying them all, even their own.

Kadmus was right; the Domain had made this—but not entirely. The priest in the vision was not in control. He'd been testing something with the Sentinel, as if looking for a cure to the taint. The Sentinel had been afflicted with it. That much was clear. Nasha had seen children die as the alleged cure was tested on them. Some of the memories burned brighter than others, like scars reminding her of losses she felt but did not understand. Had those been her friends? Even if they were enemies, that didn't justify what the Domain was doing in the vision.

Part of it was still a mystery, though. There was the question of how the Sentinel had become infected, but if Zala's taint had been affecting the Sentinels all those years ago, the dead goddess had been moving to break free from the Earth for longer than Nasha imagined.

Nasha couldn't be sure the Domain had created her curse, but they were surely the ones who'd afflicted her with it. But she'd resisted and hadn't succumbed like the other children. Had they changed something before giving it to her? Or was it she who was different?

"How did you heal it?" Shai asked.

Nasha thought back on all she'd seen, and what she'd found of herself. "You're right about the clans," she said. "We can't follow the leaders we have, but we're not leaving either. We've been resisting, Shai. All we've been doing is part of building something new, something that can be greater than people like Tomu, who judge themselves above others to gain more power. I healed it with the belief that we can make something better if we prevent Zala from taking this land from us."

Shai smiled, and the expectation that shot from the girl brought Nasha's mind back to the final part of the vision. "Bahar won't stop," she said, "and your family isn't safe, even in Azur. He's going after them." The words tasted sour and Nasha almost jumped with Shai's projected surprise.

"What? Nasha, we can't—"

"We won't let him. We'll fight back, stop him before he can get to them."

Shai watched her for a long moment. "I suppose I've trusted you up to now." She gave Nasha a smile full of good intention but weighted by concern. "Kadmus is waiting outside with Ento. Ardin is talking to the Lothrak. They'll want to speak with you too."

Nasha nodded. "Send them in."

Kadmus walked in slowly, with Ento in tow. He'd repaired most of his veil, but there seemed to be less ancestor-stone than before. He seemed eager to discuss next steps, but Nasha held up a hand to silence him.

"I've seen what I needed to see." She turned to Kadmus. "This curse, it's been manipulated by the Domain for longer than we imagined. You were right, priest."

"I'm still not a priest," Kadmus said. "But I'm glad you've recognized what must be done."

Nasha felt a strange sense of confidence from the man, but it seemed to be riding a wave of unease. She'd find whatever he was hiding soon enough, but for now, he was right.

"Bahar won't stop," she said to Ento. "He wants something with the First Tree. In my vision, the Domain were using one of the trees as well, a sap that pooled under it."

Kadmus nodded. "That is common fare."

Nasha shook her head. "I saw a priest aiding a Sentinel. The priest was bald, with a slight hunch. Thin lips. If you Domain people live as long as you say, he should be easy to recognize."

Kadmus spread his hands. "The Domain is a large place."

Nasha nodded. If Kadmus didn't know the man, she would not forget his face.

"The Sentinel was tainted," she said. "Eyes burning silver, but there was a blackness around them, like Zala's earth-spawn." That pulled a frown from Kadmus, but no words. Nasha pressed on. "They mixed his blood with the sap and something else. Whatever the priest was doing, the trees are involved."

Kadmus took a deep breath. "The trees are dying."

Ento tilted his head under the veil. "Aren't they supposed to be eternal?"

Kadmus nodded. The graveness in his posture was answer enough. Shai frowned at them, but Nasha understood. "The trees are like the pillars. They're connected. If they're dying, we need to find the source and stop it. Maybe Zala is attacking more than the pillars."

"How do you plan to stop it?" Kadmus asked.

It seemed the answer had lived within Nasha all along, and the vision from the tale Bahar had been reading told her enough. "They all run back to a single source. We need to rally the Lothrak and retake the Yltigg peak to heal their pillar . . . Then we find the First Tree."

A NOTE TO THE READER

Dear Reader,

Thank you so much for reading *A Shade of Madness*!

I truly hope you enjoyed your return to Avarin. I can't wait to show you more!

Having readers not only read my book, but also review it means the world to me. Reviews are an author's life's blood. They make sure more people get to know my book exists! If you wouldn't mind writing a review either on Amazon or Goodreads that would be amazing! I'd love to know your thoughts, good or bad.

Thank you!

Thiago

ACKNOWLEDGMENTS

The first person I would like to thank is you. Thank you for reading, and I truly hope you enjoyed the ride.

The following people are the reason this story has been put into words. I would like to extend my deepest gratitude to:

As usual, Julian Delfino, my editor at The Editorial Department, for his partnership and excitement in helping me iron out every little kink in this story. Thank you for being an integral part of this series.

John Robert Marlow at The Editorial Department for his insight and patience in dealing with my rough prose. His contributions to clarity and flow cannot be overstated.

Allen Walker for being the first to open the doors of booktube, and believing in a completely unknown author making his debut.

A very special thank you to my dear friends Andrew D. Meredith, John Mauro, Victoria Tecken, RJ Gibson, and Jordan Buxton for the immeasurable kindness in beta reading this story. Your comments and contributions made all the difference.

All of my good friends in the Indie Accords community, and all of the amazing reviewers who dedicated your time to my words. I would be nothing without you: Andrew`s Wizardly Reads, RJ Gibson, Dr. John Mauro, Tori Talks, Cassidy Chivers, Dom McDermott, Jimmy Nutts, Steve Talks Books, Kay`s Hidden Shelf, Dr. Philip Chase, Rai Furniss-Greasely, and so many more!

Mark Lawrence for the continued inspiration and dedication to the self-pub community, as well as all the friends I made through Mark`s community.

So many more who've supported me throughout this journey. I am deeply thankful.

Lightning Source UK Ltd.
Milton Keynes UK
UKHW011812250223
417666UK00004B/22/J